1.00

D1557923

Indecent
Behavior

■

OTHER BOOKS BY CARYL RIVERS

FICTION

Intimate Enemies
Girls Forever Brave and True
Virgins

NONFICTION

Occasional Sins
    (Originally published as *Aphrodite at Mid-Century:*
    Growing up Female and Catholic in Postwar America)
Lifeprints: New Patterns of Love and Work for
    Today's Women
Beyond Sugar and Spice: How Women Grow, Learn
    and Thrive
For Better, For Worse

Indecent Behavior

Caryl Rivers

DUTTON ■ NEW YORK

DUTTON
Published by the Penguin Group
Penguin Books USA Inc., 375 Hudson Street,
New York, New York 10014, U.S.A.
Penguin Books Ltd, 27 Wrights Lane,
London W8 5TZ, England
Penguin Books Australia Ltd, Ringwood,
Victoria, Australia
Penguin Books Canada Ltd, 2801 John Street,
Markham, Ontario, Canada L3R 1B4
Penguin Books (N.Z.) Ltd, 182–190 Wairau Road,
Auckland 10, New Zealand

Penguin Books Ltd, Registered Offices:
Harmondsworth, Middlesex, England

First published by Dutton, an imprint of
Penguin Books USA Inc. Published simultaneously in Canada by
Fitzhenry & Whiteside, Limited.

First printing, May, 1990
10 9 8 7 6 5 4 3 2 1

Library of Congress Cataloging-in-Publication Data

Rivers, Caryl.
  Indecent behavior / Caryl Rivers. — 1st ed.
    p. cm.
  ISBN 0-525-24867-6
  I. Title.
PS3568.I8315I45   1990
813'.54—dc20   89–27961
                                    CIP

Printed in the United States of America
Set in Trump Medieval
Designed by Earl Tidwell

Publisher's Note: This novel is a work of fiction.
Names, characters, places, and incidents either are
the product of the author's imagination
or are used fictitiously, and any resemblance to actual persons,
living or dead, events, or locales is entirely coincidental.

To the memory of my parents:

Helen Huhn Rivers
and
Hugh Rivers

and of my brother
Hugh Rivers Jr.

Indecent Behavior

■

1

■

Sally Ellenberg blinked as the elevator doors opened and the eerie quiet of the city room greeted her. It could have been a bank, with its coordinated colors and bright lights, its rows of computers purring as regiments of green letters marched across the screens. There were times when she half expected to see it the way it used to be, years ago. In fact, she had been thinking on the way up of one summer night she had come to the *World Herald* office with her father. She had visited many times as a child, so why was she thinking of that particular night? Maybe it was the sudden spurt of warm weather, unusual for spring in Boston, and the traffic jam she had just plowed through in Kenmore Square. There had been a traffic jam on that night many years ago too—the Sox were in town.

As a child she had always loved riding up in the creaky old elevator—long since replaced—holding her father's hand and inhaling his familiar aroma, equal parts cigarette smoke, aftershave and sweat, the latter a musky, comforting smell. She would wait, expectantly, for the doors to open. The scene awaiting her was as magical to a child's eye as if it had been filled with elves and trolls and dragons from her storybooks. Mere dragons, in truth, would be hard-pressed to compete with the gritty energy of the world she was about to enter.

When the doors creaked open, the sounds and sights of the room would flood in: the staccato dance of the huge black wire machines, the cries of "Copy!" that would send young men scurrying and, near her father's desk, the police radio that chattered like an angry squirrel. Men, and an occasional woman, pounded at typewriters and now and then cursed, adding to the symphony of noise. The whole room, the little girl imagined, was a giant squid, its tentacles stretched across the planet. Information was sucked like plankton into its insatiable maw: fires, anniversaries, wars, ball games, bank robberies, the crowning of queens, and the death of presidents. Nothing could escape it. By age ten, Sally knew by heart the number of bells that rang on the black wire machines and the magnitude of the events they announced. She also knew it would not be possible for her to spend her life anyplace else.

She stepped out of the elevator. It was all different now. The royal blue carpeting swallowed the sound of footsteps, and the high old ceiling that had seemed so far away was covered by vanilla white ceiling tiles, lowered on a grid a respectable distance above people's heads. The computers hummed discreetly and nobody shrieked "Copy!" anymore. Sometimes, she wished the elevator doors would open and the present would simply vanish, and there would be the room she remembered: noisy, profane, acrid, stuffy—magical.

She walked across the room toward the city desk, and saw Kevin Murphy waving frantically at her. Kevin was always in a sweat for early copy, to get as many words as possible into the sometimes unreliable entrails of the computer. Today, he seemed especially agitated.

"Ellenberg, where the hell have you been? WEEI is saying that there was a goddamn riot at Boston University!"

"Not a riot. A few busted heads, six arrests. They even dragged a few kids out of Marsh Chapel. Like the good old days."

"Why didn't you call in? I've been shitting bricks, sitting here listening to EEI."

"I did call. I talked to Neil an hour ago. I told him I was coming back to write."

"Where the hell is Neil? I haven't seen him for forty minutes."

"I saw him going out for dinner. I've got plenty of time, Kevin. It's only five."

"Where the hell's my Valium," Kevin said, rummaging around in his desk drawer. "I swear, this goddamn place is going to give me a heart attack. I'm type A, you know that! Did Samanski get any good stuff?"

"I saw her get a good shot of a cop hitting a kid. I think I can still taste some tear gas. The cops used some, would you believe? Does tear gas give you cancer?"

"Probably. How the hell did this thing get started, anyhow? I thought nobody was expecting trouble."

"They weren't," Sally said. "It was just your average Near East teach-in. The usual folks—Chomsky, George Wald, Howard Zinn. They keep on trucking."

The city editor sighed. "Sometimes I think life is a rerun. Christ, I used to go to Marsh Chapel for Vietnam rallies with those guys when I was at BU."

"Did you burn your draft card?"

"Only my food service card. I was too chicken."

"You could have relived your youth if you'd been out there today, Kevin. Hell no, we won't go! We won't die for Amoco!"

"How did it start?"

"A bunch of kids from Save Iran started to heckle the speakers. You know, 'Chommie the commie' and 'Better dead than red.' Somebody threw a punch, and the BU cops came charging in. Everything got to be messy."

Kevin scratched his head and looked at his computer. "OK, let it run. Big news hole tonight. It'll probably go off lead. There's something coming over the wires on the street fighting in Teheran. Can you give me a sidebar on Save Iran? They've been making a lot of noise lately."

"Sure." Sally went to her desk, sat down, and switched on her VDT. The Iranian situation was teetering on the brink of civil war. A coalition of mullahs still held power, but there were daily clashes in the streets between the fundamentalists and the leftists. The U.S. economy, still shaky after the recession brought on by the huge trade imbalances, still needed Iranian oil. To some American eyes, the Russians hovered over the scene like a vulture scenting dead meat.

The Iranian situation had put a pall on what had been an era of good feelings between the U.S. and the Soviet Union; old tensions resurfaced. With Eastern Europe lurching toward a market economy and German reunification possible, the Warsaw Pact was in shambles. There were growing rumbles inside the Soviet Union that the Soviet Empire must not be allowed to disintegrate. Glasnost had stalled after the riots in the Baltic states, and Soviet hardliners were vying for power with moderates. Republican president Benton Ellard, who had come to office on a peace-and-prosperity platform, was being pushed hard by Congressional hawks who demanded that the U.S. invade the Iranian oilfields to keep them out of the hands of the Soviets— or the Iraqis.

But a rising tide of dissent was sweeping across campuses and through the urban ghettos. Students, who had seemed docile and career-oriented, began to realize that they could be shipped off to the Middle East, to put their bodies on the line for oil. The quiet campuses had come alive. In ghetto streets, the word was out that this was another Vietnam. Blacks, who were slipping ever further behind in the economic battle, were going to be the first to die for white men's profits.

Sally looked at her notes and decided to lead with a good quote from one of the students. Her usual beat at the paper was criminal justice—her father's job years ago, only then it was called the police beat. But as the tempo of protest accelerated, she had been called on more and more often to cover it.

She worked steadily for an hour, turning out a piece that walked the proper line between the terse and the eloquent. "Understate," her father always told her. "If you've got a good yarn, let the story tell itself. Make it move. Be a playwright. Let your reader *see* it." Sol Ellenberg had always been known as a classy writer; the kind who probably could have written a *novel*, for chrissake. Many thought Sally had inherited his touch.

When the main story was done, she quickly put together a short sidebar on Save Iran, the conservative student group. When she finished, she got up and went to the women's room, washed her face, and grubbed about in her purse for a lipstick. The only one she could find was called Orange Punch, plucked by mistake from the bargain rack at CVS.

"Oh, what the hell," she said to her image in the mirror, and smeared Orange Punch across her mouth. The effect of a bright orange slash across her pale skin was almost clownish, under her dark mop of curly hair. She peered at herself in amusement, then shrugged and walked back out into the city room. Her choice was between tubercular and Ringling Brothers. Be a clown.

She bummed a cigarette from Kevin Murphy, who said, "Why are you worrying about tear gas when you're killing yourself with those?" She lit up, enjoyed the luxury of a deep inhale, and swore on the graves of her ancestors from Minsk that she would quit tomorrow at quarter of nine. She looked across the room and noted that John Forbes Aiken was now sitting at the desk opposite hers, absorbing a few rads of microwaves—or whatever it was the damn VDTs gave off. They had moved him to that desk when Abe Feldman retired, breaking up what Sally and Abe called Kikes' Korner. Sally knew what Jack Aiken's reaction would be when she walked to her desk and tossed her handbag on it with a loud thud. He would look up, the frown lines across his forehead bunching up in a scowl, and she could swear she could hear the sound of his jaws clenching. She wondered why she got so much delight from tormenting him. Probably because of his nose.

John Forbes Aiken had a soaring, imperious nose, with just the suggestion of a hook at the end of it, that gave his face a hawklike quality. The exact same nose—oh, maybe a millimeter longer—belonged to the publisher of the *World Herald*, Robert Storrow Ames. That fucking nose, Sally thought, would probably make Jack Aiken the editor of the newspaper one day. All he had to do was stick that lousy beak in the door and he got hired faster than you could say Myopia Hunt Club.

"Hey, Sally, want to get a couple beers?"

Joe Segal, city hall, was pulling on his coat, ready to leave.

"Thanks, Joe. Not tonight. Raincheck?"

"Sure. See you tomorrow."

Sally glanced over at John Forbes Aiken. The son-of-a-bitch not only had three names and the nose, but he could write too. Not quite as well as she could, of course. He couldn't quite make it sing the way she could.

"Sally," Joe Segal said, "I meant to ask you, could you put your hands on that story you did on Judge Adler? The librarian couldn't find it. Now that the morgue's gone electronic, you can't find shit."

"Yeah, Joe, I'll Xerox you a copy."

Joe Segal had the Ames nose too, but a fat lot of good it

would do him. Worse, Sally was indifferent to Joe Segal's nose, but she found Jack Aiken's intriguing. This, she knew, had more to do with geography than with anatomy. A Brookline nose did not have the panache of a Pride's Crossing one. That was the trouble with growing up in this goddamned town where the Yankees owned everything, and everybody wanted to be one. Even the Kennedys, deep down, probably wanted to be Yankees. Old Joe tried hard enough to turn his sons into Brahmins. Jack could pass, but Teddy was looking more and more like a guy who tends bar in Southie.

She walked over to her desk and tossed her purse down with a thud. Jack Aiken looked up, annoyance flitting across his face. He had his suit jacket draped across the back of his chair and his sleeves rolled up. Other reporters in the same deshabille looked like slobs. Why did he look like a page out of *GQ*? There was a refinement about him that always made her want to do something really gross, like pick her nose or spit.

"Hey, Aiken," she said, "know what you got with five WASPs sitting around a table?"

This time she heard his jaw clench. He gave a weary sigh of resignation. She loved needling him. He had given up wearing the sports shirts with the little alligators on them—he had one, it seemed, in every color of the rainbow—and she missed them. Little alligators were fine for snotty one-liners about class distinctions. But he hated WASP jokes almost as much.

"No, Ellenberg," he said, displaying feigned and saintly patience, "I don't know what you get with five WASPs sitting around a table."

"Price-fixing."

"Ho-ho."

"Have you ever had a WASP sub?"

"Why do I ask? What is a WASP sub?"

"White bread and mayonnaise."

"Oh, Christ."

Sally flopped down gracelessly into her chair. He was too polite to just tell her to go fuck off. Maybe that's why she enjoyed giving him the needle; a streak of sadism. It was like prodding a hamster with a sharp stick—you knew he wouldn't fight back.

She lit a cigarette—he thought smoking was disgusting—and said to him, "It must be boring to be a WASP. A preppie WASP at that."

"Why should it be boring?"

"You miss all the fun stuff. Oppression, prejudice, ethnic hatred. No swastikas chalked on your hubcaps. No rocks crashing through your windows at midnight. You've probably never even been mugged."

He leaned back in his chair and looked at her. His eyes were very blue, and clear. Why was he so goddamned perfect? At the very least, couldn't he have an astigmatism?

"For your information," he said, "my family and I once had a raging mob nearly burn down our house, just because we were Yankees. So don't tell me I don't know what prejudice is."

"You're kidding."

"No, I am not."

"A mob actually tried to burn your house down? Why?"

The frown lines deepened. His face was sober.

"I was just a kid. Do you remember the big strike on the North Shore twenty-five years ago?"

"No."

"It was a long strike. Really a bitter one. Our neighbors were the owners of one of the factories. One night the strikers marched right up our street, a thousand strong. They had torches, and they were screaming they were going to kill all of us. I was only nine years old, and I was sure I was going to die. My mother was screaming hysterically. My father got out his hunting rifle and stood by the window."

"My God!"

"He told my mother that if they got him, to take the rifle and shoot me. In the heart, so I'd die right away. And then kill herself. The mob was out of control. I guess I can't blame them, they were hungry and out of work—but they would have torn us apart."

"That must have been terrifying!"

"I still have nightmares about it sometimes. My father standing there with the gun, all those torches on the lawn. It was awful."

"What happened?"

He looked at her and a tiny smile tugged at the corners of his mouth.

"They burned an alligator on our lawn."

Sally swallowed the puff of smoke she had inhaled. Jack Aiken just smiled at her happily, as she nearly choked to death. "I'm dying!" she croaked.

"Serves you right, it's a filthy habit."

She coughed and shook her head. "You son-of-a-bitch. Torches on the lawn. Your father and his hunting rifle. Shit, you lie like an angel."

He smiled again. "I know."

Sally snuffed out her cigarette in the ashtray on her desk and said, "You're right about one thing. It is a filthy habit. Tomorrow, nine A.M., I quit."

"You won't quit. No self-discipline."

Those cool blue eyes appraised her. She felt her spine stiffen; probably because he was right. At that moment, she couldn't bear his being right.

"Yeah?" she snapped. "Just watch me." She dropped the pack of cigarettes into the wastebasket. "Discipline is my middle name."

"Ho, ho, ho."

"I suppose you have no vices? A regular Cotton Mather."

"None that pollute my precious bodily fluids."

She looked at him. His face was perfectly sober, not even a glint of ingenuousness in those placid blue eyes. They unnerved her. It was the reason she never quite knew when he was putting her on.

Kevin Murphy walked over, nodded to Jack, and said to Sally, "Parker Ames wants to see you."

"Ah, it's your lucky day," Jack said.

"Oh shit, what's he want?"

"Who knows?" Kevin sighed. "Who ever knows?"

Parker Ames was the nephew of Robert Storrow Ames, and it was said in the newsroom that he disproved the theories of natural selection. All the hardy, thrifty genes that had carried the Ameses to fortune had seemingly taken a detour when it came to Parker. It was sacred writ around the water cooler that if his name had been Parker O'Reilly, he'd still be on the police beat in Dorchester.

It was rumored that there had been an unholy row when the family proposed moving Parker from his post in sales to the managing editorship. The Ameses played things very close to the vest, but rumors did manage to seep out. Robert Storrow Ames had been unhappy with the notion, but bowed to intense family pressure. Parker got the title, but most of the real work was done by two assistants. Sally thought Parker was an idiot. Even Jack Aiken, who never gossiped about anyone, curled his lip at the very mention of his name.

She walked into Parker's office and said, "What can I do for you, Parker?" (She knew it annoyed him when she used his first name.)

He looked up, tugged at his glasses and said, "I've had a complaint about your tactics."

"Oh? Who from?"

"The Middlesex DA."

"Ethridge? Mr. Integrity?"

"He's asking us to retract the story that he's pushing indictments against the former lieutenant governor."

"Everybody knows he wants to run for governor. Hanging a racketeering rap on Curran means brownie points. But his case is thinner than pantyhose. He's got *bupkis*. Which means nothing."

"Your story implies that it's nothing but politics."

"More than implies. Ethridge has been bragging to all his buddies that he's going to nail Curran."

"He's hinting at a libel suit."

Sally laughed. "He's so full of crap. He's panicking because Senator Devon's picking up a lot of support. Ethridge needs a big score. But he won't sue us, because that would open his office up to discovery. A lot of nasty stuff would crawl out. He's a bully. He uses his office more politically than any other DA in the state, and then he hands out pious crap about cleaning up politics."

Parker Ames drew himself up straight in his chair.

"What's wrong with going after politicians who have their hand in the till?"

"You have to make a case. In law, not in the headlines. He's sloppy. Doesn't do his homework."

"He happens to teach a seminar at Harvard Law."

"That doesn't make him Louis Brandeis. Sure, he's connected. He's still sloppy."

"Can't you ever use a little tact, Ellenberg? Why do you alienate everybody?"

"I don't get paid for tact. And you don't say that to Jerry Rogers, and he gets bomb threats every other week."

"That's different."

"Because he's a man?"

"I didn't say that."

"You didn't have to. But I do my job, and I do it well. And Ethridge isn't going to sue us. If we apologize for my story, we'll be a laughingstock, all over town. The *Record-American* would get a good chuckle."

"I'll talk to my uncle about it."

"That's a very good idea."

"And please remember that you represent this paper, at all times."

"I always keep that in mind, Parker.

"Asshole," she muttered under her breath as she walked out of his office. She went back to her desk and stuffed a sheaf of papers into her briefcase and slammed it shut, hard.

"Are we losing our cool again?" Jack Aiken asked, a malicious little smile on his lips.

"Parker Ames could turn Mahatma Gandhi into the Boston Strangler," she fumed. "Two minutes with Parker, and he'd garrot the son-of-a-bitch with his loincloth."

"You're so cute when you're mad."

"How'd you like a fat lip!"

"I bet Dorothy Parker wishes she said that. Such witty repartee."

"I am going home and kick the cat. Maybe I'll feel better."

"Sweet dreams."

"Oh fuck off, Jack," she said.

REPORTER'S JOURNAL: Sally Ellenberg

This journal idea came from my father, actually. He always used to keep one. Nothing formal, just a series of scribblings in one of the notebooks he always carried around. He said that journalism was the first rough draft of history, and he thought one day he might use it for writing his memoirs. That's what he was working on when he died, in fact. His journal was a jumble of things. Sometimes it would be what happened that day, or sometimes rememberings about his past, or philosophical notes. Mine is going to be the same. Who knows what I'll use it for. When a thought hits me, I'll scribble, that's it. Today it's Jason Abromivitz.

We were both sixteen when we decided to overthrow

the government. Jason had the nicest wavy hair, and a very nice smile, even with the braces. His father did my teeth. He was a Maoist. (Not Dr. Abromivitz. Jason.)

I could never get as doctrinaire as Jason. He wanted to march all the bourgeoisie of Brookline out into the countryside to collective farms. Including his parents, who he said had the worst kind of counterrevolutionary ideas. I could see Jason, in his fatigues, force-marching his mother and father and their neighbors and half the faculty at Brookline High out the Mass Turnpike to Lincoln or Concord someplace to grow soybeans. He said he might let his father carry his high-speed drill on his back, because even stoop laborers got cavities. Jason and I would run a reeducation camp, where we would teach the proper revolutionary creeds to the cognoscenti of Brookline. Jason had visions of watching Rabbi Gershon, who did his Bar Mitzvah and wouldn't let him read a section of *Das Kapital* along with his Torah portion, grubbing in the dirt while chanting the thoughts of Mao.

Jason and I were rebels against bourgeois sexual morality as well. We used to Do It in the storage room over his father's dental office, on Saturday mornings when the office was in full swing. To this day, hearing people spit gives me a strange kind of sexual thrill.

The terrible burden we bore was that we were too young for real revolution. We'd put on our ripped jeans and go off to the marches, but we always had to be back in time to get our homework done. I mean, we were nice, middle-class Jewish kids and our parents would kill us if we didn't at least get B's on our report cards.

One day Jason decided we should make a bomb, to blow up some pillar of the bourgeois establishment. But we agreed that nobody could get hurt. This was a problem. Even if we blasted a bank or a post office late at night, we might off some security guard who was a member of the working class and that certainly would not please the spirit of Karl Marx.

Jason suggested Tufts Dental School as a target, since that was where his father had gone and probably picked up such capitalist imperialist pig ideas as driving a Lincoln Town car. I said that blowing Tufts Dental off the face of the earth would probably not hasten the forward march of the dialectical process. I thought blasting Harvard would be much better.

We decided to postpone discussions of our target and to move to the practical considerations. We went down to the North End, to the alley where we knew you could get illegal fireworks and Seiko watches hijacked from trucks on their way up from Providence. A big, hairy guy named Mario asked us what we wanted. He said he had bottle rockets, cherry bombs, Roman candles, Gucci wallets, and Panasonic tape decks.

"Plastique," I said.

"What?" Mario asked, somewhat surprised. I guess he didn't get many requests for plastic explosives.

"You know," I said, "the stuff Algerian freedom fighters used in their war of liberation against the colonial domination of the French." I used to talk like that.

"Jesus, you are talking serious shit," Mario said. "Cherry bombs are as big as I get."

"You can't blow up Harvard with cherry bombs," Jason said.

"Yeah, but a person could blow his head off with one of these babies," Mario said, hefting a large cherry bomb.

"How?" Jason asked.

"Put it in your mouth, light it, and Pow! Your head will go bouncing right down the street."

"I don't think we could get the president of Harvard to do that," Jason said regretfully.

"A person would have to be pretty stupid," Mario admitted. He chuckled. "There's some guineas around here dumb enough," he said.

I told Mario he should not denigrate his ethnic heritage. After all, Caesar's legions once ruled the world from the Aral Sea to the Nile.

Mario chuckled again and said there were some dumb

guineas in Caesar's legion who'd be stupid enough to do it too.

We asked Mario if he knew where we could find what we were looking for. He didn't know, but he did offer to get us a good buy on a couple of crates of Uzis. Through his cousin's wife's girlfriend's ex-boyfriend, who was in Walpole Prison, but still had good connections on the outside. We thanked him, but declined. We weren't quite ready for Uzis. Between what I made working at the pizza parlor and Jason's savings bonds from his Bar Mitzvah, we could probably swing a little plastique, but a couple dozen Uzis probably cost a lot. Besides, where would we keep them? In the storage room? Jason's father would have had a coronary if he went looking for the rubber stuff he made teeth molds with and found Uzis with fifteen crates of ammo instead.

But it just got too intense with Jason and me. One minute we'd be groping like crazy to the sounds of gargled Lavoris, then we'd be fighting and swearing never to see each other again. I just couldn't live like that. Besides, Jason was a more dedicated revolutionary than I was. My old bourgeois habits kept creeping back on me. Sometimes I'd sneak off to Loehmann's for designer sweaters, and I liked going to shul with my folks on the high holidays, losing myself in the ancient sounds and rituals. Jason hadn't been to shul since his Bar Mitzvah, and he loved to quote Marx about you know what being the opium of the masses. We would end up fighting a lot more than we groped, and we sort of drifted apart.

I've been thinking about Jason because I ran into him last week on Boylston Street. I asked him what he was up to, and he laughed, and said that he'd just been put on tenure track at Tufts Dental. We both giggled at that, and I said I was very glad we hadn't decided to blow it up.

Jason wasn't a Maoist anymore, but he did work for free one day a week in a dental clinic for poor kids in Dorchester. He and his wife had just joined Temple Israel, so their daughter could start Sunday school.

So it's funny how things turn out. Jason still has nice wavy hair and a terrific smile. I wonder if his wife gargles with Lavoris; maybe I ought to send her an anonymous note telling her forget *The Joy of Sex*— run out and get some of that red sweet stuff.

Who knows, maybe I made the mistake of my life not hanging around and waiting for Jason to grow out of revolution and into oral surgery. Ah well, the moving finger writes, etc.

2
■

He hunched his shoulders and pulled up his collar against the night wind. April was always unpredictable in Boston; summer weather one day and cold and clammy the next. Tonight, the chill in the air crept into your bones with the fog.

He looked up and down the street. There was no one to be seen in the darkness except an old wino sleeping it off in a doorway. This neighborhood sure had gone to hell since he was a kid. In those days, there had been nice stores—not fancy, but the people from St. Margaret's had shopped there. Now, the place was full of niggers and spics. Good thing his mother was gone. She had wanted him to be a priest. He laughed. *Good luck on that one, Ma.*

He shivered and checked the street again. "It's time," he thought, but he didn't move. He had thought it was going to be so great being out on the street again, but the fuckers wouldn't give him a decent job. He had tried, but screw it. He wasn't going to work at some stupid job that even spics and niggers turned up their noses at.

He looked around again, but still didn't move. Why was he nervous about this one? It had been a while, but this one was a piece of cake. DOYLE'S LIQUORS the sign said, but there sure as hell hadn't been a Doyle in the neighborhood for a long time. Maybe a Jew owned it now. They stayed in the stores, the cheap bastards, even after they moved to Newton. Or some black dude, getting rich and getting the hell out of here too.

He could see inside the store from his vantage point across the street. The guy behind the counter was a spic, skinny, looked as if he was just a kid. He didn't look more than sixteen, but you couldn't tell with the greasers. Some of them were little, but tough. Better than an old guy, though. An old guy would probably be the owner, and the old guys were the ones who kept guns under the counter, out of sight. Their reflexes weren't very good, but at close range they could take your head off. It had always been a belief of his, watch out for the old guys. The hired help was better. They didn't give a shit what was in the register, they just didn't want to get their asses shot off. They'd shut up and fork over.

He checked the street again. Why did he have the feeling they knew where he was? The day he was going down to Providence to cut a deal, there was the guy who showed up at the bus station to tell him he wasn't supposed to leave the state. Why would they put a tail on him? Cops never put a tail on small fry like him unless there was something big going down. There never was anything big for him. Too bad. Maybe one day.

He looked across the street and saw the spic wiping the counter inside Doyle's. No one was on his tail tonight. He had made sure of that. It was late, now, the store was probably going to close soon. Christ, there had to be at least five hundred in the drawer. Even in a crummy neighborhood like this, people spent money on booze with the weekend coming up. The spics were into cheap wine, but the niggers liked the hard stuff. Maybe there was even seven hundred in the drawer. Whatever it was, he needed it.

He walked across the street toward the store. He could feel the juices starting to flow, Christ, he had almost forgotten what it felt like, just before. It was a real high; sometimes he had done it not just for the money, but for the fun of it. He laughed to himself, softly. He noticed a faint throbbing in his head.

He stepped onto the curb in front of the store and there was a sharp twinge of pain in his forehead. Christ, his nerves must really be shot. He walked through the door, moved quickly to the counter and pulled out the blunt-nosed revolver. He felt good now. You had to move fast, but calmly. Hesitation could make somebody think they could reach for a gun or throw a punch. Hesitation got you killed.

"Empty the drawer. Now! Make it fast and you won't get blown away."

His voice was steady. Good. The young Puerto Rican clerk looked up, his eyes at first widening with surprise, and then the fear came. He saw a white man of medium build, with a face that was creased beyond his years, with eyes as cold and hard as slate.

"OK, man, I give it to you," the clerk said. "Don't shoot. Please. I give it to you, OK?"

"All of it. Don't try to hide any of it, you lousy spic."

"Man, you'll get it all. All of it. Don't shoot me."

The young man's hands shook so violently that he had a hard time trying to gather up all the bills. "Here it is, man, take it. Take it all."

The clerk reached out his hand, clutching the bills, to the white man. But the man with the gun did not grab for the money. A peculiar expression crossed his face, as if someone had asked him a difficult question and he was trying to respond. Sheer terror circled the windpipe of the clerk.

"Please, mister, here it is!" he croaked.

The gunman looked at the terrified clerk and opened his mouth as if about to speak, but only a strange sound, like a squeak, came out. Then he made a moaning sound and the gun dropped from his hands. His hands clutched at his head, and he bent over slightly, holding his head and making a sound that was half a moan, half a whine.

"Jesus, Mary!" the clerk prayed.

The man straightened up, looked directly at the clerk and then let out a howl, a terrible, animal sound, and the slate blue eyes rolled upwards toward the ceiling. He fell, heavily, like a sack of potatoes. He was dead before he hit the ground.

3
∎

Sally was still aggrieved about her session with Parker when she met her best friend from high school for lunch the next day at the Meridian. Mary Ellen O'Malley had been voted Most Likely to Succeed in their class at Brookline High School, and she took the honor seriously. She was moving up the ladder quickly in corporate law. Sally envied her the big office with the view, the Kerman rug—and the expense account—but she wouldn't have traded jobs with Mary Ellen. Newspapering, in spite of Ames, was still magic. She had that visceral connection with the beating heart of the day's events. Still, Mary Ellen vacationed in St. Barts and would retire one day to a condo on the waterfront. Sally got to Hyannis once a year and figured she would end her days in a walk-up in Allston-Brighton, pounding on the ceiling at nights to make the BU kids turn down their stereos.

Sally stabbed her fork fiercely into a greenish rotini (pasta of the day) and snarled, "Tact! I am a fucking police reporter, not Miss Manners. God forbid I should get anybody *mad*. If he had his way, I'd be writing Chatters Corner!" She sighed. "I'm a bull in a china shop, M.E. A pushy Jew in a place run by Yankees and Irish Catholics."

Mary Ellen sipped her white wine and nodded. "Try being an Irish Catholic at Carter, Palmer, Hale and Hawkins. They still expect me to start keening 'Alive-alive-Ohhh' in the middle of a brief."

"Boston is a weird town. One group was so dominant for so long. The Yankees gave everybody else an inferiority complex. Jews in New York can be . . . Jewish. Here, they try to blend into the pavement. At least the Irish can be Irish," Sally said.

"Sure. If you want to be the rep from Cohasset. Not a partner at C, P, H and H. Or Palmer and Dodge. Who was the first Irish Catholic President? Some guy with a brogue who went to Holy Cross?"

"I get your point."

"Joe Kennedy sent his kids to Harvard so they'd be Protestant enough to pass. When *he* was there, he thought he was smart enough and popular enough so they'd forget he was Irish. But he didn't get into the Porcellian Club, and he never forgot that."

"Yeah, but at least there's a lot of you. You can make noise."

"Sure, all that awful blather about how great it is to be Irish. The *Irish* Irish think we're nuts. And phony. You think Jews have an inferiority complex in this town? We run politics, but nothing else. Not the banks. Not Harvard. Somehow, we're taught to play it safe. Stay with our own. Not take too many risks. That's why Joe Kennedy didn't send the boys to Holy Cross, or Notre Dame. He wanted them to inherit that sense of entitlement you get in the Ivys. Never, for a minute, were they to think they were second-rate."

"What about the girls?"

"Oh, they could go to Catholic schools. They were only *girls*."

"How did you get to be such a ballbuster, M.E.?"

"My father was like old Joe. Kept me away from the nuns. He told me I could be anything I wanted. And he didn't have any sons."

"Neither did my father. I guess we're both the first-born sons. Carrying the family flag."

They were both quiet for a minute, and then Sally said, "But we'll never have what *they* have. The Yankees. That sense of ease. That sureness. That they *deserve* to run things. There will always be those moments, for us, when we think, 'What the hell are we doing here?' They don't wonder. They *know*. Born and bred to it."

"Which gives us an edge, Sally. We're hungry. We want it. So we'll be better."

"But it would be nice, wouldn't it?" Sally said, as she gobbled up the last bite of pasta, "not to *have* to be better."

"In our next life, maybe."

Back at the paper, Sally ran into Robert Storrow Ames in the elevator. They chatted pleasantly, his demeanor as usual polite, friendly—but with enough reserve so that you knew who was the boss and who the hired help. As they stepped out of the elevator he said, "Good story on Ethridge." That was it, nothing more. But she smiled. Good Guys, one, Parker, zip.

She spent most of the day putting together a followup story on the student protests. She was determined not to smoke another cigarette, especially not with Jack Aiken sitting right next to her. She gobbled Certs, two grubby Lifesavers from the bottom of her purse, chewed the labels off three pencils. It killed her, but she didn't have a smoke.

"The whole day," she announced to him gleefully. "Not one butt."

"You'll crack."

"Not me." She picked up the empty ashtray. "Nerves of steel." She put down the ashtray. "OK, no cancer. Now I'm off to get my CARE package from Bloomie's."

"*You* shop at Bloomingdale's?"

"No. But my sister does. I get her hand-me-downs. She thinks fashion is important. She's the kind of person who would airlift fifteen crates of Papagallos to earthquake victims."

"I'm glad to see you're getting help."

Sally looked down at her khaki skirt ($12.99 in Filene's Basement) with the frayed hem and the blue V-necked top with the yellow mustard stain just above the right nipple, from the hot dog she had bought the day before in front of Marsh Chapel, before things turned ugly.

"So I'm not a fashion pacesetter."

"Ellenberg, I give quarters to bag ladies on the Common who dress better than you do."

"We don't *all* have charge accounts at Louie's. Besides, reporters are supposed to be scruffy, haven't you heard? Carl Bernstein is my role model."

"You picked the wrong half of Woodstein. Carl Bernstein is two notches *below* bag lady. I used to see him in D.C."

"Ah, but his Pulitzer Prize goes so nicely with his complexion. Good night, Aiken. Catch you tomorrow."

"Don't remind me."

Sally got her car out of the parking lot and drove to the edge of the South End. She got a spot in front of the Recovery Room, a bar a block away from Municipal Hospital. Her CARE package was going to be delivered, as usual, by her brother-in-law, Joe Weinberg. Joe was in his last year of residency at Boston Municipal. He was an easygoing young man who was still mad about Sally's sister, tolerant of her insistence that one must do things right in this life and dress as if one could at any moment expect an inspection from *Women's Wear*. Joe had also been the source of more than one story for Sally, since anyone who got himself filled with bulletholes and left in a trunk in Boston's internecine gang warfare usually wound up on a slab at Municipal.

Joe was sitting in a booth working on his second beer when Sally walked in. She slid into the booth opposite him. "How's our favorite JAP these days?"

"Judy has discovered Zionism," he said.

"Our Judy?"

"Yes, and I think she's serious. There's this program where you go for a couple of weeks, and you gas up the tanks and serve on a military base. Some people at our temple did it last summer."

"I can't see my sister on the front lines on the Golan. They don't make Uzis in pastel shades to go with your shoes. Got my CARE package?"

He handed her a Bloomie's bag and Sally peeked inside. "Oh my God, Evan-Picone. It's nearly brand new. She's giving *this* away? You must have to slice a lot of spleens to keep up with Bloomie's."

"You put things so delicately, Sally."

"Yeah, well, that's why I am a writer."

Sally downed one beer and ordered another. They chatted for a few minutes about Judy and the kids, and then Joe said, "You know, a weird thing happened last week. I thought you might be interested."

"Weird? How do you mean?"

"On Wednesday night the ambulance brought in a DOA. A

guy was trying to hold up a liquor store and dropped dead right in the middle of the stickup. Took out a gun, asked the clerk to open the cash register, and collapsed. He was dead when the EMTs got there. They thought it was a heart attack. He didn't have a pulse."

"A kid?"

"No. Mid-thirties, I'd say. I had a look at him when he was brought in, and I noticed something peculiar. His hair was real short, almost like the shavetail haircuts they give you in boot camp. Because his hair was so short I could see the holes."

"Holes? In his head?"

"On both sides of his head. Tiny symmetrical holes. The EMTs didn't even notice."

"Why would someone have holes in his head?"

"Well, last year I did a stint in neurosurgery. One of the surgeons was doing experimental work with electrode implants in the brains of patients with temporal lobe epilepsy. The holes this guy had were the same type I saw in implant patients."

"Wait a minute. You mean doctors are putting batteries inside people's heads?"

"Not batteries. Electrodes. Tiny wires that can deliver an electrical charge. It seems they may have had some success in controlling seizures with the implants."

As she listened, Sally pulled out a cigarette. Joe frowned, but she lit up. "How can you control seizures by sticking a wire in somebody's head?"

"I'm no expert, but I do know that you can control a person's physical movements, even his behavior, by electrically stimulating certain areas of the brain. The idea, as I understand it, is to develop the hardware to allow epileptics to control their own seizures when they feel them coming on. It's pretty controversial stuff, though."

"You mean someday a lot of people will be walking around with wires inside their brains?"

"It's not so farfetched. People walk around with pacemakers inside them all the time. They've got metal ball bearings in their joints and Dacron veins. But the funny thing about this case was what happened next. He disappeared."

"Disappeared? Like he just got up and walked out?"

Joe shook his head. "Not very likely. I went down to pathology to see if an autopsy had been performed, because I was curious about those holes. There was no record of an autopsy. I went back to check the emergency room records. There was no record at all.

"Nothing?"

"Zero. Zip. I went to the chief resident, and he said the records were probably just misfiled. Happens all the time since our staff got cut back. Then I was talking to one of the emergency room nurses, and she said that the night the guy was brought in there were Feds at the hospital."

Sally leaned forward, her interest quickening. "Federal agents? Is she sure about that?"

"They didn't identify themselves, but she says she can pick a Fed out of a crowd at the Super Bowl. Her father is secret service. She says they came in an unmarked black limo, but she has no idea what they were doing. Anyhow, yesterday, I checked the records again and they were back in the right place. The cause of death was listed as heart failure. The death certificate was signed by the Suffolk county medical examiner. But if he did an autopsy, there should be a record, and there wasn't. I haven't had time to check it all out. But it seems a little strange."

"I'd say it's strange! A missing body, maybe with electrodes in its head, and federal agents swarming around—"

"Hold on a minute, Sally," Joe warned. "Don't start turning this into cops and robbers. It could be nothing. I didn't see any federal agents, all I saw was a guy with a couple of holes in his head and a file that was missing for a while."

"Well, I'd like to do a bit of checking around. Was there a name in the records?"

"Francis Xavier Brady. Address unknown. But look, protect me, Sally. I don't need *tsuris* on this."

"Don't I always?"

The next morning Sally made a few calls from her apartment before going in to the paper. The police gave her the details of the holdup from the blotter, but said that any medical data had to come from the medical examiner's office. As usual, the M.E.'s office wasn't much help. He was known for running a tight ship and having little regard for reporters, whom he had once publicly referred to as vermin. All she got out of an assistant was what Joe had told her was on the report. Cause of death, heart failure.

Damn.

She would have to make an end run to get more on the story, and it would take time. She was already behind on her series about the patrolmen's union and its fight with the mayor. Was it worth taking time out for something that would probably turn out to be a wild goose chase? Still, it was interesting, and she sensed something about it that smelled.

When she walked into the city room later that morning, she saw, standing next to John Forbes Aiken, a tall, pale blond woman. Sally had been introduced to his fiancée before. She breezed in and out of the city room from time to time, always dressed in what Sally called North Shore Imperative: real silk, real tweed, and jewelry that wouldn't turn her neck green. She was a walking example of the maxim that a woman couldn't be too thin or too rich.

Sally muttered, "I've seen bigger boobs on an eight year old." She immediately felt a twinge of feminist guilt. But she couldn't help her feelings about the blonde. Sheer class hatred shot through her at the sight of that pale hair—too delicate to be Clairol—the porcelain jaw, and the washed-out blue eyes. She remembered reading *Ivanhoe* in seventh grade in Brookline and wanting to be Lady Rowena, pale and blond and fragile and rescued by a shining knight. Instead, she got her tush pinched by dirty old men on the Green Line. When Jack Aiken's fiancée was coming out at her debutante cotillion, Sally was already into combat boots and refusing to shave her legs. In those days, she sneered at the bourgeois ritual of ballgowns and debutantes. She sneered even harder at the JAPs who tried to outdo the Brahmins, renting limousines to ferry them to fancy do's at the Sidney Hill Country Club, where the names were Jewish but the ambience was strictly WASP. Still, there were times, Sally remembered, when she had pictured herself in pink tulle, waltzing in the arms of a handsome man of the John-Forbes-Aiken genus. Thoughts like that would fill her with remorse, and she would apologize to the entire pantheon: Sorry, Che. Sorry, Mao, Fidel, Huey, Eldridge. Oh God, it was hard to be a middle-class high school radical. Did Angela Davis ever worry about what she was going to wear to the prom?

Sally walked to her desk and nodded to Aiken and his fiancée. He said to her, "Sally, you remember Miki Shelton. Miki, Sally Ellenberg."

"Have we met?" asked Miki, extending her hand.

"Probably at Myopia," Sally said, dropping the name of the

hunt club where Prince Charles rode his ponies now and then.

Miki's eyes registered interest. "Do you ride?"

"No, just plain old missionary position for me," Sally said. Jack Aiken threw her a black look. Miki just smiled vacantly. "Lovely to have met you."

"Lovely."

Jack Aiken walked his fiancée to the elevator and Sally started to work on her police union story. He came back, slid into his chair and said, "Wise-ass."

"Aiken," she said, "just what is it that Muffy does?"

"*Miki.*"

"Whatever."

"She—she's involved in a lot of things."

"Such as?"

"Well, this week Miki is organizing a crafts fair for the Ipswitch Chamber of Commerce."

"Oh."

"It's a lot of work."

"Did I say it wasn't?"

He sighed. "Why the hell is it that you can always do this to me?"

"Do what?"

"Make me feel so defensive."

She looked at him in surprise. She thought *she* was the one who was always on the defensive. He suddenly seemed less than perfect and impregnable, and she felt a throb of regret for needling him about Muffy—Miki—whatever. She realized that he was what her radical friends would have called—with a sneer—a straight arrow. There was no cunning in him. She suddenly felt an urge to explain herself to him.

"I'm sorry, Jack. It's not her fault that she sets my teeth on edge. I guess if I was from Peoria or someplace I wouldn't feel that way."

He looked at her blankly, so she said, "It's growing up around here where you people owned everything. Even the class. The style. I hated that. I hated it that people like me tried to be like people like you. My friend Sharon in high school had a nose just like Muffy's . . . Miki's. Only she got it from Izzy Bromberg at the Beth Israel. She already had a perfectly nice nose, only it wasn't WASP enough. What do you know about electrodes in the brain?"

"What?"

"Electrodes. In the brain."

"Sally, would you run that one by me again? What are we talking about?"

"Sorry, that's the way my mind works. Hops from one thing to another. Nose jobs remind me of brain implants. See, there was this guy who tried to knock over a liquor store . . ."

She told him the story that her brother-in-law had told her. "So all I can get on this guy is that he served time at Deer Island and was in Concord Reformatory for a while. Minor stuff. Grand theft auto, tailgating, and his specialty was hitting on liquor stores. So tell me, why would the Feds be interested in a guy like that?"

"Seems very odd."

"Tell me about this implant stuff. How common is it?"

"It's very controversial. More sophisticated than the old lobotomies, but a lot of people say we don't have enough knowledge to go messing around in people's brains that way. But some doctors think that brain surgery is the cure for all kinds of deviant behavior. There was a big flap back in the sixties when a couple of Boston neurosurgeons said that ghetto rioters were suffering from brain dysfunction and could be helped by surgery."

"That's crazy," Sally said. "Blacks can't get jobs and rats are biting their kids, and they riot because they have brain damage?"

"That's how a lot of people reacted. As I remember the story, the two doctors qualified their statements and the whole thing blew over. But there are still a lot of questions about informed consent. Can a mental patient, for example, really give consent to this kind of surgery?"

"You're doing stuff on mental hospitals, aren't you?"

"Yes, a series on the state hospitals. I'm going out to Westborough Hospital tomorrow.

Sally grubbed into her bag for a cigarette, remembered what he had said about discipline, and took out a Lifesaver instead. "Listen," she said, "if you have time, can you tell me more about this electrode business?"

"I can tell you what I know. How about after work tomorrow? Over a drink. I have a feeling I'm going to need one after a cheerful afternoon in the snake pit."

He went back to his work, and she watched him as he leafed through his notes for a story, absorbed in his thoughts. She was attracted to him; she admitted it, but could not for the life of her figure out why. Possibly it was his highly developed sense of order. He pasted neat labels on his files; his desk was so clean you could eat off it; and his pencils, sharpened to exactly the same length, stood in a precise row on the desktop. Maybe that appealed to her because she was still feeling bruised from Mark, whom she had lived with for two years. Mark was impulsive, messy, and fun. At first she had loved his passion for anything new and different, until she began to suspect it was merely a short attention span. She bailed out when his attention wandered to a budding Trotskyite undergraduate at Brandeis with a dogmatic turn of mind and a D cup bra. Maybe she was simply tired of ex-radicals with messy closets, messy lives, and a disinclination to grow up.

But there was something more. Jack Aiken had an air about him. "Establishment Square," Mark would have called it, but it was more a sense of quiet dignity that in some odd way reminded Sally of her father. In a business that always had its share of hacks, drunks, and has-beens, Sol Ellenberg had been a class act. He had rarely raised his voice, but people had listened when he talked. If he hadn't been a Jew, in a town where what you were had a lot to do with how far you got . . . But that was an old story. He had made his peace with it long ago, even if his daughter never had.

When he died of liver cancer five years ago, the temple had been filled with mourners. Her mother and father had one of the few really good marriages she had ever seen, where the affection and respect were mutual. She could only imagine her mother's loss, but her own was acute. She especially missed the long talks they used to have, about the state of the world in general and the newspaper business in particular.

She looked at Jack Aiken again—he was sharpening another goddamned pencil. He was not, after all, her father. Scratch Jack Aiken's vanilla wafer exterior and all you'd probably find was more vanilla wafer. Just because a man smelled nice, kept his Eberhardt Fabers in a neat row, and made you think of your father did not mean there was a basis for a relationship.

Still, there was a certain chemistry. She enjoyed watching the way he walked, not macho jock, but fluid and easy. Tennis was his sport, she guessed. She loved his hair, brown, wavy, always neatly trimmed. When she walked by his chair, she often had a mad urge to put both her hands in his hair and disarrange it. Jack Aiken's hair was as tempting as a mud puddle to a kid in white shoes.

She had never been very good, she thought with a twinge of shame, at resisting temptation. Which was why she was going to keep her hands off Jack Aiken; not that she couldn't think of interesting things to do with her hands *on* Jack Aiken. But this was the new Sally Ellenberg. Disciplined. Into chastity. No more wild leaps into the stratosphere, and no more thudding crashes at the other end. "All-the-way Sally" had been her nickname in high school, not entirely because she was the leading scorer on the soccer team.

Well, no more. "Down to Gehenna or up to the throne, she travels fastest who travels alone." She was going to have labels sewn into her underwear; an appropriate place.

She waited until Jack had left on an assignment, then reached in her purse for a cigarette. No! She had to cut out the damn things before the Big C got her. She looked at the pack. "The Surgeon General has determined . . ." it told her sternly.

"Screw the Surgeon General," she retorted, defiantly. She couldn't give up sex *and* cigarettes.

She leaned back, and lit up a filter.

4

■

Jack Aiken didn't have his mind on his story as he drove along the Mass Turnpike. He was thinking about his fiancée. He had to get this whole thing with Miki settled. It had to be done before their engagement had run longer than *A Chorus Line*. Miki was showing signs of restlessness and his mother was itching to get the wedding invitations off to the stationer's. It wasn't fair to anybody, particularly to Miki, to let it drag on—and he was the one at fault. "Fair" was his watchword in dealing with people. Whatever else one did, one had to be fair and aboveboard. He liked being engaged to Miki. He was not so sure about being married to her. But it was time to be married to someone, and Miki seemed a more than pleasant choice.

He had passed his thirtieth birthday four years ago, and things had felt unsettled ever since. In his culture, a man was not a full-grown adult until he was married, had produced heirs, and was fully in charge of his financial affairs. After a certain age, single men in Yankee families seemed somehow out of place. Their status gradually declined from that of eligible bachelor to permanent "extra man" for dinner parties and weekends, to eccentric male relative. The Irish made a lot of noise about the primacy of family—if he read one more book about the Kennedys he would puke—but it was his people who settled in and wrestled with this wild shore, tamed and farmed it and civilized it and built families whose tentacles stretched out to embrace the land and the mills and the shipping and the banks—all of it, at one time. *They* knew about family. Jack found the genial philandering of the Kennedy males somewhat déclassé—the behavior of the servant class. Yankees viewed adultery more severely—not that they never did it, but it was seen more as *The Scarlet Letter* than a bit of pinch and tickle. Not that they were prudes. Men and women had needs, and rutting could be quite pleasurable, but one did not refer to it over the demitasse. Not if one had any class.

Yes, being married would put an end to this unsettled period of his life. He was not comfortable with it. On or about his thirtieth birthday, he had taken stock of himself very seriously. He prided himself on the fact that he could assess himself quite objectively.

He saw a man who was sound of limb and possessed of a good mind, one that tended more toward the analytical than the poetic. He husbanded his physical assets with reasonable care, exercised moderately, always flossed his teeth, wore good walking shoes, did not smoke, and drank—never to excess—on appropriate social occasions. He performed capably at most tasks assigned him. Sometimes he wished he was less evenly balanced, that he did just one thing with brilliance and fire, instead of doing many things quite well. But genius was a gift from the Almighty, and there was no sense mourning what one would never have. He was doing well, if not spectacularly, in his chosen profession of journalism, and it was a point of stubborn pride that he had not climbed on the strength of his family name. He had started on a small daily in New York State, and made it to the *Washington Post* on his clips, not his connections. It was at the *Post* that he began his science specialty; it appealed to his analytical mind. He could have had a bright future there. German Jews like the Meyers and their daughter Katherine felt comfortable with Boston Brahmins. The editor of the paper, after all, had been Benjamin Crowninshield Bradlee.

But he discovered that Washington was an unsettled place, since power was based on the shifting sands of electoral politics, not the verities of class and family. While he found that exhilarating at times, he felt more at home in Boston, with its clearly defined ethnic geography, where he could read the names of his ancestors on weathered tombstones. Once he knew he could succeed on alien ground, without the connections and the cachet of his name, the tug of New England became too strong to resist. Moving to Boston was coming home. Still, he didn't feel connected the way he wanted to feel. Marriage to Miki would complete the circle.

He had to admit that he liked the stares of other men when he walked into places with her. It was the pale hair and the cheekbones that did it. She had the face of a model; had, in fact, done some modeling, but it bored her. Everything she did, she did beautifully, but little seemed to surprise or delight her. Especially, he thought ruefully, *him.*

Miki liked sex—even the sweaty, athletic sort—but she never seemed exactly thrilled with the fact that it was with him. At first he had thought it was his fault, so he dutifully plowed through *The Joy of Sex,* though he had been, deep down, a trifle embarrassed over some of the kinky bits. Miki was appreciative, but hardly overwhelmed. To Miki, sex was a natural fact of life, like eating, riding, bathing, and shopping, to be enjoyed but not to be made a big deal over. And it certainly wasn't dirty; good mental health required that notion to be consigned to the dustbin of outworn ideas. Still, lately he had been wishing for an edge of danger, or mystery in their relationship. Couldn't she do something equated in his mind with *sin*? Like wearing black stockings with garters or whispering really dirty words in his ear? If he asked her, of course, she would cheerfully and gracefully comply. Miki was a good sport about most things. If he said he wanted to tie her to the bedpost she would buy him sterling silver handcuffs—from Shreves.

Unaccountably, he found himself thinking about Sally Ellenberg. Did she like that stuff in *The Joy of Sex*? Hell, she would probably tie *him* to the bedpost.

What an aggravating woman. Anything that popped into her head came out of her mouth. Not that she was dumb—far from it. She had a mind like a laser, it cut through to the heart of things. But she certainly had no style. She dressed as if she were blind, with the most amazing color combinations, and lately she had been wearing a lipstick that was the most grotesque shade of orange he had ever seen. Against her fair skin—beautiful skin, he had to admit—it looked like a neon sign. She didn't seem to give a damn about what she looked like, and with a little care, she could be a knockout. She had large brown eyes and lashes that were like underbrush, and when she wore those V-necked tee shirts, it was hard to keep his eyes on his VDT. More than a hint of milk-white bosom was visible when she leaned forward and he tried—unsuccessfully—not to stare at it. He once typed, in a recombinant DNA story, "They seal the ring of DNA with an annealing enzyme and put the plasmid back in the breasts."

He hit the erase key with *Guiness-Book-of-World-Records* speed, and his face flushed crimson, a weakness that had dogged him since childhood. He would never live it down if she saw that one. He shuddered at the thought of how she would rag him for his Freudian slip.

"Hey, Aiken, which piece of my anatomy do you want for your story today? The right one for the SALT talks? Or maybe you would prefer the left, for Acid Rain?" Why did she love to needle him, with her stupid WASP jokes and her comments about his clothes? He hated it. Really hated it.

He swung the car off the Mass Pike at the Westborough exit. Thinking about Sally Ellenberg was . . . unsettling. He had a suspicion that she could bring out all sorts of dangerous emotions in a person like him. He was a healthy young male, he liked sex as well as the next fellow, and his relations with women had always been amiable and mutually pleasurable. Unreasoned passion had never been his métier; he found it quite inexplicable. Yankees, he admitted, tended to view an excess of passion as treacherous, a danger to property, family, trade, virtue, and the orderly proceedings of the universe. It caused people to behave in disturbing ways. Great-Great-Great Uncle Zachariah had shot a man at sunrise in a duel over a pulchritudinous young woman named Sarah Grimsby, and he had to leave Boston to pursue a (presumably) dissolute life on the Barbary Coast. Another ancestor had lusted so mightily after the wife of his partner in the shipping business that he was shot in the heart by the aggrieved husband in the midst of a midnight coupling. This left his wife a widow, his children fatherless, and the business a shambles. Passion, indeed, was to be viewed with a jaundiced eye.

And yet . . . and yet. He should have had someone like Sally Ellenberg in his past. Someplace tucked away in memory, where he could look at it as safely as peering at an old photo album.

He would have written her stupid love poems, drowned himself in drink when she so much as glanced at another man, dipped her breasts in champagne and tenderly sucked off every drop, made love naked in the surf, had furious arguments in which crockery was thrown. It would be well over, of course.

He thought about her sitting at the desk with the blouse with the mustard stain on it and wearing the terrible orange lipstick and suddenly he was kissing the orange mouth and she was kissing him back, hard, and then she was tearing off his tie and sliding her hands across his chest and running her tongue over his bare nipple—

Oh shit.

That's all he needed, to go limping into Westborough State Hospital with a hard-on. "Sorry about that, non-English-speaking shrinks and borderline paranoids, but I was just having this wonderful fantasy about being ravished by the criminal justice reporter."

He deliberately shoved bare chests and nipples of all varieties out of his mind and tried to concentrate on strands of DNA and the Watson-Crick model of the double helix. That was nearly enough to do it, and the sight of Westborough State Hospital finished the job.

He got out of the car and walked slowly toward the main building. It was a dreary old institutional structure that wore on its grimy façade the traces of generations of neglect. As he neared the door, he felt a shiver of recognition. His father had been in places like this—well, fancier maybe—from time to time, drying out. It astonished him that, as he walked, the years peeled back and he was a child again, remembering so acutely the pain he had felt, coming to visit his father.

Damn, why did he get stuck with this lousy story? Everybody knew the state mental health system was a shambles, its funding slashed, its staff overworked and underpaid. He knew he had to do these stories, but they gave him an overwhelming sense of powerlessness and frustration. He liked the excitement of the "frontier" pieces, where he could grapple with new concepts that were changing the face of science. He was acutely uncomfortable with situations over which he had no control, and this one was too close to home.

He walked through the door and up the corridor toward the admissions office. The familiar, faintly medicinal scent kept him halfway sunk in the past. He remembered how his father had looked when he and his mother had come to visit, as fragile as the old pieces of china in the cupboard, his hands trembling slightly, his lips stretched out into a painful smile, but his eyes frightened and wary. Jack had wanted to go to his father, put his arms around him and say, "It's all right. I am going to grow up to be strong and rich, and you can live in my house forever." He never did it. He stood, rigid, his hands at his sides; the pain of seeing his father this way had been so intense it had made his teeth ache.

Having a father who was an alcoholic made him different from other boys of his station. Like perfectly cut pieces of a jigsaw puzzle, they could move into places ordained for them with all the ease of a Mercedes making a turn. But what if you didn't fit? What if one of the edges was a little bit broken? Yankee families did not throw their failures out into the street with the dogs and winos. They found a place where they could die, slowly, in comfort, killed them with a chilly kindness in a place where they could never forget that they hadn't measured up. In the long run, maybe cheap muscatel and camaraderie on the Common were better.

Jack spent his childhood buffeted by two overwhelming currents: the wish to fit in and the need to be loyal to his father. His life was a series of small rebellions. He did go to Harvard, but he did not go into law, banking, or the foreign service. He chose what many in his social set saw as a disreputable, blue collar profession. Oh, other well-born young men became journalists, but they did so in a manner befitting a gentleman. They found powerful mentors, started out their careers with nice lunches at the State Department with assistant secretaries who knew their fathers, and rented chic flats in Georgetown where they served impertinent—but not showy—white wines. Jack did it like the proles did, chasing fires and broken sewer lines and living in a walk-up. He learned, fast, about misery and violence and lost hopes and the vagaries of race and class. When he'd come to the job, he was a young man with decent instincts, honed by a sense of noblesse oblige. But the early years in his trade had given him a loathing for injustice that would forever set him apart from many of the young men he'd grown up with. The sense that he would never fit did not go away, it grew more intense.

As he walked along the hallway he felt a tightness in his

throat, and fought back an impulse to simply turn and run out of this building that housed so much misery. He didn't, of course. That was one thing that being a Forbes and an Aiken had taught him. You did what you had to do, and you didn't let on that it hurt.

He introduced himself to the hospital director, a young man who had been in the job less than a year and who admitted frankly that he would not be staying long.

"I'll be honest with you, Mr. Aiken, we do our best under difficult circumstances. We're level-funded or cut in every department this fiscal year. We haven't got enough staff and we can hardly keep up with maintenance costs."

"Is it a crisis situation?"

"Pretty close. We try to give quality care, but we don't have enough people to go around. It's a revolving door. We haven't got enough beds. Know where people go when they leave here? Look on the streets, in the libraries, anyplace it's warm."

"What about drugs? Some critics say patients are over-sedated."

"We try to give appropriate therapy. Do we sometimes use meds too much? We try not to."

"My . . . somebody in my family was an alcoholic. I used to see him shot full of Thorazine. He'd shuffle, like a zombie. But he was never dangerous."

"These are forgotten people out here, Mr. Aiken. Who cares that they're getting shot full of drugs because we don't have enough staff to manage a ward? What people care about is getting another fifty bucks shaved off their real estate tax."

After the interview, the director introduced Jack to a young attendant named Bill, who offered to give him a tour of the facility. Jack dutifully trudged along. These places were all the same: bleak, institutional rooms, patients sitting in chairs staring aimlessly at TV sets or wandering through the halls. There was the inevitable Ping-Pong table. Ping-Pong was the big sport in mental hospitals.

As they entered one of the wards, a man shuffled past Jack in the corridor. He wore the same drab, shapeless clothes as most of the other inmates, and his gait was the half-walk, half-shuffle that Jack knew to be the result of drugs. But over his head, the man wore a paper bag. There were ragged holes torn out for the eyes.

Jack stopped still. "Bill?"

"Yes?"

"That man has a bag over his head."

"I know."

"Look, I know you get some peculiar behavior in here, but why is that man wearing a bag over his head?"

"He says he's afraid that people will try to cut his head."

"Paranoid?"

"Yes, but maybe he has a reason."

"What do you mean?"

"He had an operation."

"What kind?"

"Some kind of brain operation. I think he was a lot better before."

"Before?" Jack kept looking at the patient, who walked to the end of the corridor, turned, and walked back the other way. He seemed to be pacing, like an animal in a cage.

"He was here before his operation."

"Was he like this?"

"No. He was a very smart guy. A lawyer. I used to talk to him a lot. He had episodes where he would fly into rages and you had to calm him down. But when they passed he'd seem OK again."

"And now? Does he have any good periods?"

"I haven't seen any. He just walks around all the time with a bag over his head. If we take the bag away, he puts newspapers or towels over his head. He's totally psychotic."

"Could I talk to him?"

"You could try."

They walked over to the man with the bag over his head, who backed up against the wall. All Jack could see of his face was two large frightened eyes glittering through the ragged holes he had torn in the bag.

"Frank, someone wants to talk to you," Bill said, gently.

The man shrank back against the wall. "They cut me. They want to cut me!"

"No, sir," Jack said, trying to keep his voice gentle and reassuring. "I don't want to hurt you. I promise. I just want to talk to you."

"They cut me. The government!"

"Who?" Jack said.

"The government. They cut me. Please don't let them get me. They're after me."

"Bill," Jack said, softly, "do you think you could get him to take off the bag?"

"I could try. He trusts me." He put his arm on the man's shoulder. "Frank, no one is going to hurt you. This man wants to see where they cut you. He wants to make sure no one hurts you again."

The man's eyes glittered.

"Here, Frank," Bill said, putting his hand on the bag. "I'll take it off, just for a minute. Then you can have your bag back."

"Do you promise?" Frank said fearfully.

"I promise."

Bill gently lifted the bag from the man's head. Jack barely stifled a gasp of surprise. The man's head was completely shaven. On each side of his head was a small, neat hole.

"They cut me," the man said.

"I'm sorry, Frank," Jack told him.

Bill slipped the bag back over Frank's head and the man stood still, eyes staring through the holes. The fear in his eyes chilled Jack to the bone.

As they walked away, Jack asked, "What's going to happen to him?"

"He'll probably spend the rest of his life here. He's in his fifties. I don't think he'll ever get better."

"Doesn't he have any family?"

"An ex-wife, I guess. No kids, parents dead. He's like a lot of people here. The earth could swallow them up and no one would care."

"Where was his surgery done? Here?"

"Oh no. A Dr. Severn used to come around from time to time to look at him. I haven't seen him lately. There are a lot of private clinics in the area. Some of them are good. Some are just shock mills."

"Zap 'em and bill 'em?"

"More or less. We get their failures. It's a dumping grounds, here."

"Where was this Dr. Severn from?"

"I'm not sure. We get a lot of doctors in and out. I think I heard him say he had an office in Marlborough."

Jack thanked Bill for his time and walked out of the hospital. As he opened the door to his car, he found that his hands were shaking. Jack knew that the specter of Frank, with his frightened eyes staring out through the jagged holes in a paper bag, would shuffle through the corridors of his dreams in the days ahead. Could any hell imagined by a medieval muralist be more terrible? To wander, until the end of your days, seeing the demons manufactured by your mind at every turn? Jack shuddered, and pressed hard on the accelerator, feeling an urgent need to put as much distance as he could between himself and Westborough State Hospital.

He had planned to go back to the paper, but he was in no mood to write, not yet, so on an impulse he drove to Cambridge and parked his car in front of the office at MIT where Craig Letterman worked. Craig, a friend from his Harvard days, was active in Science for the People, a left-liberal group of academicians who often opposed establishment views on science policy. Craig and his colleagues could always be counted on for an intelligent dissenting voice.

He found Letterman in his tiny, littered office on Mass Ave.

"Craig, for a man *Time* magazine called America's best bet for the Nobel, you sure do work in a craphole."

Letterman looked up. There was food on his walrus moustache, and his feet, shod in L. L. Bean hiking boots, were resting on a pile of papers that might indeed one day lead to a Nobel Prize. If he could find them all.

"Hah!" he said. "If I lose one more grant to budget cuts I'll be doing my thing in the back of a station wagon. What can I do for the *World Herald*, my man?"

Jack dropped into a chair. "I've just been out to Westborough. I'm doing a story on state hospitals."

Craig made a face. "Garbage dumps."

"Yeah. By the way, have you by any chance heard of a guy named Severn, a neurosurgeon, works out of Marlborough or someplace near there?"

"That fascist pig."

Jack laughed. "I sense an undercurrent of hostility."

"A real scumbag, Jack ole buddy. He's a big behavior-control buff. He's into a lot of neat stuff. He'd lobotomize his mother if they let him."

"Into 'stuff'? Like what?"

"A couple of years back he was running a program at the Reedville Hospital for the Criminally Insane down in Jersey. He was doing aversion therapy. We filed an amicus brief when the ACLU went to court to stop it."

"Aversion therapy?"

"Yeah, they were doing it with sexual offenders. And others. The stuff was really bad."

"Is that the kind of thing where you associate something painful with a habit you're trying to break? Like putting sour-tasting stuff on your nails to keep from biting them?"

"That's the general idea," Craig said. "But a whole lot worse. You take a guy who exposes himself, for example. You show him pictures of a flasher and you make him experience pain at the same time. Ever heard of Anectine?"

"No."

Craig leaned back in his chair. "It's a neuro-muscular blocking agent. Related to curare—the poison that South American Indians use on the tips of their arrows."

"What does it do?"

"In small doses, it can be used to relax the muscles during surgical procedures. In bigger doses, it paralyzes the muscles that control breathing. It gives you the wonderful sensation of strangling to death."

"Good Lord!"

Craig got up and rummaged in a file cabinet. "I have a description here someplace of what they were doing to prisoners in Jersey. Yeah, here it is. What they do is administer the drug intravenously. While the patient is strangling, they tell him his behavior is harmful to himself and others. They tell him his behavior is responsible for what's being done to him."

"Jesus, Craig, that sounds a lot like torture."

"You got it. Listen to what one of the shrinks said on the stand about the program. Quote. The subject experiences deep terror, as if he were on the brink of death. He feels like he is suffocating or drowning. Even the toughest inmates have come to fear and loathe the drug. I don't blame them. I wouldn't have one treatment myself for the world. Unquote."

"Was this just being done to the hard cases? The guys who did sexual crimes over and over?"

"Listen to what prisoners were being subjected to the treatment for. Stealing, deviant sexual behavior, fighting, unresponsiveness to the group therapy program."

"Holy shit. You mean you give a therapist some lip and you get zapped?"

"Yeah. It makes the Spanish Inquisition look like a church picnic."

"So how was Severn connected with all this?" Jack asked.

"He was head of the medical staff. He's proud of it. He's pretty well connected to a lot of right-wing types. Does a lot of speaking about controlling deviant behavior through the wonders of science. I also hear rumors that he's been involved with CIA hanky-panky."

"I thought all this stuff was ancient history. What about all the regs that got passed in the seventies clamping down on this kind of thing?"

"This stuff goes in cycles. You can get around the regs if you have to." Craig put the folder back in the case and wedged his bulk into the chair again. "I think we're in for a big comeback in behavior control, because we're heading for another round of dissent against government policies. I think it may be worse than during the Vietnam era, even."

Jack rubbed his head, which was beginning to ache. "I saw a guy today who may have been one of Severn's patients. He had some kind of lobotomy. I'm told that, before, he had some violent episodes, but now he's a total looney tune."

"Severn is a big advocate of psychosurgery. He's pushing for research money for electrical stimulation of the brain. That's scary stuff, to me. It goes way beyond therapy. I don't like the idea of sticking electrodes in somebody's head, and pushing a little button to make him laugh or cry, or fly into a rage."

"They can do that?"

"Yeah."

"I find it sort of hard to believe that people will let doctors just merrily stick wires in their heads."

"They don't do it to thee and me, old chum. It's prisoners, mental patients, juveniles in institutions. Places where there aren't a lot of controls."

"Why do the controls fail at these places?"

"It's the great twentieth-century contribution. The banality of evil. The ordinariness of it."

"Explain," Jack said.

"Think of our images of evil. Dr. Jekyll and Mr. Hyde. Grotesque. Spectacular. We don't expect it in ordinary places. Put evil in a benign place, and call it something else, and people don't recognize it. Call it therapy, not torture. Have people in white coats around, in a place that looks like Harvard Medical School."

"Give it an official stamp?"

"Right. Give it government funds. Or wrap it in the flag. In our century, evil deeds don't get done on foggy moors with witches cackling. More often, it's over white wine in paneled rooms."

"You don't believe in the devil theory of history?"

"Oh, there have been devils. Hitler was one, certainly. But I'm always amused that people have to invent these elaborate conspiracy theories. Sinister Jews who want to control the globe. Mad scientists. The Rockefellers and their ilk who secretly control the world economy. Commie plots."

"You don't think there are conspiracies?"

"Of course there are. But they usually turn out to be run by very ordinary people who think they're doing good stuff. Or necessary stuff."

"You really think we're going to see a lot more of this behavior-control technology?"

"Crime is up, resources are scarce, people are scared shitless about violence. We're in for a nasty time, politically. This Iran situation is going to lead to more turmoil. The times are right for the behavior control buffs."

"Big Brother is watching you?"

"And me. In the Soviet Union, they had a long history of using their mental hospitals as instruments of social control. It's funny. They're stopping some of those abuses and we're going backwards."

He leaned back, scratched his moustache, and swiveled his chair around to face Jack.

"I used to think we had headed Big Brother off at the pass. That it was over, and the good guys won." He sighed. "I don't think so anymore."

5

■

When Jack finally got back to the paper, he had five calls waiting. After he'd returned them, he decided to type his notes— not that he really had to, but it was the sort of busy work that would keep his brain occupied for a while. As he was typing, he was suddenly aware that someone was leaning over his shoulder.

"Umm, Aiken, you smell so good," Sally Ellenberg said. "What is that cologne you use? Subtle, yet distinctive. Impudent, but elegant. Oh yes, of course. *Old Money.*"

He turned to look at her, a suitable comeback gathering in his mind. Then he noticed, for the first time, the outfit she was wearing.

"Ellenberg, what in God's name do you have on?"

"I think they're knickers. Why?"

"You are not supposed to wear knickers with sling-back pumps with rhinestones in them."

"Yeah, I did think it looked kind of strange. Would Reeboks be better?"

"Reeboks! Oh my God. How did you go through your whole life without learning how to dress?"

"It was my revolutionary period. When everybody else was

reading *Glamour*, I was into Che and Franz Fanon. They didn't say a lot about picking the right accessories. Where did you learn to dress so good?"

"In my family," he said, "we have three rules. One. Nothing from a test tube. Polyester gets you out of the will. All materials must be from vegetable substances or dead animals. One thousand baby cashmeres are clubbed to death each year for my family alone."

She grinned. "What's two?"

"Anything British is OK as long as it itches."

"Three?"

"Wear anything that looks like it has been within twelve miles of a disco, and the ghost of Ezekial Forbes rises from the Old Granary Burying Grounds and strangles you with your gold lamé belt."

"Was there really an Ezekial Forbes?"

"Sure. Harvard oh-four. *Eighteen* oh-four. He was a gentleman merchant."

"Was he in the slave trade?"

"No, computer microchips. He went broke. My family was never big on timing."

She laughed. She had a wonderful laugh, he noticed, deep and full.

"Actually," he went on, "the Forbeses and Aikens tried to get into slavery last year. We recruited at the Harvard Afro Center. 'Look, guys,' we said, 'the hours may be long but the bennies are swell. Cradle to grave job security.' "

"Any takers?"

"No blacks, but we did get a lot of Irish Catholics. They thought we were talking about civil service."

"Jack, you'd better not say that too loud."

He grinned. "I know."

"I didn't think Yankees had a sense of humor."

"Cotton Mather spoiled our image. Are you ready for that drink now? I could use it."

They walked to the neighborhood bar that reporters used as a hangout and slid into a booth. Over watery beers, he told her about what he had seen at Westborough State Hospital.

"It was really a weird sight, this poor guy walking around the halls with a bag over his head. And the holes—they looked like they'd been made by a drill. Ugh."

"It's odd, isn't it, to run into a couple of possible stories about people with their heads carved up? Think there could be any connection?"

"I doubt it. Brain surgery isn't all that uncommon these days. I don't even know if there's a story in this neurosurgeon. But he's been connected with some strange stuff. Oh, I brought you some material from my files on electrode implants. There's clips, journal articles, and a book. They ought to give you a good overview."

She took the folder he handed her. "Thanks. I'll get started on this tonight. You know, this whole issue of experimenting on people made me remember a series my father did, back in the sixties. Did you know that in Mississippi they let syphilis in black prisoners go untreated so they could study the course of the disease? My father was outraged. He was pretty sensitive to that kind of thing. It was hard not to be, for a Jew who fought in World War II."

Jack ordered two more beers. "They still talk about your father. They say he was one of the best."

"He was. If he hadn't been the wrong religion, he might have had a shot at being editor of this paper."

"This was a pretty prejudiced town."

"Was? It's still there, but it's subtle now. How much of a chance do I have to move into a really good management job at this paper? A woman and a Jew. Double whammy. My father had a chance, once, to go to the *Times.* They really wanted him. But we had a family life here. I think maybe he should have gone."

She shook her head and took a sip of her beer.

"When I was in Washington," Jack said, "everybody thought that Yankees were a baseball team. If I'd said I was a Yankee, they'd have thought I was hallucinating about being Don Mattingly. But I grew up being told it was very special being a Yankee. That's why I went to the *Post* before I came here. To show people I could hack it. I know what they say about Parker Ames around the city room."

She took another sip of beer, then licked the foam off her lips. She had lovely, full lips, he noticed. She said, "You can't blame people for feeling that way, Jack. They work hard, put in time and pay their dues, and then some kid sails right by them into an editor's chair because he has the right name."

"I won't do that. I'll earn what I get."

"But what about people who earn it but know they won't get it? Some people resent you. Not that they think you're not good. They know you are. But they think it's so easy for you. You picked the right father."

He leaned back in the booth and laughed. A little warning buzzer sounded in his head, but he ignored it. The beers were starting to take effect; he was not a drinker. "Want to know about my father, Sally? He was a drunk. He spent half his life drying out in institutions. That's why I didn't want to go out to that rattrap this afternoon, because I went to those places so often when I was a kid. Then I'd go home and throw up."

"I'm sorry, Jack," she said, quietly. "I didn't know. It was a stupid thing for me to say."

He took another swig of beer. "Nobody knows. It's a very well-kept secret." He was astounded that he was telling her this. "He had everything—money, family, *and* Harvard, but somehow it was all too much for him. He was a failure. But we give our failures nice offices in family firms and we pretend they're going off to work every morning. We never talked about the fact that my father was packed off to an office every day where he didn't have anything to do but drink himself pie-eyed before noon. Everyone would talk about 'your father's liver infection.' His liver got infected because he poured booze on it all the time."

He laughed, and it was a sound strange and tinny to his ear. Why in God's name was he going on like this?

"I used to try to make deals with God, all the time, to get my father to stop drinking. I kept upping the ante, when nothing happened. Finally, I told God he could make my hand get cut off if He'd let my father get better. But I'd never deal for a leg. I used to feel guilty as shit, because I figured it was my fault my father wasn't getting better because I wouldn't give up my leg."

She smiled. "I don't think God is such a hardass."

He shook his head. "This was a real Old Testament God, not your Unitarian touchy-feely God. The one that asked Abraham to sacrifice his only son. This is a guy who would take a leg in a minute." He laughed again. "It got to be an obsession with me. One day I went out in the woods and I took my Boy Scout knife and I said, 'OK, God, I'll do it. I'll cut my leg off. Unless you tell me not to.' I gave Him a *lot* of time. But he didn't show. So I took out my knife, and I made one slice, and it started to bleed something awful. And I knew I couldn't do it. I said, 'I'm sorry, Dad, you're just going to have to be a drunk.' I still have the scar. My own personal mark of Cain."

"You still feel guilty, don't you? About him."

He nodded. "He was a kind man, never abusive, even when he was drunk. He just got very quiet. I had this fantasy that I was going to save him when I grew up. He died before I had the chance. Liver failure. The family was right after all."

"No, you were right for trying. You were only a kid."

"You know, I still get angry at him sometimes. Not for being a drunk, he couldn't help that, but because he made me learn too young that the world is a very scary place. He was my father. He was supposed to protect me from that. It's not fair to get angry at him, but I do. Still, for chrissake. And I'm thirty-four years old."

He was amazed at the way the words came pouring out of him, at his anger. He had never talked about this to anyone before—not to his mother, or his best friend at Harvard. Why did it seem so easy to talk to a woman he hardly knew?

She said, "I remember once, when I was about eleven, my father and I were walking home from shul. A bunch of Irish toughs came up behind us and started to say, 'Dirty Jews! Jews smell!' I said, 'We do not!' but my father told me to be quiet and just keep walking. They were very big and very drunk and my father was right. But I always thought he could protect me from anything. And he couldn't. Those men called me 'dirty Jew.' I hated my father for a while after that. He wasn't a giant anymore. Just a person. Like everyone else."

Impulsively, he reached out his hand to cover hers. "I wish I'd been there," he said.

She smiled. "What could you have done?"

"If I had let them cut my hand off, God would have made them stop."

She laughed and he laughed too, and they were quiet for a minute. His hand still rested on hers. Then she said, "Are you ever afraid, Jack, that you'll be like him?"

"No. Yes. Hell, yes, I am. Not that I'll drink, but that I won't measure up. I couldn't fail at anything. I was on the dean's list all the way through Harvard. I was captain of the tennis team. Captain of the debating team. I had to prove I had the right Forbes and Aiken stuff. I guess I still have to."

"I had to be the best too," she said. "You had to be twice as good as everybody if you were a woman and half again as good if you were a Jew. So I figured I'd be three and a half times as good. My father had to swallow a lot, it was the times. I won't. That's why I'm up front all the time. Union committee. Women's group. Pushy broad. Pushy Jew. Damn right. I'll keep on pushing."

"Don't you ever get tired? Of pushing?"

"Do I ever! But I have to get to a spot where I can write my own ticket. I have to be so good, get so far, that nobody can dump on me. Ever."

"Me too, I guess. Maybe one of these days I'll get to the point where I can fail at something. Really mess up. And not care."

"It's funny," she said, "I thought it was all so simple for you. Easy as ice cream."

"I thought you had everything figured," he said. "You're so smart and you seemed to know exactly where you were going. Nobody ever said you got where you are because of your father."

They sat, finishing the rest of the beer in silence, feeling no need to speak. He had told her his deepest, darkest secret, the one he had spent most of his life trying to hide. He knew, instinctively, that he could trust her with it. Touching only her hand, he felt more intimate with her than with any woman he had ever known. It was a new experience, lovely, but scary as hell. He felt opened, like a can of sardines. This was crazy; tomorrow it would be back to Miki, who was so beautiful, and so safe. Thank God for Miki, it was a good thing he was going to marry her. He couldn't spend his life feeling the way he felt right now; out of control, and liking it. There was no safety here.

Still, he did not move his hand.

6

■

Sally parked her car outside of Uhuru House in Roxbury, Boston's black community, and walked to the front door of the newly renovated turn-of-the-century Victorian home. She had an appointment with Sandra Jefferson, the director and a well-known community activist.

Sandra greeted Sally at the door, wearing a stylish grey suit, her trim Afro haircut revealing a sprinkling of grey at the temples. She had been a good source in the past. Sally trusted her instincts and was certain of her integrity.

"I saw it in the police report this morning," Sally said to her as she entered the house. "Another girl missing."

"We were just talking about it," Sandra said. As the two women entered Sandra's cluttered, comfortable office, Sally saw a tall black man standing in the corner of the room. He was wearing a brightly colored African shirt over his khaki pants, and a bright red pair of Reeboks. In his mid-thirties, he was possessed of classic Afro-American good looks, enhanced by a pale scar on his right cheek; the air of menace it gave him was something he cultivated, carefully. He grinned when he saw Sally.

"Hello, *World Herald*," he said. He knew her name perfectly well, but it was a game with him to pretend he didn't.

"Didn't I see you on 'Geraldo,' Hakim?"

"No, I was on Donahue. Third transvestite from the left."

Sally shook her head. She enjoyed jousting with Hakim Abdul (née Robert Brown), ex-felon, ex–drug addict, leader of Boston's New Panthers. *Newsweek* had recently said of him, "Hakim is one of the most articulate new voices rising from the nation's ghettos. He combines nonviolence with the instincts of a born street fighter." Some white reporters thought him a con man, a media hound too fast on his feet, too good on TV to be for real. But Sally sensed that under the glitz, there was a true passion for society's underclass. Hakim might indeed be on the make, but he wouldn't forget where he came from.

"Hakim wants to help us with the missing girls," Sandra said. She picked up a photograph from her desk of a sweet-faced black girl smiling at the camera.

"Dottie West," she said. "Her mother is frantic."

Hakim took the picture, and Sally saw the line of his mouth harden. "A child," he said. "Goddamn bastards. How could anybody hurt a child like that?"

"Not a hooker this time?" Sally asked.

Sandra sat down in the chair and sighed. "Dottie's a good kid. She's run away a few times. She got mixed up with this guy who's an addict. So she turned a trick now and then, probably to buy drugs for him. Or to pay the rent on the crummy apartment they've been sharing."

"She's not an addict?"

"No," Hakim said. "She ran away the last time when her stepfather raped her. Didn't tell her mother."

"Christ," Sally swore. "Why can't we get help for these kids?"

"Who cares about poor black runaway kids?" Hakim asked. "Not the taxpayers in Wellesley."

"Do you think we have a serial killer on our hands?"

"Six young women have vanished so far," Sandra said, "and only one has been found. Dismembered, in a trash bag. These kids are not likely to be off on a weekend in the Bahamas."

"And no leads," Sally said.

"I've had our people out combing the area," Hakim said. "Nothing. The cops aren't exactly busting their butts on this."

"Sally, can you get us more ink on this?" Sandra asked. "We need to put more pressure on the police department."

"I'll try. I'll push it with my city editor. I got metro front with the discovery of the first body, but my follow stories have ended up under the obits. No bodies, the story gets buried."

"If they were white girls from Dover, they'd be all over page one," Hakim said, an edge of bitterness creeping into his voice.

"If they were white girls from Dover, the National Guard would be out," Sally told him.

"The guy from *Newsweek*, he asked me what I'm so mad about." Hakim picked up the picture of Dottie West. "This is why I'm so mad. Because kids like this just get thrown away. And nobody cares."

"Look, I could get at least Metro front, maybe page one with a serial killer story. But I don't want to get hung out to dry on a story that's not real. Do you really think that's what we've got here?"

"I can't prove it," Sandra said. "Sure, these kids could turn up. I hope they do. But I think we're either going to find them dead, or we're never going to find them at all. There's lots of places bodies can be dumped. And this guy is no Son of Sam. No note. No 'Stop me before I kill again' stuff. He doesn't seem to want publicity."

"If we had more police help, maybe we could stop him. Before some other kids vanish without a trace," Hakim argued.

"OK. I'll try to get a statement out of the commissioner about why he's dropping the ball on this."

Back at the paper, Sally lobbied Kevin for page one.

"Come on, Kev, a possible serial killer."

"Big news day. National is trying to hog the show. Lots of stuff out of D.C. on Iran. I may only get one story."

"This is the one story," Sally argued.

"The mayor gave a major speech on his housing policy."

"Old news. He outlined it last month."

"Come on, Sally, stop bugging me," the city editor moaned. "I've had a rough day."

Sally figured she had to up the ante.

"The black community is getting pretty pissed about our lack of coverage on this."

"We've been following it."

"Not the way you would if it happened in Wellesley. Hey,

the last thing we need is pickets out front carrying signs saying the *World Herald* is racist."

Sally saw Kevin's brow furrow. *Bingo.*

"You've heard some rumors to that effect?"

"Yeah, I have," Sally said, lying with the face of a cherub.

"Jeez, I don't know—"

"We get brownie points with a lot of folks."

Kevin popped a Rolaid into his mouth and sighed.

"OK, OK, I'll push for it at the news conference."

"Thanks, Kev."

She went back to her desk and, after a few well-placed phone calls, wrote a story that raised the issue of the serial killer, with outrage from black leaders and defensiveness from the police commissioner—and a promise to put more men on the investigation.

She had sent the story to Kevin's terminal when her phone rang.

"Sally?" said a voice, speaking in a half-whisper.

"Who's this?"

"It's Karen. In Frank O'Brien's office. You ought to get over here fast."

"Karen. Hi. What's happening?"

"I can't talk. Just come over."

Sally wasted no time getting a cab. Frank O'Brien was almost always a good story. The crusading DA seemed to regard himself as a cross between an avenging angel and *Mr. Smith Goes To Washington.* There were those who said that Frankie boyo could find Mafia ties in the bust of the most innocuous bookie in the tackiest East Boston storefront. He'd get ink by hinting, darkly, that the hapless peddler of tomato paste, precut salami, and tickets for the third at Suffolk Downs was a vital cog in the web of organized crime stretching to Jerry Anguilo himself. O'Brien was notorious for labeling every other cocaine bust as "The biggest strike against the murderous drug armies in the history of New England." Wags said that if you read the newspaper stories, you'd believe that the coastline had sunk two inches from the sheer weight of illegal substances Frank had seized.

O'Brien worked his subordinates hard—and gave them little credit. Which was why secretaries like Karen hated him. He also seemed to have a personal relationship with God that rivaled Moses' with the burning bush. He showed up constantly at communion breakfasts across the state, and it was rumored that he belonged to an elite, right-wing Catholic society with ties to the Vatican that practiced, on occasion, self-flagellation. Certain Catholics, mostly of the Italian persuasion, as well as a number of his underlings, said they would be delighted to assist the DA in the latter activity. Italians believed that if your name ended in a vowel, and you were over eleven years of age, Frankie boyo would try to indict you sooner or later.

Sally didn't like the DA much, or trust him—the scent of ambition hung too thickly about him—but he made good copy. When she arrived at his office, she walked in and found the outer office empty. A small group of people was gathered in the inner office, where Frank O'Brien was standing on his desk, staring up at what appeared to be a vacant spot on the ceiling.

No one noticed when Sally entered, so intent were they on gaping at the peculiar scene before them. Frank O'Brien spoke—to the ceiling, it seemed—at that moment.

"Theru apkian nolu framidian inkendu," he said.

Sally found herself standing next to Billy Devlin, an assistant DA.

"Billy, what did he say?"

Billy looked at her. "Oh shit," he said. "The *World Herald* is here."

"What's he doing?" Sally asked, puzzled.

"Speaking in tongues."

"What?"

"I think he's finally gone over the edge," Billy sighed.

"Why is he staring at the ceiling?"

"He's, uh, he's having a vision."

"What kind of a vision?"

"He says Our Lady is talking to him."

"What lady?" Sally asked, perplexed.

"The Blessed Virgin. She's there."

"On the ceiling?"

"Right," Billy said.

"She can just hang up there? Like something from *Star Wars*?"

"Sally, *I* don't see him," Billy said. "Frank does."

"Can I talk to him?"

Billy shrugged. "Why not?"

Sally approached the desk, slowly. Frank O'Brien, a tall bony man who seemed not to possess an ounce of fat on his body, was still staring, his face rapt, at the ceiling.

"Uh, Frank, can you tell me who you are talking to?" Sally asked.

Without looking at her, or losing the look of ecstasy on his face, Frank O'Brien said, "Our Lady of Perpetual Light has appeared to me. She has chosen me to give a message to all the people."

"Oy!" moaned assistant DA Sol Ginsberg, dropping his face in his hands.

"What is she saying, Frank?" Sally asked.

"She says that we must break the evil death grip of the Italian crime families, the spawn of Satan, the evil one. We must consume this wretched spawn in righteousness, or we will all perish in flame."

Billy Devlin stepped up next to Sally. He looked up at O'Brien. "Frank, why don't you come down now?"

Frank, still immobile, said, "Our Lady bids me speak."

"Maybe you could ask her into my office. Where she can have some privacy."

"With fire and iron, we must break the Italians!"

"Billy," Sally asked, "does the, uh, Blessed . . ."

"Virgin."

"Yeah. Does she not like Italians much?"

"She's not on the record on that, as far as I know," Billy said. "Frank doesn't like them much."

"Etag wurfel zaplat hignun," Frank intoned.

"What does that mean, Frank?" Sally asked.

Frank O'Brien threw out his arms, still gazing upward. His voice rose nearly an octave. "We will conquer, under her banner, the mantle of blue and white, we will break the spawn of Satan as she crushed the head of the serpent!"

"Billy," Sally whispered to the assistant DA, "you ought to get him out of here. I think he needs help."

"I know," Billy whispered back, "but we've got to get *her* out of here first."

"You think she's really here?"

"No, I mean Frank won't leave if he thinks the Madonna is on his ceiling."

"So how do we get her to leave? Ask her to click the heels of her ruby slippers three times and think about Kansas?"

"Very funny, Sally. I don't know how to do it."

"Erak blasnex klem berdad," Frank said.

Seeing the rest of the people in the room fairly paralyzed by the bizarre situation, Sally tried again.

"Frank," she said, "the Lady has to go. You have to let her go. She has an appointment. She has to . . ." She paused. "She has to get her nails done."

"No!" hissed Billy Devlin. "She doesn't do that."

"Uh, she has to go see the Pope," Sally tried.

"Right, Frank," said Billy. "You can't monopolize the Blessed Virgin. She has to appear in a lot of places."

Frank stood absolutely still, staring at the ceiling. Sally noticed that he didn't even blink.

"Frank?" Billy said.

"Frank, can you hear me?" Sally asked.

Sally moved closer to the desk and touched Frank's outstretched hand. He didn't move a muscle. Then she pinched it, hard. He didn't flinch.

"God, Billy, I think he's gone catatonic," she said.

"Karen, call an ambulance, fast!" Billy called out.

Frank O'Brien was still standing, arms outstreched, rigid as a statue, when the paramedics arrived and carried him off. Sol Ginsberg watched as the men with the stretchers exited the office.

"There goes the run for governor," he sighed.

"I don't know," Sally said. "If he could get the Blessed Virgin to do a public endorsement, he'd be a shoo-in."

"Beats Billy Graham," Sol said.

Billy Devlin sighed, a deep martyred sigh. He turned to Sally.

"I guess you'll be writing about this, huh?"

"I have to," she said.

"Well . . . don't make us look too crazy," he asked her.

"The man came unglued. And he's a powerful public figure. I can't soft-pedal this, Billy."

"He's been under a lot of strain."

"Sure. I'll say that."

"The speaking in tongues. Do you have to use that?"

"Yeah. I do. But look, I'm not going to make fun of him. People crack up under pressure. It happens."

"We had a million-dollar war chest. For the governor's race. I guess we'll have to give it back." He sighed. "Frank had high ambitions, you know. The second Catholic-American president."

"So I've heard," Sally said.

"Poor Frank. The Democrats would never run anybody who talks to invisible Virgins."

"Given their luck in the past ten years," Sally said, "who knows."

Billy sighed again. He had spent a lot of time hitching his wagon to the right political star. Now it seemed it was all for naught.

"Sorry, Billy," Sally said. "Tough break."

"In your story, would you say that I called the ambulance? I took charge?"

"Right. I'll point that out."

"It's William G. Devlin. Middle initial G."

"Don't worry, Billy. I'll get it right."

He smiled. "Maybe," he said, "I'll drop by the paper and catch the early edition."

He was still smiling when she walked out of the office.

REPORTER'S JOURNAL: Sally Ellenberg

Subject: Crooks

I get to meet a lot of interesting people on this job. Not especially nice ones, but interesting. Frank O'Brien, for instance, did not make for a dull day. But often, the crooks are the ones I remember, after all is said and done.

Crooks fall into several categories. There are the thugs, and they are a dull lot, guys who could make Darwin recant every one of his theories if he ran into one of them in a dark alley. They tend to be low of forehead, with a high steroid level, and they will tell you that the sweetest music this side of heaven is the sound of knee joints crunching. Worse than these are the sociopaths, who really make my flesh creep. The thugs, at least, are usually acting on orders, "Hey, nothing personal." The sociopaths are the ones with high I.Q.'s, Mr.-Average-Guy looks, and the inability to feel anything at all for another human being. They are the ones who pull out a handgun and mow down everybody in McDonald's because the Quarter-pounders weren't warm enough.

The druggies are a breed all their own. The dealers are mainly freelance operators; Genghis Khan started out just the way they did. They sweep down in little bands, using Hondas instead of Mongol ponies, carving each other up over turf. White guys, blacks, Cubans, Jamaicans, Taiwanese, Colombians—running their border wars and regularly plugging innocent bystanders. Most of them will have short life spans. The ones who survive, and prosper, well, their descendants will be gifting chairs at Harvard and standing with the Speaker of the House and aging movie stars at Kennedy Center galas. Most great American fortunes rest on a firm base of dark deeds and ill-gotten gains.

The guys on top today, the Mafia dons, have gone corporate. Like IBM. They're surrounded by lawyers in pinstripes who call them "my client," and make activities that are basically loan-sharking, peddling drugs and whores, and laundering money sound like a valuable contribution to the GNP. The old guys, they had the self-respect to at least *look* like gangsters. Al Capone, now there's a guy who wouldn't just blend into the wallpaper at the annual stockbrokers' banquet. You offered him a canape, six goons would reach for their pieces and he'd shove the paté de foie gras up your nose.

You know what you don't see anymore either? Gun molls. Remember the trashy dames who used to hang around with gangsters, wearing platform heels and bad dye jobs? Oh, the species is still around, but the gangsters' media consultants won't let them out in public. Your typical capo gets his picture taken, these days, with the Archbishop or the head of the UNICEF children's fund, not with Trixie or Pixie. The classic moll success story, of course, was Judith Exner, who was sleeping with both Sam Giancana and Jack Kennedy at the same time. There was a girl who really knew how to make conversation with different kinds of people.

My favorite crooks, though, are the guys who live on the fringes of crime; the small-timers who wind up not really hurting anybody very much, but who find living by their wits a sort of code of honor. They don't often succeed, but they do usually muddle through.

Big Doc Jabotinsky is an example. Big Doc is eighty-seven, and he's in the slammer now because he won't turn state's evidence in a scheme he was involved in. In the next cell is his partner in crime, Moe Levitz. Doc and Moe had a fistfight in an alley over a numbers deal that went sour. Moe is a spry seventy-eight, but Big Doc outweighs him by fifteen pounds. Moe had a quadruple bypass but Big Doc has gout and a cataract in one eye. Younger men had to pry them apart; Big Doc was screaming, "*Momser,*" as Moe tried to stick two fingers up his nose.

I talked to Big Doc in Walpole a couple weeks ago. He is stonewalling it. There's no way, he says, that he's going to be a fink. They can keep him in jail until he rots. In jail, he gets good low-sodium food, a doctor to listen to his kvetching every day, and he knows he's not going to get gang-raped.

"Honey, even the horny bastards in here aren't hard up enough to grab my bony ass," he chuckles.

Big Doc has twelve grandchildren, including two Ph.D.'s and a producer for CBS News.

Big Doc says that when he goes to his maker, he has a lot of credits to offset the black marks. Thanks to a mountain of two-dollar policy slips, the Jabotinsky clan has become a solid pillar of middle-class virtue. "God should thank me," he says. "My family alone keeps five shuls and two rabbis in bagels and *tsimmis.* If God doesn't like that, it would be a *shanda!*"

Then there's Mayo Shannahan. Mayo is a thief with spectacular bad luck. Mayo has spent forty-eight long years in pursuit of the big score. Tailgating is his specialty. Mayo once spread the word that he had a truckload of Gucci shoes to sell; he was going to set up shop in the parking lot at the back of a bar in Southie. But when prospective buyers arrived and opened the boxes to inspect the merchandise, Mayo discovered that he had five thousand pumps, all for the right foot. Somewhere on Interstate 95 was a truck with five thousand *left* shoes. He went cruising around looking for it, but finally gave it up as a lost cause.

Then there was the time Mayo lifted a couple of brand new engines from a luxury yacht at a North Shore marina. They were just there for the picking, Mayo said, and he couldn't resist. He was trying to find buyers in a bowling alley in Dorchester when the proprietor told him that two guys in dark suits had been there before him, inquiring about the whereabouts of certain engines. It seems that Mayo had heisted the engines from a yacht owned by one Jerry Anguilo, who, in the times when he was not at sea, was reputed to be the organized crime boss of New England.

Mayo got the engines back, fast, and got only his nose broken in the process. He told me he should have known better, because the Irish are terrible with boats anyhow. He is bloody but unbowed, still looking for the big hit. Last I heard, he was hustling his tush around selling microchips made in some black market operation in Hong Kong. They're no good, but they're cheap. I just hope he doesn't sell them to Jerry Anguilo.

7

■

Jack walked into the dining room at Locke-Ober's and looked around. A young man in a dark three-piece suit waved to him from a table for two in the corner of the room. Jack smiled and made his way through the crowded dining room.

"Heineken light?" Seth Chaffee asked. He was a slender man, with a shock of just-longer-than-fashionable brown hair, a strand of which tumbled across his forehead. He brushed it back impatiently. Even when Seth was at rest, Jack thought, no part of him was completely still; he toyed with his fork, he tapped his foot, he tugged at his ear.

"Heineken light." Jack slipped into the chair.

"Steak, rare, baked potato, butter, no sour cream."

"Am I that predictable?" Jack asked with a grin.

"It's your charm."

The two men had been friends at Harvard. In fact, Jack realized with some surprise, Seth had been his closest friend—which would have surprised Seth as well. Jack had been friendly with many of his classmates, intimate with none. Seth came as close as anyone to the description "best friend." They had much in common—crew, tennis, debate, an interest in things political. Seth went on to Harvard Law, and afterward to Washington.

They saw each other several times a year, catching up with each other's busy lives.

Over steaks and light German beers, they filled in the blanks. Jack asked how things were going in the Attorney General's office. Seth was guarded at first, but after a second beer he admitted his frustrations.

"It's not what I expected. I thought it was going to be an exciting place. I figured Elliott Andrews was going to be another Archie Cox. Known for integrity, the right establishment credentials. But he has all these political cronies from out west who have too much influence. These people, Jack, they've got no class. Real estate guys, ad men from California. Their roots are orange groves and *Rambo*."

"Do I detect a little effete Eastern intellectual snobbery here?"

"The word 'Republican' used to mean something. Now it's some tub-thumping TV evangelist from the Bible Belt. In school, when I was in the Ripon society, I thought the party was the future. We wanted progress, sure, but we didn't grab on to any new fad that came along the way the Democrats did—like save the gay whales."

"Harvard wasn't the world, Seth."

"So I've discovered. But I think the Reagan landslide was really the end of the party I believed in. It opened the door to the religious right, and the macho crazies who want to nuke every commie in sight. I wonder if we'll ever get the party back again."

"Who's 'we,' white man?"

"You know what I mean."

Jack grinned. "Seth, you haven't changed. You just thumped the table, did you realize that? You used to do that when we argued back in Adams House."

Seth shook his head, then let his breath out slowly.

"My problem is, I get too intense. That's what I always admired about you, Jack. You never lost your cool. You were always in control."

"What you mean is I didn't get involved. Didn't care."

"No, I didn't mean it as a dig."

"Oh yeah?"

"Maybe a little. But I did admire you. You never seemed to sweat anything. Things seemed to come to you. Good grades, pretty girls. Whatever happened to that Cliffie, by the way—the one who looked like a young Grace Kelly?"

"She married a banker. Funny thing, I envied *you*. The way you threw yourself into things head first. You had more . . . verve than I did. I was always looking on, an observer. Maybe that's part of why I'm a journalist."

"You like the work."

"Yeah, a lot of it I do. But I've never felt the way you feel, that sort of whole-soul commitment. Like it's earth-shaking."

"Maybe with me it's part self-dramatization. I'm trying to see myself more objectively. Pick my fights. Not just go flailing at windmills."

"Sometimes I think I'd like to do some flailing. Might be fun."

"Believe me, Jack, it's not."

They both sipped their beers in silence for a minute. Then Jack said, "Being in control is my thing. Always was. Because there was so much of my life that was out of control."

Seth looked up at him in surprise. "You? Mr. Cool?"

"My father was a drunk. I never knew when he'd be sober and when he'd be drunk. Not tipsy. Real, falling-down drunk."

"I never knew that."

"Nobody did. You're only the second person outside my family I've ever told. And I didn't tell the first one until last week."

"No wonder you never let it all hang out."

"To say the least."

"Have you ever thought of therapy? Children of alcoholics have a lot of baggage to carry around."

"No Forbes or Aiken has ever been to a shrink. We just clench our teeth harder."

"That must have caused you a lot of pain."

"It did. When I used to go to your house I used to wish we could swap families. I didn't know what a normal family was like."

"You didn't come very often."

"No. Because then I'd have to invite you into the bosom of *my* family, where I didn't want anyone."

"I always figured it was because I wasn't quite classy enough to be invited over. Not the A team."

"Oh Christ, you thought *that*?"

"Yeah."

"I guess a lot of people thought I was a snob. But I was just scared shitless that people would know."

"I remember his funeral. The eulogy made him sound like the leader of the Vault."

"Yes. It was all a lie, but we all had to keep pretending. Except him. He didn't have to anymore."

Jack took another sip of beer.

"I'm glad you told me, Jack," Seth said.

Jack nodded. "Yeah, me too."

"Look, we shouldn't . . . lose touch. There's not a lot of people I can talk to. Not in my office, God knows."

"You're right. It's too easy, just getting busy. Not spending any time with—with good friends. Let's not do that."

After lunch, Jack dropped Seth off at the airport and headed back to the paper. He saw Sally at her desk, and as he approached, she held up a book and waved it at him.

"That was nice light reading you gave me last night. I read about brain surgery instead of my Harlequin romance before beddy-bye."

"Harlequin romance? You don't actually read that shit?"

"Oh yeah, puts me right out. Ever heard of a Harlequin-lobotomy nightmare? 'He put his virile arms around her. He kissed her ruby lips, her swanlike throat. He went snippety-snip on her left amygdala.' "

"You did read it, didn't you?"

"What fun. Icepick surgery, that's what they used to call it. They went in through the eyes. There was one surgeon at St. Elizabeth's Hospital in D.C. who did over four thousand of them. Guess who most of the patients were?"

"Blacks and women."

"Right. Round up the usual suspects. There was this three-hundred-pound black woman who used to deck the attendants when they tried to sedate her. So they went in and burned out her frontal lobes. Listen to what the surgeon had to say about her." Sally opened the book, and read. " 'The day after the operation we could playfully grab Oretha by the throat, tickle her in the ribs and slap her behind without eliciting anything but a wide grin or a hoarse giggle.' "

"Jesus!"

"Yeah. In the seventies there was one white surgeon who

used to do the procedure a lot on black children. He operated six times on the brain of a six-year-old."

"Craig Letterman thinks we're going to see a lot more behavior-control technology. Only it's going to be more sophisticated. No more icepicks. Hey, I see they buried your story on the liquor store holdup. You didn't mention anything about possible implants."

"I couldn't. Joe is my only source and I have to protect him. He's already given me stuff that could have gotten him into trouble."

"How about the medical examiner?"

"Zilch. Nothing through official channels. I do have a source in the office who owes me one, though. I didn't get a lot, but my source did tell me that the night Brady's body came over, there was a guy she recognized talking to the medical examiner about it. She doesn't know what he said, though."

"Who was it?"

"I got it in my notes. Wait a minute. Here it is. Dr. Theodore Severn, and she thinks he's a neurosurgeon."

Jack looked at her in surprise. "Who?"

"Severn. Ever heard of him?"

"Sally, that's the guy who did the surgery on the bag man. Theodore J. Severn. He's the guy Craig says was involved with experiments with prisoners, maybe CIA stuff."

"Is that on the record, the spook connection?"

"No, just rumors."

"Jack, I think we got something here, but I'll be damned if I know what."

"I'm going to do some checking on Severn. He seems to be into some very interesting stuff."

On his way home that evening, Jack stopped at the Countway Medical Library, where he found a number of articles in various journals and popular magazines by Theodore J. Severn. He Xeroxed them and stuck them in his briefcase, before driving north on Route One, heading toward the North Shore and his Uncle Robert's house to join him for dinner. He smiled as he drove along; their frequent meetings for dinner or lunch were always a distinct pleasure.

Uncle Robert—Robert Forbes Aiken, as *The New York Times* always referred to him—had often taken the place of Jack's father, at the basketball finals, the jumping competitions, when Jack was growing up. Jack had often, and guiltily, wished that Uncle Robert, a decade older than his father, had in fact been his real father. His uncle had the sort of a career expected of Forbeses and Aikens. He was a partner in a distinguished Boston firm, and had an admirable record of public service in administrations—both Republican and Democrat—dating back to FDR. He had been one of the youngest men in the OSS during World War II, helped to put together the Marshall Plan while still in his twenties, and called every president since Eisenhower by his first name. Jack had gone against Uncle Robert's wishes only once—when he turned down Harvard Law.

Their dinners, served at home by Uncle Robert's excellent Korean chef, were accompanied by interesting wines and lively conversation, often centered on the state of the world. Tonight, Robert Aiken was in a philosophical mood.

"Jack," he said, as the two of them shared a very good bottle of sherry, "I think life is more . . . treacherous today than when I was young."

Jack laughed. "Uncle Robert, when you were young, a genuine psychopath was about to plunge Europe into war and the Japanese were gobbling up all of Asia."

"Yes, but even with that, our hopes were high. Especially during the war. We believed we were saving the world."

Jack smiled. "You were."

"No one believes that anymore. There is such cynicism all around. Such pessimism."

"I suppose so," his nephew agreed. "If the greenhouse effect doesn't fry us, and we don't all get nuked, we may just bury ourselves in our own garbage."

Robert Aiken smiled ruefully. "You see what I mean?"

"Oh, I think we'll survive."

"We used to talk of the American Century. A world where democracy and prosperity would spread out across the continents."

Jack shook his head. "I don't know that anybody's going to own the next century. Lot of folks will have a piece of it."

"Yes. Crazed mullahs, brutal dictators, both right and left, and the Russians—ah, the Russians. Still trying to struggle out of the twelfth century. A society that went from feudalism to high technology, without getting civilized in between."

"You do think the world is in a bad way."

Robert Aiken took a sip of his sherry. "Perhaps it was better in the bad old days when a few European powers divided up the world and pretty much ran things."

"You don't believe that," Jack chided him.

"Is it so much better now? Each nation, each tribe, each little group of people who feels kinship, carving up its neighbors? Building nuclear bombs, chemical weapons plants?"

Jack smiled. "Uncle Robert, you're a Tory, that's what you are."

Robert Aiken laughed. "I suppose I am."

"But there's no more Rule Britannia. Or Pax Americana. No one can dominate the world anymore."

"True. But we can't hobble ourselves with doubt, either. If you have power, you must use it. Wisely."

"That's the problem," Jack argued. "How wisely have we used it? Making Guatemala safe for United Fruit? Getting rid of Allende? Vietnam?"

"Oh, mistakes were made. Bad ones. I'd be the first to admit it. On the other hand, there's the Marshall Plan, and Jack Kennedy keeping the missiles out of Cuba, and the U.S. giving Marcos a shove. Even though Reagan had to be bullied into it by Senator Richard Lugar."

Jack looked thoughtful as he sipped his sherry. What he enjoyed in his conversation with Uncle Robert was testing his own ideas against his uncle's wisdom and vast store of experience.

"It just seems to me," he said, "that the arrogance of power gets us into trouble more than it helps. It's hubris for us to decide we have the almighty right to decide what sorts of governments other people will have."

Robert Aiken leaned back in his chair. "Jack, what if you were granted the power to travel back in time. To Munich, 1928. Would you assassinate a rising young rabble-rouser named Adolf Hitler?"

"Of course. But that's with the power of hindsight."

"But there comes a time when men in power have to make a judgment that the security of the nation—and yes, sometimes the good of the world—demands action."

"You'd condone the assassination of political leaders?" Jack asked.

"Only in the most extreme case. Like you would, with Hitler."

The shadow of a mischievous grin crossed Jack's face.

"So, Uncle Robert, when you were in government, who did you bump off?"

"Nobody, alas. But I certainly had some likely candidates."

"Fidel?"

"Oh no. The CIA made such a muddle out of that. We've been successful in containing Castro. He's really more of a nuisance, now, than a threat."

"I'm intrigued," Jack said. "Who?"

"This is all off the record, I assume. I must remember I'm talking to a journalist."

"Of course."

"The Shah of Iran."

"The Shah? But he was our good buddy. In fact, we brought him to power by getting involved in the assassination of Mossadegh."

"Yes, and for a number of years he was a decent, progressive leader. Broke the power of the mullahs. Modernized his country, dragged it out of feudalism. But his ego, his megalomania, destroyed him. The Peacock Throne—poppycock. He became isolated from the people, relying on Savak to hold on to power."

"The secret police."

"Yes. Torture of the most brutal kind. Evil, evil men."

"So you'd have offed the Shah?"

"Very delicately put, Jack. I would have used all the powers of persuasion we had to bear on the Shah. Twist his arm in a very serious way. But if he insisted on his dangerous and murderous course, yes, I'd have recommended assassination. Maybe we wouldn't have this mess on our hands now. There might be a moderate, middle-class regime, instead of these crazed religious fanatics."

"Diplomacy is a pretty cold-blooded business."

"Yes, it always has been. Machiavelli and Metternich weren't flower children. Winston Churchill was all steel under that jovial exterior. And FDR, of course, was as wily as they come. Clever. Ruthless. A master of what we now call image-making."

"I hope you're working on your memoirs, Uncle Robert. You've known most of the important figures of the twentieth century."

"I have been working on them, but I find myself pretty busy these days."

Robert Aiken finished his wine and the houseboy brought two cups of coffee.

"Well, enough about the world for now," Robert Aiken said. "How's your life going?"

"Oh, pretty good," Jack told his uncle, "the Sci-Tech section's been expanded, and that's keeping me pretty busy."

"Still enjoying being an ink-stained wretch?"

"Yes. It does seem to suit me."

"How's your mother feeling?"

"Good. You know Mother. She manages to keep busy."

"And Miki? I hope you'll bring her over for dinner again soon. A delightful woman."

Jack smiled. "Are you hinting?"

"Who, me?" said Robert Aiken. "Not hinting. Lobbying outright."

"Well, it'll be soon. I'm getting my act together."

"Good. I'd be delighted, you know, if you'd hold the wedding reception here. We could put a tent up on the lawn. Elizabeth and I used to do that quite often for special occasions."

"That's very kind of you."

"It would be my pleasure, Jack. You know that."

It was several days after his dinner with his uncle that Jack ushered Sally into a conference room at the *World Herald*, armed with stacks of papers, a book, and a videotape. He had been doing his homework.

"All that stuff?" she asked.

"He's a very prolific guy, this Severn. And ambitious. Here's the introduction to his book, *The Uncivilized Brain*."

He opened the book. " 'The brain is the new frontier of science. It is the last great mystery that the human body has kept hidden from us, but its secrets are about to be mined. Our voyages of discovery will be as momentous as those of Columbus's.' "

"Your bag man might not be so enthusiastic about all this 'voyages' shit."

"You don't understand, Sally. The casualties along the way are nothing compared with the glorious march of science."

"*Mazel tov*. So what exactly is this guy into?"

"He says he's interested in researching the functioning of the limbic system of the brain."

"What's that? Biology is not my strong suit."

"Well, in laymen's terms, the human brain is sort of like a

city that grows over time. New parts got added on top of the old ones, as we evolved. Severn describes the limbic system as a link between the higher and lower parts of the brain. Like a telephone switchboard. It can receive and transmit messages from the older brain structures—the ones involved in visceral responses."

"Like flight or fight? That sort of thing?"

"Exactly. And the newer brain structures involve thought, perception, language."

"What's so fascinating to Severn about this switchboard?"

"He's looking at how the system is involved in aggressive behavior. He talks a lot about how Soviet research is way ahead of us in this area."

"Does he know that?"

"Not really, but it's a good guess. The Soviets keep this stuff pretty secret. Traditionally, they've been able to use their psychiatric hospitals not only as prisons but as a source of research subjects."

"Severn thinks this is neat?"

"Clearly he does. Oh, he throws in the usual caveats about how people should be protected, but he seems to think elite medical groups can do that, we don't need all this law stuff. Yeah, he'd be as happy as a pig in swill in a mental hospital in Sverdlovsk."

"Nice guy."

Jack picked up the videotape. "Craig gave me this tape. It's pretty old stuff, but I thought you might be interested. It's some of the classic research on the limbic system, done in the thirties. By Heinrich Kluver and Paul Bucy. They filmed their experiments."

"On people?"

"No, this was on monkeys. They destroyed the temporal lobes and parts of the limbic systems of monkeys. The species they used was pretty wild and aggressive. But after the operations, they became very pacified."

"Like people who get lobotomized?"

"Exactly. That's what this research led to. In this film, which Kluver made, you'll see that the monkeys were no longer able to inhibit their responses, even when the consequences were painful. Watch."

Jack picked up the tape and put it into the VCR. Sally watched as a grainy black and white image appeared on the screen. A small group of monkeys moved in what seemed to be an aimless way in an enclosure. A disembodied hand put a lighted cigarette in front of one of the monkeys. The animal picked up the cigarette, looked at it curiously, then put the lighted end into its mouth. It howled and threw down the cigarette after a painful burn. A minute later, it picked up the cigarette again, once more burned itself, and threw the cigarette away. The monkey repeated this sequence over and over again.

"This is what can happen when you destroy part of the brain," Jack said.

"Like the lobotomized people," Sally said, frowning. "Their violent behavior was stopped, but they had all sorts of bizarre behavior patterns."

The grainy image flickered to black. "Severn says the lobotomies were very crude. Like shooting a flea with a howitzer. Today, he says, we're much more sophisticated. We can take precise aim at any area of the brain we want." He raised his hand to simulate a pistol. "Zap."

"Jack, what in the hell is this guy doing?"

"I don't know. The bag man could just be a botched operation. Happens all the time. But Brady, that whole thing is very weird."

"Given Severn's history of medical experiments on prisoners, I'm inclined to think he's messing around with something. And dollars to doughnuts he's at least skirting the law."

"I think you're right."

"So we should stay on this," Sally said.

"Severn is scheduled to give a lecture next Thursday night. Sponsored by the Patriot Foundation."

"What's that?"

"It's one of those right-wing think tanks. Severn's apparently been very involved in it. Want to go?"

Sally nodded. "Yeah, I'd like to get a look at this guy."

"You've got a date."

"Sure you don't want to catch the late show of *Night of the Living Dead* instead?"

Jack smiled. "It'll probably be pretty dull. I doubt if he'll bring the bag man or any of his other mistakes along to model for the folks."

"Jack, I still get nightmares from your story about that guy. God, that poor man. Living in constant terror that someone's going to cut his brain again."

"I've lost some sleep on that one myself."

"All right," she said. "Thursday night we're on. Fun with Dr. Frankenstein."

REPORTER'S JOURNAL: Sally Ellenberg

Subject: Men

I got a card from Norman the other day, one of those embossed jobbies with a mailing label on it, announcing that he is expanding his oral surgery practice in San Francisco. Can you imagine the nerve? Or maybe I was still on his Rolodex, and some secretary thought I was a root canal.

It must have been those Saturday mornings with Jason that sent me marching, like some stupid lemming, right to Norman. Getting dentistry and sex all connected in my psyche at an early age was a disaster. Who else can have an orgasm in the dentist's chair when a male voice says, "Rinse, please." I was so blinded by Norman's shiny diploma and his pleasant toothside manner that I neglected to notice that he was a faithless swine.

Norman was good—looking, he had a sense of humor and a nice steady job. Even after the nuclear holocaust, when we are crawling around in caves, dentists will still do OK because people will complain about their toothaches even if their skin is molting. And Norman taught me to ski.

I was terrified when he first took me out on the slopes. I mean, you march someone out in the freezing cold, you tie boards to her feet, and you push her down the hill. Where is Amnesty International when you need them?

But I actually learned to enjoy it. We were so into it that Norman even had drawings done of the little ski chalet we would have at Mt. Snow, where we would take the children for family weekends on the slopes. Norman loved children, he said.

My Uncle Morty from Miami never liked Norman. He doesn't trust Jews who ski.

"What is he, Swedish?" Morty said when I said Norman and I were going skiing. When I told him Norman was Jewish, he said, "Snow is for *goyim.*"

I pointed out to Uncle Morty that his grandfather lived in Russia. He must have gone out in the snow.

"Correction—he *ran* out in the snow during pogroms to get away from getting hit in the head from a cossack. You think he took a little side trip to Aspen? If God had wanted Jews to ski, Jerusalem would be in Norway."

I should have listened to Morty. When Norman went off to his residency in San Francisco, he boarded the plane pledging eternal fealty. Six months later he eloped with an heiress who gave him a suite of offices furnished in peach and dove grey for a wedding present.

And the whole time, I—the stupid *schmuck*—was being chaste, which is very hard, and not skiing, which by then I really liked, and just sort of putting my life on hold. When he called on the phone to say ''Hi, how are you, I'm getting married," I guess I made a fool of myself. I told him he'd never be safe, never for a day in his life. One day, after he'd just washed his hands, he'd turn around, expecting his 2:30 root canal, the fluorescent lights glinting off his capped teeth, and there I'd be. I'd shove a ski pole right down his throat and he'd fall to the floor gasping, and that's how he'd die, coughing up blood on the dove grey carpet.

He said I was just upset. couldn't we still be friends?

Friends? A man breaks your heart and he wants to be your friend? It's like Hitler saying to Hadassah, "Sure, but that aside, let's do lunch."

Then there was Irwin, who, it turned out, was working toward his juris doctor by selling cocaine. And I thought it was some woman he was seeing when he had those little "appointments" at strange hours. That was a short-lived affair. How many women can say they had a torrid romance broken up by the Federal Drug

Enforcement Agency? Uncle Morty couldn't believe Irwin was selling drugs.

"Jews do insider trading," Morty said, "not drugs."

I have to admit, Uncle Morty has been right on his radar about Jews, especially the ones I date. He didn't like Mark much either.

"He uses a lot of big words," Morty said.

"He teaches twentieth-century sociopolitical theory at Harvard," I said.

"A Jew at Harvard?" he asked.

"Sure, there's lots of them there now," I told him.

"Harvard is for *goyim*," he said.

Like skiing, snow, and drugs, I assumed. But he did have Mark pegged right. He *was* a phony.

I was attracted to him because he seemed so fiery, so intense. An ex-radical who hadn't sold out. (I'd dated enough of the kind who had.) He didn't ski, which was a minus, but he didn't have anything to do with dentistry either, which was a very big plus. But he did use big words. Mark had to be an expert on everything, even my field, criminal justice. He wouldn't know a subpoena from a bench warrant, and he wouldn't know a DA if he fell over one, but he lectured me about Crime and Punishment. I guess I just wasn't worshipful enough, though God knows I tried. That's why he finally left me for one of his undergraduates, a baby Trotskyite with an I.Q. and a bra size exactly the same: forty-two.

Why, I wonder, am I so *leavable*? What is it that I don't know, or I don't have? I am loyal, I am kind, I know the contents of the three best-selling sex manuals. I wonder if someone is out there who could love me for the duration. Who has as much love to give me back as I give out? Who won't walk away or run away or ski away—or be dragged off by the Federal authorities?

I guess I will survive if there isn't anyone. I'm pretty strong.

But I'd really like it if there was.

A lot.

8

■

Sally looked around at the crowd filing into the small amphitheater. There were college students, middle-aged couples, young professionals—a typical group for any of the many lectures that were a part of Boston's social landscape. You could usually draw some kind of crowd in Boston or Cambridge, whether you were talking about the leafy flora of the Galapagos (with slides) or the latest Star Wars death ray (with artists' renderings).

"Pretty good crowd," Sally said to Jack as they entered along with the rest of the audience.

"Sexy topic," he told her. "Aggression and the brain. Sort of an intellectual *Rambo*."

They walked down the aisle and took seats near the front of the auditorium. A man, neatly dressed in a suit and tie, stepped up to the microphone, tapped it, and then said, "Welcome to the second in the series of public policy lectures sponsored by the Patriot Foundation. I'm pleased to introduce tonight's speaker, Dr. Theodore J. Severn, a distinguished neurosurgeon and the author of *The Uncivilized Brain*. Copies of the book will be available for sale in the back of the hall after the talk. Dr. Severn."

A man walked out from behind the curtain and stepped to the podium. He was of medium height, dressed, Jack noticed, in an expensive suit—probably Brooks Brothers. He had a benign moon face, made more so by the wire-rimmed glasses he wore, and smiled as he said, "Good evening, ladies and gentlemen. I'm delighted to be here tonight."

"That's him?" Sally said to Jack. "He looks like somebody's nice grandfather."

"Maybe he is."

Severn began to speak, highlighting many of the same themes he had explored in his book. The world he pictured was a sunny vista of scientific progress: the elimination of mental illness, the conquest of pain, the eradication of violence and antisocial behavior through the knife, the drug, and the electrode.

"Better living through chemistry," Jack muttered. No mention of mutilating a human being into a terrified hulk or making prisoners believe they were strangling to death. Both Sally and Jack listened closely as he described the great promise of electrical stimulation of the brain in altering behavior.

"The psycho-civilized society is a phrase first coined in the nineteen sixties by Dr. José Delgado of Yale Medical School and the Psychiatric Institute of Madrid," said Dr. Theodore Severn. "It is a phrase I especially like, because I am convinced that mankind's true destiny is not his control of the stars but in the mastery of his own brain. The wonders that lie within us are more tantalizing than the outer reaches of the galaxy."

"He has a way with words, doesn't he?" Sally said to Jack.

"Yeah. Quite a showman."

"Dr. Delgado was years ahead of his time," Severn said. "He wrote, 'We have reached a critical turning point in the evolution of man at which the mind can be used to influence its own structure, functions, and purpose, thereby ensuring both the preservation and advance of civilization.'"

Dr. Severn paused, then smiled as he saw he had his audience's rapt attention.

"Dr. Delgado, a true visionary, suggested that an organized, well-funded government effort, similar to the space agency, be founded for the purpose of exploring the frontiers of the human brain. Alas, this did not happen. Perhaps one day it will."

He paused again. "Dr. Delgado was one of the few scientists able to dramatize his work so the general public could understand it. There is some clucking and shaking of heads in the scientific community when a scientist has this ability. This is an unfortunate and, I might say, old-fashioned attitude. This is the era of the mass media, of marketing and imagery. Science vies with many other competing voices for attention and funding. If science does not use the modern technologies of the media to make its case, it will be left far behind. Would Socrates have hesitated to use the televised press conference? Or Newton the talk show, had those been available to them? I think not. And Dr. Delgado can demonstrate, far better than I, the promise of technology. The lights, please."

The lights began to dim in the room as a large screen rolled down from the ceiling.

"Dr. Delgado wanted to answer a number of questions," Severn continued. "Here is what he said, quote—'Is it possible to induce a robotlike performance in animals and men by pushing the buttons of a cerebral radio stimulator? Could dreams, desires, and thoughts be placed under the artificial command of electrodes? Can the mind be physically controlled?' "

Sally and Jack looked at each other in the darkening room.

The projector began to whir as Severn continued.

"Dr. Delgado invented a device called the Stimoceiver, which can be linked to electrodes implanted in the brain. Can we control behavior with technology? Judge for yourself."

The first few frames of the film depicted a small bull ring in Spain. A man, seemingly of middle age, with dark hair and wearing slacks and a shirt, walked into the ring. With a distinct flair, he tossed the cape of a matador over his shoulders. In his hand he held a small black device, about the size of a small portable radio.

The camera panned to a group of reporters and photographers, seated near the front of the ring, watching him.

A gasp went up from the crowd in the room when they saw, on film, that a large bull had been released into the ring with the scientist. An unarmed man was alone in the ring with several tons of murderous beef-on-the-hoof trotting on the fringes of the ring. The man watched the animal for a minute, then took the cape from his shoulders and, imitating the movements of a matador, waved the red cape at the bull. The bull snorted, then shook his head. Sally and Jack watched, entranced, like the others in the room.

José Delgado, on film, waved the cape again. The bull regarded him, then pawed the ground and lowered his head. Delgado waved the cape once more, and the bull began to move, then picked up speed, thudding toward him in full charge. The scientist stood unflinching, seemingly about to be gored by the galloping animal.

Then he raised his hand, and an astonishing thing happened. The huge bull shuddered and stopped dead in its tracks, just as if it had run headlong into a brick wall. The scientist stood, his hand upraised toward the bull, the little black box in his hand. The bull stood shaking his head, and if a bull could be said to look perplexed, indeed this one did.

The man in the ring smiled, turned toward the reporters who had been observing him, and gave a deep bow, with a twirl of his cape. There, the film ended.

As the lights came up again, Theodore Severn said, "Ladies and gentlemen, there were no stunt men here. No special effects. No trick photography. Believe what you have seen—the furious charge of the bull, one of the most awesome forces in nature, frozen in its tracks by the mere press of a button. Now, I'd be happy to answer all of your questions. And please remember, copies of my book are on sale tonight."

A young man near the front of the audience leaped to his feet.

"Dr. Severn, what you've shown us are the building blocks of Big Brother. You say you are going to create the psycho-civilized society? Aren't you really creating the tools for an advanced police state?"

Dr. Severn smiled at him. "Of course technology must be used wisely. But perhaps we have passed the point in evolution where we can allow random forces to control us. For our survival, we may have to move, as B. F. Skinner so eloquently puts it, 'beyond freedom and dignity.' "

"But those are the most important concepts of our society."

"What freedoms do you refer to?" Dr. Severn asked. "The freedom to hit someone over the head and take his money? To get in a car drunk, and slam into another car at one hundred miles an hour? The freedom to beat your children with a strap? We can control these behaviors, my friend, and create more freedom for people who will no longer be their victims."

That triggered a heated debate between Severn and some members of the audience. Finally the moderator stepped in, held up his hand, and said, "Well this has been a most"—he chuckled—"stimulating evening, if I may use that word. I hope you will join us next month when Dr. Andrew Tellman will speak on nuclear survival. And our thanks to Dr. Severn for a most enjoyable and educational evening."

Sally turned to Jack as they joined other members of the crowd who were filing out.

"Could that be what's going on? Trying to control people through electrodes in their brains?"

"It's easy to talk about this gee-whiz sci-fi stuff," Jack said. "*Doing* it is something else."

"Fits the Brady case. Joe thought he'd had electrode implants."

Jack sighed. "Yeah, but why does he drop dead in the middle of a holdup? Somebody goes to all the trouble of programming some guy just to be a petty thief?"

"You're right. The Manchurian Candidate didn't knock over a liquor store." She shook her head. "Unless Brady just wandered off the reservation and went back to old habits."

"If you're doing illegal research on some guy," Jack said, "you don't give him a weekend pass."

"Well, something damn strange is happening."

"I want to look into electrical stimulation of the brain some more," Jack said. "I've got a lot of clips, but I've barely had time to scan them."

"The Brady trail is pretty cold," Sally told him, "but I still have a couple of leads I haven't tried. I'll get to it as soon as I can. Kevin has me doing a lot of the Iran protest stuff."

"This could all go nowhere," Jack said.

"I know. But let's see where it leads. If anyplace." She laughed. "We make a great team. Sherlock and Watson."

He smiled. "Dr. Watson, how about a beer?"

"Now you're talking, Sherl," she said, and she took his arm.

Miki rushed up to Jack after she stepped out of a cab, and kissed him lightly on the cheek.

"So sorry to be late, darling," she said. "Traffic is beastly."

She took his arm and said, "I'm so pleased that your uncle is joining us tonight. He's a dear man."

"He is that," Jack said, smiling.

She was dressed with her usual elegance, Jack noticed. The

blue sheath she was wearing under the fox-trimmed coat cost at least a grand, he was sure, purchased at one of the exclusive little Newbury Street shops she frequented. Her shoes matched the dress, her nails and hair were freshly done; she could have just stepped out of the pages of *Vogue*. He frowned. It had not occurred to him before how much time must go into the attainment of that level of perfection. He had always admired it before. Why, now, did he wish she had a run in her stocking? Or a piece of spinach in her teeth?

He saw his uncle waving to him as he and Miki walked into the lobby of Symphony Hall. Robert Aiken came over, embraced Miki warmly, and gave Jack a manly pat on the shoulder.

To Miki he said, "You're looking lovely, my dear. As usual. Is this nephew of mine treating you right?"

"Jack's a dear man," Miki said.

"How was Washington, Uncle Robert?"

"One meeting after another. I'm rather regretting the fact that I agreed to serve on the Commission on Renewable Energy."

"Why?" Jack asked him as they moved toward their seats.

"So much technical material. You really do have to have the wisdom of Solomon to know which scientist to believe. They all make such good arguments. For totally opposite positions."

"I don't envy you that. I'm in that position a lot myself."

"So I can imagine."

The usher guided them to the correct row and they took their seats. Miki turned to Robert Aiken.

"Did the President ask you to serve?"

"Yes, Benton rather twisted my arm. It's very hard to say no to the President of the United States. And Benton is very good at being presidential."

"You do lead such a fascinating life," Miki told him.

"Yes, I'd like to convince Jack to get into government. So far I haven't had much luck."

Jack just smiled. Miki squeezed his arm and said to his uncle, "Just keep after him. Maybe he'll give in."

"Why do I feel outnumbered?" Jack said with a laugh. He picked up his program to see which selections the symphony would be doing tonight.

"Oh, Jack, Stravinsky," Miki said. She turned to Uncle Robert. "Jack loves Stravinsky."

"I do not," Jack said. "I hardly like him at all."

Miki looked crestfallen. "But, Jack, you said you loved the album I got you."

"I *like* him some. I don't love him," Jack said.

He turned back to his program and wondered why he was being so disagreeable. It was not like him. The houselights dimmed, Seiji Ozawa came out to take a bow, and the concert began.

As the music drifted over him, Jack sat back and half closed his eyes. He began to experience an unusual sensation, almost hallucinatory. He felt as if his spirit, separated from his body, was hovering overhead someplace, looking down at his physical self watching the concert. He had the sense that he was looking into his own future, like Scrooge in *A Christmas Carol*, and that he and Miki and Uncle Robert were frozen in their configuration, rigid as ceramic figures, floating through eternity together.

Then, abruptly, he was back in his seat, acutely aware of the close confines of the row, the constricted space, and the warmth of the room. He felt trapped, hardly able to breathe. He felt an unbearable need to move.

"Be right back," he whispered to Miki. He tried not to run up the center aisle toward the rear. He hurried through the lobby, out the front doors into the night.

He felt better almost immediately, the cool air splashing against his face. What the hell was going on? An attack of claustrophobia? He'd never experienced that before.

He thought, inexplicably, of sitting with Sally Ellenberg the night before, in a tacky neighborhood bar, over a couple of warm beers. They had talked shop, traded office gossip, and talked of deep things like life and philosophy. It had been so ordinary and so . . . lovely. He wished he were there right now.

He shook his head. Maybe it was just the about-to-be-married-man jitters. Maybe everyone felt this way on the verge of a major commitment. After all, doors were closing, the roads not taken were slipping by. When you were young, endless possibilities shimmered in the mist. Maybe part of growing up was mourning them.

He took a deep breath. If that was indeed his future, beside Miki and Uncle Robert, well then, it was the one he had chosen. He was, he knew, a fairly traditional man. Wild leaps into the unknown made him uncomfortable. He thought of Sally Ellenberg, her lipstick smudged on her beer glass, her hair unruly, her skin luminous.

He took another deep breath. What he didn't need at all was some crazy affair that would lead noplace, only to broken hearts and broken crockery, because that's what it would be with Sally. If he were younger, if he were freer—

But he wasn't.

Nor was he about to risk the well-ordered life he had planned (a paint-by-numbers life, came the unbidden thought; he pushed it away) with his usual thoroughness. He was not a fool.

He went back inside and slid into his seat. Miki looked at him with concern. "Are you all right?" she asked.

"Just something I ate," he said.

She turned back to the music, and he looked at her face in profile. The straight, elegant nose, the long swanlike neck, the golden hair pinned up in a perfect French twist. Not a single hair out of place. He looked very carefully. No, not one.

He leaned over to kiss her neck.

"You were right about the Stravinsky," he whispered. "It's wonderful."

She gave him a glowing smile in the darkness. Even her teeth, he noticed, were perfect, a flawless string of pearls bedecking her mouth. Not a piece of spinach anywhere.

He was a lucky man.

9

■

Kevin Murphy waved to Sally, who had looked up from the Sunday piece she was doing on the Federal Witness Protection program. She walked over to the city desk.

"Sally," he said, "can you handle Andrews for me, at Harvard?"

The Attorney General was scheduled to put in an appearance at the university for a panel on the Iranian situation. What appeared to be a sizable protest was in the making.

"Yeah, Kev, I'll handle it."

"This protest stuff is really building. With the near riot last week in Chicago and the big demonstration at Stanford."

"Got a photog going over?"

"Gail Samanski. I think she's heading over there now."

"OK. I'm on my way."

Sally found Gail and the two of them rode the Red Line to Harvard. Walking out through the doors of the subway entrance in Harvard Square, she found the street already jammed with people. It was going to be a big crowd.

The call by the Student Alliance to protest the Attorney General's appearance had been a rousing success. Hundreds of people, most of them young and casually dressed, filled Harvard

Yard and spilled out onto the surrounding streets. The university hadn't tried to close off the yard—good thing, Sally thought, because if they had, no traffic would have moved for blocks.

Sally looked around for familiar faces. She spotted Sandra Jefferson in the crowd, and smiled. Not only was Sandra a good source on the disappearances of the young women in the black community, she had also given Sally a key piece of information when a black teenager had been shot by a cop, after joyriding in a stolen car. Sandra had found a witness who had seen the shooting, but went underground for fear of reprisal.

The black woman was talking with a young man, standing beside a banner that spelled out, in large black letters, NEW PANTHERS.

Urban blacks had not forgotten the bitter experience of Vietnam, where recruiters reaped the richest harvest from the streets of the nation's Wattses and Harlems and Roxburys. While middle-class and rich whites escaped in droves into college classrooms, it was the blacks and poor whites who had been shipped home in body bags. Was it going to happen again?

Sandra Jefferson shook her head. "No way! This time they're not going to get black cannon fodder. Die for some stinking oil field in Iran? Hell no. Give the vice-presidents of Exxon and Gulf M-16s and let them go shoot up the Persian Gulf."

"Is Hakim going to be here today?" Sally asked.

"He'll be here. I saw him this morning. Hakim wouldn't miss this one."

Sally looked around. A line of Cambridge police stood against the walls of the ivied buildings, along with perhaps a dozen trench-coated men who were obviously Federal security agents. Sally wandered around, trying to get quotes from the demonstrators and material for a color piece on the crowd. As people milled around, there were more than a few impromptu speeches and a lot of songs. The rally organizers chanted slogans through a bullhorn and a few guitarists led protest songs, while people gathered around them. While the rhetoric was angry, the mood of the crowd was benign. Sally looked around for Hakim Abdul, but didn't see him anyplace in the crowd. Hakim ought to have a juicy quote on Andrews. Without it, the story would probably run inside, maybe in Metro.

Sally turned around and nearly bumped into Fritz Diehl, a reporter on the national desk at the *Washington Post* and a classmate of hers at Columbia J School. Fritz told her that since last month, he had been assigned full time to cover the A.G. She asked him for a quick fill-in on Andrews; the *World Herald* clips were spotty.

"He's getting to be the point man for the hardliners in the administration," he told her. "The White House staff wants him on a short leash, but he and Ellard go way back."

"He's been threatening to use the Federal contempt powers to get student protesters."

"That's not just noise."

"Is this leftie-baiting just a way to distract attention from the mess the administration is in on this?"

"No, even at the height of glasnost he was still an 'evil empire' guy. He's a funny kind of cat. He seems to take all these demonstrations personally. He can be fun to cover, because he likes reporters and he can be charming when he wants to. But the protests make him foam at the mouth."

"Do you think he'll come out here?" Sally asked him.

Diehl laughed. "His press guys will probably tie him to his chair to stop him. But he won't be able to resist. He loves to lead the six p.m.'s."

The *Post* reporter proved to be right on the mark. It was only a few minutes before one of the doors of an ivy-draped building swung open. Elliott Andrews stepped out into the yard; the TV lights blazed on and the minicams whirred. The Attorney General pulled himself to his full height and faced them, his much-photographed jut-jaw at maximum jut. He was a tall well-built man who wore his finely tailored suits with more flair than the average bureaucrat.

A hail of boos and catcalls greeted the Attorney General's appearance. Andrews struck a defiant pose, one that would play beautifully on ABC news.

A voice yelled out above the din, "We're not going to die for Amoco!" Another: "No more black bodies for white men's wars!" "Fascist Pig!" came a shout.

The Attorney General shook his fist at the crowd, profile-in-courage turned to the cameras. It was rumored that he was thinking of a White House run next time if Ellard's health continued to fail.

"Spineless punks," he snarled. "There's not a real pair of balls in this whole crowd!"

Sally sighed. "Another fight with Kevin," she said to Gail, who was shooting away beside her. "I'll never get 'balls' into the paper."

A tomato came sailing through the air, and it caught the A.G. on the shoulder, dribbling its contents on the Harris tweed. A phalanx of security guards congealed around him, and formed a protective wall as they hustled him to a waiting limousine. Suddenly, without warning, the line of policemen charged into the crowd. In the enclosed space, the result was pandemonium. People trying to get out of the way found themselves trapped against the brick walls of the buildings. The police line kept advancing and people began to trip and fall, causing others trying to back up to get tangled in their bodies and to go down as well. Sally found herself caught in a surging mass of humanity, unable to break free. People were screaming all around her.

"Hey, man!" somebody yelled to the cops, "We're just trying to get out!"

"Police brutality!"

"Pigs! Lousy Pigs!"

Sally used her arms for protection and to help her keep her balance, trying to move with the mass of people and not lose her footing. It was a distinct possibility that people could be trampled, and she thought that it would be a horrible irony to be trampled to death in Harvard Yard. Her father had wanted to go there, but then, there were quotas for Jews—especially very bright scholarship boys. She tried to edge her way out of the crowd, but it was impossible. She fought back a surge of panic.

Finally, she managed to turn and break free of the crush, and she saw, directly in front of her, a policeman savagely swinging his club up and down. A young blond girl went down, dead weight, under the club. The policeman, instead of pulling back, continued to club her. The girl curled up on the ground and moaned.

He's out of control, Sally thought. She lunged toward the policeman, grabbing at the arm that was plunging up and down.

"You're going to kill her, you idiot. Stop it! Stop it!"

The arm swung around; all Sally saw was a blur, and the next thing she knew she was sitting on the ground, stunned. The whole mad scene seemed to whirl around her, a jumble of colors and sounds. Suddenly, she was aware of a splitting pain down the side of her face. She put her hand up to see if she was bleeding. Her face felt warm and sticky.

Then Gail Samanski was squatting beside her. "Oh shit! Sally, are you all right?"

Sally nodded. "Did you get that fucker's badge?"

"Yeah. I also got a shot of him clobbering you."

Sally sat still, trying to let her head clear. Gail stood up to shoot some more pictures as the police line began to retreat. Some students were being led off to paddy wagons, others were quickly streaming out of the yard to the surrounding streets. Sally got to her feet, unsteadily. "I've got to get more stuff," she said, but Gail shook her head. "We've got to get you to a doctor. You're still bleeding."

"The arrests . . ." Sally felt suddenly dizzy.

"The desk can get that on the phone. Come on."

Sally held a handkerchief to the side of her face and let Gail lead her out to Mass Ave. Somehow, in all the chaos, Gail was able to hail a cab. The cabbie saw Sally's bloodied face and he stopped and waved to the two women. Gail shoved Sally in the cab.

"Take her to Boston Municipal. Emergency room," Gail said. "Sally, are you going to be OK by yourself?"

"Yeah, thanks, Gail. I'm all right."

The attendants in the emergency room took one look at her and led her to a small treatment room. As a nurse bathed her face with a warm, damp solution, Sally's brother-in-law hurried in, looking worried.

"Hi, Joe," Sally said. "How did you know I was here?"

"The desk called me. Are you OK?"

"I guess so."

He looked at her face. "Jeez, you really did get clobbered."

"Will I need stitches?"

"No, I don't think so. Let me take a look."

Nothing was broken, as it turned out, but she had suffered a severe bone bruise and lacerations. She called Kevin Murphy and told him she was coming in to write. She took a cab back to the paper, and when she walked in, Kevin took a look at her, gulped down a Valium, and said, "Jesus Christ!"

"He was the guy who said, 'Turn the other cheek.' "

"You sure you feel good enough to write?"

"You bet your ass I'll write it. I am going to have that sucker up on charges. Goddamn Cambridge cops. Bush league!"

As she expected, she got into a fight with Kevin over the A.G.'s quote.

"That's what he said, Kevin. 'Balls.' "

"How about we say 'male genitals.' "

"Sure. Everybody's going to believe the Attorney General yelled, 'There's not a real pair of male genitals in the crowd!' Or, how about 'gonads.' "

"We can't use *balls* in a family newspaper."

"Kevin, they're going to use it on 'Nightline.' Dan Rather will use it. Peter Jennings will use balls. Even Christopher Lydon on public television will use balls. Christ, these days, they say it on 'Sesame Street'!"

Kevin went so far as to agree to "b---s." Sally considered it a victory. She suddenly felt very tired. A major moment in American journalism. The *Boston World Herald* was going to use "b---s." Eat your heart out, Scotty Reston.

She let her head rest in her hands for a minute, then sensed someone was standing beside her. Jack Aiken was looking at her, and she was surprised to see the concern etched on his face. He was transparent as Scotch tape, she thought, but the look on his face warmed her.

She tried to smile. "I knew there were quotas at Harvard, but this is ridiculous. I wasn't even trying to matriculate."

He didn't smile. He put his hand gently against the side of her face. "I'd like to break his fucking neck!" It was the first time she had heard him use that word. "What kind of a man hits a woman?" he said.

"That turkey would have clobbered Mother Teresa. He was really getting his rocks off."

"Kevin says you were trying to stop him from hitting a kid."

"Not just hitting. He was clubbing her, bad."

"You're not supposed to get involved, you know."

"Kevin's already given me the lecture. I thought he was going to kill her, Jack. She's got a multiple fracture, we hear. How could I just stand there and let him do that?"

"How do you feel?"

"Not great, actually."

"Come on. I'll drive you home. You shouldn't be driving tonight."

She put on her sweater and walked out with him. Going down the front steps, she felt a wave of nausea and grabbed for his arm. He put his arm around her and she leaned against him, gratefully. He felt so good, he smelled so good. This would be very easy to get used to, she thought.

He drove her to her apartment in the Back Bay and walked her to the door. He looked carefully at her face.

"Sally, that looks pretty bad. Are you going to be all right?"

"I'm OK, Jack."

"Do you want me to stay with you?"

The old Sally would have said, "You bet your sweet ass I do." The new, self-disciplined Sally said, "No thanks, Jack. I'm all right. But thanks."

She went upstairs, peeled off her clothes, and fell into bed. The whole side of her face was throbbing; she took another of the painkillers Joe had given her. She was very proud of herself for not letting Jack spend the night. He was too tall for the couch, so of course she would have offered him half the double bed. Since he didn't have pajamas, he would have to strip down to his Jockeys to sleep comfortably. How nice it would have been to feel his warm body next to hers. She might have asked him to give her a back rub to get rid of the tension in her neck and shoulders, moving close to his body to make it easier. She had a pretty good idea of what his body was like under the layers of cashmere and cotton broadcloth. The hair on his chest would be wavy, a shade darker than the hair on his head, and his belly would be flat and muscular, and moving right along—

She noticed another throbbing, but not the one in her face. Oh no, the day had been frustrating enough already. What she didn't need right now to complicate her life was jumping into the sack with someone. Especially Jack Aiken, who had his WASP princess, Muffy or Wuffy or whatever the hell her name was, hanging around. Very pretty. Very cultured. Very frigid. Probably thought fellatio was a minor work by Vivaldi. Thin wrists. Thin blood. Poor Jack.

Sally turned over, trying to get into a comfortable position. The pain was starting to dull, slightly. Giving up sex was not all that it was cracked up to be. It made her edgy, and she smoked more. She did not consider herself promiscuous. In fact, by her own lights, she was a very moral person. She had never—well, OK, twice, three times?—since high school jumped into bed with a man purely for libido. She always went into a new relationship with what might be called the triumph of hope over experience. She had spent all that time waiting for Norman, collecting ski brochures and staying horny . . . he should only have an entire officeful of cavity-prone AIDS patients who bite. Irwin was still in Allendale, working on his forehand, and she had simply wasted two years with Mark.

Each time a relationship came unglued, she felt that her fingernails were being pulled out, one by one. It was as if she had been through three divorces—with no community property, not even half a record collection or the family dog, to show for it.

She turned again. She thought that she could still smell Jack Aiken's aftershave; not heavy macho aphrodisiac, but subtle, elegant. Like him. She sighed.

She had the feeling she was going to do something really dumb about Jack Aiken. But she was going to be smart about it this time.

No more white knight fantasies, no more daydreams about a Beacon Hill love nest with His and Hers towels in the shower, no more picking out cute names for twins. She and Jack Aiken would never be more to each other than a brief fling. His world, of North Shore gentry and family stretching back probably to the *Mayflower*, of summers in Maine and very old silver and even older money, was as alien to her as the surface of Mars. In their generation, the gap between Yankee Brahmin and immigrant Jew had narrowed; neither group believed any longer that the other drank blood in sinister and arcane religious rituals. But she could hardly see herself chatting with old aunt Agatha about the blood lines of ponies at Myopia. And how would Jack fare, schmoozing with Uncle Morty, up from Miami (pink shirt and polyester lime-green pants), about his fortunes at the dog track?

No, this time, if anything happened, she was going to hold her heart in check. It would all be very civilized, very Noel Coward. A smile, a bittersweet melody half remembered, and that's all she wrote. No Jewish guilt, hysteria, moaning and rending of garments. She would send him one perfect rose, and a note. *"Je regrette."* She had read that Alain Delon did that once, and, oh God, *that* was class. Much better than getting on the phone and shrieking, "You lousy *putz*, I gave you the best years of my life!"

A single rose. *"Je regrette. Sally."* He'd keep it pressed in his album, and he could take it out and look at it from time to time, years later, when he had married frigid Muffy who spent her time going to garden shows and hitting the cooking sherry. Once a month she'd let him hump her—she still wouldn't have any boobs—and fake an orgasm so she could go off to sleep and he would come downstairs and open his album and touch the rose and remember.

She smiled and closed her eyes. Wasn't it nice, she thought, that she had become a realist at last.

REPORTER'S JOURNAL: Sally Ellenberg

Subject: Games Your Mother Never Taught You

I get so tired of this. I practically had to throw a tantrum so I wouldn't get my story on the Federal Witness Protection Act stolen out from under me. My story. My sources. And they wanted to give it to Jerry Rogers, because, quote, he does organized crime. I do more stories on it than he does, I'm the senior person, my sources are better. They know this. Why do they forget?

It almost made me want to go back and reread all those books about how to make it in a man's world. I read a whole shelf full of them once, and ended up being mainly depressed. It seemed that if you didn't understand football, you were doomed to the typing pool.

I myself find football intensely boring, except when they do close-ups on the tushies in the tight pants. Norman was a big football buff. We'd be sitting there, watching, and he'd rant on about offensive stats and yards gained rushing and he'd get annoyed because I'd sit there, glassy eyed, swilling down beer and now and then muttering, "Nice ass."

I could never figure out the little chalk drawings on the TV set. They looked like diagrams for some kind of chemical reaction. And the announcers drone on and on about obscure plays made in the Super Bowl in 47 B.C. by some guy who went to Southern Methodist. Or Notre Dame. *Goyish* schools, all. You never hear Brent Musburger talking about a tight end from Hebrew Union. Or the NFL draft choice from Yeshiva.

Anyhow, I do not think knowing football really

helps you with life. Do you listen to the TV interviews they do with football players? They make Tarzan of the Apes sound like Bill Buckley. But I guess it's all the male bonding stuff, and the keeping score. Men love to keep score.

I finished reading all the books, and I knew I couldn't play The Game. I didn't care about keeping score—all this concern about who is where in the hierarchy is a big bore. Basically there are two kinds of behavior in The Game—Domination and Sucking Up. And you do one of them to get to do the other. One takes all your energy figuring out who to be nice to and then being nice to them, and the other takes all your energy being mean to almost everyone. It is not a very efficient system.

I decided that the only way I could get what I wanted was just to use my talent as a battering ram. Just keep throwing myself against the dike until it gave. It's worked so far. But still, sometimes they don't see me. But it's better than The Game.

I'm no good as an imitation man. I'm not built for it, and anyhow, I find that some of the things I learned by being a woman turn out to be very helpful at work. Why doesn't anybody tell you about that?

First of all, I listen. Really listen. People tell me things they don't tell men. Have you ever noticed, when two guys get together, they circle each other and shake their antlers, sizing each other up? Male sources don't have to do that with me. They don't perceive a threat. Which is sometimes their mistake. Women tell me things because they think only another woman would understand. I think women learn to listen because they saw their mothers listening and having to fix things for everyone. It's a simple skill, but very, very useful. Men should do more of it.

Another thing I do is treat little people (not midgets, just regular people) nicely. I notice them. I *see* them. Especially secretaries. Men see secretaries the way they see socks—as basically all one size and one color. Do men ever *notice* socks? But secretaries know everything that goes on. And because men think they are invisible, they say things in front of them that they shouldn't. And secretaries call me—when there's something wrong, or sometimes just to get even for being invisible. They call me because I do see them.

There's something I don't have to do, either. I don't have to pretend I don't give a shit. Men lose brownie points if they display any emotion other than contempt or rage. It's why guys joke around a lot to hide what they are really feeling. After a big fire or an air crash, there's so many one-liners in the newsroom you'd think it was "The Tonight Show." They can't cry, so they quip. I think that must be very hard.

I can't actually cry—that's unprofessional—but I don't have to clench my jaw and toss out a one-liner. I can feel.

To do my stories, I'm often seeing people at a crisis point in their lives. If they see that I'm feeling something, they're more likely to make a connection with me, and then the reader can connect with *them.* And that's important.

There are times, of course, when somebody misreads what I'm feeling. There was the Klan guy, who really thought I was fascinated when he was explaining how easy it is to light a cross if you get the thing oiled up right.

What I was really thinking, as I nodded my head and smiled, was that I had told the switchboard to give out my home number any time of night or day. I was thinking of the call they were going to get:

"Good morning, *World Herald.*"

"Hello there, ma'am. I need to get in touch with Miz Sally Ellenberg."

"She is not in at the minute. What is the nature of the call?"

"Well, we'd just like to burn a li'l ole cross on Jew girl's lawn."

"Ms. Ellenberg can be reached at 555-3412."

"Thank you so much. You all have a nice day, now."

It's a funny thing about opting out of The Game. You see things other people are too busy to see. An outsider has this oblique angle of vision that might be worthless to the stockbroker, but it is very good for a journalist. Journalism is the quintessential outsider's profession. Sometimes, we like to think we're insiders, but basically, we're Little Match Girls, pressing our noses to the pane to see and hear things we're not supposed to see and hear.

It suits me, this job. I rather like hanging out with cops and DA's—even crazy ones like Frank O'Brien—and the assorted types who drift on the fringes of society. There's a rawness to their lives that is interesting, even honest, in a strange way. Not that I buy the romantic garbage about criminals you get in some novels. Violence isn't noble or pur—gative or honorable. Mean scum are mean scum, period. But the world I cover is one in which the usual ci—vilities that cover up meanness are stripped away; all the edges are bare. Makes for high drama, often. But it's better to be an observer than a participant.

Odd, the people who turn out to be outsiders—Jack Aiken, for one. On the surface, he's Mr. Inside. But an alcoholic father can turn a guy with all those ad—vantages into the Little Match Girl, too. Maybe it's even worse to be an outsider when everybody assumes you're not—when you *know* everybody you can see through the glass. I'd noticed that he didn't play The Game either, but I assumed he simply didn't have to. It's funny that we have that in common. Oh dear, I am so attracted to that man. What am I going to do about it?

I'll think about it tomorrow. Tomorrow is another day.

10

■

Sally told the story of almost getting her story snatched away to Mary Ellen as she took a spoonful of chocolate mousse. They were splurging and splitting a dessert.

"I get the same thing," Mary Ellen said. "I get to be 'Invisible Woman.' I'll make a point in a meeting and no one will say anything. A few minutes later a guy will make the same point, and they'll all start buzzing, like they never heard it before."

"Why do they do that?" Sally wondered.

"Men are trained to tune out when women talk. They saw their fathers do it to their mothers."

"Mark used to do that, all the time. When he didn't want to listen, he'd just go off into outer space, his own universe. That was supposed to be OK. If I did it, he'd get pissed. I always had to be tuned in."

"Have you seen him?"

"No. He called, suggested we see each other now and then. He means screw now and then. I told him to fuck off."

"Can I believe my ears? You're doing something smart where a man is concerned? Which reminds me, who was the hunk I saw you with at Dwyer's the other night?"

"You were there?"

"Brian and I dropped in for a couple of beers."

"Why didn't you come over?"

"Because you and the hunk were holding hands and staring deep into each other's eyes, that's why."

"No, we were just talking. Kind of intently."

"Yeah, kind of."

"He's just—oh hell, he's just a guy that makes my hormones twitch. Nothing serious."

"Sally, are you about to go off on another sexual toot?"

"I haven't done that in years. Come on, high school doesn't count. He just reminds me of my father."

"Your *father*? Since when was Sol Ellenberg a six-foot stud?"

"Not physically. Jack is just so . . . solid. My dad was always . . . there, you know. He'd never run off to do his thing or get weird with a mid-life crisis. He was a *mensch*. All the guys in my life turned out so flaky. Jack isn't. But we don't have anything going. There's chemistry, but talk about different worlds! Besides, he's engaged."

"Who to?"

"Some North Shore socialite. Muffy something."

"What you don't need is another smash-up."

"I know. Believe me, if anything happens, it'll just be about sex. Very safe. Condoms all the way. Who knows what Muffy sleeps with? Probably her horse."

"Sally, listen to me, your old Irish aunt, Mary Ellen. You have this image of yourself as some kind of hard-hearted sexual rebel. But you always wind up getting hurt."

"Not always."

"Am I speaking to the wall? Who is the person who had to have her stomach pumped when Norman eloped?"

"I just lost track of the Valium. And the scotch."

"Sally, just do me a favor. Do not do anything terminally stupid."

"I've learned my lesson. I take it one day at a time now. No fantasies. No expectations. I'm not *intense* anymore. Mellow, that's me."

"I'll believe you're mellow when Arafat gets bar-mitzvahed."

"Laid back, that's me, now."

"Or just *laid.*"

"That too. I hope. Why are people staring at us?"

"Have you forgotten?"

Sally put her hand to her eye. "Oh, right," she said. "It must look kind of strange."

It was a classic black eye, as if she had gone ten rounds with Marvelous Marvin Hagler. At the paper, it caused much comment—sympathy, bad jokes, home remedies. Jack Aiken couldn't help staring at it—which was better, he guessed, then staring down the front of her shirt. He was astonished at the rush of emotions that stupid black eye stirred up in him, in particular a rush of aggression that he hadn't known was in him.

Miki had told him, over dinner at Joseph's, that he seemed distracted. He had realized that while he was finishing his veal Oscar, he was at the same time relishing a scene in which he was pounding the face of a certain Cambridge cop into blood-flecked oatmeal. It was not like him at all. The last real fight he had was in eighth grade at Phillips Exeter. It was with Puddy Rhinebeck and, if memory served, both of them had retired with bloody noses and some degree of honor. He had boxed a bit as an undergraduate, but his heart wasn't in it. Basically, he didn't like hitting people; he was a very peaceful man, he told himself as he mentally stomped the heel of his foot into the bridge of the policeman's nose, grinding it into bloody paste.

Every time he looked at Sally's black eye he wanted to take her in his arms and hold her and protect her from everything in the world that could hurt her. It was strictly a Me-Tarzan, You-Jane sort of feeling. It was all very puzzling. Miki was everything he wanted in a woman: elegant, beautiful, intelligent, from the right family, the right schools. Why was he spending most of his time these past few days thinking about a woman who was sort of a leftist, foul-mouthed, a women's-libber, Jewish, funny, and dressed in outfits Bette Midler would reject? He wondered which one of those attributes would be most likely to make Uncle Robert and Uncle Josiah choke on their white bread and mayonnaise.

Sally looked up and saw him watching her.

"Gorgeous, huh? I look like the poster girl for the S and M telethon."

"I have to admit, you do look funny."

"Well, it'll be worth it if Gail gets the Pulitzer for that picture. There I am, getting smacked in the face, four columns."

"Listen, I've been doing some more work on ELS."

"What?"

"Electrical stimulation of the brain."

"Oh, right."

"There's a neurosurgeon Craig told me about, who has a tape on some of the research. He's at Harvard Med. Want to go with me? I have an appointment at three."

"Yeah, I can make it. If you don't mind being seen with me in this condition."

"I'll grin and bear it."

Sally was a few minutes late for the appointment at Harvard. Jack and Dr. Sol Weinstein had already started talking when she dashed in and slid out of her coat.

"Sorry. Just keep going. I'll catch up."

The doctor looked at her.

"Wherever you've been, I don't want to go there."

Sally put her hand to her face. "Line of duty. Harvard Yard, in fact."

The doctor nodded. "Oh. It got quite lively, I hear."

"You hear right." She sat down in a chair opposite him. "Go ahead, Jack. Sorry to interrupt."

Jack nodded to the doctor. "You were talking," he said, "about stereotaxic surgery."

"Yes. It's not difficult, with modern technology, to place electrodes in a precise spot in the brain."

"How do you get them in there?" Sally asked.

"You drill holes in the skull to allow for the entry."

"Like you'd do with a piece of wood? Just—drill it?" she asked him.

"Basically, yes," the doctor said. "You make a small hole in the bony plate of the skull, then you pierce the dura, the delicate membrane that covers the brain. Then you find your spot."

"How's that done?" Jack asked.

"You know how we use dye to find out where arteries near the heart are clogged?"

"Yes."

"We can do the same thing with the brain. We inject a radiopaque solution into a ventricle in the brain. The solution travels through the vessels of the brain and lights them up, so to speak."

The doctor reached for a folder on his desk. "Here's what a stereotaxic machine looks like. It's an old one—the new ones are sleeker—but you'll get the idea."

Sally and Jack peered at the picture.

"Weird," Sally said. "Looks like something out of a medieval torture chamber."

"Now that you mention it, it does," the doctor said. "But it's a painless procedure."

The machine in the photograph resembled nothing more than a large metal arc with a piece of metal attached, its end curving down. There were two screwlike clamps at the bottom of the arc.

"This is fitted to the skull of the patient?" Jack asked.

"Yes. And with the help of a radiologist, we can take X-ray pictures of the skull. With fast developing X-ray film, we can get a series of pictures of the interior of the brain. With our new scans and computer imaging, the quality of the pictures we get is remarkable."

"Sort of like a road map," Sally said.

The doctor nodded. "Exactly. The surgeon can adjust the controls of his machine to exactly match that map of the brain."

"The machine is something like a missile launcher, right?" Jack asked. "It fires the electrodes into the brain."

"Good analogy," the doctor said. "In this case, the 'missiles' are tiny wires along which an electrical current can be passed."

"How many can be inserted at once?" Sally asked him.

"I've heard of as many as twenty-five being done."

Sally cringed at the idea of the electrodes being plunged deep into the mysterious, spongy tissue of the brain.

"It doesn't hurt at all?"

"No. There's no pain in the insertion."

Jack ran his finger across the glossy surface of the photograph.

"When the electrodes are in, then what?"

"An electric current is passed along the electrodes," the doctor explained. "At sixty-five degrees centigrade, a number of cells around the tip of the electrode are destroyed."

Jack leaned back in his chair. "So what is this all for? That's the sixty-four-dollar question."

"Medically, the surgery is very controversial. There have been claims that ELS can help people who suffer from temporal lobe epilepsy, or disorders that cause unprovoked, random violence."

"Have you investigated some of these claims?"

Dr. Weinstein nodded. "Yes, I took a thorough look at what's available. At first, some of the progress seemed pretty remarkable. People with histories of violent attacks seemingly pacified. But when you looked closely, the claims didn't hold up. The progress seemed only temporary. Most of the people actually ended up worse off."

"In what ways?"

"They lost some of the capabilities they had before. One man had been a fairly talented painter. He lost the ability to paint. Couldn't do it at all."

"Doctor," Sally said, "as far as you know, could anyone use this technology to control somebody, like a robot?"

"At the level our knowledge is now? Not a chance. We really know very little about what can and can't be done. There's a real moral dimension to this kind of research. You're talking about the human brain. You can't subject living people to this sort of thing just to see how they're going to react. And of course, research on cadavers is useless, since the brain isn't functioning."

"You've got a videotape of some research subjects?" Jack asked.

The doctor stood up and took a reel of videotape out of a bookcase. "This is from the Radlin Institute, in Chicago. They were doing a lot of this kind of surgery."

He popped the tape into a video player in his office.

"What you *can* do with this technology is create violent swings of mood. This particular tape gives a pretty dramatic example of that."

He pressed the PLAY button and a picture appeared, of a small white room that contained only a bed. A young woman, who appeared to be in her early twenties, was lying on the bed, dressed in a green hospital gown. Her head had been completely shaved, and a series of wires protruded from it. The scene looked, Sally thought, like something out of a science fiction movie.

"You see," the doctor said, "she appears calm, almost passive. Watch as the stimulation of one set of electrodes begins."

The young woman on the bed began to move, restlessly at first, as if she couldn't find a comfortable position. Then she began to pound her fist, almost rhythmically, on the bed, and then all of a sudden she leapt up and, with an animal shriek of rage, began to pound on the bedrail, which was heavily padded. Her frenzy mounted, as did her shrieks. Her rage was total and uncontrollable.

"Now they're going to stop."

The young woman collapsed on the bed, panting like an exhausted animal.

"You see how quickly she passed from passivity to rage," the doctor said. "Now, watch as another area of the brain is stimulated with another set of electrodes."

The girl on the bed began to twitch. Then her legs started to move, opening and closing.

"Ohhh, you're doing it," she moaned. "Please, oh please!"

Sally and Jack looked at each other in surprise.

The girl writhed and moaned. "Oh, who am I? Oh, I feel so good! I feel like I'm dying. So good! So good!"

"Do you want us to stop?" asked an unseen male voice.

"No, please, don't stop. I'll be a good girl. I will!"

Suddenly, she stopped moaning and lay still on the bed. The screen went blank. Sally was still staring at the screen, horrified.

"My God," she said, "that poor girl was being . . . tormented. Like an animal in a cage. We don't even do that to animals in zoos."

The doctor nodded. "Yeah, it's pretty disgusting. There's no real medical purpose served by this."

"What happened to that girl?" Sally asked him.

"She's in an institution, in the Midwest. One of the nurses who had worked with her reported that she used to play the guitar beautifully, and have long discussions about life and art. Since ELS, she's deteriorated badly. Very depressed. Often suicidal."

"Did ELS cause that?" Sally asked.

"It can't be proven, but my guess is that it certainly contributed."

Jack frowned. "Doctor, some people say that there may be a pleasure center in the brain, and that if it could be found, it would be a powerful tool for social control."

"When you watch that tape, there clearly does seem to be a kind of pleasure when some of the brain areas are stimulated. But it's pleasure that's almost pain. If someone *could* find a pleasure center, they'd make a million bucks. Forget cocaine. People would be zapping themselves like crazy."

"Doctor, is a lot of this research going on?" Sally asked him.

"Not so much. I think that people feel, today, that the real medical payoffs will be in the chemistry of the brain. We're learning the links between neurotransmitters and certain diseases. To me, that's a more exciting area of research. It's more in the classic traditions of medicine, and it's less intrusive."

"But you're not interested in controlling people."

"True."

"Some people are."

"Oh, a lot of people are. But the regulations these days are a lot better than they used to be."

"I hope so," Jack said.

When they left the doctor's office, Jack and Sally stopped on Huntington Avenue for a cup of coffee.

"Jack," Sally said, "do you think that's what they—whoever *they* are—were doing to Brady?"

"But I don't get the robbery angle. Weinstein says there's no way they could control anybody to that degree."

"Could he be wrong? Could they be that advanced?"

"It's very unlikely they could have made that kind of quantum leap," he said.

"And if they just wanted to find out if they could kill somebody with the technology, they'd do it in some private place. Not march him into a liquor store."

He shook his head. "There's a piece missing here that we're not getting." He rubbed his forehead, wearily, and said, "What if Brady had been one of Severn's patients? And sometime after the surgery he just went back to his old life. Knocking over stores. Maybe that's why Severn was at the morgue. Maybe what we've got here is just a botched operation."

"But why did the records disappear?"

"Clerical screwup. Happens all the time. Maybe nothing illegal is going on. Maybe just your routine lousy medicine. That girl in the tape was in that place at her family's urging. All the right forms got signed."

"But Brady had been in prison. I checked his medical records. No record of surgery. If it had been done then, there would have to be some record of it."

"We just need more than what we have."

"I know. But I don't want to drop it, do you?"

"No. Let's keep going, see what turns up."

"Good," she said. "I hoped you'd say that."

"Sorry I'm running late," Jack said to Seth Chaffee, as he joined him at the Harvard Club bar, on Commonwealth Avenue. "I was on a story."

"I'm just drinking myself into a happy mood," Seth told him. "Let's eat before I fall down."

"How's it going in D.C.?" Jack asked, as the maître d' showed them to their table.

"No shop talk tonight," Seth said. "I'm just glad to be out of D.C. and back in Boston."

"I have something to ask you," Jack said, after he'd ordered a glass of white wine. "How'd you like to be my best man?"

"Best man! So you're finally going to do it, huh?"

Jack grinned. "It's about time."

"I thought you and Miki were going to be the world's oldest living engaged couple. Did she threaten to toss you out?"

"No, she's not putting any pressure on. It's me, in fact. Time to do the deed."

"Do I detect a note of uncertainty?" Seth asked.

Jack hesitated. "No," he said.

"You are a rotten liar, Jack."

Jack picked up the glass of wine that had arrived at the table and took a sip. "Miki is perfect for me," he said. "She's the most beautiful woman I've ever met. My family adores her. She'd be a terrific mother."

"There seems to be something missing," Seth said.

"What?"

"Do *you* adore her?"

Jack frowned. " 'Adore' is not the word I would use. It's not exactly . . . my style."

"Let's try *love*, then."

Jack nodded. "Love. Yes, that's better."

"This is not exactly Romeo under the balcony," Seth observed.

"I don't believe in that stuff, Seth. Blinding passion is for cheap novels. Of the ripped-bodice variety."

"You have something against ripped bodices?" Seth asked him.

Jack laughed. "I've ripped a bodice or two in my time."

"You had me worried for a minute there."

"But this is serious stuff, Seth. Marriage. Children. It's what our parents did. It's so damn . . . grown up."

"And your parents didn't do it very well," Seth said.

"No. I know what happens when it gets messed up. How so much . . . misery can just go on for years. You have to get it just right."

"You make it sound like the bar exam," Seth said. "What do you mean, get it right? This is *life* we are talking about."

"I know." Jack nodded. "That's why you have to be careful."

Seth chuckled. "You sound like a Yankee."

Jack grinned. "There's the family land to protect. Not to mention the bloodlines."

"Miki will certain improve those."

Jack agreed. "Her family thinks the *Mayflower* crowd is riffraff. Her family came later, on a nicer boat."

"So you've got it all figured out."

"I like it that way. No surprises. I had enough of those growing up. Surprise! Pater fell down the cellar stairs!"

"You'll get it right, Jack, if anyone can. You'll have two perfect children who look like Miki, a matched set. You'll join the Somerset Club and you'll change your registration from Independent to Republican. You'll serve white wine and brie at the tailgate parties at the Harvard-Yale game. You'll complain that Boston is getting tacky, with all the high-rises and condos. You will have the perfect North Shore life."

Jack sat back in his chair, and took a long deep sip of the very good white wine.

"Sounds great," he said.

11

■

Jack switched on the radio in his car as he drove along the Southeast Expressway to the paper. The morning news report was on.

"Boston police today put out a missing person alert on black activist Hakim Abdul, who did not appear this morning at a scheduled news conference." The dulcet voice paused. "A spokesperson for the New Panthers, the group headed by Hakim, says that he has not been seen for four days, and they are concerned for his safety. They are critical of Boston police for being slow to take action. In other news today . . ."

Jack pulled into the parking lot and hurried into the city room. He looked for Sally, and saw her coming back to her desk, carrying a cup of coffee.

"Sally, when I was driving in, I heard on EEI something about Hakim Abdul. That he disappeared."

"I heard it too."

"People don't seem to be taking it very seriously."

"Hakim does tend to pop up unexpectedly in one place or another. He was in Atlanta last week. But I got a call from Sandra Jefferson and she's really worried. She's a straight lady, I trust her. She's never played games with me."

"Who'd want to grab Hakim?"

"From what I hear, the line forms to the right. Maybe the government, maybe the Klan, maybe his ex-buddies at Walpole Prison, maybe his ex-wife. I'm going to talk to Sandra about it."

"Going to Roxbury?"

"Yes."

"Mind if I come along."

She bristled. He should have known she would.

"Aiken, I don't need a bodyguard. I'm in and out of the black community all the time. The only place I ever got hurt was Harvard."

"Ellenberg, I am not trying to play Sir Galahad. I was reading my clips last night, and guess who turns out to have been a key player in getting the New Jersey experiments stopped. The ones Severn was directing."

"Hakim?"

"The very same. So I really want to find him. Besides, if I stick around, Kevin is going to make me interview the twelve-year-old ornithologist who won the state science fair."

"OK. Come on, then."

They walked together out to the parking lot. "Want to take my car?" he asked.

"Which one is it?"

"The grey BMW."

"This is your car? Oh, wow! It's beautiful." She rubbed her hand across the fender, then opened the door. "Oh, that's real leather. Umm, I just love the smell of real leather." She caressed the edge of the seat. "Oh, that feels so good."

"Sally, if you want to grope my car, at least have the decency not to do it in a public place."

"Oh, Jack, I love this car. Don't you have bad taste in anything? Do you secretly listen to Lawrence Welk?"

"No. The Modern Jazz Quartet."

"Oh, well. Listen, we'll take my car. I couldn't bear to see this one in Chico's chop shop, with some guy with a blowtorch drooling on the chrome. My car, even Chico wouldn't touch it."

They took Sally's rusting Dodge Dart. She drove expertly, Jack noticed, but with a little too much speed for his comfort. A cabbie tried to cut her off on Columbia Road and she stepped on the accelerator and beat him into the lane, making a rude gesture as she did so.

"Sally, don't you think you ought to slow down?"

"It's kill or be killed out here, Jack. Boston drivers have the instincts of Attila the Hun."

"Oh my God, Sally, look out!"

A burly man in a Chevy shook his fist as Sally cut into the lane in front of him. At the stoplight he leaned out the window and let loose a stream of invective.

"Up yours, Charlie," she said, and sped off at an alarming rate.

"I just may never live to see another twelve-year-old ornithologist," Jack groaned, clutching the dashboard. "I am going to get my brains beat out by some Mafia don you mouth off to on the road."

"Don't you ever yell at people on the road?"

"No. I am a courteous, restrained driver. I have never even had a fender-bender."

"Jack, you're too civilized. Stick with me if you want a little chaos and confusion."

There was more truth than fiction in *that*, he thought. But what did she mean with that crack about being too civilized? He was not feeling particularly civilized at the moment. He wondered what she would do if at the next stoplight he pulled her away from the wheel, kissed her mouth hard until it opened under his, then kissed the soft white spot on her throat where he could see the slight throb of her pulse and—oh no! He was doing it again!

He decided to concentrate on the scenery, such as it was. They were driving down Blue Hill Avenue, the main thoroughfare of Roxbury, where only a few traces remained of what had once been a thriving Jewish neighborhood. There were a few faded Hebrew letters left on a boarded-up store; that was about all that was left. The Jews had migrated to the suburbs in the south and west, to be replaced first by the blacks and in recent years by Hispanics as well. Now, stores with Spanish lettering dotted the street. There were small stores, bodegas, shoe repair shops—but too many of the storefronts were boarded up and abandoned, each one a desolate symbol of some small entrepreneur's failed try to grab the American Dream. There was little money to be had in loans, interest rates were high, and shoppers who were mobile were drawn to the big discount stores in other neighborhoods.

The little stores, with their workaday signs, seemed to Jack like tiny vessels on a choppy sea. He wondered what it would be like to live here, to be powerless, and poor, never able to leave it all behind, the way he could. Part of him wanted to shut out the scene, simply pretend that none of this existed. Another part told him he *had* to try to understand. Yankee guilt. You couldn't just enjoy your money and, God knows, you couldn't flaunt it. You had to do good works and give as much money away as possible to hospitals and shelters and libraries and public television stations.

Sally pulled the car up in front of a small frame house on a quiet side street. Sandra Jefferson welcomed them. Sally introduced her to Jack.

"Come in," she said. "There are a few other people here. You know Mel Baker from Freedom House. This is Abdul Rajeen from the New Panthers."

"Have you heard anything at all?" Sally asked.

Sandra shook her head. "Nothing. No one's heard from Hakim. He had a board meeting scheduled this morning, after the news conference on the arrests at Harvard. He didn't show."

"Are the police looking for him?"

"They finally put out an APB. But they didn't do it until we pushed hard."

"Sandra, I'm getting noise from police sources on this. They really don't think it's foul play. One guy said to me, 'Two bits he shows up tomorrow on "Good Morning America." ' He also said that if anybody wanted to mess up Hakim, it would be the guys he used to be in the drug business with."

"That's what somebody said to me too," said Mel Baker, "but it's not true."

"Hakim has been clean for seven years," Sandra said.

"You're sure?" Jack asked.

"I know this community, Mr. Aiken. I know who's doing numbers and who's doing the dope stuff. And who's clean. Hakim is clean."

"You think there's something funny going on?"

"Who knows? The New Panthers are a threat to a lot of people, especially now. You don't see any Lennie Bernsteins giving us parties in Manhattan penthouses these days. Times are tough, jobs are scarce, we're against a war that a lot of powerful people want to see happen."

"Remember Fred Hampton in Chicago?" said Abdul Rajeen.

"Hoover gave the Chicago cops information on where the Panthers were, and they came in with guns blazing. Against unarmed men. It was murder. You think that can't happen again?"

Sandra said, "I'm hearing things from people who think their phones are tapped, that they're being followed."

"By whom?"

"Who knows? FBI? CIA? Justice? Domestic surveillance is back in a big way. I'll tell you the truth—I'm scared. Who cares if somebody in the black community just ups and disappears? What's one nigger more or less? A political leader. A prostitute."

"No more information on the missing girls, either?"

"Nothing. Though the police got more involved after your story."

Jack asked Abdul Rajeen what he knew about Hakim's involvement with Reedville.

"Hakim was really active on that one. He led the charge and testified at the legislative hearings. They shut that operation down. I've got copies of the news stories that ran at the time. Would you like to see them?"

"Yes. Did you ever hear Hakim talk about a man named Theodore Severn? A neurosurgeon."

"I sure did," Rajeen said. "He was the guy in charge of that hellhole. Called Hakim a communist, said he ought to be deported." Rajeen chuckled. "Deported to where, we wondered. Hakim was born in Hackensack. . . . Hey, I'll get you those clips."

Jack thanked him, and Sally asked Sandra for a statement on the record from the New Panthers. "You can say we're very concerned, and we demand that police make every effort to locate him."

When they left the house in Roxbury, Sally asked Jack, "Do you mind if we make a stop before we go back to the paper?"

"Where?"

"Bayside Towers."

"Talk about a change of scenery. What's there?"

"There's a source I want to check out. Mary Louise Anderson. She's the head of PUMA."

"What's that? An environmental group?"

Sally laughed. "No. The Prostitutes Union of Massachusetts. I want to talk to somebody about these prostitutes disappearing."

Mary Louise Anderson's apartment on the twelfth floor did

not live up to Jack's fantasy of all white furniture, red drapes, and mirrors on the ceiling. It was a small one-bedroom unit, furnished in Sears Colonial. Mary Louise was a disappointment as well. He had half hoped for a blonde in a leather pantsuit with six-inch stiletto heels. But she turned out to be a pleasant-looking young woman with a round girlish face, who seemed more like a college student than a hooker.

She made them a cup of tea and listened to Sally's questions.

"Yeah, I've heard about the girls. Stories are around on the street."

"What kind of stories?"

"There may be some creeps cruising around the zone in a car, picking up hookers. Now, if you're street smart, you know the last thing you do is get in a car with some john. But a lot of the girls out there today, they're not smart. They're just kids—fourteen, fifteen. Runaways, junkies. They don't know shit. It's dangerous out on the streets, and if you don't get very smart very fast, you can wind up dead."

"Any specifics about these guys?" Jack asked.

"Not many. I hear they're well dressed, and they're in some kind of black limo, three or four guys in it, and they're flashing a lot of dough."

"Any police followup on that angle?"

"No. What do cops care? One less hooker means one less problem for them. A prostitute gets killed or beat up, the public's attitude is, 'She asked for it.' But let some DA threaten to put a john's name in the paper and you should hear the stink. 'The poor man! Think of his wife! Think of his kids!' Was he thinking of his wife and kiddies when he was running around the zone hitting on whoever he could find?"

"Would you do me a favor, Mary Louise? If you hear anything more—anything at all—give me a call."

"Sure. I'll call you, Sally."

Driving back to the paper, Jack asked Sally, "How did a nice, bright woman like her get to be a prostitute?"

"She was raped by her father at six, raped by her stepfather at eleven. He had her selling drugs at thirteen. She was on the street to support her habit for a few years. But she kicked it. Now she only works out of her apartment."

"What happens to somebody like that at thirty-five—or forty-five?"

"Mary Louise is smart. She says she's getting out, and I think maybe she'll make it. A few do get out, marry, have kids. A lot of them O.D., or wind up in and out of hospitals. It's a rotten life."

He leaned back against the seat. "You sure get to meet more interesting people than I do."

"I bet there's a lot of prostitution in the business you cover—different kind, though."

"Yeah, some guys would perform unnatural acts on their white mice for an NSF grant."

They were on Storrow Drive now, and Jack noticed that the sun was sparkling on the water, the sailboats on the Charles were moving with the steady breeze, and dozens of people were skating, riding bikes, or jogging along the riverbank.

"It's a gorgeous day. Too bad we have to go to work."

"What would you be doing if you didn't have to work today?" she asked him.

"I'd ride up into the hills, away from everything. Just me and the woods and the sky and the wildflowers. It's the season for wildflowers."

"Ride? Ride on what?"

"My horse."

"I should have known you'd have a horse."

"It's a great sport. There's nothing like taking a horse at full gallop across a field, feeling the sun and the wind in your face—"

"The damp spot in your panties as you pee in them from sheer terror."

"You'd love it."

"I get dizzy when I stand on the kitchen stool to change a light bulb. I can't see me on a horse."

"I'll tell you what. I know a gentle old mare who can't walk faster than two miles an hour. I'll take you riding."

"How about you find me a horse that's dead, lying on its side in a field. I'll go stand on it."

"You'll be a lot safer on a horse than I am in this car."

"You ever hear of anybody being kicked in the crotch by a Dodge?"

"Chicken."

"Don't call me that."

He chuckled. "I knew that would get you."

"I'm not chicken. I'm just—"

"Chicken. Chicken-chicken-chicken."

"Oh, all right, I'll do it. It's ridiculous at my age, but I never lost a game of chicken in my life."

He thought of how she would look in jodhpurs, with that neat little behind bouncing up and down. He would have to help her up on the horse, and he would be able to feel the weight of her breasts through the thin fabric of her shirt—in his fantasies she never wore a bra—and she would be so overwhelmed by the masterly way he handled a horse that she would whisper in his ear, "Oh Jack, I must have you!" and they would fall together in the perfumed grass and—this was getting ridiculous.

He hadn't had such puerile fantasies since he was seventeen and in lust with Bambi Thatcher, who could make his heart stop every time she took her gelding over a jump. He had thought of making passionate love to Bambi in the moonlight in the riding ring (Oh, Jack, I must have you! etc.!). Of course, the ring was splattered with horse droppings, which would have spoiled the ambience somewhat. But droppings, like bras, could be banished at will in fantasies.

"Jack," Sally said, "I think we ought to talk about this story we have. If it is a story. Are you free later on?"

"I can be. Name a time."

"Eight o'clock. My apartment."

He rang the buzzer at five minutes to eight that night, they both went into the kitchen, and she asked him if he wanted something to drink.

"Yes, please. Perrier and lime?"

"How about a Schlitz?"

"Schlitz is fine."

She got him the beer and he said, "OK, what have we got? A man who may have had an implant in his head drops dead. His records disappear. Severn shows up at the morgue."

"And the same guy, Severn, is the surgeon who operated on your bag man. He says the government cut him."

"Hakim Abdul disappears, and he had a connection with Severn."

"And then," Sally said, "there's the story about well-dressed guys in a black limo cruising the zone, and hookers disappearing. Is that connected?"

"Could be." Jack shook his head. "I just have a hunch that all this stuff isn't mere coincidence. Hakim sandbagged Severn, and then Hakim disappears, at a time when it looks like Severn might be into more funny stuff."

"But how does this all hang together?"

"Remember, back in the fifties and sixties, the Feds were giving experimental drugs to unsuspecting people. Trying them out."

"I vaguely remember reading about that."

"Well," Jack said, "Dr. Weinstein said that there isn't much research on ELS going on in legitimate medical facilities anymore. Looking at chemical neurotransmitters was more useful, medically."

"So the source of research data for people interested in this stuff dried up."

"Exactly. And the regs tightened a lot. Today, you have to get consent forms and court orders and there are watchdog groups keeping an eye on consumers' rights in the medical field."

"Not like the days when you could just march into some local hospital and carve up the women and the black folks," Sally said.

"But if you think this research is vital to national security, who *could* you get for subjects?"

"People nobody cared about," she said. "Mental patients."

"Prisoners."

"Prostitutes?"

"Yes."

"Jack, you're right. This does sound crazy."

"I know. Maybe we're just letting our imaginations run away with us."

"It could be a series of coincidences," she said. "Maybe Hakim will show up. And how do the prostitutes tie in? A black limo in the zone? Just because there was one at the hospital? How many limousines are there in the city of Boston?"

"You're right," he said. "It's nothing."

They were quiet for a minute. "It isn't nothing," she said. "I feel it in my bones."

"I know. I have the same feeling. *Something* is going on. If it does all fit, then I don't know if I want to think about what it means."

"Let's just keep digging to see what we can find. If it's nothing, what have we lost, except some time?"

"I wonder if we should get Kevin in on this?"

Sally shook her head. "Let's get more information on our own before we take it to him. I worry about him taking it away from us and giving it to the Investigative Team."

"You think he'd do that?"

"I don't know. But remember, Woodward and Bernstein almost lost Watergate to the national desk at the *Post*. Besides, Parker Ames would love to fuck me over. I get to fight with him at grievance committee meetings, and I don't hide my feelings about him very well."

"The blood did run a little thin when it got to Parker. But he's not a good person to have for an enemy, Sally. He's a mean little prick. Vindictive."

"I really ought to learn to be more political."

"That'll be the day. Listen, I've been doing my homework on Severn, and if there was any guy who'd be linked up with something covert, it's him."

"A real Dr. Strangelove?"

"His medical credentials are top-notch, but his politics are strange. He trained at Bellevue and Johns Hopkins, he's board certified in neurosurgery, and he has a clinical appointment at the Peter Bent Brigham—that's a Harvard teaching hospital. His Marlborough clinic seems to be totally legit."

"So he's in the medical establishment."

"Yes. He's got ties with a lot of right-wing groups, but they're all legal. The Patriot Foundation, Scientists for A Free America. He does a couple of months each year on the lecture circuit. And he's done a lot of prison consulting."

"CIA?"

"Not on his resumé. As you can imagine."

"I've got a line on Brady. He was at a halfway house on a furlough program. I've got an interview set up there. Hey, you're dry—want another beer?"

"Sure."

"There's one in the fridge. Help yourself. I'm going to, as they say, slip into something a little more comfortable. I didn't have time to change after work."

His pulse accelerated a few beats as she disappeared into the bedroom. It slowed again when she came out again.

"Morgies?" he said. "You wear Morgies?"

The Morgan Memorial Goodwill shop had recently gone into the designer jeans business by sewing its own label on second-hand jeans.

"It's my contribution to the arts. I like their band."

"Sally, that's the Salvation Army. Goodwill doesn't have a band."

"Oh. Too bad. But I'm sure as hell not going to buy another condominium for Calvin Klein. I used to be a Maoist, you know." She looked at him. "When I said 'comfortable,' were you thinking black chiffon or something?"

"When Lana Turner says comfortable on 'The Late Show,' she does *not* mean Morgies."

"Actually, Aiken, it's a good thing that you're not attracted to me. Sexually. The man-woman stuff would just get in the way."

"I never said that."

"What?"

"That I wasn't attracted to you. You are, uh, I think you are quite attractive, actually."

"You don't have to make a statement for the record. It's OK."

"No, it's true. But I guess I'm not your type."

"Did I say that?"

"No, it's just something I assumed."

"Don't assume."

"This is a stupid conversation."

"I agree. What are we talking about, anyhow?"

"About who is attracted to who. Whom."

"Who's on first?"

"What's on second?"

"But who's on third?"

"I don't know."

They did the whole routine, without missing a beat, and he looked at her, astonished. "You're the first woman I ever met who knows 'Who's on first.' "

"I am amazing," she said.

He took a sip of his beer. His pulse was accelerating again. "I guess you find me pretty dull, right? Predictable. What was it you called me the other day? A Richard Nixon anal-compulsive?"

"It's because you line up all your pencils with the names face up. They're all exactly the same length, in a perfect row."

"They made us do that at Beaver Country Day."

"Sometimes I mess them up when you're not looking."

"I thought it was you."

"I take both hands and just push them around and around until they are all over the place."

"Oh God, I love it when you talk dirty!"

"Pencils?"

"Richard Nixon anal-compulsives think messing up pencils is better than sex!"

And then she was kissing him, or he was kissing her, it was hard to tell who started. Not that it mattered. Her mouth was soft and sweet and tasted faintly of beer. He kept kissing her; he hadn't had such fun just kissing somebody since Emily Lathrop—the vixen of the sixth grade—had grabbed him in her father's study when they were supposed to be doing a project on Panama. Finally, he said, "You see how I'm not attracted to you. I have fantasies about you all the time."

"Tell me," she said.

"I'm in the city room," he paused to nibble on her ear, "in the middle of a story on laser satellites. You come over and tear off my clothes."

"I like that," she said. "Come on." She took him by the hand and led him to the desk that held her Leading Edge computer. She switched it on. "Write," she commanded.

"This is very kinky," he said.

"It's your fantasy. *Write.*"

He started, reciting out loud as he typed. "Laser satellites are deployed out in space and they are aimed at Soviet missiles and Oh My God! You really are tearing my clothes off."

She dropped his shirt in a ball on the floor. When she had finished, he was sitting naked as the day he was born, in front of the computer.

"Now," she said, "do I keep my clothes on, or what?"

"Just the Morgies, for now. I have another one, by the way."

"Jack, the one you have is just fine. You don't need a spare."

"No. Another fantasy. You strip, and I'll tell you. There's you and me and my horse—"

"Jack!"

"Oh God, nothing like *that.* It's just that we go riding and we make passionate love in the grass."

"With the horse watching?" she said, as she tugged at her bra.

"He wouldn't be interested. He'd just eat grass."

"This is a very strange conversation," she said. "This is not at all like the sex talk in John O'Hara novels." She dropped her bra on the floor. "This is what I learned in journalism school. Show, don't tell. What now?"

"You'll do anything I want?"

"Within reason."

"Do you have black panties and very high heels?"

"Umm hmm."

"I'd like that."

She did, indeed, look wonderful in black panties and high heels, and knew it, of course. She teased him for a bit, and then it was his turn, and all that homework in *The Joy of Sex* paid off handsomely. Her attention did not wander for an instant. Finally she said, "I want you, Jack," and he said, "Oh yes," and he brought her slowly to the edge and then over it, and her abandon reinforced his own. Then he held her close, his breathing slowing, and hers as well, and he felt an odd sensation inside his chest, as if the physical space was too small to hold what it contained. Was it pleasure or pain?

"Oh, Sally," he said.

"Jack," she whispered, and he liked the way it sounded on her lips.

They both lay together in silence for a while and then he said, "Sally, what are we going to do?"

"Do?"

"About this."

"I don't know," she said.

"Did you want it to happen?"

"Yes."

"So did I. But I don't know—"

She put her finger to his lips. "You don't belong to me. Maybe this is just something for a little while. It's all right."

"Is that what you want?"

"I don't know what I want."

"Neither do I."

"We could just pretend it never happened, if that's what you want."

"Oh no. I don't want to do that," he said.

"I'm glad."

"I wanted you so damn much. But it's not just—when that cop hurt you, I wanted to kill him—it's not just bed. I don't know what it is."

"I don't care what it is. You're here. Hold me. Please. Don't stop holding me."

"I won't," he said.

12

■

Sally stared at the computer terminal. The story just wasn't coming. It was getting late, and she felt as if her mind had shut down; that a metal grate had just descended across all her mental energies.

The phone at her elbow jangled and she picked it up. The male voice on the other end didn't bother with the usual courtesies.

"Do you want to know where Hakim Abdul is?" it said.

"Yes. Do you know?"

At the desk opposite her, Jack picked up the tone in her voice. He stopped typing and looked up.

"OK, where should I go," she said. She paused. "Yes. Yes. I've got it. Who are you . . . oh shit."

"What was that?" Jack said.

"Some guy just called and said he knew where Hakim was. Gave me an address. Hung up before I could get his name."

"Where did he say Hakim is?"

"He said that a guy named George, at a Dorchester address, can tell me."

"Do you think this is real?" he asked her.

"I don't know. But I'd better check it out."

"I'll go with you. Come on."

As they drove south, away from the paper, Jack asked her if there was anything new from the police department on Hakim's disappearance.

"Nothing. The Panthers have got their people out looking, but he's just vanished into thin air. The last time he was seen, he was leaving Roxbury to drive out to Worcester, to meet with a group that was trying to form a New Panthers chapter out there."

"Nobody's found his car? Nothing?"

"Nothing. And I think the cops are hustling on this one, because they don't want to look bad. But a lot of them think he's just up to his old tricks. Now you see him, now you don't. They're sure he's going to show up."

Jack looked out into the darkness at the streets they were passing. "This doesn't look like a great area."

"It's not. There's a lot of drug action in this part of Dorchester."

Sally turned the car into a street filled with triple-deckers and brick apartment buildings, multifamily structures. At least a third of the buildings were boarded up; several were burned out.

"Oh, great," Jack said.

"Yeah, Crack City. I bet some of these places are just shooting galleries."

"What number are we looking for?" he asked her.

"Twenty-five. Can you see any numbers?"

Jack peered into the darkness. "Most of them are gone. Wait a minute, there's one. Thirty."

"Close enough." She pulled the car to the curb and she and Jack got out. The evening was warm, but Jack felt a chill creep up his spine nonetheless. They walked across the street and looked at the doors of the structures, trying to find numbers. On the side of one door, Jack saw 25 in the fading imprint of a house number that had long since been ripped off.

He put his hand on the knob and pushed, carefully. The door opened. There was no longer a lock.

Sally came up behind him and they stepped into the front hallway. Jack nearly gagged at the strong scent of urine and stale air, mixed with more recent cooking odors.

"Do you have an apartment number?" he asked her.

"Two-C."

"Sally, do you think we ought to go up there? What if we're being set up?"

"Somebody wants a story about Hakim. Whoever it is needs us. Nobody benefits if we get hurt."

"Why am I not reassured?"

They climbed the stairs and Jack tried to ignore the beating of his heart. He never felt like this on *his* stories; getting in the elevator to go up to the office of the director of the National Science Foundation did not give you an adrenaline high.

"Here it is," Sally announced. She pointed to a weather-beaten door, behind which the sounds of reggae music could be heard throbbing. She knocked. The music continued to blare.

She began to pound on the door and, suddenly, the music stopped.

"George?" Sally called. "Is George there?"

There was silence for a minute and then a deep male voice sounded: "Who's there?"

"Open up, please. We're not cops."

The door opened a crack, and a pair of brown eyes peered out.

"Are you George?" Sally asked.

"Who wants to know?"

"Sally Ellenberg. And Jack Aiken, *World Herald*."

The door closed.

"I was told to come here, to see George," Sally said.

The door opened, and the owner of the eyes, a large black man wearing a bright blue Hawaiian shirt, stood facing them.

"Can we come in?" Sally asked.

The man nodded and Jack walked into the apartment behind Sally, mentally visualizing the headline: MAN FROM DISTINGUISHED BOSTON FAMILY PERISHES IN CRACK HOUSE.

In the foyer of the apartment Jack looked around. It was sparsely and cheaply furnished, and clothes and old food containers lay on the floors. The man walked into the kitchen and Jack and Sally followed him.

"OK, what do you want?" George said. His tone was not hostile but wary. There was a hint of a Jamaican accent in his speech, and his arms were thickly muscled. Jack decided not to speculate on what he did for a living. Sally seemed perfectly at ease, Jack noticed, as if she spent any number of social evenings in shooting galleries with Jamaican drug dealers. He looked at her with a new respect.

"I was told Hakim Abdul might be here," she said to George. "He's not."

"Do you expect him?" Jack asked. The words sounded absurd as soon as they came out. Drug dealers probably did not have social calendars.

"Who knows?" George said.

"But he's been here recently, right?" Sally said.

George smiled, showing a row of gleaming teeth, all capped. Jack decided not to speculate on where the originals had gone.

"Maybe," he said.

"But you know him," Sally persisted.

"I know him. He's a big shot now. On the *TV*."

"Is he dealing drugs?" Jack asked.

George chuckled. "Lots of folks would like to know."

"It's real important that we find him," Sally said.

George leaned against the drainboard, observing them. "I've seen him. Down here. Dealing."

"When?" Sally asked.

"Yesterday. He was down here yesterday."

"After he disappeared," Jack said. George chuckled again. "He's very good at that, my man. Hakim is very good at disappearing." His voice curled into a snarl. "Ask his old friends."

Jack heard a car pulling up in the street outside, but paid scant attention. There was the sound of a door slamming.

"You're certain of that?" Sally asked George. He nodded and smiled.

All of a sudden a staccato noise came from the street outside; at first Jack thought it was firecrackers going off.

"Oh shee—it," George said. "It's the Colombians. They're crazy!" He bolted from the room. Jack just stood there, dumbfounded, and Sally dropped to a squat, grabbing Jack's wrist and taking him down too. She crawled quickly to the window and peered out. Four men, armed with Uzis, were advancing on the house, firing as they came. There were screams from other apartments.

"My God, they're shooting!" Jack croaked.

"We're going to get out of here," Sally said. "Come on!"

He ran behind her to the foyer. The front door was open.

George was nowhere to be seen. There was more gunfire; someone in a downstairs apartment was shooting back.

"There must be a back way out," Sally said, and he followed her as she ran to the rear of the apartment. An open window led to a rusted fire escape; obviously George had already made his exit. The Uzis blazed away. It sounded to Jack as if the Third Army had just descended on a crack house in Dorchester.

Sally scrambled out on the iron grating of the fire escape and started to climb down. Jack looked back to see if anyone was coming up the stairs.

"Jack!" Sally hissed. "Come on, we've got to get out of here!"

He turned and followed her down the iron stairs, tightly grabbing the railing so as not to lose his footing. Something whizzed by his ear, and then he felt a stinging sensation in his earlobe. Sally dropped the four feet to the ground and he jumped down too. "I've been shot, I think!" he said, and she grabbed his hand and they ran down an alley away from the house. Suddenly, the sound of a wailing siren split the night.

"Are you all right?" she asked him.

"My ear. Something went right by it."

She put her hand to his earlobe. "It's not bleeding," she said. "The bullet must have just grazed you. Come on, let's circle around the block and get to the car. I don't want to have to explain to any cops why we're here."

They hurried down the alley to the next street, then walked up the block and through another alley that led back to the street where the car was parked. By now, three police cars had pulled up in front, their lights flashing. The scene in front of the apartment building was chaos; people were milling around on the street, and the cops had several men in "the position" up against the side of a cruiser.

"I think we're parked far enough away so we can get out without being noticed," she said. Jack had already imagined a new headline: MAN FROM DISTINGUISHED BOSTON FAMILY ARRESTED FLEEING DRUG WAR SCENE.

"You don't think we should tell the police what happened?" Jack whispered.

"No. We are going to be far, far away from here. Come on, Jack."

They got into the car very quickly, and Sally started the engine without turning on the lights. She backed slowly down the street until she came to the intersection. She turned the car around, and then gunned it as she drove as fast as she could in the other direction.

When they were a dozen blocks away, she pulled the car to a stop, and turned on the interior lights. She put her hand to his face and turned it, so she could look closely at his ear.

"Does it still hurt?"

"Stings a little."

"I think you've got a burn. I'll put something on it. I don't think you need a doctor."

She switched the light off and started the car up again.

"Sally, what are you going to do with this story? Do you think he was telling the truth?"

"I don't know. It all just seems too pat. But I'll write it, with a lot of hedging about the source. We don't know who wants this story out. Or why."

"You know, we could have been killed in that place tonight."

"Tell me about it," she said.

"My first gunshot wound." He looked at her, his eyes drawn to a spot on the side of her neck where he thought he could see the pulse throbbing. He leaned over and kissed it.

"Wounded, but still horny," she said.

"Oh, my God!" he said. "I *am* turned on. All that shooting and violence. This is awful. I am not that kind of a person."

After he said it, he stuck his tongue in her ear. Then he gave her neck a nip.

"Drive fast," he said. "My place."

"Oh, I will. I will. Bite me again."

He did. As soon as they got inside his apartment, he began to tear her clothes off and throw them on the floor, and even in the midst of his sexual frenzy, he remembered that he never threw Miki's clothes on the floor. One silk designer blouse would be a week's salary at the *World Herald*, and he had too much appreciation for the value of money to treat it so cavalierly.

He carried her, naked, to the bed, and threw her on it, roughly, and then there was a great deal of groping and pinching and even a slap or two on appropriately padded places. He was astonished at himself. He had always regarded sex as an epicurean delight, to be approached with subtlety and restraint. It was not seemly for a man of his tastes to be rutting like a brute. Perhaps he should withdraw for the nonce.

Then she bit him.

"Ow!" he said, and he pinned her arms to the bed and growled, "Do you know what I do with bad little girls who bite?"

"No," she said. "Show me."

"You asked for it!" He showed her, and the ensuing racket could have awakened the entire citizenry of the Old Granary Burial Grounds. She screamed. He bellowed. It was by far the noisiest sex he'd ever had. And the most exciting.

Afterward, she lay entangled in his arms, making little cooing noises of contentment. He felt sweaty, exhausted, and sensational. Gunfire did wonders for one's social life.

"I should have warned you," she said, "about the biting. But it's your fault. You just got me so carried away."

"It's all right. I liked it, actually."

He was quiet for a minute and then he said, "I didn't hurt you, did I?"

She smiled. "If that's pain, you can hurt me a lot."

"You were pretty amazing out there tonight," he told her. "Cool as a cucumber."

"Are you kidding? I was petrified. Colombians really *are* crazy." She laughed. "You were pretty good yourself. For a guy with a gunshot wound."

"Do you suppose I'll have a scar?" he asked, with hope.

"No."

"Oh, well," he sighed. "I think," he said, "that hanging around with you is going to get me in trouble."

13

■

The halfway house was located—as such places usually were—in one of the poorer neighborhoods of the city. They sure as hell weren't going to plunk it down in Manchester-by-the-Sea, Sally thought, as she pulled the Dodge up in front of Transition House.

She had a 3 P.M. meeting with the director, Michael Kallow. He had not sounded particularly eager to meet with her when they talked on the phone. That was strange, she thought, since most such organizations were hot for publicity in an era of budget cutting. She had told Kallow she was doing a story on halfway houses in general, and had mentioned the Brady case only in passing. She noticed a perceptible chill in his voice afterward. He was not likely to want to dwell on one of his failures.

A secretary ushered her into the small, cluttered office. Michael Kallow stood up to meet her. He was informally dressed, in slacks and a sweater, but Sally noticed that he wore businesslike black shoes.

"What can I tell the *World Herald* about Transition House?" he asked.

"I'm particularly interested in the furlough program for inmates—how long it's been going on, how successful it's been."

He began to explain the program to her. Sally flipped on her Sony, and watched him as he spoke. There was something disconcerting about him. He was a young man, well groomed—his nails were manicured, Sally noticed. He was articulate, but something was off kilter. The way he spoke sounded just a bit too formal. She had been around the sorts of people who worked in these programs long enough to know that they were often of a type—young liberals or ex-radicals, the kind of people who had wanted to save the world, once. That idea had been knocked out of them, but they had learned that there were places where they could make the system move in small ways to help people. Such people gravitated to social work, prison reform, urban politics. They were good sources because they saw the press as an ally, a possible vehicle for kicking the system to make it move another inch. They were often funny, angry, willing to talk about problems. Michael Kallow seemed a different breed. Why?

The way he dressed, the way he spoke, was too studied. He tossed the usual prison lingo into his speech from time to time, cracked a joke, but it all seemed forced. There was a word to describe him that Sally was looking for. What was it?

Bureaucrat.

He had a GS-9 manner about him, a man choosing his words carefully, as if a superior were just outside the door. He talked a great deal without revealing much. Sally knew she wasn't going to get anything important from Kallow.

"Let's talk about some case histories," she said. "I understand your rules about privacy, so I'll be happy to agree to disguise identities."

"Well—"

"Randy Jackson, for instance. He's done very well. He's going to graduate from Northeastern in January."

"It is our policy not to discuss individuals. We do have the privacy of our clients to protect."

"Of course. That's why I suggested not using real names. But it's no story without people." She could usually charm, persuade, or bully people into getting specific. The *World Herald* had the power to make or break careers in Boston.

"I can only speak in terms of our program."

"And I'll be able to interview some of the men, of course."

"I would have to see about that. I would have to get approval."

"Could you do that as soon as possible, please?" She knew

he was ducking. He didn't want her talking to anyone. He wanted her out of the place, the sooner the better.

"There was one inmate who didn't do well," she said. "Francis Xavier Brady. He was killed, as I understand it, in the middle of a holdup."

"Yes, unfortunately."

"Did you have any sense that he was having problems? How closely can you monitor people in the furlough program?"

"That's a difficult issue for us. Of course, there is a risk with the kind of population we serve. I can explain our counseling service, which I think is quite effective."

"Was Brady seeing a counselor? What sorts of problems was he having?"

"As I said, I can't talk about specific cases."

"Why not this one? Brady is dead. There's no issue of privacy."

"I'm sorry. It is simply not our policy to discuss individuals."

The buzzer on his phone sounded. He picked it up. "Yes, Miss Greenfield, I'll be right there." He said to Sally, "Excuse me, there is an emergency I have to deal with. I'll be right back."

He left, and Sally surveyed the room. Behind his desk was a grey metal filing cabinet. It was a good bet that what she was looking for was in that cabinet.

With only a faint twinge of conscience, she got up and pulled out the A-D drawer. It was in there: *Brady, Francis X.*

Only a single page form was in the file, with basic biographical data. Parents deceased; divorced, no children. There was his record of incarceration, starting with a notation that there was a juvenile file. Her eye caught one line on the form halfway down the page. Work Sponsor: Neurodyne Inc. Bradley, Ma.

She closed the folder and slipped it back into the drawer. She found that her hands were shaking, and her pulse was racing. She sat back down in the chair, taking deep breaths to try to relax. Stealing things was not her usual style.

Kallow came back into the room, and she hoped her voice would not betray her nervousness. He said, "I'm sorry, but I have to leave shortly. Are there any questions I haven't answered?"

She thought, You haven't answered anything, you son of a bitch! But she said, "You mentioned that each client has a work sponsor, whether he's on furlough or he's been released. Could you explain that to me?"

"If inmates are going to have a chance to rehabilitate themselves successfully in the mainstream of society, a job is the most important facet of that rehabilitation. Our sponsors agree to take one of our clients, to give him a training program, and to either give him a job at the firm or to find him a job in a similar firm."

"Who's been good about taking prisoners?"

"Digital has several. Also Stop and Shop. I'm sorry, but I really do have to go."

After she left Transition House, Sally decided to visit a probation officer she often used as a source. He looked chagrined as she walked into his office.

"Oh shit, Sally, what is it now? One of our guys knock off a Brink's truck?"

"No bad news today, Charlie. Just a couple of questions, if you've got a minute."

"Shoot."

"What do you know about Transition House? And a guy named Michael Kallow."

"I haven't had a lot of dealings with them. I have called over a couple of times, because I hear they have a good work program. But it's hard to get placements. I only talked to Kallow a couple of times. Seemed like a prick."

"What do you know about him?"

"Not much. He's out of D.C. One thing I do know is that Transition House seems to have a lot of money. They don't seem to be grubbing along like a lot of the halfway houses."

"Transition House is strictly a private contractor, right?"

"Yeah. They do some work for the state, a fair amount for the Feds. I get the sense that a fair amount of private money goes through that place. It's well run, I hear. But Kallow is real standoffish."

"Charlie, have you heard anything about medical experiments on prisoners that might be going on in the state?"

"No, not recently. Some questionable stuff was going on at Bridgewater a few years back, but that was stopped. Why?"

"Nothing, really. I've just picked up a few hints that something could be going on. It may not add up to anything. But I'd appreciate it if you'd keep your ears open."

As she drove back to the paper, Sally wondered if Jack was getting anyplace with his digging on Theodore J. Severn.

She smiled. *Jack*. She liked the sound of his name; it was

so solid, real, honest. They were still at the stage where they couldn't keep their hands off one another. He was particularly inventive about finding ways of touching her—leaning over her chair at work, pretending to read something she was writing while his hands oh-so-casually massaged her back. She finally had to say to him, "Jack, this is not exactly subtle. We might as well be doing it on the copy desk."

"Great. I was thinking of the supply closet, but the copy desk is roomier."

She was surprised at how inventive he was about sex, and how gentle and loving he was afterwards. He had a capacity for giving that she would not have expected. He sent her flowers one day, with a note saying, "Let a thousand flowers bloom. Love, Mao." No one had sent her flowers since she got a wrist corsage from Nathan Blumberg for the Brookline High School sophomore social. She had told him that corsages were bourgeois capitalist symbols of patriarchal oppression, but she would wear it anyway since he had paid six bucks for it.

Jack. She shook her head. This was not the sort of man you seduced and abandoned. This was a man like her father, who made commitments and stuck to them. This was a man you made babies with. She saw her belly swelling, felt him putting his hands on it and laughing. Yankee names were like Jewish names, Biblical; Noah, Adam, Sarah . . .

Vey is meir. A pregnancy fantasy? How had that snuck in? She had never had one of those with Mark. But then, she would never trust Mark to take care of a guppy, much less a kid. She had never really trusted a man enough to think seriously about babies—not since Norman, anyhow. He probably had a pack of them by now, with the realtor's daughter. Irwin would have had the tots snorting coke, and Mark needed to be babied himself, she could hardly imagine him changing diapers. Jack could be a father. She could see him striding along with two moppets in tow, a large sheepdog bounding along behind.

There was something wrong with this picture. The children were blond, like Miki, who had had them and then dumped them on a nanny while she glugged down sherry. A sheepdog had no place in Sally's fantasies, especially since a foul-tempered one named Raoul bit her in the thigh when she was seven. Uncle Morty always said, "Jews don't have dogs. Cossacks have dogs. You like pogroms, you'll love dogs."

No, Jack was the marrying kind, but he would marry somebody else; if not Miki, then someone like her, some Cliffie who
had the requisite Protestant genes. Sally's pregnancy fantasy
probably had something to do with the biological time clock and
all the stupid Disney movies force-fed her as a child, where all
the moms were cute and the dads were stupid and the kids looked
Norwegian and the only one with any smarts was the dog. None
of the kids in those movies even looked vaguely Jewish; Tin-
kerbell was certainly not a Semite. She was, Sally thought, a
victim of middle-American white-Protestant cultural imperial-
ism. Sheepdogs. Feh! She raised her fist and shook it at a lowering
sky. "Walt Disney, wherever you are, stop fucking with my
mind!"

14

■

Jack took a bite of his steak sandwich and looked closely at Seth Chaffee. There were dark circles under his friend's eyes. Seth only toyed with his food.

"The guys around Andrews," Seth said. "They say they want less government, but they don't. They want to use government to line their pockets. Public service is just a feeding trough. It's disgusting!"

"That's always gone on. The spoils system."

"Politics as a way up for people who were the underclass, sure, I understand that. But not for people who are already rich and use government to get richer. Where are the ideals of service? Honor? They used to mean something."

"Seth, you sound positively Roman."

"That's not a bad analogy, Jack. When the Roman Senate was the province of the old aristocracy, it was uncorrupted. The Senate and the Roman People. Then you got the Empire, with all the types from the provinces rolling in. The whole structure started to rot."

"It was probably the Californians."

Seth grinned. "I have a theory. Snow and ice produces character. Good weather is bad for the soul."

"Elliott Andrews is from Maine."

"Yeah, but he spent the last twenty years in Phoenix. Surrounded by all those new-money Republicans."

"You really don't like them."

"My daddy raised me to be a god-fearing goo-goo," Seth said. Jack smiled at the word. It was the taunt that Irish pols used to refer to reformist, "good-government" Yankees. "The Chaffees were in every good government cause as far back as the family goes. Public service was our duty. We voted for Leverett Saltonstall, Christian Herter, and Frank Sargent."

"So did we," Jack grinned.

"None of those men thought getting rich in office was what it was about. Getting favors for friends. Fattening up their client lists for PR firms they were going to start. Peddling influence."

"You really sound discouraged."

"I thought the civil rights division would really make a difference. But we're in limbo. Andrews is just obsessed with the protests. Everything else is on the back burner. And he's got this thing about blacks. He's convinced that Libyan or Syrian money is getting funneled to the protests through them."

"Any evidence of that?"

"It's mainly in Andrews's head. He spent so many years on the golf course in Phoenix that he's out of touch with what's going on in the cities. He sees subversives everywhere. He's trying to get wiretaps and he's giving protestors forced immunity so they can rot in jail."

"So they can't plead the Fifth Amendment?" Jack asked him.

"Right. They're given immunity from self-incrimination even though they don't want it. So they can be held indefinitely in contempt of court. It stinks. Meanwhile, the voting rights cases and the real work just piles up. Nothing gets done."

"Seth, you look lousy. Are you OK?"

"Last year, I was . . . sick for a while, but I'm all right now. I got myself in a stew about my work, then I decided just to do the best I can. I've transferred out of the division, and I'm looking."

"Boston?"

"I've had it with government. I want to come back home. Where my roots are."

"Yankees are like some wines. We don't travel well. It would be great to have you back—like old times."

Seth sighed. "Nothing's going to be like old times. That's when I was happiest, at Harvard."

"It was a great time, but we have to move on," Jack said, gently.

"I might like to teach. I think I'd like the life."

"You'd be good at it."

"I just know I'll feel a lot better out of D.C.," Seth told him.

When he left Seth, Jack drove to Cambridge to spend several hours in the Widener Library at Harvard. He was on a fishing expedition in the collected works of Theodore J. Severn. As he read, he found himself muttering. "What bilge! Garbage!" An Indian student across the table glared at him, so Jack decided to read silently. Could the man really believe this nonsense? But he had to admit that Severn's world view did have appeal, especially in a time when resources were scarce and class tensions high. Severn's was a world in which the benign application of scientific technology could forever banish the twin scourges of crime and civil strife, in which an elite of technological guardians created a Pax Americana under which civilization and peace would flower. It was an assumption that many of the boys Jack grew up with—who were now men in positions of influence—could accept. He might have as well, were it not for his father, who, when he was sober, was a very smart man.

"Ask why, Jack," his father had always told him. "Never just accept."

Jack's odd sense of being both part of an elite and yet separated from it had given him an unusual perspective. He was not awed by his own kind, and wondered why they assumed they had a right to run things. The whole idea of elite groups, even his own, troubled him. There was a question to be asked, the one posed by Juvenal centuries before: Who shall guard the guardians?

He yawned and turned to another article, "The Prisons of Tomorrow" in *Penology Review*. One paragraph seemed particularly intriguing.

Today, prisoners are put into cages like animals. Many men live out their entire lives in these enclosures, because they are too sick, too vicious, and too warped to be allowed out in society. But an electronic monitoring system could change all this. Suppose we had an effective monitoring system, by which we could follow the movements of such men every hour of the night and day? In this case, we would not have to cage prisoners, we could control them. We could monitor and mediate their behavior while they walked among us. And we could protect society at the same time. How much more humane this would be. How much more cost-effective. An electronic surveillance system would cost only a fraction of what it now costs to maintain an extensive system of prisons. This technology should be available to us in the near future.

There was a footnote following the paragraph indicating an article in the *Criminal Justice Review* by associate professor Joseph Bottomly of Boston University. Jack hunted down the article and started to read it, his interest quickening with every paragraph. When he finished it, he said "Holy shit!" and the Indian student glared at him again. He went to the phone and called BU.

Thirty minutes later, he was sitting in Bottomly's office on Commonwealth Avenue.

"Professor," he said, "you wrote that this new technology grew out of the automated battlefield first used in Vietnam. Could you explain that?"

"In Vietnam, where much of the fighting went on at night, often in dense jungle, there was a big problem with directing firepower. You didn't know whether you might be firing on your own men. In fact, so many American casualties were caused by friendly fire that a system was devised so combat troops would wear devices—like wristwatches—that sent out electronic impulses. They could be monitored so the position of friendly forces would be known at all times."

"And you say this technology might be adapted to keep track of men on parole?"

"Since I wrote that article, it's already been done."

"How does it work?"

"It's been used mainly with people waiting for trial, or with people put under house arrest because jails are overcrowded. Usually, the prisoner has to wear an electronic bracelet on his wrist or ankle that sends off an electronic impulse."

"Which is tracked by computer?"

"One computer could be programmed to track any number of prisoners, based on the signals."

"But if you really wanted a foolproof system, you'd need something the person couldn't take off, right?"

"Yes. The bracelets give off a signal if they're unlocked, but I would guess somebody with sophistication in electronics could find a way around that."

"But an implant would be permanent."

"Unless you went to a surgeon. The more radical proposals involve the sending as well as the receiving of signals."

"Tell me about that."

"Suppose you've got this guy with a long string of breaking and enterings on his record. Prison hasn't been able to change his behavior pattern, but he's not the kind of prisoner who's so violent you want to keep him in a cage forever."

"So he gets an implant in his brain."

"Right. And he's told that he's being constantly tracked."

"That might not stop him," Jack said. "This guy's compulsive. So one night, at three A.M., the computer tells you he's in the jewelry section at Jordan Marsh, what then?"

"Somebody presses a button. A mild electrical impulse makes him confused and forgetful. He would be incapable of continuing with his plan."

"And you send the paddy wagon to pick him up."

"That's the idea."

"Could you send the signal over a long distance? Across a city?"

"We send signals to turn our space probes passing Jupiter."

"Good point. So what happens to our thief? Does he suffer brain damage?"

"Supposedly not. But we really don't know a lot about what happens to the brain when it's manipulated in this way. The idea, of course, is to use it as a deterrent. Once the man realizes he can't rob anyplace, he'll stop trying."

"What if somebody gives him more juice than he's supposed to get. Could it kill him?"

"Conceivably. Or he could have a weakness in an artery no one suspected. People who advocate this kind of thing say that we could find out the right signal, which could deter him but not injure him. That's not so simple. I don't know of anyplace this research is being done. It may never be."

"Why? I'd think a lot of people would jump at the idea."

"They would. But who are your guinea pigs? Can you imagine what would happen if some parole board announced it was putting electrodes in parolees' heads? The ACLU would be in court so fast it would make your head swim."

"Could all this be done today?"

"Do we have the technology? Yes. The bugs would have to be worked out, but it could be done."

"Should it be?"

"I don't think so. Some people argue that it could be more humane than jails. But look at the possibilities for abuse. Could it be used on draft resisters? That's a crime. Civil rights protestors? They've ended up in jail too. It could be a terrifying system of thought control."

"Supposing you wanted to do this kind of thing. Who could design the hardware for you?"

"Just drive out to Route 128. One of those firms that does biotech stuff could do it. Boston is a good place for it."

Later that night, Jack told Sally about what he had learned. "As soon as I saw that article, it clicked. *Brady,*" he said. She nodded excitedly.

"It has to be! It's the missing piece of our puzzle. Everything fits. He's got the implants, somebody is watching him. He tries to hold up a liquor store, and they try out their hardware. He drops dead."

"But why kill him? That's not the idea. A mistake?"

"Getting the bugs out. Isn't that what the guy at BU said?"

"But who? Who's doing this? If somebody really *is* doing it, then people in law enforcement have to be in on it."

"Yeah, it's got to be the white hats," she said. "Unless the boys with the violin cases have suddenly gone in for brain surgery. I got an interesting lead on Brady. I found out that his work sponsor was a place called Neurodyne. Ever heard of it?"

"No," Jack said. "Did they tell you that at the halfway house?"

"Not exactly."

"What do you mean, 'not exactly'?"

"I stole a file."

"Oh shit, Sally!"

"Don't worry, I put it back."

Jack started to pace around Sally's small living room. "You know, it troubles me that we haven't got anything really solid yet. Something to take to Kevin to knock his socks off. Everything is so—what should I say—scattered. There are pieces that fit here and there, but I can see Kevin taking our story apart, piece by piece."

"That's right," Sally said. "Joe says he saw the holes. But

he's not a neurosurgeon. And the coroner's report doesn't say anything about holes in his head. We can hardly go grave-robbing."

"We've got a source at the morgue who said she saw Severn." Jack kept pacing. "How surprising is it that there's a doctor in the morgue? We have a mental patient who had an operation, done by this same guy, but so what?"

"And we've got a lot of sci-fi stuff about a tracking system." Sally opened a beer. "And there's Hakim, and who knows where that fits in? Except he was an opponent of Severn's."

Jack stopped pacing and got himself a beer. "Can we go in and say, 'Kevin, we think somebody's grabbing people to do brain implants on them?' He'll think we're ready for the funny farm."

"I know, Jack. In my more rational moments, I think maybe we just want a story so bad we're seeing connections that aren't there."

"Do you believe that?"

She laughed. "Then I keep remembering that people said the President couldn't be involved with a bunch of Puerto Ricans in a second-rate break-in at the Watergate. Ridiculous!"

"All right, let's assume this is going on. That we're not paranoid. People pretty high up have to know about it. The question is, how high? Who's paying for it? Where's the money trail?" Jack asked.

"It's not hard to keep something like this under wraps. Fund it covertly. Dummy corporations. Ollie North ran the whole contra war through straws. From the basement of the goddamned White House."

"This would be much smaller in scale. Much easier to hide."

"Right," Sally said. "A few people could be in charge of the details. If they're in the right place, they'd get cooperation. Like North used his White House influence to get things he wanted. Law enforcement agencies cooperate with each other. They have to."

"Like the medical examiner? What if somebody at Justice, or the FBI, calls and says, 'We've got a hot investigation going. Clam up on this one for us.' He'd do it, right?"

"Sure. Then somebody owes him a favor, and he hates the press anyhow."

"Severn is our link," Jack said. "He's the key to this whole story. It lives or dies with him. So we don't want to tip him off that we're on to him."

"Kallow knows I've been snooping around the Brady case," Sally said. "But that makes sense, because it's a good story. A con in a furlough program goes bad."

"One reason I'd like to get to Kevin pretty soon," Jack said, "is that if this story turns out to be what we think it is, things could get hairy."

"That thought has crossed my mind. But people don't go around knocking off reporters for major newspapers."

"Remember Gordon Liddy? He thought he'd been told to assassinate Jack Anderson. How many Liddy clones do you think there are in Spookland?"

"Oh damn. This story is making my head ache," Sally complained.

"Me too. Let's go out and catch a movie."

"Can you stay tonight?"

"Yes."

That meant he would not be seeing his fiancée tonight. Miki's name was never mentioned, but still, she was a presence. Like Mr. Rochester's first wife, locked in the attic, Sally thought. It could be awkward to bring up the subject. Miki was a ghost— a beautiful, rich ghost with the right bloodlines and monogrammed silver. She wondered if he was still sleeping with Miki. Probably; they were engaged, after all. What did they do when they were together? Go to elegant little dinner parties? Did they ride together in the woods? She realized that she had never met any of Jack's friends from outside work. At the paper, he was friendly with many people, but had no close "buddies." In her worst moments, she pictured him describing her to his Harvard chums, each with a porcelain nose, high forehead, and leather patches on his sleeves.

"She's amusing. A hot little slut."

"Everybody should get some Jewish tail. Get it early, before they go off and marry doctors and join Hadassah."

"But you wouldn't think of marrying her, Jack."

"Of course not. You don't marry them."

"No. You don't even let them in the Corinthian Yacht Club. One must retain *some* standards."

She knew it was absurd. Jack didn't seem to have a shred of prejudice of any kind in his bones. He was a gentleman. He had never been, she thought, the sort to go in for locker-room bragging.

It was growing up in Boston that made you paranoid. She

could trace her lineage, after all, five thousand years back to the city of Ur, where Abraham came from, and compared to that, the *Mayflower* crowd were parvenus. But still, she had seen her father lose out to lesser men with half his brains and talent because they had the right names.

If there was to be a contest between Miki and herself (and there wasn't) Miki would win because she would fit so neatly into a life of privilege. No one would have to explain Miki at the Harvard-Yale game or the Hunt Club Ball. Besides, Sally had discovered that Miki wasn't the pea-brained rich bitch she had imagined. This month's *Boston* magazine featured an article on Miki titled "The North Shore's Renaissance Woman." Miki had graduated summa from Radcliffe, painted respectably enough so that her watercolors hung in a Newbury Street gallery, and rode in competition well enough to have a wall full of trophies. She was buddy-buddy with the heads of the city's arts establishment, and was a good enough organizer to whip up a fund-raiser in no time. Sally gritted her teeth as she read Miki's quotes. The woman was bright, insightful, and she even betrayed a hint of a sense of humor. Who wanted to compete with a woman who spoke three languages and looked like a goddess in the saddle?

No, there was to be no competition. It was all very simple. Jack was a nice, funny, warm, and lovable man. Very good in bed. She was going to enjoy it while it lasted, and not think about tomorrow. Or Miki.

When they came back from the movie, she took a long hot shower and came back into the bedroom to find Jack in bed, reading. She climbed in beside him, to discover that he was naked, and the book he was poring over was one of her sex manuals, by an MD she thought of as Dirty Doctor David.

"This man is *sick*," Jack said. "Look at this chapter, 'Fun with Foodstuffs.' "

Sally read over his shoulder. "Yeah, who wants to go to the gynecologist with pesticide poisoning? 'See, Doc, I had this prom date with a cucumber.' "

"This looks like fun. You spray Kool Whip all over each other and lick it off."

"Fattening."

"Chapter Five. Home movies."

"We don't have a movie camera."

"We'll just play casting couch."

"Mr. Mogul, suh, ah know ah am jes right for Scarlett. Ah would do any ole thing to get that part."

"Well, young woman, let's see what you can do."

She pulled the covers away from his body.

"Umm," he said. "That certainly shows promise. Oh. Ohhh. Ohhh."

"See?"

"Very good technique. Where did you learn that, Miss, Actors Studio?"

"No indeedy. I learned that l'il ole thing in the back seat of a car in a drive-in in Charlotte N'oth C'lina."

Then he pulled her to him; they were playful at first, and then got down to serious adult sex; lovely combat they both enjoyed completely. She loved the way he seemed to know when to be rough, and when to be gentle. He had the knack of being in tune with her body; he enjoyed her pleasure as much as she. Afterward, when they were lying close, she thought of a time that he would not be there, and a rush of desolation overcame her. She burrowed against him.

"I like to wake up and find you next to me," she said. "It's nice."

"I like it too."

"You can stay whenever you want."

He was silent.

"But you don't have to," she added.

"You make me feel . . . things I've never felt before," he said.

"That's good?"

"I'm not sure." He was quiet again. "I like to be in control of things. To know where I'm going. I don't, with you."

"Maybe it's not important."

"Yes, it is."

"Don't you ever just cut loose? Go where the current takes you?"

"No. I never do that."

"I do."

"I know."

"We're very different, aren't we?"

"Yes. We are."

"Whenever you want to go, Jack, you're free."

"I don't want to go. You're like a rabbit, always ready to bolt. Did I say I wanted to go?"

"I thought that was what you were saying."

"Oh God, no. I don't want to go. I want this to be forever. To sail off like Wynken, Blynken, and Nod, sail off on a silver sea. Just you and me, nothing else, here in this bed forever. Shit, isn't that juvenile and stupid?"

"No. It's lovely. But nothing is forever, Jack."

"No," he said. "Nothing is." And he put his arms around her and in a few minutes she was asleep.

REPORTER'S JOURNAL: Sally Ellenberg

Subject: Childhood

I dashed into a store the other day, and wound up by mistake in the toy aisle. There they were, lined up in their little cellophane packages, dozens and dozens of them: Barbies. Did that bring back memories!

Mary Ellen and I used to play with our Barbies all the time, for hours on end. We were both flat as boards then, and Barbie was reassuring. We figured we'd grow up to look like her. (Which shows you how dumb kids can be. Barbie was nine inches high and made of plastic. Her boobs were so hard you could drive nails in with them. Sometimes we did.)

Since I was already enchanted by my father's stories of cops and robbers, my Barbie games had a distinct law-and-order theme. I turned Barbie's Town House into Sing Sing. It was the only federal penitentiary in the world done in coordinated decorator pastels. My Barbies plea-bargained on the green and pink couch, or sometimes, Barbie Town House became the scene of a mass murder. I'd put nail polish on the dead Barbies and the detective Barbies would wander around in their slutty clothes and say things like, "There's a mad dog killer loose, but we'll get her."

Justice did prevail. Once, we staged an execution of a mad dog killer Barbie. Mary Ellen and I lynched her with twine. She twisted slowly, slowly in the wind from the bathroom doorknob. (Fashionable to the end,

Barbie chose a red halter-top dress with matching handbag and shoes for her execution.) Mary Ellen had her priest-Barbie say the last rites in Latin, but mad dog killer Barbie never cracked. "I'll never talk, dirty coppers!" she snarled, putting on lipstick as she stepped to her doom.

Mary Ellen was in her nurse phase then, and so we had a Barbie clinic too. It's a good thing Mary Ellen went on to law school instead of med school. My friend's idea of health care was fairly macabre. There were a lot of amputations at Barbie Clinic, done with Mary Ellen's manicure scissors. We patched our patients up with airplane glue, but they were never quite the same. Especially when we glued their legs on backwards.

We created a whole Barbie world with our imaginations. Barbies were the judges and the juries, the cops and the robbers, the adventurers, the mommies, the movie stars, and mad dog killers. In the grown-up world, men may have been in charge, but in our world, the Barbies ran the show.

We did have a few Kens, but they led a dog's life. They got kicked a lot by Barbies in spike heels, and drowned in Barbie's pool, and if there was a mass murder, the Kens always had their throats slit. Good thing the Kens weren't anatomically correct. Mary Ellen would have had them castrated.

Let's face it, when it came to sheer star power, Barbie—with gold lamé miniskirts and her perfect plastic hair and indestructible boobs—made dowdy old Ken pale by comparison.

I went through a stage when my feminist consciousness was raised when I thought Barbies were dreadful sexist toys and ought to be banished. I have since reconsidered. I now believe that Barbie is the modern reincarnation of the primitive female goddess, a symbol of female fertility and power. Barbie is Aphrodite or Astarte in a pink bra, green jumpsuit, and heels.

And her values, while somewhat Yuppified, are not so bad. Look at GI Joe. His only wardrobe is fatigues, he spends all his time trying to kill people, or getting his own innards splashed across the landscape. His big hobby is death.

Barbie drives a Corvette, is a gourmet cook, water skis and scuba dives—all life-affirming, if expensive, pursuits. Give GI Joe a couple of days with Barbie, and she'd have him in a French lamé swimsuit, eating crêpes in Barbie Kitchen, followed by a dip in Barbie Pool. He'd be an asshole if he went back to his hand grenades and rocket launchers. (And since he wasn't anatomically correct either, he wouldn't have to worry about Mary Ellen and her manicure scissors.)

I wonder if Jack ever played with GI Joe? Or is that too declassé for Yankee families? Maybe they have little plastic bankers and lawyers and corporate CEOs. Their war game is called zoning, and they put up barricades to keep out the little plastic Jews, Italians, and Irish.

Jack didn't have much of a childhood, I guess. He had to grow up so early. It makes me sad, thinking of him, this little boy, trying to be a man—the only real glue in a disintegrating family. No wonder he never wants to feel that things are out of control. I make him laugh a lot and that's good. But I can never give him back the childhood he never had. Maybe that's why, in the end, he'll go back to Miki. Because there's no surprises there and, maybe, no passion. But it's safe.

I could never live that way. I'd rather hit the bumps, full force, than not get on the ride at all. Mary Ellen thinks I steer for the bumps, but that's not it, really. I don't like getting hurt any more than anyone else. But if you stop taking risks, you start narrowing the possibilities. Life narrows down, to a small, airless tunnel. I'd hate to think of Jack that way, growing older, carefully, in a small, dim room. He has such capacity for joy, and warmth. But the tug of safety, oh, it must be awfully strong. And when it comes in a flawless package like Miki, who pees nothing but pure golden apricot juice—do I have a chance?

I think I see one of those bumps coming. I guess I'll just have to hang on.

I'm getting good at that.

15

■

You realize you've been talking about him nonstop for twenty-five minutes," Mary Ellen said. Surprised, Sally stopped her forkful of chicken salad halfway to her mouth.

"Have I?"

"Yes."

"Well—"

"You're sure this is nothing but a quickie? Nice sex, good times, that's it?"

"Sure. What else could it be? Those Yankee families guard their bloodlines like the gold in Fort Knox. And Jack's blood is pure blue, back to the goddamn *Mayflower*. Besides, the word 'love' has not been mentioned. On either side."

"Sally, I don't think this is good for you."

"You're as cheerful as the witches in *Macbeth* where my love life is concerned."

"I think you're falling for this guy, hard."

"No, it's just very nice. For now. Then he'll go off and marry Muffy and I'll send them something silver as a wedding gift. I'll have nice memories."

"No more Scotch and Valium sandwiches?" Mary Ellen asked.

"I promise."

"I'm thinking about getting pregnant. Now that I've made partner. Brian and I have decided that now's the time."

"Pregnant. That's a big step."

"It *is* time. We're not kids anymore. At this age, my mother had two daughters already. And she's itching for grandchildren."

"I think my mother's given up on me. Judy is doing the settle-down-have-kids bit, thank God. Takes the pressure off me."

"Maybe you ought to start thinking about the future a little, Sally. This live-for-today business is fine when you're nineteen."

"I'm *not* Grandma Moses, M.E., come on!"

"Don't you feel the old biological clock ticking?"

"No." Sally took a bite of chicken salad, a defiant sip of white wine.

"I always know when you're lying," Mary Ellen said. "Your lower lip sticks out. I've known that since you were ten."

"Oh, all right, now and then I think about it. But I have rotten luck with men, you know that. Some people just do. What if I'd married Norman? I'd be divorced, probably with a couple of kids, paying lawyers a fortune to pry money out of his second wife's bank account to pay for pablum. And Mark? He wanted to make a baby just because he said we ought to experience primal creativity. But marriage was too bourgeois for old Mark. I have *not* been stupid, M.E. Having a kid isn't something you do just because some hormones are stirring. Not for me, anyhow."

"I just don't like to see you wasting your life on some guy who's just taking you for a ride."

"It takes two to tango. I make my own decisions."

"Suppose he got serious. What then?"

"That's not going to happen."

"But if it did?"

"It won't."

"But you'd like it to."

Sally sighed. "Since I can't lie to you, OK. I'd like it. He's the best thing that's happened to me for a long time."

"So if it does get serious, what then?"

"I don't know. I'm sure there would be problems with his family."

"Screw his family."

"Family is very big with Yankees. His world is a total mystery to me. Very closed. Inbred. They like it that way."

"Yeah, I know what you mean. I don't get asked to tea with the partners' wives. I've never even *seen* Mrs. Hale or Mrs. Hawkins."

"The North Shore yacht clubs are still restricted. They don't share their ocean with *Jews*."

"Why do we stay in this goddamn town?"

"Because everybody knows the Irish and the Jews are into pain. It's our *tradition*."

Solemnly, they raised their glasses in a toast.

At that precise moment, the subject of their conversation was walking along Arlington Street, frowning, deep in thought. Had his neat, predictable, well-planned life suddenly come all unglued? No. He was going to marry Miki, they would honeymoon in Europe, buy a place near her parents in Pride's Crossing, settle in to raise horses and children who would ride the horses and go on to Phillips Exeter and Harvard and one day take their places in the secure world of Boston's North Shore.

Miki was perfect for him. Everybody said so. His uncles. His mother. Her mother. Everybody's aunts and uncles. It was all perfect. Except for Sally Ellenberg.

For a minute he felt a flash of macho pride that he had two beautiful women coming to his bed. But it passed, and he felt swinish for it. A decent man did not trifle with the affections of good women.

He had thought that once he had gone to bed with Sally, he would be satiated, that his fantasies came from the allure of forbidden fruit. It had been that way in the past. He'd be attracted to some girl, and then bored, once he'd bedded her. Not that it happened all that often, and he always let them down gently. Usually, they stayed friends. It never hurt much.

But now he felt as if he had a knife in his gut much of the time. His moods swung back and forth; at times he felt an elation so intense he could feel it even in the tips of his fingers. Other times he fell into a black funk that made him want to kick dogs and snarl at children. If this was love, he wondered if he could survive it. Once, when he was seventeen, he was half in love with love and looked desperately for someone to fall in love with. He read novels and played old Frank Sinatra records and tried to cultivate a brooding, haunted stare. It didn't take. He stayed cheerful—though horny—and didn't fall in love, even with Bambi Thatcher, who only had eyes for her horse anyhow. He decided some people were just not built for it. How absurd, at thirty-four, to feel so intensely for the first time. The Romans regarded romantic love as a fever; one just had to grit his teeth and it would pass.

The best thing to do, the sensible thing, would be to marry Miki fast and forget all about Sally Ellenberg, let her fade into memory so his life could go back to the old, pleasant routine. Sally had an escape hatch ready for him. All he had to do was step through it, and he wouldn't have to hurt anymore.

And suddenly there she was, in his mind's eye, lovely and vulnerable and naked in his arms. His erection was instant, pushing against the fabric of his trousers. Luckily, he had a raincoat with him, which he draped strategically. Jesus Christ, a hard-on right in front of Burberry's, heading toward the Ritz. Close to sacrilege!

No woman had ever touched him the way Sally had. She could be a sprite, a wanton, a grown-up, a child—and under it all was her tough, ready intelligence. Oddly, he liked her ambition. She was so different from the girls he had grown up with: bright young women, many of them, but cushioned by affluence from the jagged edges of a life they would never know. While they had sailed through one of the Seven Sisters, with Harvard weekends and summers on the shore, Sally had sweated her way through BU on scholarship, getting her fanny pinched on weekends by tipsy men in the bars where she had worked as a cocktail waitress. On thing was sure about Sally. No man would have to give her a life. She would make her own, thank you. His mother's tragedy, he had just begun to understand, was that she had waited, half-formed, for a man to come and finish her. When his father had been unable to do that, she stayed incomplete, like a painting abandoned and left in a corner with its colors half filled in. Miki was stronger than that. But for all her intelligence and charm, she merely dabbled at things. She never seemed to commit herself to anything sustained. He had a sudden chilling thought. Was *he* the final hue in her completion?

His erection, he discovered, had vanished. He had thought, as a child, that manhood would at last offer safe harbor. In the chilly depths of his childhood, it glimmered in the future, serene and golden. Sally had asked him if he ever drifted with the current. When you had an alcoholic father, your whole world was a floating iceberg. You tired of surprises; they were seldom pleasant. Better the calm of the harbor, where nothing unexpected ever popped up out of the sea.

He walked across Newbury Street and through the front door of the Ritz. He was meeting Uncle Robert for lunch, and he had the feeling that his uncle would not take long in bringing up the subject of Miki. He was right.

Two sherries had already been ordered at their table in the main dining room. His uncle smiled and said, "Jack, I thought your series on the new AIDS research was splendid. Just the right tone. Informative, but not hysterical."

"Thank you."

"When are you going to bring Miki over for dinner again?"

"Uh, soon, I guess. I don't know."

Robert Aiken looked at his nephew sharply. "There isn't any trouble, is there? With you and Miki?"

"I, uh, not really."

"I know you, Jack. Something's up."

"What would you say if I told you I was ... involved ... with another woman?"

"Someone totally unsuitable, by the tone of your voice."

"Someone—different. Very unlike me."

"I'd say that sowing your wild oats is probably healthy. If you know when to call it quits. Family is important, Jack. Maybe the most important thing there is. Although, God knows, these days it hardly seems so."

"The world I work in, Uncle Robert—well, who your family is isn't so important. It's pretty democratic. All sorts of unsuitable people. I like it. I can hack it there. I don't need the protection of my name. My class."

"It's a proud name, Jack. It stands for something."

"I know. I know that, Uncle Robert."

"Jack, you're at a difficult age. The rest of your life will hinge on choices you make now. So whatever you do, consider it. Don't be impulsive."

"Impulsive? Me? You know me better than that."

"You remind me of myself, years ago. I was young, there was a war on, and I couldn't wait to get away from dull old Boston. I did get away. But I found out that there was a part of me that could have slipped into a life of chaos. A wild, undisciplined part."

"And that worried you?"

"Very much. I had a few friends who slipped over the brink. Their lives have been a trail of wreckage. I came back to what I knew. It was the saving of me."

"Were you in love with Aunt Elizabeth when you married her?"

"We . . . suited each other. It worked out very well. I miss her. There's a good woman behind every successful man."

"What if the woman wants to be successful too?"

"Ah, you *are* the modern generation. I think Miki is accomplished in many areas. She would not be a millstone, Jack."

"I didn't mean Miki."

"I was afraid you didn't. Compatibility is very important, Jack. When you're young, the blood runs hot, but over the long haul, shared values, traditions are what count."

"Maybe our blood's running thin, Uncle Robert."

"Possibly. Or perhaps we stand at the gates, and the barbarians are coming. Perhaps we are the last centurions of a world where honor and scholarship and tradition had meaning."

"Yes, but only ours. *Our* scholarship. *Our* tradition."

"You always did like to argue with me, Jack. You never take anything on faith."

Jack smiled. "Maybe that's why I became a journalist. I get to ask questions."

"Yes. But you're a Forbes and an Aiken, Jack. In the end, you'll do the right thing."

"Yes," Jack said, taking a sip of sherry. "Yes, I guess I will."

"And you'll come to dinner soon. With Miki."

"Yes. Yes, I'll do that."

Later that evening, as he picked Sally up in front of her apartment, he saw her for a moment through Uncle Robert's eyes. Fresh and pretty, to be sure, but without the polish that generations of being in the ruling class can bestow. He thought of Miki, cool and elegant at the fund-raiser for the Boston Symphony, chatting with Seiji Ozawa. He loved showing her off. Like a prized possession, he thought. She could always be counted on to behave impeccably. What would Sally Ellenberg say to Seiji Ozawa? "Is it true, Seij, that the Teamsters are trying to muscle in on your shipping contracts? Got any fiddlers who've had their kneecaps shot off?"

He chuckled, as they drove along. She asked him what was so funny.

"I was just picturing a conversation between you and Seiji Ozawa," he said.

"I would tell him," she said, "that they were very weak on the Stravinsky last week and, for God's sakes, don't do any more of that dreadful modern Italian stuff. It's so atonal people were climbing the walls."

He looked at her, astonished. "I didn't know you knew music."

"Who are the great musicians of the world, Aiken? Is Itzhak Perlman a Yankee? My father used to take me to the rehearsals when I was just a little kid. They were cheaper than the concerts."

"You never fail to amaze me," he said.

"Good. You need to be amazed."

They drove for a while and he said, "I don't know how much we'll see of this place. But at least it will still be light when we get there."

Jack turned off the pike and began to drive along a winding road bordered by fields and patches of woodland.

"Sally," he said, "I know this road. I think it goes out to the old Stevens School. They closed it down about five years ago, and I heard they had sold it to some research outfit."

"What's the Stevens School?"

"If you couldn't make it into Choate or Andover, your parents shipped you off to Stevens."

"A school for dummies."

"Rich dummies."

"No blacks, Jews, Puerto Ricans."

"A few Jews. Dumb ones."

"There *are* no dumb Jews."

"Sy Bernstein, night copy desk."

"OK. One or two, maybe."

"I think the old school should be just ahead, around this bend. Yes, over there. On the hill, see. That brick building used to be the administration building," he said.

"It's really out in the boonies. Looks like the whole place is fenced in. Did that high wire fence used to be there?"

"Not that I remember. But it's been a long time. They used to have riding competitions out here. There should be an entrance around here someplace."

"There it is. 'Neurodyne Inc. Private Property.' "

Jack turned the car into a small, private roadway. They drove slowly for about a hundred yards up the winding drive, which was thickly forested on each side. Abruptly, they came to a locked chain-link fence which stood twelve feet high and was topped off by three rows of barbed wire. The sign that hung on one side of the gate said, NEURODYNE RESEARCH CENTER. VISITORS PLEASE SUMMON GUARD BY PRESSING RED BUTTON ON CALL BOX.

Jack and Sally got out of the car, and Jack pressed the button on the box that hung on the gate. In less than a minute, a Chevrolet sedan, marked *Arrow Protective Services,* pulled up to the other side of the gate. A security guard got out of the car and ambled up to the gate. He was wearing a gun, Jack noticed.

"Hi, folks, can I help you?" he asked jovially. He was a young, beefy man whose manner was anything but menacing.

"Hi," Jack said. "I used to go to school here, back when this place was the Stevens School. I've told my wife all about it, and I just thought I'd show her around the place."

"I'm Buffy," Sally said brightly. "Gerald has told me so many fun stories about Stevens." She took Jack's arm and looked up at him, adoringly. "Remember, darling, the time you put the toilet paper all over the headmaster's dog? Wasn't that fun!" She said to the guard, "Oh, could we please look around?"

"I'm sorry, folks, but this is private property now. You'd have to call the director to get permission to go through."

"Oh, just a little peek," Sally wheedled. "We'd only be a minute."

"I'm very sorry, Miss. I'd like to, but I have orders."

"What kind of a place is this now anyhow?" Jack asked.

"Oh, they do some kind of medical research. I've only been on the job a couple of weeks, so I don't know too much about it."

"I guess they don't get a lot of people way out here," Sally said.

"You'd be surprised. A fair number of people come and go."

"Is it like a hospital? Do they have sick people here?"

"I think they have some patients. They've redone one of the old dormitories. I haven't been inside, but from the outside it looks real nice."

"Arrow Services," Jack said. "Are you on contract to Neurodyne?"

"Yeah. I work for Arrow. We just do the perimeter work. They have their own people inside." The guard suddenly realized he ought to be suspicious. "Why do you want to know?"

"I run a company," Jack said, "and I need good security people. The ones I have aren't working out."

"Call my boss. Mr. Nelson. We're in the book, in Allston." The beeper on the guard's belt suddenly sounded and he said, "Sorry, folks, but I have to go. Sorry I couldn't let you in, but you understand."

Jack and Sally got back in the car and Jack turned the BMW around and steered it slowly back down the drive. When they came to the main road he turned to Sally.

"Buffy, darling, how would you like it if I toilet paper your mouth after I get through with the headmaster's dog?"

"I thought I did pretty good, Gerald dear. You expect me to come on like Sy Hersh? The guy would have been so suspicious he'd have told everybody in sight about us."

"True. I think this road circles around the property. Maybe we can see something."

"It certainly is a perfect place to be doing things you don't want anybody to know about. Look at that fence. Is it electric?"

"Could be. Whatever this place is, we're not going to stroll in."

"Not hardly."

"Well, that's about it. We're back where we started. We're not going to see much anyhow. It's getting dark."

"Jack, you know something? I'm starved. I was so busy I forgot to eat lunch."

"I'm hungry too. You know, there's a great little place that's not too far from here. Mik—uh, I ate there once. A small place, not fancy, but terrific food. You like nouvelle?"

"Beats the shit out of old vel."

"You know music, but you don't know food."

"I know food. I don't know vel."

"It's French."

"The French are anti-Semites. *J'accuse.*"

"But they have great food."

They went into the restaurant and were seated, and Jack ordered a carafe of the house white and examined the menu.

"Let's make a pact," she said. "Let's just enjoy our dinner and not talk about brains or electrodes or anything like that."

They finished the carafe of wine and had started on another by the time the meal arrived. Sally told him stories about Big Doc and Frank O'Brien and Mayo Shannahan. Jack found he was laughing more than he had in a long time. When people turned to stare, he ignored them.

After the meal, they lingered over dessert and brandy, trading gossip about who was doing what to whom at the *World Herald*. Finally, Jack turned around to signal the waiter and, as he did so, noticed three men sitting at a nearby table. One of them looked very familiar. Then it clicked.

"Sally, look what we've got. At that table over there."

Sally craned her neck to see the table. "Oh, God!" she said. "It's Theodore J. Severn!"

The waiter came to the table and Jack said to him, "There's a man at the table over there who looks very familiar. Does he come here often?"

"Oh, you mean Dr. Severn? He's one of our best customers."

"Does he live around here?" Sally asked.

"He works at Neurodyne. Up the road."

The waiter took the check and Jack said to Sally, "Bingo!"

"But, Jack, this means there was a legitimate reason for him to have been at the Coroner's. If Neurodyne was Brady's work sponsor. Maybe he was identifying the body."

"Or maybe checking out why his hardware failed?"

"I just keep trying to play devil's advocate. Like Kevin would do."

"I know. With all this wine sloshing around inside me, I don't think I can be very logical tonight."

"Me neither. Come on, let's go home."

They drove along the dark, wooded road. Jack flipped on the car stereo. He was feeling the wine more than he realized. He was also acutely conscious of Sally's body next to his. Frank Sinatra started to sing "Night and Day" and that didn't help because it was the most erotic song Sinatra had ever done to Jack's way of thinking. He reached over with one hand and began to caress her knee. It wasn't long before he found his hand moving a few points north.

"Umm," she said.

"I wish," he said, "that it wasn't such a long drive home."

"Who needs home?"

He noticed that she was wiggling in the seat next to him.

"Sally, what are you doing?"

"Taking my clothes off."

"Oh my God!"

"Jack, have you noticed? You say that a lot."

"Only since I met you. You weren't kidding. You are taking your clothes off."

"The trained observer has noticed."

She moved closer to him.

"Sally, if you keep doing that, I won't be able to drive."

"Want me to stop?"

"No."

"Park the car."

"Park? Where?"

"Jack, we are surrounded by zillions of miles of woods. Anyplace will do."

Jack pulled the car over to the side of the road and an extended period of groping immediately followed.

"I remember," he said, "why I didn't like this. I don't fit in car seats."

"Let's get out."

"Out? Outside? You mean do it on the ground?"

"Where's your sense of adventure?"

"Oh my God!"

Later, when everything stopped spinning around, he noticed that the smell of pine needles on the damp earth was overpowering. He also noticed another familiar sensation. Pain.

"This is the forest primeval," she whispered in his ear. "The murmuring pines and the hemlocks."

"I think I have the entire forest primeval jabbing me in the ass."

"Let's see. It's just a burr. Only a flesh wound."

"Next time, we'll do it in bed and I'll spray you with Pine Sol."

"I thought you Yankees were great outdoorsmen."

"We hunt. We fish. You can do those with your clothes on. Where's my pants? Yuk."

"What's the matter?"

"Caterpillar. Out you go, chum."

She dressed quickly and gracefully, and he struggled back into his pants and shirt, hoping there weren't any more slimy creepy things in his clothes. "Oh-oh."

"Problems?"

"My goddamn zipper's stuck," he said.

"Let me see if I can get it."

Just then, a blinding light struck Jack in the face. He looked around to see a squad car that had pulled up a few yards away by the side of the road.

"You there!" said a voice. "Come out here!"

"Oh my God!" Jack said.

"What are you kids doing out here?"

Sally and Jack walked sheepishly into the light. Jack's fly was still unzipped.

"We are naturalists, officer," Sally said. "There are many species of bird that are nocturnal. We observe them in their habitats."

The policeman chortled. "Aren't you people a little *old* for this?"

"Officer," Jack said, "we were just leaving. We are going to get in the car and drive far away and never come back here again."

"Just do your bird-watching someplace else from now on, buddy."

"Yes, sir, you bet. Get in the car, Sally. We're leaving, right now."

When they got back into the car she began to giggle; his heart was still pounding.

"What is so goddamned *funny!*" he demanded. "Do you realize we almost got ourselves arrested?" He was driving along the road as quickly as he dared.

"We must have hit the local lover's lane. I didn't think he'd believe me, but it was worth a try."

"Don't you think," he said, "that Robert Storrow Ames would have been a little bit upset if his science correspondent and his criminal justice reporter got thrown in the slammer for exposing themselves to squirrels?"

"I suppose."

"He'd send us to Bangladesh for five years."

"Nothing that nice, Jack. He'd send us to Chicopee for the rest of our natural lives."

She started to giggle again, and suddenly the absurdity of the whole situation hit him and he started to laugh too. He was laughing so hard that he had to pull over; the two of them sat there, laughing like a pair of loons until their ribs ached. Then she nestled next to him. He could still feel the pine needles in his underwear and God knew what creepy crawlies were taking a stroll on his private parts. John Forbes Aiken, member of the National Association for the Advancement of Science, winner of the Lasker Award for the definitive article on laser surgery, scion of two of the most respected—and most discreet—families in the Commonwealth, had just missed getting arrested for screwing naked as a jaybird in the middle of the woods. It was crazy, absolutely crazy.

"Jack," she said, "I have certainly messed up your life, haven't I?"

"Yes," he said.

"I'm sorry."

"No, you're not," he said.

"You're right. I'm not."

It felt wonderful, just sitting, not talking, holding her. Wonderful, but scary. Like being at the very top of the big roller coaster at Canobie Lake, just before you took the plunge and your stomach came right up into your throat. Everything was out of control, and it was crazy, dizzying. It was the ride of your life, but it had to come to an end, sometime. How could you live with the world always spinning out of control? With the colors so bright they were almost blinding?

No, it would have to end. One day. But not now. He had the odd sensation he often had with Sally, of wanting to stop time, to just drift on forever on the sounds of a warm spring night and the smell of her hair and the feel of her body against him. It was magical.

Magic wasn't real. It vanished in the light, and the light would be back again. It always came back.

But not now. Someday. Soon. But not now. Not just now.

REPORTER'S JOURNAL: Sally Ellenberg

Subject: Being Stupid

    I make a complete asshole of myself when I fall in
love. I just sort of jump right off the dock,
whooooeee!, and my butt hits the water before my

brain. Men say they like that. They say they dream of this uninhibited woman who is sexually free and will run naked with them in the surf. This is not true.

Oh, they like it at the time, but when it comes to Getting Serious, which they think of in capital letters, their brains turn into old TV reruns, and they go looking for Donna Reed or Mrs. Brady.

Men are by nature very conservative. It was Adam, not Eve, who had all the second thoughts. I mean, he took the bite of the apple, and we all know what that means, and then he was the one who bailed out.

"Jesus Christ, Eve, we can't do this!"

"Why not, it's fun."

"For heaven's sakes, cover yourself! Put on some leaves!"

"Why? This is the way God made us, Adam."

"But He certainly didn't want us rolling around in the dirt and grunting like pigs and, oh God, it's so *dirty!*"

"You liked it, I know you did. You had this big grin on your face and you gave this loud shriek when you—"

"Don't *say* that. *He* might hear you. Besides, it was you who tempted me with your nakedness and I couldn't help myself. Go put some leaves on, woman!"

"You mean we can't do this again?"

"We can, but only in the dark in a cave and we can't tell anybody about it and we have to feel very, very guilty."

"I don't see why."

"Because God is a man, and that's the way He wants it. It's all your fault this happened. If you weren't such a slut we wouldn't have these problems."

"What's a slut, Adam?"

"It is a person who doesn't wear leaves and talks to serpents and learns things nice people don't know about."

"But the multiple orgasm sounded so interesting."

"Ahhhhhhrrrggg! Now He's going to get us for sure!"

156

I probably played it all wrong with Jack. I should have been an ice princess, drawing near, then pulling away, making him really sweat, not just dropping my britches the first time he dropped a hint. I am sure Miki was not such a pushover. She probably had the diamond ring on her dainty little white finger before she let him into the stable, so to speak. (She is a very horsey person, so this is probably how she thinks.)

But I thought I was being so clever. I picked a totally unavailable man so it would be uncomplicated, and decided we'd just have wonderful sex because I liked his hair and his clothes and the way he walked. I was not going to be so idiotic as to think this would last, and I certainly was not going to start making cooing little nesting noises, because this would only be Fireworks and Farewell.

I didn't bother to calculate or play games, not that I ever do, because I am an idiot, but I just decided to let this thing go wherever it would lead. One of the places it led was to the forest primeval in the middle of the night, humping away while the birdies and the squirrels looked on and said to each other, "Strange customs these large white people have, and they make a mess of the grass." I think Jack was really traumatized by that one—even though he had a big grin on his face and let out a shriek. But afterwards, he wanted me to wear leaves.

I was so focused on my libido that I forgot about my heart. The little sucker just snuck off and did stuff while I wasn't looking. I started out wanting Jack in my bed and ended up wanting him in my life. I feel like a fucking Tammy Wynette song. I want to "Stand By My Man" and "Not Take My Love To Town" and "Hold Him When He's Hurting." I want to cook his breakfast—he should only learn to like bagels—and rub his back and have his babies. This is so, so stupid. At least with Norman I would have had a chance, if I'd had the presence of mind to buy him a dental suite. And I figured Mark might grow up someday instead of just being the world's oldest Jewish Peter Pan. No such luck, he is chasing after Wendy with her

40-inch tinkerbells. But at least there was some reality in those affairs. Why did I have to go and pick a man who has already given a ring to a Nordic goddess who has more shoes than Imelda Marcos and as many ponies as the Aga Khan? I should have my head examined.

Because he is going to end it. I know that. I'm living on borrowed time. I never thought that I'd fall so much in love with him that on the nights he's not beside me I hug my pillow and pretend it's him. I try to imagine my life without him and it seems like an endless walk on a windy shore, all grey and grainy and hard. (Brokenhearted, but she still does great alliteration.)

Oh, I do love him, and it hurts so much it makes my teeth ache. This was not how it was supposed to be.

This is Being Stupid.

16

◼

You are looking especially lovely tonight, my dear," Robert Aiken told Miki as she and Jack walked into the foyer of his home. A butler, hired for the evening, took her cashmere coat and carried it to the closet.

From the living room just beyond came the clatter of glasses and the jovial hum of cocktail hour conversation.

"Come on in, you two, there are some people I'd like you to meet," Robert Aiken told them, taking Miki by the arm and guiding her toward the living room.

"I didn't realize this was going to be such a big deal, Uncle Robert," Jack told him. "You just said a few people were dropping by for dinner."

"It is just a few, really. But I felt festive. I haven't had a party here since Elizabeth died. I thought it was about time. Miki helped me choose the menu and the decor."

Jack looked at his fiancée. "You didn't tell me about this."

She smiled. "I wanted to surprise you, Jack."

He frowned and she said, "Darling, I thought you'd be pleased."

He saw a shadow flicker across her lovely face and he immediately felt a throb of regret. He gave her what he hoped was an apologetic smile.

The shadow skittered away and she smiled back. She did have a beautiful smile, he thought.

As they entered the living room, a waiter came by carrying a silver tray filled with long, slim glasses of champagne. Jack took one, and made a quick visual check of the room. Some of the faces were familiar, longtime friends of his uncle. Others he did not know, though some looked strangely familiar.

Robert Aiken steered Jack and Miki toward a group of people standing by the window. As the introductions were made, Jack knew why the faces were familiar. He had seen them in the pages of the *World Herald*. One was a Pulitzer prize–winning playwright, another a director for the American Repertory Theater. The people in the room, Jack realized, would have graced the guest lists of the most discriminating hostess in the Boston area. In fact, some of them would have hocked the family jewels to have this group assembled under their roof. All Robert Aiken had to do was ask.

The director and Miki immediately fell into a lively discourse on the merits of David Mamet. As the discussion grew more animated, Jack was certain that he saw the director, a reed-thin young man who wore his hair fashionably—and artistically—long, peer down the front of Miki's dress. An emotion stirred in Jack that he did not immediately recognize as jealousy. He stepped closer to her side.

Uncle Robert was right. She did look uncommonly lovely tonight. The blue taffeta dress set off the flawless white skin of her shoulders and the gentle curve of her bosom. If the dress cost a fortune, well, what was money for, if not to showcase perfection? Her perfume drifted into his nostrils. Light. Delicate. Like her.

Several other men had joined the group, drawn, Jack realized suddenly, by Miki's beauty. He put his arm around her shoulder, casually but possessively. One of the men shot him a look of unmasked envy. Jack smiled at him, charitably, and wondered why he was behaving like the lead gorilla in the pack, warning the other male primates to keep their distances.

Miki looked up at him and smiled. How did she keep her skin that way? It was as white and smooth as pond ice. And her eyes were such a deep blue. Were they always quite that blue?

No, it was the dress. Her eyes picked up and reflected its color.

As dinner was announced Robert Aiken walked over to Jack and said, "She's a treasure, Jack. A lot of men would like to be in your shoes."

"I know, Uncle Robert," he said.

At dinner, Jack and Miki were seated next to the playwright and the former ambassador to one of the French-speaking African countries. Miki had studied theater and spoke perfect French. During the meal, she chatted with the ambassador in beautiful unaccented classical French and traded *bon mots* with the playwright. It suddenly occurred to Jack that Uncle Robert had staged this tableau, all to allow Miki to shine. Jack should have been annoyed, but the champagne had created a mellow glow, and he had to admire his uncle's cunning. No wonder he was such a superb diplomat. And Miki was playing his Eliza to the hilt. Jack found to his surprise that he was enjoying himself very much. Uncle Robert's stagecraft was superb. The food was elegant—not trendy but light and classic, done to perfection. The conversation was relaxed, witty, unforced. Jack let himself relax and drift with the pleasant sensations.

Uncle Robert, you old fox. This was how it always should have been. It was how life—North Shore life—had been for Uncle Robert and his wife. In Jack's family, of course, there had been no parties, no lovely talk, and, certainly, no champagne. Uncle Robert was giving him a preview of what his life could be, with Miki.

Jack was aware that the buzz of the champagne and the very good food nestled in his digestive tract were creating an unfamiliar ambience. For the first time in one of these grand houses, Jack felt at home. This was his place, among his people, his roots, his family. It was the kind of life he could have; the life, he realized, he had spent most of his energies running away from.

"Jack's the science correspondent for the *World Herald*," Miki was saying to the former ambassador. "He's a *wonderful* writer." Such words of praise, from a lovely creature, made several of the other male heads swivel toward him.

He smiled at her. Adoration certainly went well with dessert. He had forgotten how good Miki was at that. It was not a fraud. For all Miki's abilities, what he did was something she could not do. Would never think of doing.

For the first time that night he thought of Sally Ellenberg.

Adoration was certainly not her strong suit. Hell, she wrote better than he did. She did a lot of things better than he did.

Miki looked at Jack again, then dipped her head and looked up at him from lowered lashes, her eyes bluer than ever. It charmed him, utterly. She was a remarkable woman. He underestimated her. She could dazzle a Pulitzer prize–winner with her knowledge of contemporary theater. She could select the perfect wine to go with the meat; she could sit a horse like a queen. He felt a sudden rush of love for her. *His* Miki. The very ring on her finger proclaimed that.

Banished by the wine, the setting, the talk, were the uncertainties about Miki that had nibbled at Jack like a swarm of gnats. Why, with all her talents, didn't Miki really do much of anything? Why did she have to pay a grand for a dress?

No, at the moment he was entranced by her elegance and grace. Was ever more perfect a woman created for the edification of mankind? He thought about less-than-charming places on the female anatomy. The backs of the elbows. Spots usually disregarded by women, hung with little rough patches of hippopotamus skin. He devised a test for her. Could she be perfect there too? He watched as she rose from the table, turned to say good evening to the ambassador. He looked at her elbows.

God. They were smooth and lovely. That did it. He would marry her. As soon as possible.

As the guests were preparing to leave, Jack went up to his uncle. "Thanks for a lovely evening."

"Did you enjoy yourself, Jack? Really?"

"I haven't enjoyed a social evening like this in ages. Thank you for going to all this trouble."

"I couldn't have done it without Miki. She's a love."

"I'd like to take you up on your offer, by the way."

"My offer?"

"To use your house for the reception," Jack said.

Uncle Robert took on the look of the cat who has just eaten the canary. "I'd be delighted, Jack. Just delighted." He paused, and put his hand on Jack's arm. "It can be a good life, Jack. Really good."

"I know," he told his uncle. "Well, I guess I didn't know."

"Now you do."

"Yes. Now I do."

On the way home in the car, Miki leaned against him and

he once again inhaled the light, slightly flowery scent of her perfume. The full moon hung low in the sky, floating over the darkened tips of the evergreens. He was young. Anything was possible.

"Hey," he said to Miki, kissing the top of her head. "Let's do it in the car."

"What?"

"Right here. Right now. I'll tear your clothes off."

She laughed. "Oh, Jack, don't be silly. We'll do it, as you call it, at my house."

"Come on, in the car."

"Jack, we're not teenagers. There's a lovely big bed at home."

"Well—"

"And a fireplace. And coffee. All very civilized, Jack. And *you* are a civilized man."

Her perfume curled up into his nostrils. Yes, she was right. Dumb idea, thrashing around in the car like a couple of horny high school kids. Strictly lower class. She was so perceptive. She knew what he wanted before he did. Wonderful woman.

"Home it is," he said.

17

■

Sally had an interview with the drug enforcement division in the morning, and she arrived at the paper just before noon. She picked up a copy of the latest edition from the front desk, and stepped into the elevator. The door opened and she stepped out—what she saw gave her a sudden cold knot in the pit of her stomach.

Jack was sitting on the edge of his desk, and there beside him, looking as cool and fresh as if she had just been unwrapped, was Miki. Sally had been trying not to think of her; it was a magical thought of the sort one has as a child, that your mind has the power to undo people completely. Just don't think about them, and poof!—they're gone.

Obviously, it hadn't worked with Miki. She had definitely not gone up in smoke. She was clad in a pink and white silk dress, with shoes to match, and the silk scarf that held her chignon in place matched as well.

Jack was smiling at her as she spoke, animatedly. Sally walked slowly to her desk. Jack looked up, and what she saw in his eyes let her know instantly that her first reaction was dead-on.

"Miki, you remember Sally Ellenberg," Jack said.

Miki's blue eyes rested on Sally. There was no glimmer of recognition.

She doesn't know, Sally thought. The insight gave her a sudden, and chilling, idea of her status. She was so insignificant to Jack that his fiancée didn't have a clue that anything was happening. And Miki was anything but stupid.

"Hello. Nice to meet you," Miki said.

"We met once before, remember?"

"I'm sorry," Miki said. "Of course. How are you?"

Then she turned to Jack, dismissing Sally utterly. Sally sat down at her desk and pulled out a notebook, pretending to leaf through her notes. She didn't even try not to eavesdrop. Miki was debating about what restaurant they should choose for tonight's "special" dinner. What was so special, Sally wondered.

She decided on Maison Robert. "The rack of lamb for two. How does that sound?"

"Fine," Jack said, "that's just fine." He paused. "Darling."

The "darling" went straight to Sally's heart, a dart.

"I'll order a Vouvray. I'll have them chill it beforehand."

"That would be very nice."

"I love doing things for you, darling," she said. She kissed him lightly on the cheek and said, "Until tonight."

As she walked briskly to the elevator, most of the heads—male and female—turned to watch her. This fact was not lost on Sally.

Jack sat down at his desk and they both pretended to work for a while. Then Sally could stand it no more.

"Jack," she said, "do we have to talk?"

"Yes. But not here."

She walked beside him to the parking lot, feeling a certain kinship with the death row inmate doing the Last Mile. She got into the car beside him, and they drove in silence along the expressway, into the city. Finally he pulled the car up beside the river, on Memorial Drive. "Let's walk for a bit," he said, and they both got out and began to walk slowly along the Charles. The sun refracted off the river, sending shimmers of light skidding along its surface. The day held the promise of a fine summer to come. They walked closely, but their bodies deliberately did not touch. His face, she thought, looked like a thundercloud.

"You don't look so great," she said.

"I don't feel so great."

He was quiet for a minute and he said, "Sally, I'm a very . . . uncomplicated person. I like things cut and dried. I don't handle ambiguity very well."

"Is that what *we* are? Ambiguity?"

"I guess."

They walked more and then she said, "Jack, what do you want?"

He shook his head. "I don't know what the fuck I want."

"I think you do."

"Do you? Tell me, oh omniscient one."

"You want the life you were born for. The one you've been rebelling against all these years. You want to marry Miki and have a couple of kids and ride at Myopia. You want your wine chilled. You want the whole ball of wax."

He frowned as they walked along.

God, don't let me be right. But she knew she was. "Am I right?"

He didn't speak for a minute, and then he nodded. "Yes. I think you are." He looked at her. "But what about you, Sally? What do you want?"

I want you, asshole, what do you think I want? She shrugged. "I said from the beginning that you didn't belong to me. I never had any illusions."

"I heard you say that. I guess I didn't believe it."

"Believe it."

"Just fun and games? Was that it?"

No. It was never fun and games. "More or less."

He seemed to be thinking about that.

"Was that what I was doing?" he asked her. "Fighting off everything I really wanted? Really needed?" He shook his head again, as if the motion could clear away cobwebs of thoughts. "My uncle gave me a dinner the other night. For the first time I didn't feel like . . . an outsider. I felt like I belonged. It was . . . nice. I don't think I ever felt that way before. Not at home. Not at Harvard. Only at the paper. Not in . . . life."

"I know," she said.

"Was I using you? Like some kind of aptitude test for what kind of life I wanted? I swear to God, Sally, that's not what I meant to do."

"Maybe that's what you were doing subconsciously. But not

to be cruel, Jack. That's not what you'd do." *You idiot, you sound like Dr. Joyce Brothers.*

"I never meant to hurt you. God, if I thought that was what I was doing—Sally, I wasn't jerking you around. I didn't know what I felt. I was so damn . . . confused."

His brows knitted together in a frown, and an unruly lock of hair slipped down across his forehead. He looked, at that moment, very young and very miserable. She wanted to brush the hair back from his forehead and kiss his sweet warm mouth and tell him to forget about Miki, the cold bitch, and her fucking chilled white wine.

"So what are you going to do?" she asked him.

"What, ah, what do you think we should do?"

Elope to Las Vegas. Fuck our brains out. Kill Miki. Jack, Jack, I love you! What do you want me to say? "Your call, Jack. You're the one who's engaged."

They walked some more in silence. She thought, we are going to do the whole fucking Boston Marathon.

"Maybe it's best if we just cut it off clean," he said. "Before it hurts more than it already does."

No. Wrong answer. Wrong! "Well, that does seem to be best. I guess it's the best thing."

More walking. Her feet began to hurt. The Last Mile had become a road race.

"This is going to sound pretty stupid," he said, "but can we be friends?"

"Sure. I mean, it's stupid not to be. We sit right next to each other. And we've got a story to do. You don't want to junk that, do you?"

"No. No, I don't."

"OK."

More walking. She didn't feel anything. She felt numb, suspended in some strange, blank place, where nothing was real.

Then he said, "I think I'll marry in the summer." She almost didn't get past that one, but she clenched her fists until her fingernails dug into her palms. When she knew her voice would not tremble, she said, "Well, Jack, I'll dance at your wedding."

Then there was nothing more to say, except what he did say. "I guess we'd better be getting back."

As they drove along Memorial Drive she said, "Jack, will

you drop me at my apartment? I think I'll finish my story faster on my PC without Kevin breathing down my back."

"Sure. No problem."

In front of her apartment he pulled the car to the curb and turned off the ignition. She looked at him. He was struggling to find the words. She didn't want to hear them. Men were either very good or very bad at making speeches when they dumped you. Either way, she didn't want to hear it.

"Listen," she said, "it's been one of those things. No hard feelings."

"Sally, are you OK? Really?"

"Me? Sure, I'm fine. See you tomorrow, Jack."

"Yeah. Tomorrow."

She went inside and made herself a cup of coffee. She poured it into a mug, and raised it up, in an ironic salute to the victor. "Hail, Miki. We who are about to die salute you. May you choke to death on the rack of lamb. May a horse walk on your face. May you be gang-raped by the entire string section of the Boston Symphony. Miki, you bitch, you won, and you didn't even know it was a fight. I didn't lay a glove on you."

She took a sip of coffee. "Oh, yeah, you'll plan his menus and you'll chill his wine and you'll buy his clothes and they'll fit perfectly, won't even chafe in the crotch. You'll bear his children—you should only be sterile but no such luck—and you won't even work up a sweat doing it. You'll feed his horses and you'll charm his friends and you'll probably make little fucking French sandwiches for the Harvard-Yale game.

"But, Miki, babe, one thing. One fucking thing. You'll never love him like I do."

And she put her head in her hands and wept.

REPORTER'S JOURNAL: Sally Ellenberg

Subject: Breaking Up Is Hard to Do

I don't do breakups well. This is a fact. With Norman there was the Valium and Scotch sandwich. And I could only get a few words of venom in to Irwin as he was dragged off by the Feds. It's hard to feel very good about reviling a man when he's handcuffed.

I had more than a few choice words for Mark. He called me a *yenta*. I should have sent him a letter bomb. Dear Mark: Up yours, *putz*. Powie!

But at least when those guys were gone they were gone. (Especially Irwin. He had to get the permission of his parole officer just to phone.) But I have to see Jack every day, sit next to him, exchange pleasantries as if our bodily parts had never been involved, so to speak.

You know what my worst fear is? That I am going to turn into Glenn Close in *Fatal Attraction*. I have so far resisted the temptation to call Jack on the phone using fake voices or to sit in my car outside his apartment all night or to steal things from his desk. I have thought, quite a lot, of sending Miki a python in the mail all wrapped up as a present. When she opens it, the python will leap out, grab her around the throat, and squeeze until her eyeballs pop out. They will drop right on her desk, roll across the menu for the benefit ball for lepers she is planning, and plunk!—fall into the wastebasket. But I suppose lugging a Python—Pak to Fed—Ex would be quite a chore, and of course I would be caught and executed, which would be bad for my perm.

On the surface, I am doing very well. I think. Does my laugh sound a tad too high and tinny? Just on the edge of hysteria? Will my cheeks crack from the permanent smile implant? Oh, I am just so witty and cheery and bonhomie it makes me want to puke.

At home, I do bizarre things. I put little dabs of his electric shave lotion on my cheeks. I sleep in his old shirt. That's very odd, but it smells like him, and it helps me sleep. I fondle things he's left, like a half—empty jar of talcum powder, and a tie, like icons. I am in mourning, I guess, but no one has died. But why do I feel as if they have?

At work, I try not to look at him when he is not looking at me, try not to remember things like how soft and sweet his mouth is, and the feeling of the bony part of his shoulder against my cheek, and how amazing it feels when he's inside me. His body is so beautiful. You're not supposed to say that about men, but it's true.

Miki has come in a couple of times. There is no imprint of a horseshoe on her face, so I guess my curse did not work. Her eyeballs seem secure in her sockets. There's a guy I could hire, who wouldn't really hurt her much, just break her kneecaps. Probably wouldn't even slow her down. She'd keep on chilling wine and doing horse shows and not even notice her knees are on backwards.

Sometimes I feel like everything hurts, that there are pins and needles in the air. I can't breathe. I keep thinking I am going to wake up one day and the pins and needles will be gone, I'll be my old self again. But it doesn't happen. And I can't cry anymore. I'm all dry inside, like Death Valley. Arid. *Barren.* Now there's a Freudian idea for you.

This bump was the real big one. I saw it coming, but I never knew how big it was. I keep hanging on, just hanging, tight. I don't know what else to do.

18

■

Sally was staring at her pasta salad as Mary Ellen said, "Come over for dinner tonight, Sally. I'll fix a big pot of chicken soup. We'll put Woody Allen on the VCR. We'll have fun."

"No thanks, M.E."

"You haven't eaten a bite of lunch. Are you turning anorexic on me?"

"I just don't feel very hungry."

"I hate the bastard," M.E. said.

Sally put her fork down. "Come on, M.E., be fair. He never lied to me. Never made any promises."

"He was using you. That sucks."

"I seduced him. I got exactly what I asked for."

"Sally, you deserve a lot better. You are a nice person. Why do you always get mixed up with losers?"

"Jack's not a loser."

"In my book he is. Anyone that treats you the way he did is a, a . . . *putz!*"

Sally smiled. "M.E., do they let Jews become nuns?"

"These days, they let in ax murderers. Pickings are slim."

"Maybe that's what I'll be. A nun."

"Sister Sally of the Most Stupid Heart?"

"Something like that. God, M.E., it gets harder as you get older."

"You really are in love with this guy." M.E. shook her head.

"I didn't expect this," Sally said. "I thought I could manage a nice little torrid affair. Good sex, then, hey, here's hoping we meet now and then."

"I hate him."

"I don't. I wish I did."

Back at the paper, Sally immersed herself in the story she was working on for Sunday. She tried to ignore the fact that Jack was working right across from her. It was some time later when he said, "Sally, there's something we ought to do."

Her heart took a little skip. "What?"

"Stanley Green, who wrote the book on the MKULTRA project, is in town."

"On what?"

"Remember I told you about the CIA experiments in the sixties?"

"Oh. Right."

"I think we ought to go talk to him. Get some more background. Want to come with me tonight?"

"Yeah, sure. That's a good idea."

Driving to the Hyatt Regency that night, she was acutely aware of the nearness of his body in the front seat. She tried to sit as near the door as she could. She had the odd sensation that even the touch of his flesh would burn her. He hadn't changed his cologne. She blocked out the images that that particular scent brought to mind.

There was a long and awkward silence as they drove.

"Uh, Sally," he said, "how are things?"

"Oh fine," she said, brightly. "Never better. And with you?"

"OK."

"That's good," she said, and stared at the dashboard.

At the Hyatt, Stanley Green greeted them cordially in his suite. He was in town, he said, to do some interviews on the new book he was researching on nuclear waste. "Another cheery subject," he said.

They relaxed on the sofa and he offered them something to drink. Jack took a Perrier and Sally ordered a Diet Coke from room service, and then asked Stanley Green how it all got started.

"It was actually launched in the fifties," Green said. "During the Cold War paranoia, the CIA got really interested in the psychotropic drugs that were coming out of the labs. A patient at New York State Psychiatric Institute died after he got a mescaline derivative from a secret drug development program run by the U.S. Army Chemical Corps. Then, in '53, a civilian biophysicist had LSD slipped into his after-dinner brandy at a CIA party. Three days later he jumped to his death from a ten-story building."

"All this was done with no knowledge on the part of the people who werc given the drugs?" Sally said.

"Yes. In 1957, the CIA began paying one Dr. Ewen Cameron, a Canadian psychologist, to experiment on patients to develop a system he called psychic driving."

"What's that?" Jack asked.

"You'll love this one," Green said. "Cameron believed he could erase a patient's personality and substitute a completely new one. He would drug patients to sleep for twenty-two hours a day. One patient was forced into electroshock therapy three times a day, at voltages far higher than normal. Combined with that were long periods of sensory deprivation—not being able to hear or see anything."

"That was supposed to erase the personality?" Sally asked.

"Right. Then, they were forced to listen to hours and hours of tapes, telling them what kind of people they were supposed to be."

"How many people did this guy experiment on?" Sally asked.

"More than a hundred. At Tulane, patients were subjected to electrode implants and psychoactive drugs. A Marine colonel tried to join the CIA in 1966. He told his wife he had been given some kind of drug at the interview. He killed himself two days later. I think there were thousands of people involved in this stuff, at dozens of institutions. But we'll never know the full dimensions of what happened. The CIA destroyed most of the records on MKULTRA in 1973."

"How did you get your information?" Sally asked him.

"I got seven boxes of stuff the CIA hadn't destroyed through the Freedom of Information Act. But I couldn't find out who the people were who planned all this. There was a court case in the mid-eighties, brought by a Nader group, that tried to find out who ran MKULTRA. The Supreme Court ruled that information was privileged on the basis of national security and intelligence."

"So we'll really never know the full extent of what went on. And nobody will be punished," Jack said.

"That's right. A few people got monetary settlements through lawsuits. The money didn't replace their dead husbands or fathers."

Sally shook her head. "It's hard to believe all this stuff goes on in a democratic socety."

Stanley Green got up, poured himself another drink of Perrier, and sighed. "There's the whole gestalt of what I call 'Spookland.' You have to be very sane and well grounded to work in Intelligence and not let it take over your head. It's like with a cop on the vice squad. After a while he starts to think the whole world is pimps and drug dealers and scum. He gets terminally cynical."

"Yes, I've seen that," Sally said, "that's my beat."

"Something like that happens in Spookland. Superpower— and not so superpower—dealing is a slimy game. Double agents. Triple agents. It's a game, a serious one, but a game. It can take over your life to the point that normal morality doesn't exist. Common sense goes down the tube. All that matters is getting one up on the other guy."

"So you wind up selling arms to Iran?" Jack suggested.

"Exactly. In a little room in the White House basement, it sounds like a great idea. Get some dough from the Ayatollah, slip it to the contras. A big score, a big yuk on the Ayatollah. But get it out in the light of day, tell the average citizen, and he says, 'You did *what*?' It sounds nuts. But in that little airless world it makes sense. In a bizarre way."

"Have you heard of any of the MKULTRA-type experiments going on lately?" Sally asked him.

"No. But if there were any, they'd be deeper underground. The outcry in the seventies and the new regulations make this harder to do."

"But not impossible."

"Hell no. If people want to get it done bad enough, they'll find a way."

On the way back in the car, Sally said, "I wonder if it could be Neurodyne where this stuff is going on."

"Not necessarily. There are lots of places, especially around

Boston, that have the right stuff. This is medical high-tekkie heaven."

"So what's our M.O.?"

"Keep on doing what we're doing, tracking down every lead. Hakim. Severn. Brady. Anybody that has a connection. The prostitute disappearances. People who work at Neurodyne. We're going to find what we need. Not fast. But we'll find it."

Jack pulled the BMW to a stop in front of Sally's apartment. There was another awkward silence, and then she asked, "Want to come in for a cup of coffee?"

Jack looked at her. She could not read what was in his eyes. He seemed to take forever to answer, but he said, "No, I'm sort of beat. And I've got a NASA report to plow through tonight."

"Right. I'll keep pushing on Hakim. Somebody's got to know *something* about where he is."

"Well—good night, Sally."

"Good night, Jack. See you tomorrow."

"Yes. Tomorrow."

19

■

Jack walked to the cash bar and ordered himself another Scotch. It was his second. Or his third. The bartender handed him the drink and Jack turned around, leaned against the bar, and, as he did so, spilled a third of the glass of Scotch on his tuxedo jacket. He cursed and wiped it off with a napkin.

He surveyed the room. The ballroom of the Copley had been done in a silver and white wonderland theme for the big fund-raiser for the symphony. Couples twirled about the dance floor, the men in tuxedos, the women in long gowns from Fiandaca, Blass, St. Laurent.

He took another sip of his drink. The Scotch tasted bitter in his mouth. He downed it quickly and ordered another one. He had lately taken to having several highballs in the evenings. They barely affected him. It was just that—what? It was just that there was, located at some unspecified place within his chest, an undercurrent of pain that never seemed to go away. The liquor dulled it. A couple of drinks and he barely noticed it.

He looked across the room and saw Miki with her co-chairman, talking intently. There would be a brief ceremony honoring the top fund-raisers of the year, and Miki would introduce them. She was stunning in her silver and blue Fiandaca.

She had very efficiently taken charge of the plans for the wedding. He had hoped for something small and intimate; her idea seemed more like classy Cecil B. DeMille to him. It was true, her family and his family had been around a long time. Lots of distant relatives not to piss off, lots of social debts to pay.

They argued about stupid details, and then Jack decided, what the hell, why argue. It was her thing, really. "You only do it once, Jack," she told him. "It should be memorable."

"We are not doing *Gone With the Wind*, Miki. It's our wedding."

"I haven't come up with the theme yet. I think I'll surprise you."

"Theme?"

"Jack, theme weddings are what's in this year. They're such fun."

"Good. Let's do 'Star Trek.' "

"You know, that could be quite amusing. Space as the theme. It would be so witty, with your job."

"You think you're marrying the captain of the *Enterprise*?"

She laughed. She always did when he said anything remotely witty.

"Maybe we could beam some of your relatives to Rigel 7," he said. She did not think that was so funny.

He took another drink of Scotch, and idly munched on a few macadamia nuts. He thought about Sally Ellenberg. He took a couple quick swigs of Scotch, in order to not think about Sally Ellenberg.

His first reaction, on breaking it off with her, had been relief. She had certainly been very nice about it. It had been the right decision. His life had slowed to its old tempo. He never just laughed out loud for no reason. He didn't want to kick dogs. He didn't feel like weeping when Sinatra ballads came on the radio.

No, he wasn't made for that kind of topsy-turvy life. He was a creature of the shallows, not the surf. No darting silver fish he; he was a brown, flat fish, settling happily in the mud. He smiled. He liked the image. It suited him.

The pain had puzzled him at first. He wondered if it could be a virus, or, God forbid, some kind of aberrant heart condition that would cause him to drop dead at forty. It took him a while to figure out that it had something to do with Sally. If only he didn't have to sit next to her, aching to reach out and touch her, to feel her sweet lips against his, and her breasts, oh God! her breasts . . .

He was suddenly hard as a rock and he groaned. More Scotch. It was hormones, that was all. A pure chemical reaction to be expected in the male of the species when carnal knowledge was suddenly terminated. He had made the right decision.

He looked across the room at Miki. Beautiful Miki. Yes, she was right for him. With Miki, he didn't have to feel much of anything at all.

He shook his head. No, that wasn't right. That was not the thought he had been gathering in his mind. He tried to figure out what he did mean.

Ah, fuck it. He took another drink of Scotch.

The liquor did not taste great, but it was making him feel better. No. Mellow. *Dulled.* He wondered, idly, if that was why his father drank. To turn the volume down. Dim the colors.

He walked over to the table where Miki was standing with Mrs. Bennett Preston. The room seemed very hot, and a little out of focus.

"Your Miki is so clever, Jack," Mrs. Bennett Preston said. "Did you know she designed all the centerpieces?"

He looked at the center of the table. The centerpiece was a miniature silver tree, beautifully shaped, and from its branches hung tiny, perfect little violins, French horns, and trumpets. He picked it up, looked at it closely. Then, all of a sudden, he shook it fiercely, and the little violins and French horns and trumpets were hurled outward, clattering to the floor with a metallic ring.

"Jack!" Miki gasped. Mrs. Bennett Preston's mouth gaped open. Jack just stared at the little tree in his hand.

When Miki spoke, her voice was cool and controlled. "Jack, why did you do that?"

"I don't know," he said.

"Are you drunk?"

"Yes."

"Jack, I think you ought to just go home."

He just stood still, not saying anything.

"Jack, this is not like you," Miki said.

"I know."

"You just get into a cab, Jack. Promise me you won't drive like this."

"I won't drive," he said.

He went out of the ballroom, through the lobby, and into the street outside. He began to walk, aimlessly, he thought. By the time he got to Sally's apartment he was not drunk anymore, but not exactly sober either.

There was a look of surprise on her face when she opened the door. He probably did look peculiar, standing there in his tuxedo.

"Jack?"

"Can I come in?"

"Of course."

He walked in and took off his jacket and put it on the back of a chair. "I have to pee," he said.

"You know where it is."

When he came out of the bathroom, she looked at him, wrinkled her nose and said, "You smell like a brewery."

"Drank some," he said.

"Yeah. Want some coffee?"

"That would be nice."

They went into the kitchen and she put the water on to boil. He looked at her. She was wearing his shirt and old jeans, she didn't have any makeup on and her hair was a mess. He looked at the backs of her elbows. They were rough and scratchy.

She gave him a cup of coffee and he drank it while she watched him, quizzically. Then he said to her, "Why did you make it so easy for me?"

"What?"

"Everybody told me what I wanted. That Miki was perfect for me. She told me. Uncle Robert told me. I told myself. And then when you said the same thing, hell, what was I supposed to think?"

"You *wanted* to be told that. You were asking for your walking papers. What did you want me to do, chain you to my car?"

"It was just a fling for you, right? Something to pass the time."

She did not answer him.

"How come it's so easy for you? I mean it's like nothing's happened. You come in. 'Good morning, Jack.' We chat about the weather. 'Lovely day. Yes. A bit warm for the season. Yes, but not much rain. No, very little rain.' I mean, for you, it's like nothing. We talk about our story. We talk about the paper. You're so goddamn happy all the time. For you, it was nothing at all."

"You bastard!" she said.

He blinked in surprise. "What?"

"You bastard, what do you mean it was nothing at all? Why do you think I wear your lousy old shirt? Because it's the only way I can get near you. I kill myself to smile, so I don't show you how much it hurts, I cry alone in my bed at night, you bastard, you think that's nothing?"

"No," he said. "I don't think it's nothing." He shook his head. "I don't cry, I drink," he said. "I never used to but it sort of . . . dulls the pain."

She leaned against the refrigerator and said, "Jack, Jack, what the hell do you want from me? I can't live like this!"

"I don't think I'll be happy with you," he said, "but without you I'm just so . . . wretched. I love you, Sally, and that's the plain damn truth. But I don't think you love me. Do you, Sally? Love me?"

"Of course I love you, you asshole!" she screamed at him.

He smiled. "Well, that's a relief. I didn't think you did."

"God, Jack, why did you think I was giving you up? Because I love you, and I thought you'd be happy with Miki and the Myopia and all that and I didn't want to take that away from you."

"That was *really* stupid," he said.

"I know."

"Will you move in with me? My place is bigger."

"What about Miki?"

"No more Miki. No more anybody but you."

She walked over to him and sat in his lap in the kitchen chair, resting her head on his chest.

"Oh, I missed you," he said. "I missed you so much."

"I missed you too." She laughed. "Oh God, Jack, you do reek!"

"I suppose you'll just have to take my clothes off."

"Did your nanny feel you up when she undressed you for your bath? I never met a man who wanted his clothes ripped off so much."

"I didn't have a nanny," he said. "But you can feel me up."

"Like this?"

"Oh. Oh. Oh God!"

"My, my. For a little boy you certainly have a big—"

"Ohh!"

"I like being a nanny. It's a lot of fun."

"Take your bra off, nanny, so I can see your boobies."

"I think," she said, "we have another fantasy here."

20

∎

A chic, slim blond woman stood at the corner of Newbury and Exeter, and she caught his eye as Jack crossed the street. At first he thought it was Miki Shelton; the woman had her erect carriage, her innate sense of style. But he had been a free man for three weeks now. She had given him back his ring. She had no need of it anyhow, she could buy rings for every one of her fingers, and her toes, if she wanted them. Miki had been a very good sport about it. In fact, Jack had been somewhat chagrined at the equanimity with which she regarded the dissolution of their engagement. She seemed more perturbed that she didn't have an escort to the Children's Hospital Charity Ball than that she would not be sharing his bed for the rest of her life. And after he'd learned all those positions, just to impress her. He hadn't imagined there could have been so many ways to "do it," though some of them demanded a musculature that was beyond his ken. After all that homework, she could have seemed just a little bit distressed about losing his services.

She'd sighed and said she could probably get Robin Hunter to take her to the Hospital Ball. A friend had mentioned to Jack a few weeks earlier that he had seen Miki and Robin together at dinner at Copley's, but Jack had not been surprised. They were old friends.

He frowned.

Friends. Or were they more than that? Much more.

The harlot! Had she been deceiving him all this time? He had a sudden vision of Miki, holding Robin Hunter's private parts in her hand and cooing, "Robin, dear, you're so much bigger than Jack. And you know one hundred and fifty positions, and he only knows fifty-seven."

"Fifty-eight," Jack muttered. He felt a pall of gloom descend as he walked along, worrying about his genitals. From years of locker room glances—discreet and sidelong—he had determined that in the pantheon of male genitalia he was someplace between Hung Like a Horse and Pathetic; more *hung* than *pathetic*, if the truth be told. In fact, he was quite adequately equipped, so why was he, in God's name, obsessing about his penis at the age of thirty-four. Still, another two inches and Miki wouldn't be making snotty remarks to Robin.

He sighed. This was all ridiculous. It had worked out well. He was pleased it had been amicable with Miki. Did he really want her to tear her hair and throw herself to her knees before him and clutch at his trousers, sobbing that her heart was broken?

Yes. That would have been lovely. Damn.

Well, one part of his life was over, another was just beginning: Life with Sally. She had moved into his Beacon Hill apartment, bringing her astonishingly few possessions—including a cat named Fidel and her classical albums—with her. She was frightfully untidy; he was always picking up after her. She left half-eaten apples on the antimacassar and smudgy fingerprints on the refrigerator. But she liked his penis, a lot.

"It's so beautiful, Jack," she said one night when they were making love, and he was a bit startled to hear that. He had always been fond of his penis, and would have missed it dreadfully if it had had a mind to depart, but *beautiful?* Sally said she loved the feel of it on her lips, her breasts, her hair. She made him feel wanted as no woman had before, and delighted that his maleness could give so much pleasure. He even had begun to understand how Great-Great-Great Uncle Zachariah could have been so enamored of Sarah Grimsby that he shot off half of a rival's lower jaw.

Now there was a fantasy Sally could appreciate. Her given name, after all, was Sarah. He wondered if she had a high-necked blouse and a long skirt and a brooch.

"Yeah," she said, later. "I do. How come?"

He said that she could be Sarah Grimsby and he would be Zachariah Forbes, and he would tear her bodice open and kiss her bare breasts for a long, long time and then ravish her by the hearth.

"Oh, neat," she said, and so he did. Afterwards, they lay naked on the rug and she said, "You are very good at fantasies, Jack. You must have had a lot of practice."

"No. I never did it before. I was very traditional, Sally, before I met you."

"I'm glad," she said. "I'm glad you're doing things with me for the first time." She smiled and touched his face. "Oh, I do love you, Jack. I do. But—"

"But?"

"We're from such different worlds. There's so much I don't know about where you come from."

"I want you to know more about it. I want you to meet my family. Did you think I was keeping you away?"

"I guess I was afraid of that."

"Don't be."

"How will they react to me, Jack? I mean, I use the right spoon and I don't talk with my hands. But I'm not like Miki."

"They'll love you. Like I do, once they get to know you."

"You can't tell me your mother will be thrilled that she's getting me in a one-on-one trade for Miki."

"My mother will be very polite. Very proper. She'll warm up in about five years or so. She's a nice lady, but she's not big on warm."

"Oh, Jack, that must have been rough on you, growing up."

"It wasn't her fault. She was so disappointed over my father that she didn't seem to have much energy left for me. In some ways, my Uncle Robert was both my father and mother at times. He didn't have any kids, so I guess I was his son, really. At least, he was always there when my parents weren't."

"Speaking of uncles—"

"Umm?"

"What did Uncle Morty say to you when he got you in the parlor at my mother's the other night?"

"He asked if I was circumcised."

"Oh God, he didn't!"

"Yes. He seemed very relieved when I said I was. And he asked me if I drank. I said not very often. And he said he liked my shirt."

"Uncle Morty is very big on lime green. He wears it with a pink tie that says 'Miami Nice.'"

"He invited me to the dog track."

"You're not *going*?"

"Sure. We're going to Wonderland. To test the *putz* theory of dog racing."

"The *what*?"

"Your uncle Morty says that the dogs with the biggest putzes run the fastest, because they have more hormones. They want to *shtup* the rabbit."

"Jack, do you know what *shtuping* is?"

"Sure. What we just did."

"Five thousand years in my tradition, and he meets Uncle Morty and all he knows of Jewish culture is *putz* and *shtup*."

"It's a start," he said.

Later that day, Sally stopped in at the Secretary of State's office to check out the board members of Neurodyne Inc. Theodore J. Severn was Chairman of the Board, and another familiar name popped up on the Board of Directors, S. Michael Kallow. So the link between Transition House and Severn was more than just a con on a furlough program. How did Hakim tie into all this? Or did he? There were a lot of reporters trying to track him down, including her. She had made calls all across the country trying to see if anyone had a line on him, but no luck. Every call drew a blank.

When she walked into the office she saw Kevin Murphy waving at her, so she went up to his desk.

"Sally," he said, "we just got a call on the crime tip line. A couple of kids stumbled over a body while they were setting off firecrackers in the Belle Isle marsh."

"A mob dump?"

"No. A woman. Black."

"I'm on my way."

She drove along Southeast Expressway, through the Callahan Tunnel to Beachmont Road. On her right was the Atlantic Ocean, and on her left the marsh, a swampy area that had been saved from development by local activists and wetlands conservation laws. Across the flat expanse of weeds and marshland, she saw a police cruiser pulled up on an access road. A small knot of curious onlookers had already gathered. On the ground, under a sheet of canvas, lay what Sally knew was a human form.

She walked up to the ranking officer on the scene.

"Sally Ellenberg, Lieutenant. *World Herald.* What have you got?"

"The victim is a black female. Appears to be maybe sixteen, seventeen."

"How did she die?"

"The victim was . . ." The formal police phraseology failed him. He shrugged. "I think we have a real weirdo here."

"What happened?"

"Somebody cut the top of her head off."

"Good God."

"Yeah."

"Lieutenant, can I see the body, please?"

"It's not pretty."

"I know. I've seen them before."

He walked over to the canvas and lifted its edge. Sally was prepared for the sight, but the reality of it hit her like a blow in the stomach anyhow. The top half of the young woman's head had been neatly severed, leaving the grey matter inside her skull exposed. Sally looked, then turned away, feeling the taste of bile in her throat.

"You wonder what the hell is wrong with people," the lieutenant said.

"That had to have been done with some sort of power tool," Sally said. "Part of her skull was cut away. A chainsaw?"

"Like I said, we've got a weird one on our hands."

"Any idea who she is? One of the missing prostitutes?"

"Wouldn't surprise me. Matches the description, as best as we can tell. If it is, we'll get an ident on her pretty fast."

"Have you ever seen anything like this before? This elaborate?"

"I've seen some killers who mutilated their victims in strange ways. But not like this, no."

By the time she had gotten back to the paper, the police had made a positive identification on the victim. She was indeed one of the missing prostitutes. Sally did the story, and then she talked to Jack about it.

"Oh Christ, it sounds gory," he said.

"It was. Jack, the top of her skull was sliced clean off. Like she'd been run through a buzz saw."

"Are you thinking what I'm thinking?"

"Of course. How do you hide the evidence of brain surgery?"

"The police have any leads?" Jack asked.

"They're working on the idea that it's a psychopath."

"That's possible, of course."

They were quiet and he said, "Sally, any chance we could get somebody to do a search at Neurodyne?"

"On what evidence? There's nothing to link the prostitutes with Neurodyne, except our hunch. And who knows if that's where it's being done? *If* it's being done."

"Maybe we ought to lay this all out for Kevin, right now."

"I'd like one piece of solid evidence to take to him. Everything's so damn . . . amorphous."

"If we could work on the link with Hakim—"

"I've tried. Nothing so far."

"Maybe he doesn't fit at all. If you were trying to do outlaw research on people, why grab somebody as well known as Hakim? That would be stupid."

"I know," Sally said. "It doesn't seem to fit. *Except* for the link with Severn."

"If nothing breaks in a couple of days, we'll go to Kevin, right? I don't like the feeling of being out there all alone on this one."

"OK, it's a deal. Maybe he won't laugh us out of the room."

"They'll make a mistake. They'll do something dumb. And we'll be waiting."

"I just hope," she said.

21
■

Sally looked up at the huge grey Tudor house that seemed to loom against the darkening skyline.

"My God, Jack," she said, as he pulled the BMW into the drive, "this place is like a castle. You didn't tell me."

"I never liked it much, to tell you the truth," he said. "It always seemed too much like the places in my storybooks. Where they locked up people and ogres put out their eyes."

"I'd rather think of it as the castle of a handsome prince."

"*They* always got their eyes put out by ogres."

"There must be some happy memories here for you."

"Not a whole lot. I can't imagine why my mother stays here. I tell her she ought to sell the place, get a condo. But she never does," he said. He shook his head. "I can dredge up some good memories. But things got pretty grim, at times. Sometimes, when I walk in that front door, I feel this sense of . . . dread. It's a haunted house, Sally. The ghosts are broken dreams and lives that never really got lived. Real ghouls and demons would be better."

"That's the past, Jack. Your life won't be like theirs."

"Keep telling me that."

Inside the house they were greeted cordially by Jack's mother. There was politeness, but no warmth in her greeting. She shook Sally's hand, stiffly, like a man, and pecked Jack lightly on the cheek. This was not a family, Sally observed, that went in for bear hugs.

"How are you, Mother?" Jack asked, and his mother smiled and said she was fine, she had spent much of the day in the garden. She was a tall woman, quite attractive, really, Sally thought, but she was attired in a way that made her seem not sloppy or disheveled but rather unconscious of her physical self. Her dress was neat, her hair combed, but her clothes seemed merely necessary coverings. It was not that she had no sense of style; it was that the whole issue had simply not occurred to her. It seemed to Sally that she thought of herself as invisible.

"Would you like to see the garden?" she asked Sally, and Sally said she would enjoy that very much.

The garden was so unlike the woman that it made Sally give a little "Oh" of surprise. The colors were lush, warm. The plants were grouped together so that their colors splashed against each other in riotous profusion.

"Do you garden, Miss Ellenberg?" Jack's mother asked her.

"No, it's not a talent of mine, I'm afraid. Cement thumb."

"I find it's a very pleasant way to pass the time. I love to see all the colors in the morning when I rise."

"They are beautiful," Sally said. "You really do have the touch."

"Yes, I suppose I do. Tell me, dear, did you grow up in this area?"

"In Brookline."

"A lovely town, Brookline. Very clean." Mrs. Aiken bent down to twist off a dead leaf from a green stem.

"Yes it is. Clean."

"I was on a committee for the floating hospital once with several ladies from Brookline. Mrs. Levine and Mrs. Shapiro. Lovely, lovely ladies."

"I, ah, don't think I know them. I haven't lived in Brookline for a long time."

"And now you work for the *World Herald*. That must be very interesting."

"Yes, it is."

Just then Jack appeared to take her on a tour of the stables, and when they finished, Robert Aiken's car pulled into the driveway. Jack took her arm, very deliberately, and introduced her to his uncle.

Robert Aiken took her hand, gave her a warm smile, and said, "My dear, it's lovely to meet you. Jack's been singing your praises."

She was taken aback, by his physical presence and the warmth of his greeting. For an instant, she really did believe he was as delighted as he seemed. Then she remembered he had been a professional diplomat. He could probably make a head of state feel like an old buddy from Harvard at the very moment that Delta Force was landing to knock off his palace guard.

She looked at him, and was struck by the thought that this was what Jack would look like in forty years. His uncle's hair was silver grey, his carriage as straight as a West Pointer's. He was thicker in the chest and shoulders than he had been as a young man, but was still what would be referred to as a fine figure of a man in his impeccably tailored Savile Row suit. The Aiken men, she thought, were the peacocks in the family. She suddenly felt self-conscious about the black wool dress she was wearing ($59.95 in Filene's basement and a little tight in the butt, but it did come from Neiman Marcus and had the name of some fake Italian count on the label).

Inside the house, they sipped very good sherry and Jack and his uncle chatted for a while, and then the housekeeper appeared to announce that dinner was served. The food was a roast beef (slightly overdone, to Sally's taste) and plain roast potatoes. At one point in the meal, Sally was conscious that Robert Aiken had focused his attention solely on her. It was flattering; never before had she been given the third degree whille being made to feel she was the most interesting, attractive person in the room.

"Writing about crime must be quite a challenge," he said to her.

"Well, criminal justice covers everything from the Supreme Court to street thugs, so it's never boring."

"How did you ever get interested in such an unusual specialty for a woman? You certainly don't look like the crime reporters one sees on television. Tough guys with caved-in hats."

She laughed. "No, I don't. But my father covered the same beat at the paper, so I guess it's in the genes."

"Young girls today are so . . . fearless," Mrs. Aiken said. "It's quite remarkable."

"Maybe," Sally said, "it's because we found out there's not all that much to be afraid of."

"Well," Mrs. Aiken said, "that's an interesting thought."

Robert Aiken poured Sally more wine and said, "Don't you think, Miss Ellenberg, that we've rather gotten into the habit of coddling criminals?"

She looked at Jack, and he shot her a grin that said, "You're on your own on this one, babe."

"No," she said. "I don't."

"Oh?" Robert Aiken said. That clearly was a call for her to explain herself.

"Your average felon," she said, "will be in prison for from five to twelve years. We can let him sit and rot, so that when he gets out he'll not only be as mean and vicious as when he went in, but out for revenge. Or, we can try to give him some education and a sense of self-esteem, which he didn't have, so when he's back on the street he can make a decent life for himself. And he *will* be back on the street."

"Whatever happened to the idea of punishment?"

"Being caged up day and night, even in a humane cage, is punishment. We can't build enough jails to keep everybody in them. Not with the deficit."

Robert Aiken gave a small smile, sipped his sherry, and looked at her.

"And the death penalty. Do you oppose that?"

"Yes," she said.

"You don't feel that some crimes are so vicious they deserve the death penalty?"

"Yes. Some do. But all the studies show that a man who is poor and black is many more times as likely to get a death sentence as a white man who commits the same crime. That's not equal justice under the law."

"Even so," he said, "if vicious crimes could be prevented, perhaps that outweighs even inherent racism."

"The death penalty isn't much of a deterrent," she said. "Especially for the kind of random violence people fear most. The guy who takes your wallet and shoots you in cold blood is not thinking about the death penalty. He may not be capable of thinking beyond the impulse of the moment. Or he might be crazy high on drugs. States that have the death penalty don't have lower homicide rates."

"Well, you certainly do know your business, Miss Ellenberg," Uncle Robert said.

"Call her Sally, Uncle Robert," Jack said.

"Of course. Sally."

"She's a fine reporter," Jack said. "Writes like an angel."

Sally turned to Robert Aiken. "Your nephew is no slouch in that department either, I can assure you."

"Well," Uncle Robert said, "you two do seem like quite a mutual admiration society."

Sally smiled at Jack. "It's true. We really support each other."

"I hate to intrude on all this mutual admiration," Robert Aiken smiled, "but we have other important matters to discuss. Which port shall we have with the dessert?"

Later, on the way home, Jack turned to Sally and grinned. "I was showing you off, you know. You knocked their socks off."

"I'm not sure that's what they wanted," she sighed. "Maybe I should have just talked about the wallpaper."

"They're just going to have to get used to somebody who says what she thinks."

"I was not a hit with the horses."

"You'll get used to them. They're skittish, at first, with people they don't know. Especially at night."

"Well, it was a very nice evening. Your uncle was very gracious. He tried to make me feel comfortable."

"Uncle Robert is good at that. I always used to like it when he was there. It made me feel connected to that big world out there that he was a part of. But even he never talked about—our problem. When my father wasn't there, we just didn't mention him. It was like he didn't exist. We did talk about the wallpaper. Maybe it was because the truth was just—too awkward."

"Can you blame them, Jack?"

"Yes." There was a glint of anger in his voice. "I can blame them. You can't fix things you won't look at. Nothing changes that way."

"Could things have been fixed?"

"Maybe not. But it's too easy to pretend things are fine when they're not. I do that. A lot."

"It's hard not to sometimes," she said.

He shook his head in disagreement. "I knew that what Miki and I had wasn't real. But pretending it was seemed to make everybody happy. And that was my job. Making everybody happy."

"But see how far you've come, Jack," she said. "Taking me home didn't make everybody happy."

"Except me."

She reached up and caressed the back of his neck, gently.

"And that's the one who counts."

22

■

So how was it?" Mary Ellen asked. They were lunching at the Boston Harbor Hotel, with the panorama of the harbor, and beyond it the runways of Logan Airport, stretched out before them. It was a quite agreeable place, except that parking cost seventeen dollars for two hours. Sally wouldn't put it on her expense account. If anybody at the paper wanted to nail her, she wasn't going to give them any ammunition, no matter how small in caliber.

"Remember that scene in *Annie Hall*? The one where Woody Allen goes to Diane Keaton's Protestant family for dinner, and he turns into a Chassid, with a long black coat and beard?"

"It wasn't that bad!"

"Jack says it wasn't. He says I did fine. I don't think so. I babbled. Whenever there was a moment of silence, I felt I had to jump in and stomp it to death."

"Who was there?"

"His mother. And she's so polite, and so kind. She hated me."

"You're exaggerating."

"No. I could tell. She'd ask me questions about my job, and I'd answer, and she'd say, 'That must be so interesting.' If I'd told her I slit the throats of *goyishe* babies and sprinkled their blood on the *bimah*, she'd say, 'That must be so interesting!' I felt like I was the visiting delegation from China. You know, one must be polite to foreigners, but of course they're not like us."

"So you struck out with Mom."

"I don't blame her. She figured she had Muffy practically in the family, with her horses and her tweed and all those pale blond genes."

"Learn about horses. Maybe it'll help."

"Big smelly animals. They drop enormous turds on the ground. Ugh."

"Forget horses. Who else was there?"

"His Uncle Robert, who is just so charming. Knows everybody. Drops names of presidents, but not in a tacky way. Like they really were his buddies. If there's an American aristocracy, he's it. Averell Harriman got him started in government. He worked for Rockefeller on Latin American policy."

"Did he hate you too?"

"No. He liked me. I made him laugh. But that doesn't mean he's happy about me and Jack. I think he sees me as a youthful indiscretion. Charming member of the somewhat lower classes, but not the sort that his nephew ends up with in the rose-covered cottage."

"What was the cottage like?"

"Impressive. Big old stone thing. Not what you'd call cozy. And no plastic covers on the sofas or wax fruit. No linoleum anywhere."

"Some people don't know how to live."

"Antique furniture, the kind that makes you sit up straight. Faded Orientals and *real* oil paintings of people in the family, generations back. No tinted photographs. A few Fabian Bachrachs here and there. Very classic, soft lighting. There was stuff from the China trade. I'd call it *chozzerai*, except it's very old and expensive."

"What does Jack's mother do?" Mary Ellen asked.

"Various good works, I guess. And garden. She's very attractive. Good posture. Thin. Grey hair that she doesn't bother to cover up. No sense of humor. Jack teases her, and it's sort of like she doesn't get it, you know. But she's very smart and very well informed. I have the feeling that there's this interesting person inside her who never fully grew. I don't know, I can't figure her out."

"But Uncle Robert was different."

"Oh yes. Nothing stilted about him. He's done everything. He was an ambassador—one of the Caribbean places, I forget which. He and Jack have a very nice relationship. Jack's respectful, but throws in a zinger now and then. And Uncle Robert obviously thinks the sun rises and sets in Jack. He didn't have any children, and Jack of course didn't have a father a lot of the time, so there's this natural bond. But they're not touchers. They shake hands, they don't hug."

"I like huggers."

"So do I. Jack likes to hug. He says he has lots of hugging time to make up. He says he's going to hug his kids a lot and give them messy stuff to play with because he never had that."

"Kids?" Mary Ellen raised an eyebrow. "This *is* getting serious." ·

"Oh, we just talk about kids in general; that we both want them someday. We don't say *whose* we want. Sort of in theory. Like if I happened to be married to this unnamed person, how would I want my kids raised."

"Is Jack rich?"

"By the standards of Brookline High, Jack is rich. But not *rich* rich. He has to work, there's no huge fortune there. Jack's father didn't exactly fatten the family coffers. The places they sent him to dry out cost an arm and a leg. But Jack's the only heir between his mother and his uncle, so he'll never be on welfare. Even the horses will eat."

"Did you meet the horses?"

"Yes. I met them."

"So?"

"They're big. And they make funny snorting noises with their noses. They hated me."

"Horses are not anti-Semitic."

"But they know stark raving fear. With Jack, they nuzzled and made nice. They took one look at me and said, 'Kill! Kill!' "

"If you are going to be serious about this man, you are going to have to learn to like horses," Mary Ellen said.

"Just shut up, *kemo sabe*."

After lunch with Mary Ellen, Sally dropped by her Uncle Morty's apartment before going back to the paper. Morty returned each spring, with the robins, closing up his Miami condo to head back to Brookline. When the leaves turned green and the forsythia bloomed and the dogs started to run at Wonderland, Morty was in his element.

He opened the door when she rang—natty as ever in his "Miami Nice" pastels—and ushered her inside. She asked how it had been going at the track.

"Ah," said Morty, "the dogs. They aren't all that smart, dogs. I had my money on this *meshuggah* dog, he's running like there's no tomorrow, and then he sees a cat. The stupid dog, he runs right off the track after the cat. Cost me forty bucks."

Morty shrugged his shoulders, with a sigh that sounded like the resignation of Job. "What can you do? They're only dogs, they're not Einstein."

Sally took a covered dish out of the shopping bag she had been carrying. "Mom baked you a noodle kugel, Uncle Morty."

"Your mother's kugel"—Morty put his fingers to his lips and made a kissing sound—"the best."

He took the dish and she followed him into the kitchen. He put it on the counter and then turned to her. "It would have been Solly's birthday tomorrow," he said.

"I know." She suddenly noticed how thin he seemed, how frail. She had never thought of him as old.

"You miss him a lot, don't you?" she said.

"It's not right; the older one should go first. I'd never have believed that Solly would be gone and I'd be here." He sighed again. "Me and Solly. Did I ever tell you the story about how me and Solly took on most of Revere High, almost single-handed?"

Sally smiled. She had heard the story many times, and she would hear it again. With each retelling, the heroism of the Ellenberg brothers increased. Someone had yelled an ethnic slur outside the school. Sol and Morty, like the Maccabees of old, had shown true grit. They offered to take on all comers, of which there were more than a few. But they had a surprise ally.

"This Eye-talian kid, he was as big as a mountain," Morty said. "And he said, 'I stand with these guys!' And oh, did we make short work of the whole crowd! Then, years later, I saw him on Beacon Street, and by then he was"—Morty paused for dramatic effect—"the Lieutenant Governor! A fine gentleman. An Eye-talian, and he stood with us. I told him I always voted for him." Morty grinned. "Twice, one year."

Sally laughed, and then Morty said, "I like your fella."

"But he's a *goy*, Uncle Morty."

"Watch your mouth. Jack is a fine gentleman."

"It doesn't bother you that he's not Jewish?"

"Times are different now. Not like when me and Solly were growing up. Then you stuck with your own. Now, it's all mixed up."

Sally nodded.

"Besides, the Jewish fellas you went with"—he made a face—"so many nice Jewish men around, how come you always found *shkutzim*?"

"I could never figure that out myself," Sally said.

Jack took a bite of watery Indian pudding and frowned. Why did Uncle Robert like to eat here? The food at the Harvard Club on Commonwealth Avenue was the worst in town. But Jack could not lure his uncle to one of the fancy new yuppie eateries where the waiter told you his name and the chef did exotic things with fruits and poultry. It had to be Lock-Obers, one of the Harvard clubs, or maybe the Bay Tower room if he was feeling modern. A glass of port and a cigar followed dessert. Uncle Robert did not regard his after-dinner cigar as smoking, despite Jack's grim warnings about cancer. Certain habits one did not change.

Robert Aiken leaned back in his chair and said, "Civil rights are all well and good, but we could have an epidemic on our hands."

"We've been hearing that for years. Hasn't happened. AIDS has been declining in the gay population over the past decade. The decline has proved that education can change behavior."

"People have a right to know if their health is in jeopardy."

"No one's health is in jeopardy if they're working with someone who has AIDS. Even this new strain. Unless there's an exchange of blood. We've known that for years. AIDS patients have a right to keep their jobs. We seem to have to fight this battle over and over."

"We're not going to agree on this one, are we?" Robert Aiken sighed.

Jack smiled. "No, I guess not."

"We rarely used to disagree."

"The world is getting more complicated."

"I suppose it's natural. A young man grows up, moves away from the old family ideas. Values."

"I haven't done that. I think we still see eye to eye on most things." Jack shoved the Indian pudding, only half-eaten, to the side.

"Things have changed since I was young. The notion of 'society' is completely gone. Most of the rules don't exist anymore. It's rather more . . . democratic."

"You don't approve?"

Robert Aiken lit up his cigar despite Jack's frown.

"Perhaps it's just my age, but I was more comfortable with the way it used to be. Things were . . . clear. Hardly fair, I suppose, but you did know your own and how they would behave."

"Are we talking about Sally?" Jack's voice had an edge to it.

"I suppose we are. Yes."

"I thought you liked her."

"Oh, I did. Quite a lot. Very smart. Quite pretty. Very different from Miki."

"Yes, she is."

"Miki has, oh, such an ease about her. I would think she will make some man a wonderful wife."

"I'm sure she will."

"The right wife can be a real asset, Jack. A man's career depends on it, more than he usually likes to admit."

"Not in my business, Uncle Robert. I'm an ink-stained wretch with a press pass in my hat."

"You're young. Who knows where life will take you?"

"I like journalism. I'm good at it."

"Yes, indeed you are." He motioned to the waiter. "Two glasses of the port, if you please."

"Miki would be wasted on me anyhow," Jack said. "I'm not social. I never really enjoyed dragging off to all those benefits."

"This young woman—Sally—you and she come from such different backgrounds."

Jack laughed. "Yeah, I went to the dog track with her Uncle Morty. I won, too. I bet it was the first time a Forbes or an Aiken ever set foot in Wonderland."

"Dog racing is a pleasure I have missed," Robert Aiken said, no regret in his voice.

"Sally's good for me. She makes me feel—alive."

Uncle Robert sighed, a deliberate sound meant to convey a wisdom-of-the-ages sagacity. "Unsuitable young women always do, Jack."

"You make her sound like *Molly, A Girl of of the Streets*."

"Hardly. But Jewish people are very clannish. I don't mean that in a demeaning way. Their traditions are important to them—as ours are. Do you know that when someone marries outside the religion, the family says prayers for them as if they were dead?"

"Only if they're very Orthodox, Uncle Robert. Sally's Reform. But not very religious."

"Ah, well, it's not so important, after all. Today, men and women have many relationships before settling down."

Jack nodded and sipped his port. It occurred to him that he didn't really like port. He should have ordered a beer.

"I was correct, wasn't I?" Uncle Robert asked.

"About what?"

"You and Sally."

"Well, I don't know."

"Your mother is rather upset. She loved Miki."

"No, they just got on well. Did mother ask you to talk to me?"

"Not in so many words."

Jack put down his glass and shook his head. "*Now* she's worried about me."

"That's not fair, Jack. Your mother has not had an easy life."

"I know. I didn't mean that the way it sounded."

"I just want you to know about her concerns. She is your mother."

"And I'm a grown man. I don't want to hurt her in any way, Uncle Robert, but I have to live my own life."

"I know that. You always have. I'm only asking you not to rush into anything you might later regret. Of course, Jack, you'll do the right thing. Did I tell you, by the way, that I stopped off to see the Fords when I came in from the coast? Gerald looks wonderful. All that skiing keeps him young. And Betty has done a wonderful job with her clinic."

Uncle Robert began a tale of his latest trip, with bits of tantalizing—and sometimes elegantly malicious—gossip about the high and mighty. The discussion about Sally was over.

Later, walking down Commonwealth to the T stop, Jack

detected a vague feeling of annoyance—with his uncle, his mother, and himself. Uncle Robert represented all the things he had rebelled against, and at the same time envied. It was so seductive, his uncle's world. Despite his resistance, he had been captivated by his uncle's tales of ex-presidents and present-day power brokers. As a journalist, he was always on the outside looking in, trying to pry pieces of information from people not always willing to give it. The world of the insider had a definite appeal. It could have been—no, could *be* his world. Uncle Robert had made it very clear that he would use his connections to open the door to it whenever Jack wanted. A recent suggestion was a very high post at the Harrison Ellard Foundation. The Foundation was a powerful player in the health care and biomedical field, with the Ellard fortune at its disposal. A perfect spot for Jack, with his science writing background. Discreet inquiries were made. Yes, the job was available. It could lead to a top policy post in government one day.

As always, Jack had said no. There was the usual love-hate scenario with his uncle's world, and was he, deep down, afraid that, like his father, it was a world in which he was doomed to fail? But there was also the fact that for all its cachet, the job was really about pushing papers. At the *World Herald*, he felt closer to the action. The job gave him a chance to write, and that was when he was happiest. Of his potential talents as a bureaucrat, he was unsure. He did not, he suspected, have the patience.

But Uncle Robert always managed to make him feel as though he were somehow letting down the side. Not that he meant to; his uncle's affection for him was real. No, it was Jack's problem. He had never quite made the break. Perhaps rebellion, in some perverse way, only attested to the power of his uncle's— and his father's—world. Maybe he would only be free when it no longer mattered, when he could reject it—or accept it— whichever pleased him. He wondered if he would ever arrive at that fair place—he was a far distance from it today.

His mood did not improve after an interview with a scientist from MIT who was trying to protect his tenure and say very little about his controversial research. By the time Jack arrived back at the apartment Sally was already home and in the shower. He walked into the kitchen, opened the dishwasher to get out a clean glass, and discovered that it was still loaded with dirty dishes. When she walked in, her skin damp and glowing from the water, his mood was so foul that he was not charmed by the sight.

"Damnit, Sally, you didn't run the dishwasher. You said you would."

"Oh, I forgot. I'll do it now."

"We don't have any glasses."

"We have lots of paper cups."

"I hate paper cups. I want a glass!"

And so they had a row. He called her irresponsible and flighty. She accused him of being tight-assed and making a mountain out of a fucking molehill. He stomped out, walked around the block a few times, kicking cans and calling them rude names. That made him feel better. When he walked back in the apartment, she was still pouting, her lower lip thrust out. They avoided each other for a while, and then he said, "This is stupid."

"Yes, it is."

"I'm sorry I blew my stack."

"What was going on, anyhow? This wasn't about glasses, was it?"

"No. I had lunch with Uncle Robert."

"Oh?" she said.

"He can always make me feel like I'm ten years old again."

"Was this about me?"

"Only partly."

"Jack, I don't want to come between you and your family."

"My family," he said, and marched off to get a beer. When he came back in the living room she asked him, "Want to talk?"

He sighed. "Remember that series I did last year? On adult children of alcoholics? As you can imagine, I had an ulterior motive. I was trying to find out about myself."

"Did you?"

"Yeah. They have this list of roles that alcoholics' kids fall into. Some are martyrs. Others rebel, get into trouble. Then there are the caretakers. That's me. I read that, and I recognized myself."

"The one who keeps everything together?"

"Yeah. It's role reversal. The child becomes the parent. I remember one day—I was nine years old—and my mother had gone to bed with a migraine. But she didn't have enough of her medicine, so I called the doctor, got the prescription refilled. My father was off someplace drying out. Then the man we used to do our gardening came to the door and said he had to know right away where to plant the new bushes. So I went out and picked a place for the goddamn bushes. He was three feet taller than I was, but he was calling me sir, as I told him where to plant the bushes. I remember thinking, 'It isn't fair, I shouldn't have to do this, I'm only a kid!' Nine years old, keeping things from going to hell in a handbasket. Well, no more. I retire from the caretaker business."

"Can you just say it, and make it happen?"

"No. But if I keep saying it, maybe."

"Those experiences go deep."

"At some point, it's time for *me*. I took care of my father, I take care of my mother—do all her finances. I haven't disgraced the family name. That's enough."

"I think that's right. It's enough."

"*You* are just for me," he said. "Not for them, for me. What *I* want. To hell with what they think."

"Maybe you won't always think that way."

"Yes I will. I will. I know it."

"Well," she said, "we'll find out."

23

■

The Hakim story was as cold as a day-old bagel. Sally could hardly stir more than a shrug from the desk. Still, she kept plugging. Few of her sources in law enforcement seemed any more worried about his fate than the city desk was. A few privately admitted they would shed no tears if the activist disappeared from the face of the earth. Hakim had been the driving force behind more than a few "police brutality" protests, some quite legitimate, others questionable. To a lot of cops, he was simply an apologist for thugs and druggies. Also, Hakim had the ability to disappear into ghetto streets when it suited him. Now, flyers were being circulated by the New Panthers with his picture on it, but not many people took them seriously.

Sally had a cup of coffee with a member of the New England organized crime strike force, and his attitude was typical.

"I don't buy this 'disappearance' bit. Unless he's gotten involved with the shit that's going on with the Hispanic gangs. They shoot everybody. It's a slaughter out there."

"You think Hakim is still involved in drugs?"

"Once a druggie."

"But is there any new evidence? Lots of old stuff, I know."

"Nothing I could prove. But his file is pretty thick. Does a dude like him really get out of the business? Or does he dip into it when he needs more bread for his operations?"

"Hakim's friends swear he's out."

"The money's too good, too fast. I don't believe it."

"Look, Bill, I won't print this, but have you heard anything about the Feds going after Hakim?"

"Off the record?"

"In this case, yes."

"FBI had him under surveillance some time back. Look, all these new radical groups have ties to some strange folks. If you ask me, the guys in D.C. get paranoid over every crazy with a homemade sign, but it's not surprising that Washington's interested. This guy's gotten to be a big deal."

"Does this cause some flack in the Boston Bureau?"

"I hear some grousing from the local guys, who think they ought to be spending their time on real crooks, not chasing students in knee-pants around."

The rest of the day Sally was tied up with a big drug bust announced by Justice, and other work kept her occupied most of the week. But she did finally shake loose for a meeting with a source at the Bureau, an agent who owed her one for a piece of information she had gotten but didn't print for forty-eight hours. They walked along the Charles late one morning—who knew what bugs existed in the crevices of the cubicles in Federal buildings?

"Sally," he said, "you know I'm not supposed to make any comment on a pending investigation. If there is one."

"Come on, Fred, I'm calling in my marker. You're looking into the New Panthers, right? Off the record on this. I'm not trying to look at your investigation. I'm still trying to get a handle on the Hakim story."

The agent walked in silence for a minute, shoving his hands into the pockets of his windbreaker.

"OK. Off the record, there's been some questions about the New Panthers and foreign agents."

"Foreign agents?" Sally asked. "Who are we talking about?"

"I never told you this."

"Right."

"Middle East, I hear. Terrorist types. Libya, maybe Iran."

"Documented?"

"All I know is that there have been reports. How solid, I don't know."

"Look, I think it's important that this issue gets aired in public. Just a story saying *maybe* there's a connection. That could smoke out Hakim, if he's just being cute."

"Jesus, not from the Bureau."

"Of course not. How about 'Federal agents'?"

"Still too close. Make it look like it came from D.C."

" 'Sources close to ongoing terrorist investigations'?"

He smiled. "Yeah, that sounds like the spooks."

"Do you think there's any truth to this?"

"Hard to say. D.C. hasn't let the locals touch this one. Strictly a topside operation."

"That pisses you off."

"This is our turf. What the hell, we could handle something like this. Nobody likes to be made to feel they're bush league."

Sally was grinning to herself as she headed back to the car. This was the first break in the case. Terrorists ought to make the desk perk up. Maybe it would go page one, jump to metro. The Federal suspicions made Hakim a story again. Sometimes you just had to chip away, a crack here, a fissure there, to blast the whole surface away. Good reporting wasn't the big one-shot scoop. Good reporters had a lot of ferret in them.

But before she could write, Sally had a curious engagement. She had gotten a phone call from Robert Aiken, who in his courteous—but magisterial—way had invited her to join him for lunch at the Harvard Club. Her first instinct was to decline, but her curiosity was piqued. She wondered just what his approach would be.

He had reserved a table for two, and he pulled out her chair and stood until she was seated. His manners certainly could not be faulted. He made some suggestions about the menu, and during lunch entertained her with just the sort of light but pleasant anecdotes that must have been perfect for an embassy party, where one did not want to say too much, but had to be amusing. It was only after the food had been cleared away, and coffee and fruit served, that he got down to business.

"You didn't tell Jack we were meeting?" he asked.

"No. As you requested."

"This is rather awkward for me, Miss Ellenberg. I suppose I am here to ask you about your intentions."

"My . . . intentions?"

"Yes. Toward my nephew."

Sally had to laugh. "Mr. Aiken, excuse me, but aren't you supposed to ask the *man* that? When you think he's a fortune hunter or something?"

"I suppose it does sound a bit like Henry James."

"Yes, it sure does. But if you want my intentions, OK, here goes. I'm in love with Jack. Yes, it's serious, no, we haven't talked marriage, but we might. As for me, I've got no debts, no diseases, and I earn thirty-eight thousand dollars a year. I am financially self-sufficient. Jack and I live together, but we share the rent and expenses. I don't need or want his money. I am not a fortune hunter."

"I never really thought you were. But I'm concerned about Jack. He has a very bright future, that young man."

"So do I," Sally said tartly. "Perhaps in your day women didn't have futures, but now we do. I'm very serious about my work. Just like Jack is. That's one of the things we have in common."

Robert Aiken sipped his coffee, regarding her levelly. "Please understand my . . . interest. Jack is like a son to me. He's his mother's only son. The last male child in our branch of the family."

"You'll pardon me, but you make it sound as if what's at stake is the Crown."

He could not help a tiny smile. "Yes, I suppose we do get obsessive about family matters. It's important to us."

"Important that the right . . . stock . . . is maintained?"

"I know a fair amount about you, Miss Ellenberg. Your father was a respected journalist, your mother from an old German Jewish family. Your 'stock,' as you call it, is impressive. But of course—"

"I'm Jewish."

"Yes."

"And that's a no-no for the Forbeses and Aikens?"

"I'll be frank. It's a concern. I consider myself unprejudiced. I've worked with the finest Jewish men in public life. Arthur Goldberg was one. I certainly believe myself no better than they. But our traditions are so different."

"Jack's a grown man now, Mr. Aiken," Sally said. "Don't you think he ought to make up his own mind on all this?"

"I'm sure he will do that. I guess I am here to ask *you* to reconsider the relationship."

"Why should I?"

"Has it occurred to you that you are a part of Jack's rebellion against his family?"

"I think it's more than that," Sally said, sipping her coffee, but she felt her stomach flutter. Uncle Robert was on target with that one.

"He's wanted to go his own way, achieve on his own. But at some point, I believe he will feel a strong pull. He will want to go back to his roots. You could be in the way of that movement, and you could be hurt."

"I'm a grown-up. I can take care of myself."

"I have no doubt you can. Quite well. I only ask you to look at certain realities."

"All right, let's be frank. What kind of hardball are we playing? Are you saying you would disinherit Jack if he married me?"

"Would that change your mind?"

"The money? I said it doesn't matter to me. But to see Jack cut off from his family—totally estranged—yes that would bother me. Because it would hurt him so much. Particularly to be out of favor with you. He loves you, a lot."

Robert Aiken was silent for a minute. "You do care for him, don't you?"

"Yes, I do. And to tell you the truth, it piss—it really gets me angry to see you trying to manipulate him this way. He deserves better. He's a very capable man. He's an adult. Why don't you treat him like one?"

Robert Aiken's eyes opened a centimeter wider. "Are you lecturing me, Miss Ellenberg?"

"Yeah. I am."

"Interesting. Much against my better judgment, I really do like you. I assure you, I would never disinherit Jack, no matter what. But I will continue to oppose this match, for all the reasons I've stated."

Sally looked him directly in the eye. "And I won't be scared off or bought off. Where Jack and I are headed, I don't know."

"Well, we have both been candid. In the end, I will respect Jack's decision. But I thought it only fair that you know where I stand."

"I do."

"And you will not speak of this to Jack?"

"No, I won't, because it could wreck the relationship the

two of you have. It's important to Jack. But if you want to keep that relationship, you're going to have to understand who and what he is. Now. Today. Not when he was a child."

"You are a very direct young woman, aren't you?"

"I sure am."

Sally left the meeting with a strange mixture of anger at—and respect for—Robert Aiken. The old boy didn't pull his punches, which she preferred to surface politesse that papered over contempt. The Yankees didn't run things in Boston for several centuries by gladly letting other folks in. On the other hand, she reflected, it was Yankee parsimony and shortsightedness that had helped drive the economy of the region into the ground by the mid–twentieth century. With a sudden throb of ethnic chauvinism, she thought, Jews would have been smarter. *Goyim* always mess up.

She told Mary Ellen that the encounter had been very strange indeed.

"I felt as if I should have been wearing a shirtwaist and a Gibson Girl hairdo, M.E. He asked about my *intentions*."

"And you didn't tell him to shove it up his ass?"

"It wasn't that kind of conversation. It was all put so . . . civilly. I guess this is how diplomats do it, when they explain gently over tea that they're taking over your country because United Fruit profits are down and you can either play ball or wind up with cement overshoes. 'Oh, and by the way, one lump or two.' "

"Sounds like you handled it well."

"Well, I didn't hit him. Or tell him that *goyim* don't know shit."

"You told me that once, in seventh grade." M.E. said.

"I did?"

"Yeah. After I said Jews couldn't go to heaven."

"Oh, I remember. I was really pissed. One more restricted place."

"But the stuff about Jews being smart—I envied you on that for a long time. Nobody said that about the Irish. I used to think 'dumb Mick' was one word."

"We were smart, but sleazy. We'd cheat you in a minute even if it was only a nickel."

"We were honest, but we were drunks," Mary Ellen said.

"We didn't drink, but we couldn't play sports."

"We could play sports, but we got into office by getting dead people to vote."

"We drew up the legal papers for the dead people."

"Why didn't we get together? We would have owned this town."

"Because we killed Christ."

"Yeah, and he couldn't vote in the district."

When Sally arrived home, Jack was at the computer putting the finishing touches on a story. She wondered what he would say if he knew about her lunch with Uncle Robert. He would probably be furious. She had a sudden impulse to blurt out the truth, but didn't. She had given her word. Let Robert Aiken tell the tale, if one was indeed to be told. Instead, she filled Jack in on her conversation with the FBI man.

"Do you believe that? Middle East terrorists?" he asked.

"Hakim had a lot of third world contacts. But he's pretty sophisticated. I can see some of the black street gangs taking that kind of money—and I can sure see it being offered—but Hakim was going mainstream. He had to know that if anything like that got out, he'd be discredited."

"Maybe he didn't know. Maybe there was a front. And Hakim didn't push too hard to look into it."

"That's certainly possible. He can be careless."

Jack frowned. "It introduces a whole new cast of characters into the story. Makes it less plausible that Severn was involved."

"You think some Libyan gunman could snatch Hakim on Dorchester Avenue? Come on."

"Remember when he showed up in Algeria last year? He floats in and out of third world countries, you know that."

"That's true. He figured his visibility and his leftish politics made him invulnerable. Anybody with a grudge against the U.S. wasn't going to grab Hakim."

"But let's say he was taking money. If it came from one faction in Iran, or Libya, maybe the other faction offed him for political reasons," Jack suggested.

"So we have terrorists who might want to grab him."

"Or drug dealers, if he's into that scene."

"Right," Sally agreed. "Or somebody in one of the black gangs who had a score to settle."

"White crazies. Skinheads. The Klan. The *Newsweek* cover piece made him really visible."

"The Feds," Sally said, "especially the CIA, if he's involved with terrorists."

"Then there's Severn and his pals, because a link is there. It doesn't seem very likely, but it's there."

"This is making my head hurt," Sally said.

"It's not like this in the spy novels," Jack sighed. "By page one fifty, the hero has figured out that the Mossad has ties with MI-Five to foil the plan of the president of Pakistan who is working with the Islamic Jihad which is sending money to transvestites in the Village who are laundering the money through a Rotary Club in Duluth."

"And you know the good guys win," Sally said. "In life, it's more complicated."

"My head hurts too. Want a beer?"

"That's a good idea."

REPORTER'S JOURNAL: Sally Ellenberg

Subject: Uncle Robert

It was very odd, having somebody trying to buy me off elegantly. I mean, I've been offered a few snorts of coke to change a lead, but never over a demitasse at the Harvard Club. I could indeed have been the Little Seamstress summoned to meet the Rich Uncle. Of course the Little Seamstress would never say to the Rich Uncle, "Shove it, pal. I make 38 grand a year and I'm not playing dead for you or your *goyishe* money." Which is what I did say. But politely.

The whole episode did give me an insight into the way the world used to be. A lot of people are around who are nostalgic for the old days, when people had "values" and life was one big Norman Rockwell painting. The good old days. When Jews couldn't buy houses in certain neighborhoods and there were quotas at schools and law firms and businesses. Nobody talked about it much. There was a "Gentlemen's Agreement." In Uncle Robert's world, I can imagine how they used to talk about Jews—grudging admiration tinged with contempt. Smart, but pushy. Loud. Flashy.

You might want a smart Jew lawyer for your firm, but for God's sake, don't have him to tea. Blacks, of course, you wouldn't hire except to haul the trash, and women were OK in their place—which was cooking and shopping.

The interesting thing is that in the "old days," the people who agreed to stay in their places wound up thinking, deep down, that the other people really were better. You can't accept those kinds of limits without somehow accepting their legitimacy, no matter how hard you fight the idea. If Harvard doesn't want me, can Harvard be *all* wrong?

There are people who hate the sixties, all the chaos and the extremes; nobody seemed to do anything except to overdo it. But growing up in that era, I believed its promises. The old order didn't have any magic anymore. *We* were the future. We wanted to make our own rules, our own destinies, our own new world.

It was an illusion, of course. But because of it, I went to my meeting with Uncle Robert without the whalebone corset. Not really awed by him or his world. Oh, I appreciate his accomplishments. But it was what he's done that impressed me, not where he came from. I was not the Little Seamstress, though he didn't know that at first. I like the idea that the granddaughter of a tailor from Odessa could have lunch with a descendant of the Henry James crowd and not tip her hat or tug at her forelock. If he gets me in the family, *he* will be the lucky one. The old Yankee genes could use a little sturdy Jewish stock.

I think I rather surprised him. He expected to overpower me. But I've had DAs and mob bosses and wardens try to do the same thing. I don't overpower easily.

It must be hard for the people who used to run that world that was held in place by so many little treaties. Those "agreements" immobilized people, like flies caught in spider's webs. It's sort of surprising when the flies kick their way out, knock on your door and say, "Here's your goddamn web back, and who the fuck are you, anyhow?" Or when the seamstress not only comes to tea but wants her initials on the family silver.

Oh no, Uncle Robert, there's a new set of rules. A whole new ball game, in fact. The people who used to stay in the bleachers are now right out on the fucking field.

24

■

The switchboard at the office of the county medical examiner's office was aglow. George Rittenhouse had ordered that all calls from the press be greeted with the same message: No comment. The examiner will issue a statement.

It was too hot a story to keep quiet for long. The body of a black male had been found in an abandoned building in Roxbury. Next to him were a can of Sterno, a spoon, a piece of rubber, and a hypodermic needle. Someone in the first police cruiser on the scene had recognized Robert Brown, AKA Hakim Abdul. The examiner would complete the autopsy, but he was in no hurry to throw red meat to the pack.

There were times that a man in Rittenhouse's profession stepped out of the obscurity of the medical laboratory to become headline news. This was one of those times. There was high drama raging about this case, unusual interest from a great many parties. The thought of it made the hairs on the back of his neck tingle. The timing was perfect. He was still smarting from a very damaging series of articles by the Investigative Team at the *World Herald* that had brought to light certain questionable procedures and sloppy methods in his operation. Thanks to three decades of careful cultivation of powerful men in the state house and the governor's office, he had managed to survive in his job—but it had been close. Robert Storrow Ames held a special place in his pantheon of enemies, and they were not few.

Let the press wait. He would stage the news conference, on his terms, his time.

He announced that his office would have something to say at six. At seven, he said that a report would be forthcoming in the morning. In the morning, with the pressure mounting and the press at a fever pitch, he announced the time of his news conference: twelve noon. He smiled as he gathered his notes and prepared to face the cameras. He was ready.

George Rittenhouse had a true instinct for drama. His press conferences were well attended, and he knew precisely the words that would get the cameras from 4, 7, and 5 to click on. Drop a name. Hint darkly of nefarious deeds. Display a snappish temper.

Sally watched the medical examiner as he strutted to the microphone. He was a small man with a thatch of white hair that stood up as if it were made of wire; his movements were jerky, aggressive. He reminded Sally of a bantam rooster. He loved to perform for the cameras; he would dole out bits of information that the press would devour like snapping dogs tantalized with pieces of meat. Secrets were his trade, those hidden in bits of gristle or bloodied tendon. The secrets yielded up by corpses were the source of his power, and he luxuriated in it. His word was law in his office, and he had been known to fire summarily those who questioned him. So he had enemies, some of whom had tried to bring him down by talking to the *World Herald* Investigative Team. He would not forget that.

He stepped into the glare of the TV lights, and paused, as the room hushed.

Jack nudged Sally and whispered, "Is he always like this?"

"Oh yeah."

Rittenhouse wiped his brow. He wanted the pack really hungry when he fed it.

He shuffled his notes, then he looked directly into the TV cameras. "I have completed my examination in the case of Mr. Robert Brown, also known as Hakim Abdul. Mr. Brown died of an overdose of heroin, injected directly into the vein by a hypodermic needle. Are there any questions?"

Sally asked, in a loud voice that drowned out the man from

the *Record-American,* "Any marks on the body that would indicate a struggle?"

"None. No signs of a struggle, or violence of any kind."

"Hakim Abdul hadn't done drugs for years," said a reporter from *The Black Voice.* "You expect us to believe he killed himself with heroin?"

"I am simply reporting the medical evidence," said Rittenhouse. "His motivations for injecting himself with heroin are not known to me, and could not be."

"Isn't it possible," Jack asked, "that he could have been given the drug?"

"I find no evidence that would lead me to suspect anything other than self-inflicted overdose. Given this man's past history of drug abuse, his manner of death is not unexpected."

"Was anyone else present in the attic when he died, as far as you can tell?" asked the woman from ABC.

"There is some evidence that others were present. But police officials can tell you about that."

"Doesn't it seem a little strange to you," said the reporter from the *Phoenix,* "that a guy who has a reputation as a national leader of the New Panthers suddenly O.D.'s in an abandoned house?"

"The man was an *addict,*" said Rittenhouse, his mouth pulling into a small "O" of disdain after it formed the word. "He had two convictions for dealing drugs. Mr. Brown was a felon."

"His name was Hakim Abdul," said the reporter from *The Black Voice.*

"That was his alias. His *Christian* name was Robert Brown."

A series of questions followed, with *The Black Voice* reporter trying to goad the examiner into revealing some hint of wrongdoing. George Rittenhouse treated him as if he were a not overbright child. He let the reporter's questions buzz about him as if they were a somewhat bothersome fly. Sally knew that Rittenhouse would not be tripped up. He was a pro at this game.

The TV lights snapped off. "That's it," said the WBZ reporter to his camerman. "Another junkie snuffs himself. We'll get a minute thirty if we're lucky. Shit."

Sally looked around and saw Sandra Jefferson, who had been standing in the back of the room watching Rittenhouse's performance.

"What do you think?"

The black activist shook her head. "I can't believe Hakim overdosed. I think somebody did it to him."

"You think Rittenhouse is withholding evidence?"

"We've had plenty of trouble with him before. He doesn't like us much."

"I've heard a lot of things about Rittenhouse, but not that he's a racist."

"Not your classic Klan-type. Blacks are OK in three-piece suits. But it's more than that. He's so pro-cop. He thinks anybody in law enforcement is a noble centurion manning the barricades against the scum. He has no understanding of what happens to kids who grow up in neighborhoods where families are disorganized, where the dope dealer is the big man on the block. I think he *wants* to believe Hakim O.D.'d. I wonder if he'd even see any evidence to the contrary."

"This case ought to start unraveling in a few days, if there *is* more to it."

Sandra shook her head. "No, you're wrong. This case is going to sink like a stone. Oh, maybe the *Phoenix* and *The Black Voice* will keep doing columns on it. Nobody else. Wait and see. If it had been a white college student—but Hakim was no Harvard boy."

Sandra Jefferson turned out to be right. Two days later, stories about Hakim Abdul were nowhere to be found in the establishment press. Sally's article about the reaction of black leaders around the country got buried on page 65. But it didn't make sense. Hakim Abdul was too smart to overdose like that. Even if he was back on drugs, why would he shoot up in an attic? Hakim had developed a taste for creature comforts, Sally knew, and his lecture fees had tripled in the past year. Hakim might have gone out on a coke high in a suite at the Sheraton, she thought, but in a filthy attic? She had been there, and it was not Hakim's style. Not at all.

On a hunch, Sally dialed the home number of her source in the medical examiner's office. A woman answered.

"Hello. Zevner residence."

"Grace, it's Sally Ellenberg."

"Oh, how are you, Sally? I can guess what you're calling about."

"You're right. Grace, is there anything you can tell me about the Hakim autopsy that Rittenhouse didn't let out? Anything at all?"

"Well, it was heroin, no doubt about that, from the report."

"You saw it."

"Yes. I typed the notes."

"Anything about marks on the body?"

"No. Nothing that I saw."

"Anything else? Even if it's a detail, a small one."

"Only one thing I did notice. Trace amounts of two chemical substances. But I guess they weren't important. They weren't in the final copy at all."

"Do you remember what they were?"

"Oh yes. I have a photographic memory. Everything I type, I remember. But I can never remember where I left the car keys. Isn't that odd?"

"Can you give me the names?"

"Well—"

"It's probably not important. I just want to check them out."

"All right. You helped me, Sally. I like to help you when I can."

"You know I'll cover for you, Grace."

"Yes. Mr. Rittenhouse doesn't know I gave you that stuff on the kid who died. He thinks it came from the police."

After Jack came back from an interview at Harvard Medical School, she asked him about the drugs her source had mentioned to her.

Jack pulled out his directory of chemical substances. "OK— phrenylphine Hydrochloride." He leafed through the book. "Here it is. Common ingredient in nose drops. Nothing there, unless somebody's come up with killer nose drops. What's the other one?"

"I'm not sure how you pronounce it. Here's the spelling."

"Succinylcholine. Never heard of it. He thumbed through the book again. "SA—SC—SUC—OK, I've got it. A muscle relaxant. Used in some surgical procedures in which a reduction in skeletal muscle tone is required. Trade names—oh my God!"

"What is it?"

"One of the names under which the drug is marketed is Anectine."

"Anectine?"

"The drug Craig told me about. The one Severn was using

on the prisoners. That Hakim helped stop. That's it. Anectine!"

"Jack, could that have gotten in his body by anything he would have injected himself with? Any street drug?"

"No way, Sally. It's a deadly poison. It's the same as curare, the stuff South American headhunters put on the tips of their spears."

"Doctors use this stuff?"

"In tiny doses, it can relax the muscles during surgery. But there is no way, Sally, *none*, that Anectine could have gotten into Hakim's body unless somebody gave it to him."

"My God!"

They stared at each other.

"Jack, this is one hell of a story."

"You bet it is!"

"This ties Hakim to Severn."

"Maybe not. Lots of people know about this stuff."

"But if somebody used it on Hakim Abdul—no matter who—that's a story we can go with."

"Yes, we can."

"What are we waiting for?"

Sally told Kevin, briefly, the outline of the story. Then she and Jack worked on it together, under a joint byline, saying that reliable sources had revealed that traces of a drug used experimentally on prisoners had been found in the body of Hakim Abdul. It also told about the New Jersey experiments, how the drug affected the human body, and about the ACLU court fight against it. When they had finished, the city editor called the story up on his VDT. Jack and Sally watched his face as he read it. Kevin Murphy's face started to redden. The proximity of a good story affected his red corpuscles faster than a pint of gin.

"This stuff is dynamite!" he said. "I want a conference on this."

The city editor called the national editor—who was in charge of the news operation while Robert Storrow Ames and Parker Ames were in Washington for a meeting of the American Society of Newspaper Editors. They met in Robert Ames's office.

"Who has the source in the medical examiner's office?" asked the national editor, Adam Wetherall. "Yours, Sally?"

"Yes."

"How solid?"

"As a rock. Remember the beat we got on the Evans kid?

That he was actually killed by a blow on the head, not what the cops on the scene said? We got that before Rittenhouse released it. That was from my source. I'd stake my reputation on her."

"Jack, what about the drug stuff? All nailed down?"

"It's all in court testimony. On the record."

"This story is going to raise hell," Wetherall said. "I wish Bob Ames were here." He turned to Sally. "You're absolutely certain about your source?"

"Absolutely."

"We also have indications that this is linked to other stuff going on. Experiments," Jack said. "We can't nail that down yet, but this story will be the crack in the dam."

"Anybody else have this?" Wetherall asked.

"Not that I know of. But I'm not the only reporter with sources in Rittenhouse's operation. Levy at the *Record* gets a fair amount of stuff."

"All right, we'll go with it," Adam said. "Let's remake page one. Put the Supreme Court below the fold."

Driving home that night, Sally and Jack were unusually quiet. Then Jack said, "Sally, this is a once-in-a-lifetime story. This is big."

"I was thinking about that."

"I mean really big."

"Like how big?"

"Woodstein?"

"Oh, Jack, I don't even want to think that way."

"It's funny, but Watergate got started just the way this one did."

"How do you mean?"

"Well, it was just luck that your brother-in-law happened to be at the hospital that night. And it was just dumb luck that a police reporter from the *Post* happened to be at police headquarters when the Watergate burglars were caught."

"That's true. Woodstein got all the glory, but if that reporter hadn't picked up Howard Hunt's address book—"

"And seen the initials W.H. and knew it was the White House number—"

"And wondered what on earth a second-rate burglar would be doing calling the White House—"

"I wonder," Jack said, "how we will handle all this. I suggest no obvious gloating. A becoming modesty."

"We will become a household word. *Aikenberg.* How does that sound?"

"Your name should go first."

"I thought of that. It sounds weird. *Ellenken?* Sounds like a German beer. Besides, if you hadn't found out about the prisoner stuff, we'd never have been able to put two and two together."

"But you got the tip from the medical examiner's office."

"We're both wonderful."

"Hell, yes!" he said.

When they got home, he opened up a bottle of champagne.

They sipped it sedately at first, trying to contain their elation. After all, this story was littered with bodies; ought they to be so jubilant?

Half a bottle, and jubilation was the clear winner. Sally raised her glass and said, "To Aikenberg. We're going to blow this story wide open."

Jack was grinning as he raised his glass. "Aikenberg. The Pulitzer."

"The Nobel!"

"Think we'll topple a president?"

"Why not? It's been done before." She giggled. "I am not a crook."

"When did he know it, and when did he forget it?"

They both giggled, and glugged down more champagne.

"We've got it," he said. "Nobody else has it!"

"I'm getting schnockered," she said.

"Oh. No more champagne. Too bad."

"Too bad."

"Damn," he said, his words slurring a bit, "I still feel like celebrating."

"So do I."

"If pressed," he said, "I could think of a way."

She smiled. "And I know exactly where to press."

25
■

George Rittenhouse looked at the initials on the typed copy of the autopsy report. He would never have suspected, except for something he heard her say. "I have a photographic memory. I remember everything I type."

"Bitch. Fucking bitch." He said it to no one in particular. He was alone in his office.

She had not called a member of the press from the office, nor had she been called by one. Unbeknownst to employees, their calls were monitored. Ever since the Investigative Team story, he had been cautious. But she would not need the form in front of her. She had a photographic memory.

She was the leak on the Evans story. He was sure of that now. He had busted his balls to find it, and he never had. Until now he had never suspected her.

"Bitch."

He looked at the papers in the file in front of him. He made it a point to know as much as he could about his employees. Her husband was on permanent disability. She had one child, a son. He was in a special school because his eyesight was very poor. He was almost legally blind. She was the one, had to be. He had narrowed it down.

"Cunt."

He picked up the phone and dialed a private number at the Federal Bureau of Investigation.

26

■

The story was a sensation. When the early edition of the *World Herald* hit the streets, phones began ringing in news organizations in Boston, New York, and Washington. The *Times* and the *Washington Post* were left to play catch-up the next day. The "Today" show displayed the front page of the *World Herald*, and Bryant Gumbel discussed its possible implications. "Nightline" started working on a show for later in the week. The attitude in the *World Herald* newsroom was the usual mixture of envy, admiration, and sour grapes. Sally tried to take it all in stride, but she did wish her father had been alive to see it. "I did good, Dad," she whispered to him.

At midday, Sally got what she thought was a hot tip on the prostitute murder. But after a frustrating round of interviews, the lead disintegrated. No one was able to give her anything solid. It was just after six when she came back into the city room. She saw a knot of people gathered around the color TV set near the city editor's desk.

Kevin saw her and motioned her over.

"It's Rittenhouse. He's denying our story."

"What?"

"I tried to get hold of you. He called a press conference at five for six o'clock. I sent Cunningham. Jack's out."

On the television set, the medical examiner had assumed his combative stance, the one he knew would guarantee that they would put him on live at six.

"I have here," he said, waving a paper theatrically before the cameras, "the detailed autopsy report on Mr. Robert Brown, also known as Hakim Abdul. Copies have been made available to the press. You will note that nowhere in this report is the drug succinylcholine mentioned. The only substance that was not included in my summary of findings the other day was phrenylphine hydrochloride. What is that, ladies and gentlemen? It's what you use when you have a stuffy nose. It is the common ingredient in nose drops. There is no other drug on the list. There was no other drug found in the body. Any report to the contrary is a lie. A bald-faced lie."

"Are you saying the *World Herald* story is completely untrue?" a reporter asked.

"Absolutely. There is not a word of truth in it."

"The story came from a reliable source," said Bob Cunningham.

The examiner snorted. "The only people who knew the truth are in my office," he said. "No one in my office gave out any information. However, there are those in the community who are eager to discredit anyone who works in law enforcement. Those people often have their own paranoid fantasies, which they mistake for fact. I suggest they are the source of this story."

"Do you mean the black community?" asked the *Record* reporter.

"I don't know where this alleged story came from. But I repeat, there is not one shred of truth in it. I want an apology from the *World Herald*. This is the most shameful and irresponsible piece of journalism I have seen in all my years. I am familiar with one of the reporters who wrote the story. Well, let me tell you, that name should have read 'Janet Cooke.' We have our own Janet Cooke, right here in Boston."

"That son-of-a-bitch!" Sally said. The other reporters were quiet around her. But the reporters at the conference were scribbling like mad. They all knew Janet Cooke—even if some of the viewers of the six o'clock news were mystified—as the young reporter for the *Washington Post* who won the Pulitzer Prize for a story about an eight-year-old heroin addict. When it was discovered that the story was a fabrication, the Pulitzer was withdrawn, resulting in no small embarrassment for the *Post*.

"We're going to get a lot of heat on this, Sally," Kevin said.

"Let him deny it. My source is solid."

The controversy exploded in the Boston media the next day. Rival newspapers and television stations—which had been careful to run the story only by attributing it to the *World Herald*, had begun to salivate. The *World Herald* was big, powerful, arrogant. The prospect of the paper getting caught with its pants down on a major story whetted appetites all over town. HAKIM STORY A FAKE? headlined the *Boston Record-American. The New York Times* ran the story on page one.

Sally and Jack tried to concentrate on other stories they were working on, but they could hardly ignore the pressure the story had put on the *World Herald.*

"Can we get another source to back up our story from the examiner's office?" Jack asked her.

"Rittenhouse has really put the clamps on. I'm going to steer clear of Grace for a while. I don't want to jeopardize her right now."

"I wish we had a Xerox of that original report."

"So do I. But if we hang tough, Jack, the pressures will start to mount on Rittenhouse. People are going to start asking questions."

"That was a cheap shot, that crack about Janet Cooke."

"He figures he owes the paper one. He was just getting his licks in."

"But the TV guys are picking up that quote and running with it every hour. Whose side are they on, anyhow? They act like they'd rather dump on us than get on the story."

"Because it's our story. They don't like the idea that we got it and they didn't. Besides, a lot of people in town hate the paper. It represents the power they don't have."

"Rittenhouse says the press is like a pack of dogs. Maybe he's right. Except they're coming after *us*. It's a strange feeling."

"The paper will back us up. Like the *Post* did with Woodstein. Don't worry, Jack."

The rumors flew in the city room all through that day and the next: the *World Herald* was going to write a front page editorial backing up its story; the ombudsman for the paper had been assigned to do a full-length investigative story; the paper was going to back off the story; the CBS Evening News was going to bring its cameras into the city room. The story changed every five minutes.

Jack tried to work on a follow-up he was writing about Hakim's involvement in stopping the experiments with Anectine. He found it hard to put one sentence after another. His stomach felt as if it were knotted into a fist. He gobbled Tums and tried not to think about flying rumors. Sally was calm. One thing she knew, the *World Herald* would never back off the story. Her father had been in tight places like this; Robert Ames's father, John Storrow Ames, and then later, the son, had stood firm.

Late in the afternoon, Kevin Murphy went into Robert Ames's office, followed by Parker Ames and Adam Wetherall. Jack looked at Sally.

"What in the hell is that all about?"

"Us, I'd guess," she said.

Fifteen minutes later, Kevin came out of the office and motioned to Jack and Sally. They went into the office; the tension inside the room was so thick it was a presence. They had been arguing, Jack knew.

"Sally. Jack." Robert Storrow Ames nodded to them. "Sit down, please. This is a serious situation, I'm sure you are aware of that. You heard the medical examiner. You saw the *Times* coverage. There are charges that your story is a fabrication."

"Yes, we know," Sally said. She seemed perfectly at ease. Jack determined not to let his own nervousness show.

"This was your source, right, Sally?" Robert Ames asked.

"Yes."

"You assured Kevin that it was solid."

"It is."

"OK. Can you identify your source for me? I am only asking this because of the pressure we're under."

"Yes, I can, as long as it doesn't leave this room."

"I assure you, it won't."

"Grace Zevner. She's a records clerk and secretary in the examiner's office. Two years ago, you remember the story about the cop who had been crippled trying to break up a robbery? They were going to cut him off disability and I did a story about it. They didn't cut him off. He was her husband. She feels that she owes me one. She's been a solid source. She gave me the lead on the Evans case."

"Will she back the story up publicly?" Parker Ames asked.

Kevin Murphy scowled at the question. Kevin and Parker had been going at it, Jack guessed. There was no love lost there.

"Of course not," Sally snapped, making no effort to hide the fact that she thought the question idiotic. "She'd lose her job. It may be in jeopardy already. I wouldn't have a source left in this town if I fingered Grace."

"All right," Parker Ames said. "Then get her to confirm it to me. In confidence."

"Wait a minute," Jack said. "She gave you the name of the source. That ought to be good enough."

"We're being publicly accused of fakery!" Parker Ames was using his most patrician voice. "This is serious business."

"Just because the *Times* is playing this big, Parker, is no reason for us to panic," Kevin told him.

"My source is good. I named her. I don't want to go any further." Sally's voice was steady.

"I'm afraid I have to insist." Parker Ames tugged at his glasses. "In confidence, to me. It won't put her in jeopardy. Just one word—yes. On the phone."

Sally looked at Robert Ames. He was quiet. Clearly, he was not going to intervene. Kevin looked away, still scowling. For the first time, Jack saw a trace of uncertainty in Sally's face. She had been so sure of the support of these men.

"Nothing on the record. I promised her."

"Nothing on the record," Parker Ames agreed.

Sally shrugged. Parker Ames handed her a telephone. Sally dialed Grace Zevner's number.

"Grace, it's Sally. I have a problem here. I need you to verify, in confidence, what you saw on the record. For my editor. It will be in absolute confidence, I promise."

"Sally, I've had calls," Grace Zevner said.

"Calls? From who?"

"I don't know. They mention my boy, they know where he goes to school." Fear rippled through her voice.

"Grace, no one will know."

"Please, he's my only child. My baby, he's only eleven!"

"Only my editor will know we talked."

"I can't, Sally. I'll deny everything. I'm so sorry, but I'm so afraid!" The woman's voice indicated that she was near hysteria.

"Grace, just one word. Yes. Just say yes. One word."

"I'm sorry. Oh God, I'm so sorry." The woman was weeping now.

"Grace, I promise—" But the line had gone dead. Sally stood very still for a minute, and then she hung up the phone. "She's afraid even to talk on the phone. She's had calls, threatening her son. Mentioning his school. She was nearly hysterical."

"So she won't confirm?" Parker Ames looked smug.

"No."

"How convenient," Parker Ames said.

Sally looked at Parker Ames, curiously. Jack knew exactly what he was saying. But it seemed so inconceivable to Sally that she wasn't hearing it. "What do you mean?"

"Janet Cooke couldn't find her source for her editors either."

Sally's eyes narrowed. "Parker, that's a load of shit! I found my source. I gave you her name. I just talked to her. The woman is scared to death."

"Parker," Jack said, trying to hold his temper, "neither of us ever faked a story. We never would."

"I'm not accusing you of anything, Jack."

"My name is on that story. I'm just as responsible for it as Sally is. I stand behind every word of it."

Just then, the door to the editor's office opened, and an assistant city editor motioned to Kevin Murphy. Kevin went to the door and the man handed him a piece of wire copy. "This just came over UPI," he said. "I figured you'd want to see it right away."

Jack only had to look at Kevin's face as he read the wire story to know it was bad news. Kevin handed the piece of copy to Robert Storrow Ames.

"The story just came over," he said. "An independent pathologist who did an autopsy for the FBI says no trace of succinylcholine was found in Hakim Abdul's body."

Jack felt his stomach lurch. He looked at Sally. Her face had gone dead white.

"It's a fix," she said. "Rittenhouse is tight with the Bureau. Everybody knows that."

"So now the FBI is hiding evidence." Parker Ames fairly sneered.

"The FBI would never do anything like that, Parker," Jack snapped at the managing editor. "Pat Grey never put Watergate papers in a burn bag."

"It goes high," Sally said. "This story goes way up high. Even to the Bureau."

"Do you know what this makes the paper look like?" Parker

Ames took the piece of wire copy from his uncle and waved it in Sally's face. "We're standing here with shit all over us!"

"My source was good," Sally insisted. "Why is she being threatened if somebody doesn't want to put a lid on this whole story?"

"Remember Woodward and Bernstein," Jack said.

Kevin looked at him. "What about them?"

"They were out there all alone, for a long time. Half the press in Washington were saying they were just a couple of young, eager reporters on a wild goose chase. If the *Post* hadn't stuck by them, Watergate would just be the name of a hotel."

Robert Storrow Ames stood up. He sighed, deeply. Everyone in the room looked at him.

"Did you ever consider the possibility," he asked Sally, "that you were being set up?"

Jack and Sally looked at him in surprise.

He looked somber, the lines on his forehead deepening.

"Rittenhouse has had it in for us ever since our Investigative Team series. He's talked about getting even. You've even heard him say that."

"Yes, but—"

"It's the way the game is played in this town. Don't get mad, get even. Maybe he's been planning something like this all along."

"My source wouldn't do that," Sally said. "Grace Zevner wouldn't be part of something like that."

"She wouldn't have to be. Suppose Rittenhouse knew she was your source on the Evans case. And I'll bet he found that out. He's very thorough. All he'd have to do was let her have false information, and sit back and wait. He'd know you'd come to her again. That she'd give you the information. Then he'd have us right where he wanted us."

"You think he *planned* that leak?"

"I do. He's very smart, very devious. Hates us. I think he's been scheming for two years for a way to get back at us. And now he's found it."

Sally shook her head. "No. Because Hakim's death is part of a pattern of events Jack and I have been looking at."

"There's more to this story," Jack said. "We think there have been a number of disappearances that are linked. Hakim is only one. There are the prostitutes, and a holdup man—"

He stopped. Kevin Murphy was staring at his knuckles, Adam Wetherall gazing at his shoelaces. It all sounded so crazy. They weren't going to buy any of it. Jack saw what was happening and a sinking feeling coiled inside his gut. They were backing away, cutting their losses. They figured they had been hurt enough. A false story tainted everyone connected with it.

"I'm afraid," Robert Storrow Ames said, "that we are going to have to issue an apology."

"No," Sally blurted out. "You can't do that!"

"I don't think we have a choice," the editor said.

"There is more to this story. Hear us out," Sally argued. "I know my story is good. For God's sake, don't apologize!"

"Nobody who knows Hakim Abdul thinks he O.D.'d," Jack said. "It's too pat."

"He was an addict, Jack," Kevin said. "Eight arrests for dealing and possession."

"Give us time to put the details together," Sally said. "I know we can convince you. Don't let them bury this story along with Hakim."

"Ellenberg," said Parker Ames, "this is not *The Village Voice*. We can't throw paranoid fantasies around."

Sally ignored him. "Just don't repudiate the story. Say we're investigating. If we apologize, the story on Hakim will die. If we stay with it, more will come out. Maybe I can get Grace to confirm if the threats stop."

"Sally, we can't just stonewall," Adam Wetherall said. "I've been putting people off all day. Ted Koppel is calling. The Chicago *Trib* is on us. Not to mention the *Post* and the *Times*. We have to make a statement."

"Just say we stand by the story," Jack urged him.

"How can we? Sally's source won't confirm. The medical examiner has issued copies of the report that contradict us. The FBI pathologist backs him up. There's just no way we can support this story," Wetherall said.

There was no sound in the room after the national editor made the statement. Adam was fair, and inclined to take chances. He wasn't a man who always walked the safe and narrow path. And he wasn't buying it. They had lost, lost big, Jack thought. The FBI-backed pathology report had nailed the coffin lid down. Without that, they could have made a case—or at least bought more time. He thought, wincing, of the champagne last night. "Aikenberg" was going under, and there was no way to save it.

"I assume," Sally said, "that if we can come up with a confirmation from other sources that Hakim did not overdose on his own, you'll run that story."

"Not with an unattributed source," said Robert Ames. "If you can nail it down, then yes."

Sally stood up, wearily. Her face was pale, and she looked very small and vulnerable. But her shoulders were erect.

"I stand by my story, even if my newspaper won't," she said. "I won't ever apologize for it."

Jack walked to her side. "The same goes for me."

"I'm sorry," Robert Storrow Ames said.

They both left the room, went to their desks, and sat, silently, for a minute. Other reporters tried not to stare, but the room was already buzzing with the news.

"Shit!" Sally said.

She could think of nothing else to say. Others could; the story had already reached the mailroom and the telephone operators. Robert Storrow Ames was going to write the apology for the *World Herald*. It would run on the front page the next day. He was convinced the paper had been suckered by the medical examiner—though he would not say *that* in his measured fustian prose.

Jack looked up and saw Parker Ames motioning to him. He was standing near the door of his uncle's office. Jack walked over.

Parker put his hand on Jack's shoulder in a brotherly fashion. "Jack, I'm sorry you got dragged into this."

"I didn't get dragged into anything. My name was on that story. And I'd write it again."

"Just a word of friendly advice, hey, Jack? You have a future at this paper. This will blow over. Nobody is going to blame you for this story. What you wrote was accurate."

"The whole story was accurate, Parker."

"Look, you know you can go right up the ladder here. But watch your friends, Jack. Especially Sally Ellenberg. She's ambitious, not to say pushy, eh? She's already hurt you by association. You want to fuck her, fine, but for God's sakes don't write any more stories with her."

Jack looked at Parker, in sheer astonishment at first. The managing editor had a tiny smile on his face, the sort small boys wore when they told dirty jokes. The sight of that smile ignited a bolt of animal rage in Jack.

"Parker, you prick!" he yelled, and grabbed Parker Ames by the collar and jammed him so hard against the wall that Ames's glasses tumbled off. They bounced to the floor. Jack kept shaking him.

"You open your rotten mouth about her one more time—"

Suddenly, half the city room descended on them. Kevin Murphy and three reporters dragged Jack away from a badly shaken Parker Ames. Jack tried to shake them off. He had decided he wanted more than anything just to land one good punch on Parker's pale face. But Kevin Murphy had a firm grip on his arm.

"Jack, for God's sakes, you can't kill the managing editor," he said.

"Not that it isn't a swell idea," said Bob Cunningham, who had hold of Jack's belt."

"Little fucker!" Jack said, but by then Parker Ames had retreated into his office and shut the door.

"OK, guys, you can let go of me now," Jack said. The rush of adrenaline had faded, and he suddenly felt very tired.

"No more Marvin Hagler?" Cunningham still gripped his belt.

"No. I'm not going to hit anybody."

They let go of him and he walked over to his desk. "Asshole!" he said.

"What did he say that set you off, Jack?" Sally asked.

He looked away.

"Why do I get the idea it has something to do with me?"

"He said it was fine to screw you, but not write stories with you."

"Sound vocational advice, at this point." She sighed.

"He won't open his fucking mouth about you again. At least not when I'm around."

She put her hand up and touched his face. "My Galahad. And you're the one who told me *I* should be more political."

"You know what? Knocking his goddamn glasses off was worth wrecking my career for."

They drove home, both of them exhausted, and undressed and got into bed. They lay close together, not for passion this time, but for comfort.

"Oh, damnit, Jack! I worked so hard to be credible. A woman on the police beat, that's still not easy for some people to take.

I was so careful. I *couldn't* make a mistake. I never even got a middle initial wrong. And now—was I set up, Jack? Did Rittenhouse sucker me?"

"No. You know that isn't true. I can see how Bob Ames believes it, though. The story is still out there. We know that."

"Who's going to believe us now?"

"We'll make them believe it. Somehow."

"I thought they'd back us up. Never in a million years did I think they wouldn't back us up. I worked so damn hard, and is this how I'll be remembered? Boston's Janet Cooke?" He could hear the tremor in her voice.

"It's all right," he said. "Let it out. Don't keep it in."

"Reporters don't cry," she said.

"Sure they do. Sy Hersh wails every time they change a comma. David Halberstam blubbers. Come on, Sally, that's it." He held her and stroked her hair as she wept, her face against his chest. All the anger and frustration poured out of her. When her breathing became nearly regular again, he reached over and grabbed a box of Kleenex from the night table and handed her one.

"Feel better?"

"Oh yeah. But I think your way is better."

"My way?"

"Punching out Parker."

"That did more for my health than five years of Primal Scream. I recommend it. You were great in there, you know. A lot of people would have buckled."

"But it didn't do any good, Jack. They didn't believe us. Somebody murdered Hakim Abdul, and they're going to get away with it."

"No, they won't. We know. And we'll keep after them."

"Damn right!" she said. "We know. And we'll make somebody believe us."

REPORTER'S JOURNAL: Sally Ellenberg

Subject: Credibility

Credibility is all you've got in this business. It's your currency. It's your power. There are sev-

eral ways of getting it. Access is one. If you're close
enough to people in power that they tell you things
and return your phone calls, you're credible. But
it's a tricky business. If the word gets around that
you're just somebody's mouthpiece, you're on borrowed time, because when your source is out of office,
or out of the loop, you're as cold as yesterday's mack-
erel. To be "wired" and to be independent too takes
some intricate footwork.

Sometimes you get credibility because you work
hard and you never get it wrong. Your sources will talk
to you because of that, and because they know you'll
play fair with them. The quotes staring at them in the
A.M. will be right, and not out of context and not
splashed in the lead if they were just tossed off. You
won't burn them just to get a score, because you have
to come back to the well.

That is the kind of credibility I had. I never
tried the Sucking Up route to power—mainly because,
if you're a woman, the Sucking Up is literally done on
your knees. I've seen women move up by sleeping up,
but that's risky. When the man gets tired of you, it's
off to the bureau in Nome. If he gets fired, you're a
sitting duck. The women are pissed at you because all
the guys now believe that that's how women get ahead—
and they say so. The guys are really pissed at you
because you played a variety of the Sucking Up Game
that they couldn't use. (Not that some wouldn't try,
if they'd move up a rung.) Those who are without sin
cast the first stone at you, but the sinners are right
there in the second row, heaving rocks.

Part of credibility is having a powerful institution behind you. When I say "*World Herald,*" a lot
of doors open that otherwise would be slammed in my
face. I play that card, hard and often. In this state,
looking like an asshole on page one of the *W.H.* can
send your career right down the tubes. Sometimes, I
have to remind people of that.

But I was so worried about credibility that I
really messed up on this one. Jack wanted to go to
Kevin earlier with what we had, and he was right. We
would have been dealing from strength then, even if

our stuff did seem far out. We were two reporters with a lot of chits to call in. We were credible.

But I had to have it nailed. I always do. I'm a woman, on a man's beat, and one slip, and all of womankind goes down with me. ("Broads can't do these stories.") It made me too careful. So I got sucker-punched.

The story about Hakim dealing drugs in Dorchester was a setup. I knew it smelled bad at the time. I tried to write it very carefully, but it still came up aces for whoever planted it. Hakim was linked, publicly, with drug dealers. So when his body was found, the stage for that scenario had already been set. And I set it. My buddy George has vanished into thin air. Paid off and shipped out, I'd guess.

Right now, nobody wants anything to do with us. We went big and public with a story, and it didn't hold up. Our own paper had to back down. This was not only a corporate embarrassment, but a personal one. I can imagine the barbs Bob Ames is going to hear (wearing a pained grin and choking back the impulse to kick someone in the nuts) at the next editors' meeting. There's nothing newspapermen like better, ghouls that they are, than tossing flaming torches on the funeral pyre of a colleague who got burned on a story. The line between being a hero and a goat can be pretty thin. If Nixon had never made those tapes, do you think Woodward and Bernstein would have had their own movie?

If we'd been able to make the story stick, we'd have been in the lead of a charging pack. Reporters would have been all over the Hakim case. The pressure would have started to build, and with any luck at all, the seams would have started to buckle. One source would crack, and then the others would have been like rats trying to stay afloat.

But nobody wants to go charging up the hill we just got knocked off. When powerful people want something covered up, they've got more than a good shot at doing it. For every skeleton that gets hauled out of the closet, there are a hundred others that will never see the light of day.

I try to keep up a good front in front of Jack. I tell him, and try to convince myself, that we'll come out of it OK. One of these days, they'll play their cards wrong. Make a big misstep.

But I have this clammy hand clutching at my windpipe. People are blaming me, not Jack. He's just seen as the unlucky chump who went for a ride on a story with a partner who got suckered. Who was naïve and stupid. Cardinal sins. It will be remembered as my story, not his. Boston's Janet Cooke.

God, why does that sound like a line from my obit?

27

■

"his is big-time hardball," Sally said, pushing the mushrooms from the quiche around on the plate. She had no appetite. "I don't know if I can play this game."

"You're certain he was murdered?" Mary Ellen asked. A man at the next table looked up and stared at her. Murder was not the usual lunchtime conversation at the Bennett Street Café.

"No doubt about it. My source was right. They leaned on her." She looked around. "I'm getting paranoid. Half the guys in the room look like Feds."

"This is Cambridge. Half the guys have earrings."

"Them especially."

"I wish I could do something to help."

"Thanks for the hand-holding. That helps," Sally said. "Besides, what could you do? I screwed it up good."

"How?"

"I should have gone to Bob Ames a lot earlier. But I've never thought I could just walk in the top guy's door and be believed, just on my say so. I had to have every 'i' dotted. Every comma in place."

"Because you're a woman."

"Yeah. It's funny, I still feel I have to keep proving myself. My right to be where I am. When does it stop?"

"It doesn't," Mary Ellen said. "We wave our resumés like flags, hoping they'll look at them, not *us*."

"Yeah. I feel so . . . naked, without the paper behind me. I *know* that rotten stuff is going on, and that it goes high up. But we've been frozen out. Who's going to believe us?"

"You're sure Bob Ames is wrong? That you didn't get set up by Rittenhouse?"

"Rittenhouse is not that smart. He's a little man. A tyrant, but not subtle enough to pull off a scheme like this. He's a bureaucrat at heart. He's Eichmann—just following orders."

"How about Congress? Can you stir up any interest there?"

"I called a friend on Senator Ryan's staff. He let me know that once the paper backed off, that was it. Jack and I have the stench of failure about us. A couple of dumb reporters who got suckered. We're a laughingstock."

"What about the black community?"

"They have no power. Hakim wasn't Mr. Popularity around town. He pissed off a lot of the black establishment. His style wasn't Boston. Too much flash."

"If what you're saying is true, *somebody* must want it out."

"It gets out, there's a stink. Nobody wants that. And a lot of heavies don't seem to want it out. Besides, who cares about a left-wing black guy? Or prostitutes? They're invisible."

"What do you plan to do?"

"Keep going until we get something solid. It's easy to get a reputation as a nut, real quick—in the same category as assassination freaks and people who carry antivivisection signs at subway stops."

"Just be careful, Sally," Mary Ellen warned. "Frustration can make people take risks they shouldn't take."

"A fat lot I've got to lose at this point."

Back at the paper, Sally looked for Jack, and found him having a cup of coffee in the cafeteria.

She joined him, noticing that people who might ordinarily have come over to the table now headed to a far corner of the room.

"Jack, do you hear bells?"

"Bells?"

"Little ones. They tinkle. Unclean. Unclean."

"Something like this lets you know who your friends really are."

"Maybe they think their typing fingers will turn yellow and fall off if they have coffee with us. Did you have a talk with Kevin?"

"Yeah. I laid it all out. Neurodyne, Brady, the works."

"What did he say?"

"Punched holes in everything. Thinks it's all sci-fi. But he knows the whole story isn't out on Hakim. Adam does too. But they felt they were boxed in and had to apologize. At this point, they're not saying we have to stay away from the story. If we could give them something real, they'd go with it. But it's got to be solid."

"Bob Ames is really convinced it was a setup." She shook her head and sipped at the coffee. "All my leads on the prostitute just melt into thin air. I think I have something, then *pouf*—it vanishes."

"I've been checking out the Neurodyne board. They're all guys who have been involved with the Patriot Foundation one way or another."

"We've got to figure out a way into Neurodyne," she said.

"But we've got to be really careful," Jack warned. "As of now, nobody but Kevin knows anything about Neurodyne. If we let on that we think it's the site of brain implants, they could close the operation down overnight. Move it someplace else."

"If we hold back, more people may die."

"I know. Craig Letterman will be back from Geneva soon, and he'll help us. We've got to get some kind of a feel for how big this thing is, Sally. How far up does it go?"

"I don't know. The FBI is in on it—or somebody there. I'm afraid to talk to some of my sources. I don't know who the bad guys are anymore."

"That's where Craig comes in. He's got good sources in the government. People who don't like Big Brother stuff."

Sally took another sip of coffee. The dregs, now, but she hardly noticed. "By the way, did you know that Parker Ames tried to get me fired?"

"Who told you that?"

"Adam. He said that Parker told his uncle it would prove the paper wouldn't tolerate faking stories."

Jack frowned. "Want me to hit him again?"

"Do you want to get sent to Antarctica for an in-depth series on penguins?"

"Still, I'd love to smack the little *putz* again."

"Your Yiddish is improving."

"Half the words I learned from Uncle Morty apply to Parker."

"And I can think of plenty more."

After the coffee, Jack went back to his terminal to finish a piece on the space shuttle for the Sci-Tech section. Sally had an interview out of the building. Jack was halfway through his final edit on the story when his phone rang. The voice on the line was familiar.

"Jack. It's Seth."

"Seth? Are you in town?"

"Yes. I'm calling from a pay phone. I saw your story on Hakim Abdul and I flew up to talk to you. It's important." Seth's voice sounded tense and strained. "I don't want to say where I am. Sorry for being melodramatic, but remember where we used to meet? You and me and Jeff?"

Jeff was a friend of Jack's and Seth's who had gone to MIT.

"Where *Trojan* lived?" Jack asked. *Trojan* was the name of Jeff's racing shell.

"That's right. Can you meet me there at eight?"

"I'll be there."

The last daylight was fading from the sky when Jack drove along Memorial Drive and found a parking place by the side of the Charles. He walked to the front of the MIT boathouse and waited. In a few minutes, Seth drove up, parked, looked around carefully, and then got out of the car. He did not look good, Jack thought. The dark circles around his eyes were deep and a weariness had settled about his shoulders like an invisible cloak.

"Jack," Seth said as the two of them walked by the side of the river, "this is going to sound really strange. Bear with me."

"I'm getting used to strange things."

"Why did the paper back off the story?"

"Our source wouldn't confirm. She was threatened. And the FBI report nailed it shut."

"You still think the story is true."

"Yes."

"Well." Seth walked quietly for a minute. Then he spoke. "You remember I said I got out of the civil rights division."

The darkness closed around them as they walked by the

river; the lights of Boston, on the far shore, began to dance in the eddies of the dark water. Couples strolled by, hand in hand, and several joggers puffed by.

"I didn't have much to do. So I started playing around in the files. Andrews is away a lot, and his secretary thinks he's a pig, so I got to see stuff I wasn't supposed to see."

"What sorts of stuff?" Jack knew that Seth needed to talk things out, so he curbed his impatience. He remembered the arguments at Adams House, where Jack would want to grab Seth and shake him and holler, "Seth, get to the goddamned point!"

"I saw memos," Seth said. "Pieces of things here and there. If you put them together, you start thinking something very peculiar is going on."

"Like what?"

"I think—and this is the part that sounds crazy—I think there are a group of men, all pretty high up in the bureaucracy, who have secret meetings and an agenda that only a few people know about."

"What sort of agenda?"

"Well, I don't know a lot about it, but I think they are involved with something called a behavior unit. All the stuff I saw was very cryptic. A lot of initials and code words. But it has to do with this unit, whatever it is."

Jack felt his heartbeat quicken. "Tell me what you know about this unit."

"Well—sometimes I think I'm nuts. This all sounds so crazy. That's when I'm at home. When I go to the office I can feel the paranoia. People are seeing enemies all over the place. It's like the sixties, when they were keeping tabs on every lesbian group in Cambridge that had a mimeo machine. Remember COINTELPRO? J. Edgar sent Feds out all over the map against anybody who dissented on damn near anything. I think it's going to happen again."

"But the unit, Seth, what about it?"

"I first saw the words 'behavior unit' in a memo that Andrews wrote. Then there were cryptic memos that had the initials R. B. in them a lot. I didn't have any idea who R. B. might be, until I saw your story. I read that Rittenhouse always referred to Hakim by his old name, Robert Brown. The dates on the memos fit the time when Hakim disappeared."

"What did they say about R. B.?"

"It was shorthand, but one memo said 'R. B. secure.' A lot of stuff about R. B.'s Libya connection. And how it was top priority to identify it."

"Anything more specific?"

"No. But I picked up from the memos that there was a big shitfight about R. B. Somebody must have argued it was too risky, because one of Andrews' memos was clearly trying to calm somebody down. It said the operation had deep cover and several layers of safeguards."

"Seth, was there any reference to where this behavior unit was?"

"No. But there was something about work on a memory inhibitor proceeding well. Do you know what that is?"

"No, but I think research on a lot of behavior-control techniques is going on. Did you see any reference to a man named Severn? Or a place called Neurodyne?"

Seth shook his head. "No full names, just initials. But the memos went to people in the FBI, the CIA, the State Department. I'm working on figuring out who the people are. But my boss seems to be the head honcho."

"Can you get copies of those memos?"

"I've got handwritten copies that I made."

"Not good enough. We need actual copies of the memos themselves."

"Well, I think I could do that. I'd have to be careful."

"Good."

"You don't think this is crazy?" Seth asked.

"No, it's not crazy." Jack told Seth the whole story of what he and Sally had pieced together. Seth listened, his eyes alight with a nearly manic excitement. At the end of the story he shook his head, and the weariness settled in on him again.

"These are bad times, Jack. There may be a war, and I think we're going to see a crackdown that's going to be worse than the Vietnam era. These guys, like my boss, they're true believers. They wouldn't see anything wrong with this kind of stuff. They see themselves as patriots."

"Does anybody else know about this, Seth?"

"No. I haven't told anybody. I—well, I didn't think anybody would believe me. Like I said, I was sick for a while. And it wasn't until I saw your story that it all came together in my head."

"If I have Xerox copies of those memos, I can blow this whole story wide open."

"You really need something official, right? Not just my telling you what I saw."

"Yes. The smoking gun. We've got to have that, Seth. Otherwise, it's just your word. They could do a number on you, deny it all."

Seth straightened up. "I'll get the copies," he said.

"We need them, Seth. We've got to get our hands on the memos."

Seth suddenly grabbed Jack in a quick—and uncharacteristic—hug. Jack was startled at first, but then returned the embrace.

"Oh, Jack, you give me courage to go on! I was getting so goddamn down! But we'll nail the bastards, won't we. We'll nail them!"

They agreed to meet in one week in the same spot. Seth said he would not contact Jack unless a major hitch developed. In a week, he would bring Xerox copies of as many of the memos as he could get his hands on. Then Seth turned and vanished into the darkness, leaving Jack alone by the river. Jack walked quickly back to his car, his excitement gathering as he did so. Finally, he could not resist it; he gave a tiny whoop and a small dance step as he approached the BMW. "Eat shit, Parker!" he chortled.

When he told Sally the news, her whole face brightened. She had been putting up a brave front, but he knew how much the paper's apology had hurt her. He knew, too, that while his name had been on the story, it was her source that backed down, and her reputation that had been most damaged. She grew thoughtful when he told her about the initials, and the men to whom the memos had been sent. "Seth doesn't know exactly who they are yet, but he says he can figure it out."

"My God, Jack, how big is this? How far do the tentacles stretch?"

"I don't know. It's Seth's impression that this is a maverick operation."

"Like the one Ollie North ran out of the White House basement?"

"Yes. Or maybe it has approval higher up. But it sure as hell is illegal."

"If we had those memos! They'd have to believe us then! If we had it on paper! The smoking gun. That would be proof that it wasn't just Rittenhouse setting us up."

"I had to push Seth a little bit to make him promise to get them for us. He looks lousy. But he'll come through. Seth always did. One year, in the head of the Charles, he had a temperature of a hundred and two. But he rowed his ass off anyway. We won, and *then* he fainted. I never knew Seth not to come through."

"He's got to get them! Did you let him know how important it was?"

"Yes. I sure did. And you're right, we've got to have paper. Our credibility right now is about as good as Chicken Little's."

"The sky is falling! The sky is falling!"

"And it *is*, damnit."

Later, in bed, they lay close together, and he felt her shiver. "Are you OK?" he asked.

"I keep thinking about how big this is, Jack. Funny, I always used to feel so safe, living in this country. I'm an American. I have rights. And all of a sudden I think I know how people feel when the knock on the door could come any time."

"Yeah, I feel that way too."

"Are you scared?"

"Yeah. A little."

"We're sort of out on a limb."

"Sort of?"

She laughed. "Understatement is my forte."

"We're going to be OK, Sally. Whatever the hell is going on, they wouldn't be so stupid as to come after a couple of reporters."

"That would be dumb, wouldn't it?"

"Yes. And no one knows what we know, except Kevin and Seth. Neither of them are going to tell. One of them doesn't even believe it."

"It's going to work out all right, I think."

"It is, Sally. It's going to be fine."

"Tell me that again. And hold me. I like it."

He kissed the top of her head. "Everything is going to be fine."

28

■

Jack flew to Washington the next day, for a NASA conference on the new space shuttle. But he had trouble concentrating on payloads and heat tiles. He resisted the temptation to call Seth Chaffee; better to play it safe. He found himself wishing he could accelerate time, to fast forward it to the morning when he was to meet Seth by the MIT boathouse again and get the memos.

He had been astonished by the paper's backing off the story. He was not used to having his word questioned. He had not made a mistake. The story was good, and he had simply expected he would be given the opportunity to prove it. His family name, his wealth, and Harvard all added up to acceptance. Certain doors simply opened. He had never really understood before how so many other people had to scratch and scramble for the things he took for granted. The realization gave him a sudden empathy for Sally's drive. He was going to be vindicated if he had to tear somebody's head off to do it. It was a new kind of hunger.

His class had always been a bit leery, in this town, of all those Irishmen and Italians and Jews with their hungry eyes. It had been a long time since Brahmins had known what it was to be outside the magic circle of money and power and place. Well might they worry about all those other folks on the make. When you're hungry, you push hard. Very hard, he thought, grimly.

He flew out of Washington on a Thursday morning, went right to the paper and spent the day working on a Sunday wrap-up story on the conference. It was nearly dinnertime when he finished. Sally was out on an interview and wouldn't be back until after seven. He packed up his briefcase, chatted with the Sunday editor, selling his story for the lead piece, and then walked out to the parking lot. He opened the front door of the BMW; it was in the rear of the lot, the only space available when he drove back from Logan Airport. He tossed his briefcase on the front seat, and since the evening was warm, slid out of his jacket and threw it on the seat. As he did so, he was suddenly aware that someone had moved up behind him. A voice hissed in his ear.

"Just be quiet now, and you won't get hurt. You'll be giving us your wallet now, boyo."

One of the reporters playing a prank, Jack thought. Probably Frank Shanahan, who could do the voice of a stage Irishman with perfect pitch.

"Hello, Frank," he said. But as he turned around, he saw two men, both youngish, wearing leather jackets and cloth caps. They looked so absurd his first impulse was to laugh. They looked like central casting's idea of Irish thugs.

"You've got to be kidding," he said. "I gave to the IRA at the office." Then he realized it was a dumb remark if these guys were serious, but it all seemed too bizarre to be happening.

One of the men shoved Jack against the car. Jack was not used to being shoved, and all the anger and frustration of the past week that had been slowly building inside suddenly erupted. He smashed his fist, hard, into the face of the man who had shoved him, feeling a savage delight as he felt the bones in the man's nose crack under the force of the blow. His pleasure was short-lived, however, when the other man expertly kneed him in the groin and Jack doubled over in pain. The man then grabbed his arms and held him as the other man, blood streaming from his nose, began to pound him with swift, savage blows to his midsection. The pain ripped through him, and when the man let go of his arms he slumped to the ground, retaining enough presence of mind to try to curl up and protect himself. One of the men barked "Get the briefcase!" Jack tried to roll over and get to his feet, but one of the men kicked him, hard, in the head.

"Hurry it up!" a voice said, and he tried to get up once again, but then a pain exploded in his head, and he saw or heard nothing more.

When he regained consciousness, his first sensation was of something sticky against his face. It took him a while to realize it was his own blood, and that he was lying, face down, in the parking lot beside his car. He tried to raise his head, but a wave of pain ripped through it when he tried to move. He thought it peculiar that he should be lying on the ground. He moaned, or someone did. He lay still for a time, he wasn't sure how long, and then he heard voices, moving toward him. He tried to call out, but only a strange grunt emerged from his lips. "Shit!" he thought.

"Did you hear something?" said a voice.

"Here!" Jack finally managed to get a word out. "Over here." He tried to get up again, but the pain returned, so he lay still.

"Oh, my God!" said a voice, very near now.

"Who is it?" Another voice.

"It's Jack. Jack Aiken." The first voice again.

One of the voices was Kevin Murphy's. The other belonged to Bob Cunningham. With an effort, Jack pushed the upper half of his body off the ground. Kevin leaned down to help him. The two of them turned him over, then gently let him down again, with Kevin supporting his head and shoulders.

"What happened, Jack?" Bill asked.

A thought was trying to swim through the confusion into Jack's head. Something important. What was it.

"Seth!"

"What, Jack? What is it?" Kevin was trying to wipe Jack's face with his pocket handkerchief.

"Have to call Seth," Jack said. "Tell him."

He tried to struggle up, but Kevin held him back.

"Jack, take it easy, you've lost a lot of blood."

"Have to."

"Jack, lie still," Bob Cunningham said. "We're going to call an ambulance. You're bleeding again."

"No, you don't understand. I have to . . . I . . ."

And then the darkness descended again.

It was an hour later when Sally arrived at the *World Herald.* The night security guard was at the door as she came in.

"Miss," he said, "if you parked in the lot, be careful when you go back out. There was a mugging tonight. I knew this was going to happen. I told them not to cut the force down."

"A mugging? Who?" Sally asked.

"That nice young fella. What's his name? Tall, sort of a big nose. Yankee."

"Jack? Jack Aiken?"

"Aiken. That's right."

"What happened? What happened to Jack?"

"He got beat up pretty bad."

"Oh God! Where is he?"

"The ambulance took him to Municipal. He was all bloody when they took him on the stretcher."

"No! Oh God, no!" She turned and ran as fast as she could to the parking lot. She climbed into the car, gunned the engine, and tore out onto Morrissey Boulevard. She drove at breakneck speed down the expressway, pulled up beside the emergency room doors at Municipal, and jumped out of the car. She was running so fast into the emergency room entrance that she nearly collided with her brother-in-law.

"Joe! Where's Jack? What happened to him? Where is he?"

"Take it easy, Sally. He's going to be all right. We did some X-rays. I'm just going out to make a phone call. Calm down, he's OK."

"Where is he?"

"Room Three. Over there."

Jack was getting five stitches in his head when Sally came in. She hurried into the room, pale as a ghost. He gave a wan smile as he saw her. "Hi. I'm OK. Looks worse than it is."

She went to his side and put her hand on his arm. "Oh, Jack, I was so scared. They told me they had to carry you off."

"Yeah, I was out for a while."

Joe walked back into the room and stood next to Sally. "He was a mess when they brought him in. Blood all over the place. Those superficial head wounds bleed a lot, but they heal quick. They hit him pretty hard, the bastards."

"Did they steal anything, Jack? Your wallet?"

"My briefcase. They didn't take any money."

"Jack, the X-ray shows you've got a small crack in one rib," Joe told him.

"Was there any answer at that number, Joe?" Jack asked.

"No. I've called twice. No answer."

"Damn!"

Joe shook his head. "A couple of vicious punks, Sally. From Southie, probably."

"They weren't from South Boston," Jack said, quietly.

Sally looked at him. "What do you mean?"

"They sounded like they were from the cast of *The Informer*. Who do you know from the D Street projects who talks like that?"

"They weren't muggers?"

"No. Trying to act like Southie thugs, and doing a lousy job."

"Feds?"

"Could be."

"They took your briefcase? What would they want?"

"I don't know. Unless—"

"Seth! The stuff he was going to give us. Oh God, we've got to call him."

"Joe's been calling for me. There's no answer."

"Jack," Joe said, "let me have a look at your ribs."

"Sally, call Seth again. There's a pay phone in the hall."

Sally left the room as Joe carefully pressed on Jack's ribs. Jack stifled a cry as the doctor probed a tender place.

"Hurts, huh?"

"Yeah. At least I got a good one in before they started on me. I think I broke the sucker's nose."

Sally came back, shaking her head. "I let it ring. No answer. Maybe he's in Boston. You were going to meet him tomorrow."

"That's what I was thinking," Jack said. "My guess would be that he's here. But I don't know where he would be staying."

"Jack," the doctor said, "I'm going to give you some painkillers. You're going to feel like hell tonight. That rib will heal on its own, but I want you to rest. Stay in bed tomorrow."

"Can I take him home, Joe?"

"Yes. And make him take it easy, OK, Sally? Jack, I want to see you in a few days to make sure that rib is healing right."

When they got back to Jack's apartment, he said to Sally, "Try Seth again." She did, and let it ring for a long time, but there was no answer. Jack was struggling out of his clothes, so she hung up the phone and went over to help him. He winced as he sat down on the edge of the bed.

"How do you feel?"

"Like I just got hit by a truck."

"Do your ribs hurt a lot?"

"Yeah, and my head is pounding."

"Come on, Jack, lie down."

He got into bed, feeling dizzy and nauseated. She got in bed beside him.

"Hold me, Sally."

She put her arms around him, gently. "Try to sleep, Jack."

"Who were those guys? Did they know I was going to get something from Seth? How did they know?"

"Maybe it wasn't about Seth at all. Maybe they wanted to see if we had anything more on Hakim."

"That could be it, couldn't it? Not about Seth at all. How could they know about him?"

"He'll be here tomorrow."

"Right. Tomorrow. Oh damn. Everything hurts."

She rubbed his back. "Try to sleep, Jack."

"I can't," he said, but she rubbed his back and said, "It's OK, love, I'm here. I'll be with you." He started to say something to her, but he couldn't remember what it was. He felt himself drifting away from consciousness; finally, he fell into an exhausted sleep. He did not dream.

29

■

Jack pulled up the collar of his London Fog jacket; the day was raw and clammy; there had been a steady drizzle all morning. He paced in front of the MIT boathouse. Seth Chaffee was supposed to have been here thirty minutes ago. But it was such a lousy day, maybe Logan was socked in. On a day like this, fog rolled in quickly along the Massachusetts coastline. Or Seth could have been tied up in traffic, if he was driving or coming by cab from someplace else in the city. It was early still.

He leaned on the railing; his ribs ached from standing and his head was still sore and tender. Sally had wanted him to stay in bed and go in his place, but he had insisted. She didn't know Seth, and he didn't know her. No, Seth might cut and run if someone else was waiting.

He walked back and forth again, and then looked at his watch. Forty-five minutes. He paced some more. After an hour had passed, he went to a nearby public phone and tried calling airlines. Seth was not on Delta or Eastern or U.S. Air—none of the morning flights. But then, he might have used a false name if he thought someone was on his tail. Where would he stay? His parents had moved to Florida, and his brother was in D.C., so he had no family left in Hamilton anymore.

Jack called Sally at the paper to see if Seth had phoned there.

"Nothing, Jack. I told the operators to send all your calls to my line."

"OK. I'm going to stay here for a while."

"You shouldn't be on your feet too long."

"I'm OK, Sally. I just want to wait here a while longer."

He walked back to the boathouse, his legs shaky and the pain in his ribs getting worse. He gave a small groan as he leaned on the railing again. Why hadn't he set up a more detailed plan with Seth? He should have met him at the airport, at least known where he was going to stay. He paced some more, his sense of foreboding growing deeper with every minute. Finally, when another hour had passed, wet, aching, and weary, he climbed into his car and drove back to the paper. He walked into the city room and Kevin Murphy took one look at him and shook his head.

"Jack, for God's sake, what are you doing here? You ought to be home in bed."

"I'll go home early, Kevin."

"Look, I'm doing what I can on the Hakim story. I think something may turn up. You take it easy for a while."

Jack turned and saw Sally sitting at her desk. When she saw him, she got up and walked over to him. She held a newspaper in her hands. He just had to take one look at her face to know that something was very, very wrong.

"Jack," she said.

She handed him the newspaper. "I picked up the desk's copy of the *Washington Post*," she said. "I just happened to look at the metro section."

He took the newspaper. The off-lead story in metro said, JUSTICE DEPARTMENT ATTORNEY A SUICIDE.

"No. Oh God no."

"They fished him out of the Potomac, near Haines Point. He left a note."

Jack felt his legs starting to buckle. She grabbed his arm and steadied him, and he walked back to his desk and sank into the chair. He read the story, shaking his head as he did so. "Somebody got to him. They killed him, Sally."

"It says in the story that Seth was severely ill not long ago. It says he was committed to Shepherd Pratt in Baltimore by his family after a mental breakdown. Did he say anything about that to you?"

"He said he'd been sick. Said he'd gotten himself tied up in knots over what was happening at Justice."

"The story says he left a note in his apartment, saying he couldn't go on any longer, things were looking too black. Jack, could he really have been mentally ill?"

"Sally, the man I talked to was as sane as anyone I've ever met."

"Jack, you look awful. I'm going to drive you home."

Back in the apartment she made him a cup of hot tea and tried to persuade him to get in bed; he didn't want to, despite his aching body. He sipped the tea and tried to sort things out.

"They must have known he was taking things out of the files. They must have been following him."

"Maybe the pressure just got to be too much. Maybe he broke down again."

"Then why those goons who jumped me last night? They were looking for something. Seth was the only one who knew what he was giving me."

"How could they have killed him without making anyone suspicious? The D.C. police said there were no signs of foul play."

"There must be a million ways of doing it—and what better victim than a guy with a history of mental problems. But Seth Chaffee was sane, Sally. I *know* that."

"I believe you."

"Sally, I pushed him. Hard. I made him try to get those memos. He was wavering, and I leaned on him. Said we had to have the smoking gun."

"Don't blame yourself."

"I wasn't thinking about Seth. About any danger. I only knew I had to have those memos so we could show everybody. It was for *me* I was doing it, Sally. Not for truth, justice, and the American way. For *me*."

"You were doing your job, Jack. You never thought he'd be hurt."

"I should have warned him to be careful. I know how Seth is. Was. He gets on to something, he does it all the way. I told him I needed the stuff fast, so he probably took chances he shouldn't have. A good man, and he's dead. Because of me."

"*Not* because of you. You didn't kill him."

"But he's dead. And there are no memos. Nothing to prove they ever existed."

"We know."

"Yes, we know. And we know that somebody killed Hakim Abdul. We know a lot of things. And what good does it do us?"

Seth Chaffee's funeral was held three days later, in the church in Hamilton where he had been christened. Jack saw Seth's younger brother, Paul, whom he had known at Harvard, at a small gathering after the funeral.

"How sick was Seth, really?" Jack asked him.

"He was real depressed for a long time. Then he had a break."

"A break?"

"Yes, he was psychotic for a time. Out of touch with reality."

"Paranoid?"

"Yes. He thought he was going to create world peace. He even had a series of shock treatments, but they didn't seem to help. Then, all of a sudden, he seemed much better. He was able to go back to work, he seemed OK. Then . . . this. It's a hell of a shock."

"He didn't send you anything before he died? Papers of any kind?"

"No. Seth and I sort of went our own ways. I was busy with work—I wish I had been able to be more help."

"I'm so sorry, Paul."

"So am I."

"Paul . . . Seth might have left some papers for me—something that might be important—in his apartment. Do you have a key?"

"No. I guess I'll have to get a locksmith to open up the place. But not for a while. I'm going on vacation for a couple of weeks. I need to get away. I'll deal with Seth's stuff when I get back."

As Jack and Sally drove back to Boston, he said, "We've got to find out where Seth put those memos. We can't let him die for nothing. They can't get away with it."

"If you were Seth, wouldn't you have made more than just one copy? Of something so important?"

"Yes."

"So we've got to get into his place. See for ourselves."

"You don't think it's been gone over with a fine tooth comb?"

"But maybe they missed something. Something that would give us a clue."

"How do we get in? Paul hasn't got a key."

"I'll think of something."

The next day, they were on a flight to Washington, under assumed names. Jack said to Sally, "What is that stuff you picked up this morning? And how does it get us into Seth's apartment?"

She pulled a plastic container out of her purse.

"Fleet's enema? I hate to tell you, Sally, the door is locked, it is not constipated."

"Remember the guy I did a feature on last month? The one who used to be into breaking and entering, but now he's a big security consultant for companies? I called him and asked if this theoretical person wanted to get into this theoretical locked apartment, what was the best way to do it?"

"I don't think I want to hear this."

"We ran through a couple of M.O.'s and this one seemed best. See? She pulled another Fleet's enema container out of her purse.

"This is making no sense."

"Two different chemicals. By themselves, harmless. Squirt them both into a lock, and the insides corrode. Takes three, maybe five minutes."

"You sure he knows what he's talking about?"

"He ought to. He was doing ten to twenty at Walpole when they paroled him. He only got caught because his cousin finked on him."

When they landed at National Airport, Jack rented a car and they drove to Seth Chaffee's apartment on Connecticut Avenue. They went inside, walked quickly into the elevator, and Sally pressed the button marked 12. The elevator door opened and they stepped out into a long, carpeted hallway. They walked along its length to 1205.

"It's a good time," she said. "Most people are probably at work." She pulled a pair of rubber gloves out of her purse and slipped them on.

"Oh, great. What if somebody comes by?"

"Act nonchalant. We'll pretend we're locksmiths."

"Locksmiths always open doors with Fleet's enemas."

Sally squirted the contents of one of her enema bottles into the lock. A peculiar smell wafted through the hallway.

"Oh Christ," he said. "It smells like rotten eggs."

"He didn't tell me about that."

"Shit, we're going to asphyxiate the whole building!" Sally

squirted the other chemical into the lock, and they stood in the corridor, inhaling noxious fumes, while Sally anxiously checked her watch.

"Five minutes. Let's try."

Jack pushed on the door handle. The door didn't budge. "So much for your Walpole Houdini."

"Give it another couple of minutes."

She rattled the door. "Jack, I think it's coming!"

He pushed, hard, on the door. "You're right, Sally, I can feel it giving. Maybe one good push—" he shoved hard and the door popped open. "Son of a gun!"

They walked quickly into the apartment and closed the door. The apartment was neat, with everything in order. There were no signs that anyone had been looking for anything in the rooms.

"I'll start in here," Sally said. "You take the bedroom."

"It's so strange. I can't believe he's dead. I was talking to him a week ago. Sometimes I think this is all a bad dream. That I'm going to wake up and find out none of this happened."

"It's not a dream, Jack."

He put his hand to his head and felt the stitches. "I know."

Sally methodically started to go through Seth Chaffee's books. She found nothing there, so she began to search under sofa cushions and in cabinets. Jack was throwing clothes out of the drawers. Then he pulled off the bedcovers. The mattress, he saw, had been neatly slit by a knife. *Bastards,* he thought. There was nothing inside the mattress. Then he went to Seth's closet, and began to go through the pockets of the clothes. Jack felt an acute sense of violation as he reached his hands into the pants pockets of Seth's flannel slacks. But then he thought of how Seth Chaffee had died, and searched even more intently. In the pocket of a suit jacket, he found an appointment book. He flipped through it and found nothing unusual—women's names, lists of things he was scheduled to do. Jack took the small black book and slipped it into his pocket, just in case.

He went through everything in the bedroom, to no avail. Sally had gone into the kitchen, after finding nothing in the living room. She rifled through the kitchenware, and examined the stove and the refrigerator. Finding nothing, she went out onto the small balcony that led off the living room. She noticed that each apartment on every floor had an identical balcony. Then her gaze wandered to the street below.

"Jack! There's a black-and-white down there!"

Jack walked onto the balcony. "It's empty. Could they be on their way up here?"

"That smell could have made somebody suspicious. Let me check the hall."

She went to the front door, opened it a crack, and peered out. As she did so, she saw, down the hallway, the elevator door sliding open.

"Jack, they're here! On the floor. They're checking doors!"

"Oh Christ, can we say we're relatives?"

"With the lock melted off and all the clothes on the floor?"

"We are up shit's creek!"

"The balcony," she said. "Come on!"

He followed her out on the balcony.

"Jack, we can climb down to the balcony below."

"We're twelve floors up! I get vertigo."

"You only get it if you look down. Watch!"

She threw her leg over the railing, gripped the bars near the bottom, and nimbly swung her legs down over the railing of the balcony below. She dropped easily onto the floor of the lower balcony.

"Come on, Jack, it's easy. You get up on horses!"

"There aren't any horses twelve stories high!" he hissed "And I have a fucking broken rib."

He looked down, and felt his stomach drop to his shoes. But he heard a sound by the door, so he swung his leg over the railing, gripped the bars, and tried to swing his legs over the railing below. He missed, and his feet swung out away from the rail, out into nothingness. He looked down and saw nothing but air and—far below—the street. Everything started to spin, and he closed his eyes and gripped the bar with a desperate strength.

Sally grabbed his legs. "I've got you, Jack!' She pulled his dangling legs back over the railing and he dropped down.

His legs buckled under him as he felt something solid under his feet, and he wound up sitting on the floor of the balcony.

"Jesus Christ!" He pulled himself to the middle of the small balcony. "Sally, if they even look down from that balcony up there, they're going to see us!"

"You're right," she said. "I will create a diversion!"

She stood up, peeled off her skirt, and then her blouse. She was wearing a matching leopard skin–pattern bra and bikini panties that left very little to the imagination. She grabbed a chaise lounge that was sitting by the door to the balcony and rolled it into a patch of sun right by the edge, and then hopped onto the chaise.

Jack sat huddled by the door, gripping his knees, his ribs aching fiercely. He tried to curl up into a small ball and make himself invisible, listening to the pounding of his heart, so loud it seemed it could be heard three blocks away. He heard the door slide open to the balcony above, and then footsteps over his head.

"Hello, miss," said a male voice.

"Hi theah!" said Sally, wiggling her body voluptuously and letting her voice slide into a syrupy drawl.

Oh God! he thought, *she's doing Scarlett O'Hara!*

"Miss, did you hear or see anything unusual up here in the last hour?"

"Oh, no, Officer, I didn't hear anything. I've just been out here for a few minutes trying to get a tan. I don't really tan, though. I just burn."

"Well, you look just fine without one," the voice said.

"Why thank you! Is anything the matter, Officer?"

"There's been a break-in up here, I'm afraid."

"Oh, my!" Sally sat up straight in the chaise. There wasn't much of the bra to start with, and the view from above, Jack thought, must really be spectacular. Despite his thumping heart, he began to notice another sensation. The science writer in him marveled at the persistence of the human species; his body was signaling *procreation,* while his mind was thinking five to ten at Lorton Reformatory.

"You're sure you didn't hear anything, Miss?" the voice asked.

"Oh no, Officer. Not a thing."

"Well," said the voice, "it really is a nice day."

"Oh yes. So nice and warm." She stretched luxuriously on the chaise.

"They say we may get some rain."

Jack waved at her, frantically. Then he drew his finger across his neck. The guy on the balcony was probably getting the same message from his private parts that Jack got as he gazed down on what she was almost wearing. One more wiggle and he'd be down in a flash, but a ménage à trois was not what he had in mind.

"Oh dear," Sally said, "I guess I'll have to be getting ready for work."

"Well," said the officer, "I guess it's back to work for me too."

They waited until the sounds of footsteps died away. Jack stood up and Sally hopped up off the chaise and started to put her clothes back on.

"What was that accent anyhow?" Jack asked as she buttoned her blouse. "Miss Honeydew Melon?"

"You want I should do Molly Goldberg? It worked, didn't it? He didn't notice you."

"With that panoramic view, he wouldn't have seen the Fifth Cavalry if it had been right beside me. Come on, it's time for another enema. I can't see myself rappeling down another eleven floors of balcony."

In a few minutes the door to the apartment below Seth's opened; the smell from the chemicals wasn't so bad in the open air. Jack pushed the balcony door ajar and Sally walked through it, a few steps ahead of him. He nearly bumped into her as he followed her into the living room. She had stopped dead in her tracks.

"Hurry up, Sally, we've got to get out of here."

She grabbed his arm so hard that he could feel her nails digging into him. Her eyes were riveted to a spot across the room. A large German Shepherd was standing by the side of the couch, its fangs bared, growling.

"It's a dog!" she said. "Oh God!"

"Don't make any sudden moves. Just stay still."

"I'm terrified of dogs. Look at him! He's slavering."

"No, he's not vicious. Dogs are territorial. He's just protecting his territory.'

"Nice puppy," she said.

"No good. He can tell you're scared." Jack moved a step closer to the dog. "Easy, boy. Easy now. Good dog." He extended his hand, palm down, fingers curled. The dog growled, but the hackles on the back of his neck did not rise.

"Good dog! Oh, you're a good dog. See, he's not going to attack." He kept moving toward the dog, talking softly and soothingly all the time. Finally, he was so close he could almost reach out and touch the dog. "Come on, fella," he said, putting his hand to the dog's nose, "let's get acquainted."

He let the dog sniff his hand for a while. Then the dog licked his hand, and Jack reached out and scratched it between the ears. "Oh, you're such a good dog."

"I don't believe it! You've got that monster eating out of your hand."

"There's a good dog. Oh, you want me to scratch you? Right there. You're a beautiful dog. I think he may be pedigreed. Look at his lines."

"Jack, we've got to get out of here. Tell Lassie goodbye."

"Lassie is a collie."

"I don't care if Lassie is a giraffe. Jack, come on!"

"Walk slowly to the door. No sudden moves."

She walked to the door, eyeing the dog suspiciously all the way. She stood by the door and Jack got up slowly.

"Goodbye, boy. You're a great dog!" The dog wagged its tail and followed Jack as he walked to the door. Jack ruffled the dog's fur again. "Oh, good dog!" he said, then stepped into the hall and closed the door behind him.

Sally looked at him in awe. "How did you do that?"

"It's all in knowing how." He saw that she was deathly pale and trembling all over. He put his arm around her and they walked down the hall together. "Didn't you ever have a dog?"

"No. A gerbil named Meyer. The cat ate him. Uncle Morty says dogs are anti-Semitic."

"Morty likes dogs."

"Only at the two-dollar window. Jack, let's stay over in Washington tonight. I'm not up to getting on a plane right now."

They walked out of the building to the rental car. Jack pulled away, and said, "Sally, I'm going to drive for a while. Just in case."

"You think someone could be following us?"

"I don't think so. Watch out the window to see if any car stays with us though. We ought to be careful. They could have had Seth's place staked out."

"I don't see anybody."

"I'll go through the park. I know it pretty well."

Jack drove the car through the hairpin turns of Rock Creek Park while Sally watched the traffic in the rearview mirror. He roared around the turns until he was sure no one was on their tail. Then he drove to the Jefferson Hotel—small, but elegant— and gave the car to the doorman for valet parking. They checked in as Mr. and Mrs. Jonathan Cabot. The clerk gave Jack a fisheye when he said no luggage, but a twenty-dollar bill made him smile and assured a room with a view. As soon as the door of the room closed behind them, they both felt a flood of relief that was so intense they felt almost giddy.

Sally flung herself down on the bed and said, "Oh, it's so

good to be here!" Jack laughed, the anxiety draining out of him like receding floodwater. The sense of safety the hotel room offered was spurious, he knew, but there was no denying it. He felt a surge of euphoria.

"Jack, are you hungry? Do you want to get something to eat?"

"No. Later."

"What do you want to do?"

"Know what I would really like?"

"What?"

"An encore of that little performance you put on for the capital's finest."

"Liked that, did you? Degenerate!"

"Lust in my heart."

She slipped off her skirt and blouse. "Hi theah!" she said. Then she caught a reflection of herself in the mirror by the wall, and she put her hand to her breasts, barely covered by the bra.

"Do you think they're overdone?" she asked. "Tacky?"

"Good heavens, no. What makes you think that?"

"I always wanted to look like those models in *Vogue*. You know . . . thin. Rich. Arrogant. It never worked. I always looked like the same thing, whatever I put on my back."

"What's that?"

"Remember the Italian starlets they used to import? With the boobs and the broken English? They stood around in rice paddies with their boobs hanging out. 'I am earth mother. We make love.' "

"I loved Italian starlets. After I outgrew baseball cards. Thirty-eight–twenty-six–thirty-eight was more important than Willie Mays' three-sixty-seven."

"I do look better than Willie Mays in a bra."

"But how are you in the outfield?"

"I never did it in the outfield."

"The rug is green. Imagine short left field in Fenway."

"I am earth mother. We make love." She unhooked the 38-C.

"Oh, not tacky. Not tacky at all." He nuzzled her breasts.

"We make love?"

"Oh yes," he said.

30

■

Know what we got, Jack?" Sally said, leaning back in the seat of the airliner. "*Bupkis.* Nothing. We need somebody inside. Maybe some of Seth's friends in the civil rights division? Somebody who could get those memos nailed down."

"I think those memos went into the burn bag or the shredder. And have we got a right to ask somebody else to do what Seth did? He helped us. And he's dead."

"We know that Elliott Andrews is involved. Maybe we can get somebody in the Washington bureau to start snooping around."

"Sally, nobody wants to have anything to do with us—or our story—right now."

"I know. But we've got to find a way to crack this thing. Did you get more on Neurodyne?"

"Yes. They're doing legitimate work out there, interfacing electronic hardware with the human body. They've got a contract with the Veteran's Administration to work on an advanced prosthesis, an artificial leg."

"So it's a perfect cover. And they have access to mental patients through Severn's connections with the State Hospital.

A perfect place to find forgotten people. Who no one will miss."

"Exactly. Very neat. Did you get any leads on Transition House?"

"Yeah, I've been working on it. I bought somebody."

"You 'bought' somebody?"

"An embezzler. I figured he'd be smart."

Jack shook his head. "Who is this guy?"

"He's in the furlough program at the house."

"How much do embezzlers go for these days on the open market?"

"A grand."

"What do you get for a thousand dollars?"

"He's going to go through the files for me, see if anyone else gets sent out to Neurodyne."

"Can you trust him?"

"A thousand bucks worth."

"Think he can do it?"

"He took Compumatics for a half million. He also does computer fraud. Jack, I only buy class criminals."

The flight attendant came by with the drink tray and Sally got a gin and tonic and Jack a glass of white wine. He sipped it slowly and said, "Sally, we have to be very careful from now on. They killed Seth. We know how far they'll go. If they knew how much we know about them—"

"Jack, they wouldn't kill reporters. Too risky."

"Nobody was suspicious when they found Seth's suicide note."

"But *we* haven't been in a mental hospital."

"But we have been rejected by our newspaper. Accused of faking a story. Our careers are not exactly golden at this moment. What would people say if they found us with the gas on and a suicide note right beside us?"

"I never thought of that."

"It's something we'd better think about."

"But they don't have to bump us off. We've messed up enough already. We're a laughingstock."

"Still, Seth talked to us. They know that."

"They don't know what we have on Neurodyne and Severn."

"No. That's why we have to be circumspect. We don't want to tip our hand. We're all alone right now, Sally. It's not like we have the paper behind us."

"We could just forget it. Say we gave it a shot."

"Could you do that?"

"No."

"Neither could I. Not after Seth. They're not going to get away with killing him. I swear to God they're not!"

She sipped her drink thoughtfully. "I still wonder, Jack, could he have cracked under the strain? Could he have found all this out, and it proved to be too much for him?"

"They beat me up. They slit the mattress in his apartment. He didn't break down, dammit, they murdered him."

"They must have panicked, Jack. To kill Hakim, a revolutionary, I could see them rationalizing that he's the enemy. But Seth? Jack, he was like *them.*"

"And we're like them, Sally."

"So we have to get them, first."

They were quiet then, and Sally rested her head, wearily, on Jack's shoulder. Lulled by the drone of the engines, she was asleep in a few minutes. He reached over and touched her hair, gently, careful not to wake her. The thought of anyone harming her made his throat constrict. He had tried not to dwell on the details of how Seth Chaffee died. He thought of the hug Seth had given him, and the way Seth had said, "You give me the courage to go on!" Now all that intensity was still and cold in the Hamilton earth. The bastards. The *bastards!*

He remembered that he still had Seth's appointment book in his pocket. He took it out and started to leaf through it. He turned to the page marking the day he and Seth had been scheduled to meet. He saw his name penciled in, in bold, firm letters, and the sight brought tears to his eyes. Oh Seth, dammit, why did you ever call me? Why didn't you just forget all of it and go out and find some nice firm in the private sector where you could do pro bono and not die until years and years from now surrounded by grandchildren? But Seth never could have done that. He was bred to a tradition that was perhaps part of a dying culture. As *he* was, Jack thought. A world where honor, and decency, stood for more than the rewards of mammon. A tradition perhaps honored more in the breech than otherwise, but valuable nonetheless. The old Yankee ideals seemed quaint and old-fashioned in the America of the early 1990s. But as often as Jack had railed about the parochial notions and elitism of his class, he was steeped, too, in its traditions of honesty and hard work and public service. Seth Chaffee was one of the best that tradition had to offer. And the men who killed him? Did they believe they were patriots? Undoubtedly. He thought of a line from Yeats: "The worst are full of passionate intensity."

Idly, he leafed through Seth's calendar. It was under "M" in the address section that he found it: a set of letters and numbers, neatly printed, one under the other.

He shook Sally's shoulder to awaken her. She had been sound asleep, and for an instant, her eyes registered confusion.

"Are we there yet?"

"No. Sally, look at this." She peered at the book, and read:

```
TK   24  18  26
HW   8   7   26  7   22
JL       21  25  18
EA   17  5   8   7   18  24  22
```

All in all, there were nine sets of numbers and letters in the book, lightly printed in pencil.

"Jack, would that be it?"

"Seth said there were no names in the memos, only initials."

"The numbers? What are they?"

"A code of some kind, I think."

"It would be a simple one," she said. "Why would he do anything complicated? Just enough so that anybody who happened to look at the book wouldn't know at a glance what it was. Try 'A' equals one."

They tried that simple code and it didn't work.

"Backwards? Z is one?" he said.

They tried the numbers this way, with Jack writing on the back of an envelope from his pocket.

"T.K.—CIA," he said.

"That's it! We got it!"

"And this one. H.W.—State."

"It's Seth's list! The names."

"Yes," he said. "Now we won't be shooting in the dark. We'll know who they are. Some of them, anyway."

"Jack, it's the break we need. It's the crack in the dike!"

When they landed at Logan, Jack made a phone call. Robert Ames's secretary said yes, he would see them, at two. They had, in fact, been on the editor's mind that day, though Jack and Sally could not know that. His copy of the *Columbia Journalism Re-*

view had arrived that morning, ruining what had been a fine breakfast. The item was in the "Darts and Laurels" section.

Dart: To the Boston World Herald, *for jumping the gun on what turned out to be an unsubstantiated story.*

The review then went on to lay out the details of the Hakim Abdul episode. And then, there was the conversation with Ben Bradlee, editor emeritus of the *Washington Post*. Both men were on the Freedom of Information Committee of the newspaper editors' association. Ben had called, ostensibly to chat about a committee matter, and as always he had been witty and charming. But he hadn't been able to resist getting in a few digs about the Hakim case, and Bob Ames, trying not to let the annoyance show in his voice, had to swallow it.

So, when Jack and Sally were ushered into his office, he was in no mood to roll out the welcome mat. He was courteous, of course, and listened as they spun a tale that seemed to him rather fantastic. He had a tough budget meeting coming up, which made him a bit impatient with these two young staffers. He could understand their eagerness to find a real story in this mess, of course. He had been sucker-punched once as a young reporter, and he knew how intense the thirst for vindication could be.

Jack Aiken handed him a typed list with initials and numbers on it.

"This is it. Seth Chaffee's list."

Bob Ames sighed and sat down on the corner of his desk. "Look, I know this has been rough on you."

"This isn't a personal thing," Sally told him. "We are right on top of what could be the biggest story of the decade."

"All right," Ames said, "let's look at what we've got here. There isn't a credible source in your whole package. Let's start with Seth Chaffee."

"He had a solid record in the civil rights division," Jack said. "Check with Dershowitz at Harvard. He'll tell you. Seth worked on the LA busing case—"

"He was a man who was getting shock treatments in a mental hospital six months ago."

"But he was as sane as you and I when I talked to him."

"Was he ever paranoid? Did he ever think people were out to get him?"

"Well, yes, when he was sick, but not when he talked to me."

"He wasn't dreaming this up," Sally said. "It all came from memos he saw in the Justice Department files."

"You *saw* those memos?"

"No," Jack said, "but Seth was coming to Boston the night he died to give them to me."

Bob Ames looked down at the typed list Jack had given him.

"Look at this stuff! Letters. Numbers. Codes. A secret cabal. Do you know what this is? This is just like the stuff they found John Hinckley had written before he shot Reagan. This is classic paranoia. Conspiracies. Plots. The product of a disturbed mind."

"If you'd seen him, talked to him—"

"I'm sure he could appear quite rational. But this man had been a mental patient. Do you have any idea of how many calls and letters I get from people who tell me they know about government takeovers or invasions from Mars?"

"But this dovetailed with what we'd been hearing. About a behavior unit!" Sally said.

"Of course!" Ames barked. "Where do you think he got the idea? It's a classic symptom of paranoid behavior. Paranoids build up elaborate systems from small clues. They read something. Hear something on the radio. They build up the most complex theories in their heads."

"What about the goons who beat me up in the parking lot?"

"Come on, Jack, you were the third person in six months to get robbed out there."

"They didn't take my wallet. They took my briefcase!"

"Because a lot of people keep valuables in a briefcase. You think just because they screwed up, it means something sinister? We've got the dumbest white crooks in this town that you can find anywhere."

"What about Brady?" Sally said. "The guy who dropped dead in the middle of a holdup. He had the marks of an electrode implant."

"You saw them?"

"No. But my brother-in-law did, and he interned in neurosurgery."

"But the medical examiner said he died of a heart attack. Is he lying?"

"Yes. I think so."

"And lying about Hakim Abdul."

"Yes."

"The FBI pathologist. He was lying too?"

"A coverup," Jack said. "There's an FBI name on that list."

"These electrode implants," Ames said, "what was that supposed to be about?"

"A tracking system," Jack said. "Electronic surveillance through the use of surgery and computer technology." He realized, as he said it, how absurd this must seem to anyone hearing it for the first time.

"You got this idea from a professor. And he couldn't tell you where any of this was going on. *If* it was going on."

"Yes, but—"

"Science fiction. Make a good movie of the week."

"Why did the prostitute have her head sawed off, if not to disguise brain surgery?" Sally asked.

"What about the psycho we had last year who cut prostitutes' feet and hands off? Come on, Sally, it's Jack the Ripper. Sexual mutilation. Not that unusual. As for this mysterious right-wing doctor of yours—he operated on some guy's brain? So what? He's a neurosurgeon. It's what he does for a living."

"He was at the morgue the night Brady was killed."

"You told me he was this man's work sponsor. He probably had to identify the body."

"Severn keeps popping up in all of this," Jack said. "Hakim got his program stopped in Jersey."

"But you have no later connection between Severn and Hakim Abdul. Except the one leaked from the examiner's office. Did Seth Chaffee mention Severn?"

"No, but—" Sally bit her lip in frustration. It all sounded so crazy; the editor was taking their story apart bit by bit, and she couldn't think of a way to make it all sound convincing.

"By the way," Ames said, "how did you get Seth Chaffee's notebook anyhow?"

Sally and Jack looked at each other. He decided that honesty was the best policy.

"I got it from his apartment."

"I see. And how did you get in?"

"We broke in."

Robert Ames slammed his fist down on the desk in anger.

"Goddamn it! Haven't the two of you caused enough trouble already?"

"You printed the Pentagon Papers," Sally said. "They were stolen."

"That was different. My reporters didn't steal them."

"But Dan Ellsberg did," Jack said. "That's a pretty fine line."

"Just for a minute," Sally said, "please, just for a minute, assume that everything we've got is true. Don't you see what it adds up to?"

"Put yourself in my place, Sally. What have you given me? The ravings of a mental patient who committed suicide. A story about the murder of a black leader that was completely discredited—and humiliated this newspaper. Secondhand reports about people who may have had electrodes in their heads. Prostitute murders. A right-wing doctor who, as far as I can tell, has done nothing—I repeat *nothing*—out of the ordinary. His politics are rotten, but that doesn't make him part of a conspiracy. You haven't given me one piece of solid evidence, not one, that there's a story here."

"I know it sounds crazy. But Watergate started with a little book with initials in it," Jack said.

"There are just too many connections here, too many things that fit, that can't just be coincidence," Sally argued.

Robert Ames sighed, loudly. "What I see is two young reporters—good reporters, I might add—who got burned because of a man who has played the political game with consummate skill in this town for years. You want this to be a story. You want it so bad you can taste it. But right now, you haven't got one. Bring me some real evidence, and I'll listen."

"Will you at least get the Washington bureau to help us out? Get a line on who these people might be, what their politics are?"

"I'm understaffed by two in the bureau," Robert Ames said. "I've got a hiring freeze to buck and Congressional elections will be coming up in the fall. I'm not sending my people off to check out the conspiracy theories of some poor sick young man."

"At least let us keep on the story full time," Sally said. "We'll get you the evidence you want."

"I can't afford to lose you two on other stories right now."

"We can't back off this story," Jack said. "A good friend of mine was murdered. I know that."

"You're going to be on call to your regular editors. You'll

be handling assignments. Anything you do on this so-called story will have to be worked in. And that's generous on my part. I could say hands off completely. I'm not doing that. But I want a few things understood. You will not steal anything. You will not break into anyplace. You will not use fake identities. Everything is going to be on the up-and-up. Nothing will go into print unless I can see incontrovertible evidence. Not secondhand. Not your hunches. There will be a two-source rule on anything you get, and those sources will have to be nailed down, solid. Do you understand that?"

They nodded.

"Everybody makes mistakes. I won't say that I'll forget about the Hakim affair. But you can erase it—if you keep your noses clean. But if either one of you embarrasses the paper once more, that's it. I want that understood."

In the cafeteria later, Sally and Jack swilled down coffee and tried to second-guess their performance.

"God, we fucked it up," Sally said. "I thought he'd be so excited by what we found, I didn't think of how to present it."

"Would that have helped? I can't blame Ames. He's right. We still don't have anything that's the smoking gun. He's still convinced we were had by Rittenhouse."

"But he didn't order us off the story. At least we got that."

"The first thing we have to do is I.D. these guys," Jack said.

"Sure, but then what? How do we nail them? We can hardly waltz into their offices and say 'Any comment on the murders and the brain implants?' "

"I know where we can get help, now."

"Where?"

"Uncle Robert."

"Your uncle? You think he would help? Or would he just say what Bob Ames said—that we got suckered and our imaginations are working overtime."

"I think he'd listen to me. He knows I don't go off half-cocked."

"He doesn't know that about me."

"He's been around, Sally. He was in OSS when he was a young man. He knows the kinds of things that can go on in government. I wouldn't go to him if we had a choice—I've never liked trading on his connections—but we need them now."

"Jack, I think there's something I ought to tell you."

"Tell me in the car. I'll call Uncle Robert and let him know we're on the way."

It was getting dark when Jack gunned the BMW out of the *World Herald* parking lot and onto the expressway heading north. As they left the skyline of Boston—its lights blinking on—behind them, Jack said to her. "What was it you wanted to tell me?"

She took a deep breath and told him the whole story of her lunch with Uncle Robert at the Harvard club, his position and her response.

"I promised him I wouldn't tell you," she said. "I kept my word, but now—well, that's it. I just thought you ought to know, now."

He was silent for a long time. She could not gauge his reaction.

"Jack?"

"It's so typical of my uncle. He's so used to running things, he thinks he's got some kind of divine right."

She looked at him; his jaw was clenched, tightly. She wondered if she had done the right thing. Maybe now was exactly the wrong time for a strain between Jack and his uncle.

Suddenly, Jack started to chuckle. "God, what a scene. He really asked you about your intentions?"

"Yeah. He did."

"What in the hell century does he think he's in?"

"Late nineteenth, I'd say."

"You should have told him to stuff it."

"He was really very nice about it, in his way. Besides, I think it's sort of hard to tell Robert Forbes Aiken to stuff it."

"Not many people have tried." He chuckled again. "The old fox. I didn't know what a manipulative bastard he could be."

"You're not mad at him?"

"Pissed as hell, but you have to admire his *chutzpah*. You should have told me. I'd have straightened him out. He always tries to run my life. I never let him do it."

"Well, I did give my word. I don't know why. I guess he sort of made me feel like I'd be behaving like lower-class swine if I didn't."

"Uncle Robert could make the Sultan of Oman feel like lower-class swine. He's good at it."

It was nearly an hour's drive to Robert Aiken's house on

the North Shore, an old stone Tudor very much like the one Jack's mother lived in. When they arrived, Jack's uncle greeted them cordially at the door and ushered them in. He took Sally's raincoat as she slipped it from her shoulders. He looked at her quizzically—he probably assumed this was going to be *Gunfight At the OK Corral* over his meddling in Jack's love life, she thought—but he was as gracious as if he were greeting the Queen of England.

Jack told his uncle that he had a very serious issue to discuss with him. Robert Aiken invited them to take a seat in the living room, and poured glasses of very good sherry. Nothing was so important that the creature comforts should be ignored.

He listened intently as Jack outlined the whole story. He drew in his breath, sharply, when Jack described how Seth Chaffee died. That seemed to disturb him especially. Not surprising, Sally thought. *One of our own.*

"So you don't think Seth Chaffee was just paranoid?" he said.

"I'd bet my life on his sanity, Uncle Robert. I knew Seth since Harvard. Sure, he'd had a breakdown, but he had recovered. He was as sane as you and I."

"What do you want me to do?"

"We're in a tough spot," Sally said. "They're probably keeping an eye on us. They know Jack talked to Seth. That's why he was killed. But they also know we don't have the memos. If we did, we'd have gone public."

"I don't think they have any idea that we know about Neurodyne," Jack explained. "So they think their behavior unit is secure. But if we start bird-dogging the guys on this list, they'll know we're on to them. They'll close up shop—open it somewhere else where we'll never find them."

"You know who these men are?"

"Before we came out here, we did a quick check in Federal directories," Sally said. "We think we know who some are."

"We need to know more about them," Jack told his uncle. "How much power do they have? What are their politics? Could the president be involved?"

"Elliott Andrews is the big cheese. The Attorney General. How high up does this go?"

"Elliott Andrews has been a fine public servant," Robert Aiken said.

"I've been researching him," Jack said. "He used to be middle of the road. Rockefeller-type Republican. But he's been hanging out with the hardliners in recent years. Guys who are into some wiggy stuff."

"Wiggy?"

"Slang. Means weird. Nuke freaks. Guys who talk about the American Empire. See commies behind every bush."

"You are certain that this behavior unit not only exists, but it is being used to get around restrictions on human research?"

"We believe that's what's happening, yes."

Robert Aiken frowned, and took a slow sip of sherry. "These are very serious charges," he said. "Something like this could bring down a government."

"Very serious, Uncle Robert. People have been murdered to protect this unit. If certain people knew what Sally and I have, we'd probably be among them."

"Good God!" Robert Aiken said.

"We have no allies," Sally said. "Nobody wants to touch this story. We're suspect. We need the help of someone whose reputation is beyond reproach."

"I find this very disturbing," Robert Aiken said. "That a young man like Seth Chaffee could have been murdered in cold blood—"

"He was my friend, Uncle Robert. He was one of the most decent human beings I ever knew. Somebody has got to pay. For Seth. And the others."

Robert Aiken frowned, and stared intently into his glass of wine. For a long minute, he said nothing.

"Will you help us, Uncle Robert?" Jack asked. Sally heard just the touch of a tremor in his voice. He really was their last hope.

"Yes," Robert Aiken said, "of course I'll help you."

Sally's saw the tension slide out of Jack's jaw. The cold knot in her own stomach seemed to unclench, slightly.

"The first thing I will do is to go to people I trust implicitly. To find out for myself the facts of the matter."

"Be careful," Jack warned him. "We have no idea how deep and wide this thing goes."

"I will be extremely circumspect. But because of that, it may take some time."

"Take the time you need. This has to be done right. My fear

is that they'll crawl back into the woodwork and we'll never find them," Jack said.

"I'll be in touch with you," Jack's uncle told him. "As soon as I have something to report."

Riding home in the BMW, Sally let out a long sigh and leaned on Jack's shoulder. "For the first time, Jack, I feel that we've really got somebody on our side."

"I never asked for anything before," Jack said. "I tried to ignore all those connections of his. Now they'll save our ass."

"Yes. People can't ignore *him*, the way they did us. In the hallway, I looked at the pictures. Every president since Eisenhower had his arm around him."

"Uncle Robert wasn't partisan. When a man became the president, he stopped being Republican or Democrat, as far as Uncle Robert was concerned. He was Mr. President."

"You're lucky to have relatives like that. What could Uncle Morty do for us?"

"Get us a couple of secondhand guard dogs. Cheap."

"Great. They could trample the bad guys to death—if they happened to be standing in front of a mechanical rabbit."

"I think we've turned the corner, Sally. He knew we were telling the truth. He knew it was going on. I could see it in his face."

"Oh God, it was *so* good not to be written off as kooks, or dumb reporters who got suckered."

"You can say that again."

"All of a sudden, I feel safe, Jack. I haven't felt like that in a while. It's a good feeling."

31

■

"Low are you holding up?" Mary Ellen asked Sally, noticing that her friend's pale skin seemed even more translucent than normal, and dark shadows were visible beneath her eyes.

"Not great. But things are looking up."

"Maybe you need to get away for a little while, take a vacation."

"Not now. We've got a solid lead, M.E. We're going to crack this thing!"

"A few days at the Cape. How could that hurt?"

"No, not with this story heating up again!"

"How about you and Jack. How are things?"

"We're working on it together."

"I don't mean the story. Has Mr. North Shore said anything about marriage yet?"

"We've been so involved with this whole mess we haven't had time to think about that."

"You know, this is a perfect time for his family to turn the screws—'She's bad news, make the break now!' "

"Jack wouldn't do that."

"Not right away, no."

"You like him. You know he's not the kind of guy who'll cut and run."

"I like *him*. It's his class that worries me. When number one son got Bridget the upstairs maid pregnant, they didn't call the priest."

"I'm not Bridget. And I'm *not* pregnant."

"*You* don't think you're Bridget—but Uncle Robert does."

"I'm not sleeping with Uncle Robert."

"It just makes me antsy that he's lurking around out there, trying to break you two up."

"He won't succeed."

"He'll keep chipping away. Sally, the man influences presidents, you think he won't know how to get to Jack? He'll use all that old-school-tie-we-go-back-to-the-*Mayflower*-class-loyalty shit. He's probably got Muffy bound and gagged in the back seat of his Lincoln Town Car, just keeping her on ice."

"Miki is engaged to somebody else," Sally said. "I saw her picture in the society section of the paper the other day, at some charity ball. She *is* gorgeous. She never goes to the bathroom or gets cellulite."

"I hate her. And I don't even know her."

"She has a big rock on her finger from her new beau. I gather that Jack gave her a nice little number too. Some women attract diamonds."

"Why hasn't he given you one?" M.E. asked.

"I don't care about jewelry."

"It's not that. Jack's a traditional man. He gets married. He gives diamond engagement rings. When he's serious."

"Jack's serious about me."

"I think he is, but why hasn't he made a commitment?" Mary Ellen noticed that Sally had eaten hardly a bite of her steak. "Eat that, you're getting too thin."

"Oh, all right," Sally said, taking an unenthusiastic nibble.

"Back to Jack. And commitment. This is not a guy who sleeps around. Why hasn't he made some kind of gesture? His frat pin. An I.D. bracelet with your name on it. A few measly stocks and bonds?"

"We're very different. You don't rush into these things."

"I am not talking 'rush.' I am talking little baby steps."

"God, Mary Ellen, you are turning into a *yenta*."

"I just don't want him—or his family—thinking of you as

the upstairs maid. A smart, educated upstairs maid, but still the hired help."

"Uncle Robert is never going to welcome me with open arms."

"Well, you ought to fight him."

"Right now, we need him."

"After right now."

"He's like a father to Jack. I don't want to destroy that relationship."

Mary Ellen sighed. "I remember when you were ten, always dragging home stray cats. Feeling sorry for them. Sally, Uncle Robert is not some scruffy tabby cat. Neither is Jack. How about looking out for number one for a change?"

"I'm not great at that, M.E."

Mary Ellen sighed. "So tell me something I don't know."

As Mary Ellen and Sally were talking, Robert Forbes Aiken was pacing back and forth in his study. He had already spent several sleepless nights. He turned on his heel and said, to no one in particular, "Damn Richard Nixon!"

It had been Nixon's fault. A man of no class, no breeding. It would always tell. His instincts on foreign policy had often been good, but he had tolerated—no, encouraged—the scum who were always attracted by the scent of power. It was the job of a leader to keep them in their place. Nixon hadn't done that. The vermin had come out of the woodwork and public trust in the executive branch, and in the intelligence community, had been destroyed. Reagan, another damn Californian, had let a lieutenant colonel run his own foreign policy, had let the intelligence community once again be tarred with crazy ex-generals and right-wing old ladies from California and unreliable Latins. No government could operate without effective intelligence, but it was Nixon who first opened the door so that the radicals could start to dismember what had once been a proud and honorable arm of government. It got worse after Iran-Contra. Now there were magazines publishing names of agents and Freedom of Information suits cutting into the guts of intelligence operations. None of this would have happened if the men at the top had set the tone.

Damn Richard Nixon!

Robert Aiken reached over to the wall and took down a

framed photograph that had been hanging there. It was one his nephew had seen many times over the years, but he had forgotten, or taken little notice. But if Jack Aiken had looked closely at that picture tonight, it would have given him pause.

The photograph, still bright and glossy under the glass despite its age, was of two very young, slender men in Army khakis, their arms thrown around each other's shoulders in a brotherly fashion, smiling at the camera. One was Robert Forbes Aiken, with a head of sandy hair that had long since turned silver. The other man was an inch taller, well-built, with broad, well-muscled shoulders and a torso that tapered down to a narrow waist. The inscription read, "To my best friend Bob. With friendship and my deepest respect. Elliott."

Robert Aiken and Elliott Andrews had traveled different paths since they served together in the OSS. Andrews had gone into the private practice of law, made a considerable fortune in the Southwest, and come into government with the new administration. But the two men had maintained their friendship over the years, although it had been a long time after the war before they got in touch. Only after Robert Aiken was safely back in Boston, married, surrounded once again by the world that had nurtured him, did he dare make contact. The old, easy friendship returned. Neither man probed beneath its surface.

But they found their paths crossing, often. They were the kind of men who were always tapped for weighty assignments in the public arena, the kind of men who, in truth, *were* government. They outlasted presidents, they transcended political parties. They knew the secrets and they kept them. Perhaps they could be forgiven for thinking, at times, that theirs was something of a divine right to rule. They did it so well.

Robert Aiken picked up the phone.

He had been surprised, but not overly so, when Elliott Andrews had come to his Watergate suite one evening. If their situation had been reversed, it was he who would have gone to Elliott. Andrews was a man of character; Robert Aiken had learned, in the OSS, that the most important decision was choosing the right men. Not the wild-eyed ones, who saw conspiracies behind every rock, who had no traditions to cling to; and not the Hamlets, who could never make the hard decisions that had to be made, who were so paralyzed by the moral ambiguities that they were never able to act. In the OSS Elliott Andrews had sent men to their deaths, but only in the service of a noble end. Yes, innocent people sometimes suffered, but only when that could not be helped. You limited the damage to the degree that it was humanly possible.

The intelligence that Elliott Andrews had laid out, on the coffee table in that Watergate suite, had been especially disturbing. Soviet gains in the areas of mind control were progressing at a rapid rate. With this technology, the KGB could keep track of its agents at all times. Not only could they be tracked by computer, but devices inside their heads could be the instruments of their own destruction. Who could be persuaded to turn over if there was a time bomb in their brains? Even more chilling was the possibility that with their new technology the Soviets could create a programmed agent, unaware of the fact that he was controlled, who could slip past all the safeguards of U.S. intelligence. The outer parameters of this research were unknown. Yes, it all sounded like science fiction, but, as Elliott Andrews reminded him, so in 1942 did the idea of a single bomb, powerful enough to blow a city apart. What was necessary was a measured but effective response.

The plan that Andrews outlined was simple and possible. A small unit, knowledge of which was to be limited to a few trustworthy men high in government. The president would not know. There had to be complete deniability. Others would take the fall if the worst happened. That was the way it worked.

The scientific personnel would have topnotch medical credentials. You had to watch some of these scientific types, they could get carried away. Doctors had worked in the Nazi death camps.

The subjects were to be carefully chosen on the basis of expendability. No dumb tricks like slipping LSD into the brandy of a civilian employee. How in God's name had anyone at the CIA been so stupid?

No, subjects were to be found only among hardened felons, mental patients for whom the prospects for recovery were dismal, and prostitutes, especially those who were already wasting away as drug addicts. People for whom the promise of a happy, productive life had already slipped away. They were to be treated in the most humane way, given good medical care, fed and clothed well, housed in a comfortable dormlike environment. Termination would be ordered only when absolutely necessary;

if memory-blocking drugs could be perfected, not at all. Return to a hospital setting, where they would be cared for until they died, was the best outcome. That was of course not always possible. Numbers of subjects would be limited. One did not need masses of people for this research, just a selected few. Yes, lives would be lost, but how did those lives compute in the arithmetic of the cold truth of world politics? Against the devastating impact on American intelligence that Soviet advances would surely mean?

Robert Aiken frowned, the phone still in his hand. Was it possible that he had misread Elliott Andrews? What was the word that Jack had used? *Wiggy?* He should perhaps have been more skeptical, Robert Aiken thought. Andrews had been so convincing about the impact of this technology. Was the situation really as bad as Elliott had pictured it? Something else he had learned in OSS. Decisions made on the basis of flawed intelligence, from people whose advocacy of a cause blurred their ability to be objective, were almost always failed decisions.

Robert Aiken mentally cursed himself for being sloppy. He had been distracted, by the press of his assignments, and that had been a bad mistake. He had been in Paris when the decision had been made by the unit's operators to use it to interrogate Hakim Abdul. God, what a blunder! Using a covert, narrowly focused research operation to deal with a highly visible political dissident was not only stupid, it was morally wrong. He had said so at the time, but of course it was too late. It gave the KGB the ultimate compliment, to become just like them. And, of course, when the man died under interrogation, the unit's operators were given no choice but to make his death seem like an overdose. The medical examiner's close—one might say slavish—connection to the Bureau made that possible. What a dreadful piece of bad luck that one of the reporters who had stumbled on the story had been Jack.

And there had been Seth Chaffee. Good God, what a mess!

Incredible bad luck. But it happened. Sometimes it did. Murphy's Law. When it did, in intelligence, you moved quickly to cut your losses, cover your tracks. You were a professional.

He dialed a number in Alexandria, Virginia. A male voice answered the phone.

"Hello, Elliott," Bob Aiken said.

"Bob. How are you?"

"Is this a secure line?"

"Yes. You can speak freely."

"We're hemorrhaging, Elliott. Time to apply the tourniquet."

"Bob, there's no need to panic. We had a close call, but we're clear. The book on Hakim Abdul is closed. A newspaper got suckered by an old enemy. It flies. As time passes, the story will only be a memory. A curiosity."

"No, Elliott, it doesn't fly. There is something you never told me. Seth Chaffee found memos. And he was not a suicide."

There was a silence on the other end of the line: finally Elliott Andrews spoke.

"I deliberately did not tell you, Bob. I made the decision on Seth Chaffee myself. Only me. If this ever came to light, Bob, I wanted you to have complete deniability. I swear to God, my old friend, that's why I didn't tell you."

"Elliott, there must have been another way! He was a young man, with a brilliant career ahead of him!"

"There was no other way. He knew about the unit. He had the memos. He was very close to putting it all together. Bob, I agonized over it. But in the end, there was no other way."

"Elliott, the unit is finished. The memos have surfaced."

There was another silence on the line.

"Your nephew?"

"Yes. He not only has names, he knows the exact location of the unit. At least he thinks he does, and he's right."

"My God! He has the memos!"

"No. But he has Seth Chaffee's notes on them. How fast can you dismantle the unit?"

There was another silence. "A week. We can get everything down in a week. But your nephew, Bob, what will he do?"

"He has no solid evidence. His editor dismissed Seth's notes as the ravings of a madman. When the unit has been aborted, there is no story. He goes on to other things."

"There is still time to get out clean."

"Yes. I can tell him my investigation came up dry. Perhaps it would be possible to get him into Neurodyne. To show him there was never anything there but a normal bioresearch facility."

"Will he believe that?"

"Probably not. But the trail will be cold. Leading nowhere."

"I see."

"Elliott, he is like a son to me. You understand that."

"Of course. My God, Bob, of course I understand that!"

"All the records must be burned."

"Yes, Bob. We could all be destroyed."

"The unit will vanish without a trace," Robert Aiken said. " 'Snow upon the desert's dusty face.' "

Elliott Andrews chuckled. "Like the old days."

"Yes. Like the old days."

"Bob—can you believe how long ago that was? It seems like yesterday."

"We've grown old, Elliott. We didn't think we ever would."

"No. Not us."

"Please give my love to Milly," Bob Aiken said. "I think of her often."

"And she of you. And Bob, I will see that things are taken care of."

"I trust you will, Elliott. Your word is all I need."

The Attorney General hung up the phone. A memory hovered in his mind, one he had not thought of for a very long time. A night in the desert; the stars had been so brilliant, stabbing points of light in the dark North African sky. Two young men in their sexual prime, away from all the compass points of civilization and home, engaged in a struggle that they were certain would change the face of the globe forever. Oh, how bright the stars were. He could see them yet, so many of them, so dazzling. How it had happened, exactly, he could not recall. Nothing had been so intense for him, before or since. He could still feel the sand beneath his knees, the feel of another body in his hands that was a mirror image of his own. It was two souls, not merely bodies, blending in utter silence on a star-blurred night in a place so alien as to be another planet.

It had never happened again. They had never spoken of it, not in all the years since. Robert Aiken left soon afterwards, running, Elliott Andrews thought, from things inside himself he could not explain or comprehend.

The Attorney General thought of his wife, Milly. She had been loyal, always loyal, for forty years. Recovering from cancer surgery but still frail, she had moved to Washington to spend more time with him. Leaving her privileged world of shopping and golf and cultural events in Arizona was hard for her, but she did not complain. But she could shatter, so easily. His two sons, both lawyers now, loved him and were a bit in awe of him still. He liked that.

He picked up the telephone and dialed a number. He spoke for a moment in low tones to the person on the other end of the line. Then he listened and, when he spoke again, for the first time a tinge of panic vibrated in his voice.

"I can't go to jail. I'm not young anymore. The scandal would kill my wife!"

The voice on the other end of the line was calm. Elliott Andrews listened, quietly.

"Yes," he said, "yes, I agree." He hung up the phone.

He sat staring into space for a minute. Then he opened a drawer and took out a photograph. It was the same one that hung on the wall in Robert Aiken's study.

Oh, God, was he ever so young? So idealistic? They were as immortal as the sun, as the desert winds, and as strong. They believed that *they* would never make compromises, never betray the best that was in them, never grow old and sour. So young. All of life stretching out before them. And one desert night, wartime, something that would never happen again.

He remembered. And he buried his head in his hands.

32

■

I'm beginning to like Dirty Doctor David," Jack said. He was stretched out on the bed, nude, and Sally, also naked, was lying on top of him, absently playing with a lock of his hair.

"And we're only on page eighteen," she said. She put her head down on his chest. "Am I hurting your rib?"

"A little, but don't go away," he said. "I used to have a Golden Retriever who used to lie on me like this. But he didn't turn me on the way you do."

"I should hope not, Jack. Even Dirty Doctor David would say that's a no-no."

"I think Dirty Doctor David didn't get enough to eat as a kid," he told her. "He's very oral-fixated, have you noticed?"

"He does think shoving veggies in every available orifice is lots of fun, which I, personally, find repulsive."

"You like other things in your orifices."

"That is different." She caressed him, teasingly. "This is not a carrot."

"Thank God."

"Then you'd only be a turn-on for Bugs Bunny." She tickled him. "Eh, what's up, Doc?"

"*Stop* that!"

She giggled.

"You're going to get me turned on again, and then we'll never get to work."

"I'll put on my black panties and say filthy words in your ear."

He moaned. And came erect.

"I haven't even said them yet."

"Say them."

"Do you know what I want you to do to me?" She whispered in his ear.

"Oh God!" he said.

She smiled and slowly moved her lips down his body. He moaned again, and forgot all about work.

Afterwards, while they were showering, he said to her, "I never had the nerve to ask a woman to talk dirty before. I felt like a prevert."

"You are a *prevert*, Jack."

"I could never say any of those words when I was a kid. I'd get my mouth washed out with soap."

"That's why you like them now."

"Today's kids don't get their mouths washed out with soap." He gently soaped her back.

"No. Today, they call each other motherfucker while they're coloring in preschool."

"I think they'll miss something. The excitement of forbidden words."

"Maybe *clean* words will turn them on. Golly willickers. Oh heck."

"Oh, babe, lay some more filth on me!"

"Oh, *darn* it. Gee whiz!"

"Gosh, I'm getting in the mood to perform an act of sexual congress with you."

"Congress me! Congress me!"

He laughed and kissed her damp mouth. "Oh, Sally, you make me laugh. No one ever made me laugh the way you do. I love you," he said. "In all this mess we're in, that's the one good thing."

"I love you too, Jack."

"Marry me."

She stopped rinsing herself off and looked at him. "Do you mean that?"

"Yeah. I do."

She was quiet for a minute. "There are a lot of things we haven't talked about."

"I know."

"I kid around a lot—about what I am. But it means a lot to me. I'm not very religious, but I—"

He put his fingers to her lips. "I don't want to change you."

"What about children? I'd like to have children."

"Lots of people work it out. They'd be Jewish Yankees. A good combination."

"I have a strong feeling about—well, Jews have been around for five thousand years. I couldn't see my kids as Unitarians."

"I wasn't raised as much of anything. As far as religion went. Church a couple of times a year. I like what I've seen of Judaism. I'd be willing to raise the kids in it, then, when they're grown, let them choose whatever they want."

"Uncle Robert made it very clear he'd oppose your marrying me."

"My uncle will come around. He's a pragmatist. Once he sees that he can't change my mind—or scare you off—he'll come around. So will my mother. I'm the only son she's got."

"You have been thinking about this, haven't you?"

"Yes. I have."

"My mother really likes you. Uncle Morty says for a *goy,* you're a *mensch.*"

"Morty likes me because I bring him luck. We win more on my hunches than on his dog *putz* theory."

"If it was up to Morty, we'd get married at the two-dollar window."

"A honeymoon in Wonderland. That would be a first for the Forbeses and the Aikenses."

The phone rang, and Sally wrapped the damp towel around her and walked to the phone.

"Hello. Yes? You have something? Great." She grabbed a pencil from the night table. "William Corrin, age thirty-two, address—that's in the South End? Right. OK. Very good work. What? Oh yeah, I'll have the check for you Thursday. Same place, four o'clock." She hung up the phone. "Jackpot!"

"Our embezzler?"

"Yep. He says one of the guys who went to Neurodyne from Transition House is out on furlough. He went out there three weeks ago. Now he's living in a rooming house."

"That's enough time for an implant."

"Yes. Oh, Jack, things are finally starting to come our way. Your uncle checking the Washington end of the story, and now maybe we can get one of the actual subjects to talk to us."

The address Sally had been given turned out to be a down-at-the-heels rooming house in the South End, an area in Boston where renovated town houses for the gentry and run-down tenements stood cheek-by-jowl. She and Jack climbed two flights of stairs to room 2B and knocked on the door. There was no answer. They waited.

"Damn!" Jack rapped hard on the wood. "He's not here."

"Let's keep checking. What do you have on for today?"

"I have to be at Harvard at one. How about you?"

"Police chief has a press conference at eleven-thirty."

"OK. I'll swing by on my way to Harvard. You stop before the press conference. If we don't find him, we'll stake the place out tonight."

But William Corrin didn't return to the rooming house that afternoon. He wasn't there when Sally climbed the stairs and knocked before the police chief gamely tried to defend the mayor's budget or later, when Jack pounded on the door again. They both hurried back to the paper to write their stories quickly so they could get back to the South End.

It was six o'clock by the time they got back to the rooming house. They knocked on the door again, with Jack calling out, "Mr. Corrin! Mr. Corrin!" A door opened down the hall, and a woman with a heavily lined face leaned out the door.

"Cut out that damn racket. He's gone. He left about an hour ago."

"*Damn!*" Jack curled his hand into a fist in frustration.

"Did he say where he was going?" Sally asked.

"No. Didn't say nuthin'."

"This may sound like a strange question," Sally said, "but is Mr. Corrin bald?"

The woman looked thoughtful. "I never saw him without that hat he always wears. Like taxi drivers wear, you know? But yeah, I think maybe he is bald. Or else he's got real short hair. Funny, a young guy like that, he should be bald." She looked suddenly suspicious. "He hasn't got cancer or anything?"

"No," Jack told her.

"I wouldn't want nobody with no cancer in my place."

Jack and Sally walked out to the car. "Let's wait for him," she said.

"It may be a while."

"I know. But if we find him, and he does have electrodes in his head, there's our proof."

"This guy may not want to come trotting along with us to play show and tell with his electrodes."

"Jack, I'll bet he doesn't know what he's got in his head. Brady didn't know they were tracking him. Otherwise he'd never have held up the liquor store."

"How did they know he would try a stickup?"

"I think they try to pick losers. Brady was in and out like a revolving door. Or maybe they try to set them up. Use another con to get them to do a job. Who knows?"

"When we find him, we just tell him right out that he's got electrodes in his head? Then what?"

"Joe's on tonight. We take him right to the hospital, prove it to him. X-ray."

"But if they're tracking him, they'll know what's going on."

"They'll only know he's at Municipal. Maybe he had a cough. Or crabs. They wouldn't know he's with us."

"If they get suspicious, all they have to do is push a button. He's got a time bomb in his brain."

"But weren't they going to kill him anyway? I don't think they plan to let any of these subjects live. Unless they do what they did to the bag man you saw at the hospital. And that's worse."

"His only chance might be with us."

"That's right." She stretched, then said, "Jack, I'm hungry. There's a deli we passed on the last block. You go and get some sandwiches and I'll keep watch."

They sat in the car and ate the sandwiches, as the light began to drain from the sky and the sounds of the streets began to still. An hour passed, then two, three. At midnight Jack said, "Maybe we ought to take turns trying to get some sleep."

Sally said she wasn't tired yet, so Jack stretched out in the back seat and slept fitfully for several hours. Then it was Sally's turn. When she awoke, dawn was starting to streak the sky, and in a little while the neighborhood began to awaken. People started to come out of the buildings; some of them got into cars, others walked to the bus stop on the main thoroughfare at the end of the block.

"All night, he didn't come back. I wonder where the hell he is?" Sally asked, stretching her sore muscles.

"Maybe he's got a girlfriend."

"We'll have to check him later. We can't wait here all day. Bob Ames has been watching us like a hawk."

They went home, changed clothes and showered, then took one more swing by the rooming house on their way to the paper. There was no sign of William Corrin.

As they walked into the *World Herald,* Jack said, "I could go for some breakfast."

They went through the food line in the cafeteria and sat down at one of the tables. As Jack dove into a plate of ham and eggs, Sally picked up a copy of the morning paper. She was scanning the metro section when a headline caught her eye: THE CASE OF THE ABSENT-MINDED BURGLAR.

"Jack! Look at this!"

He picked up the paper and began to read: "A robber with larceny in his heart but a short attention span apparently forgot what he was doing in the middle of a holdup in Jamaica Plain last night.

"According to Robert Garcia, the owner of Garcia's Groceries on Highland St., a man walked in around midnight, pulled a gun, and ordered him to open the cash register. Garcia said that he did so, but when he tried to give the man the money, the gunman just looked at him in a confused way and said, "What?" The holdup man was still clutching the gun, but appeared dazed and walked out of the store. Garcia said he followed the man to the door, then watched as he strolled up the street. Then, he said, a grey sedan pulled abreast of the man, the door opened, the gunman got in it, and the car sped away."

Jack looked up at Sally, who had a stricken look on her face.

"They did it!" she said. "It's Corrin!"

"We missed him! Oh shit, we missed him!"

"It had to be him. They were tailing him too. They couldn't risk another mistake like Brady."

"It looks like the system worked perfectly. They just gave him enough juice to confuse him, stop him from doing what he set out to do."

"Jack, should we tell this to Bob Ames?"

"Know what he'd say? Just another dumb crook."

"You're right. Last week we had the bank robber who hid under his bed in Charlestown. First place the cops looked."

"He's a dead man. Corrin's a dead man now."

"Maybe they'll use him again."

"Maybe. But he has to know, now, that something is really wrong. Now he's dangerous to them."

Sally shook her head, wearily. "I bet he'll be found, fished out of some river—who knows when?"

"Let's get back to the rooming house anyway. Maybe there's a chance they let him go back there."

But when they arrived in the South End, the door was still locked. They saw the woman with the lined face, carrying a basket of laundry up the stairs.

"Have you seen Mr. Corrin at all?" Sally asked.

"Moved out."

"Moved out? When?" Jack asked her.

"Some friends moved him out. Just a little while ago. A couple of men came for his things, paid up his rent. Dressed real nice too. Who would have thought Mr. Corrin would have such fancy friends?"

Back in the car, Sally leaned back on the seat and closed her eyes. "We lost him. Oh, I can't believe it! Everytime we get close something happens and we're left with nothing. Damn. *Damn!*"

"They still don't know we have a line into Transition House, Sally. They'll use that connection again."

"Maybe not. Maybe they want to spread things out. Who knows where the next one will come from? Some private clinic someplace?" She sighed. "And my embezzler wants more money."

"Give it to him. It's a chance."

"Your uncle is our only hope now, Jack. Thank God he's helping us. When do you think you'll hear from him?"

"I haven't been pushing it, Sally. I know he has to move carefully."

"It's been almost two weeks. He must have found out something."

"If I don't hear from him today, I'll call. I've been doing some research on the guys we think are on the list. The Deputy Undersecretary of State, Harold Williamson, was in Army Intelligence before he went to State. If you read between the lines, it looks like he was involved in covert stuff. His first overseas assignment was Guatemala in the fifties. He was in and out of Chile before Allende was overthrown."

"What about the FBI? How about our candidates there?"

"There are two guys who could be possibles. I'm checking further on that."

"I do have a good source at the Bureau. But I hate like hell to use him on this. It's too tricky."

"I think you're right. The one thing we can't let them know is what *we* know. They have to think we had the Hakim story, and that's all," he said.

Jack stayed by his desk all day, waiting for the phone to ring. But his uncle did not telephone, so late in the afternoon he picked up the phone and dialed Robert Aiken's home number.

"Uncle Robert, it's me," Jack said.

"Jack, I'm working on our . . . project. It's going to take a little time."

"I have some research I've done that I want to talk to you about."

"Well—"

"I really do need to talk to you, Uncle Robert."

"Of course. Why don't you stop by about eight."

As they drove out toward the North Shore that evening, Sally said, "Jack, what we need is one person to crack, and the whole thing will come pouring out. Could one of the men on the list be the weak link?"

"Maybe. But to crack one of them we'd have to have something real. Otherwise, they'd just stonewall."

"We've got no paper trail without those memos," she said.

"And now we've got a two-source rule from Ames. Unless we get somebody real high up, we can't write anything. We can't smoke people out."

"If your uncle comes up with something, Bob Ames would believe it."

"That's for sure." He shook his head. "Uncle Robert was really shaken by the idea that Seth could have been murdered. He has this notion that everybody ought to share his ideas of service and loyalty."

"Better than living for the buck. Selling your soul to some multinational."

"Yes, but it can cloud your vision. It's very easy to confuse what's good for your class with what's good for everybody. I think that Uncle Robert really believes that people from good Yankee families are as honest as he is. And as fair-minded. It's funny, he's so sophisticated on most things, but on this he can just be so blind."

"Like how?"

"We have a cousin named Forbes Richardson who got involved in stock fraud. Uncle Robert said he was certain Forbes couldn't have done it, that he was a victim of some shady operators. But everybody knows Forbes is so crooked he makes a pretzel look like a ruler."

Jack pulled the BMW into the long, curving drive of his uncle's house. He and Sally got out of the car and walked to the door. Jack rang the bell, but there was no answer. He pushed on the doorknob and the door swung open. They walked into the hallway. The lights in the foyer were out, but there was a gleam of light from a half-opened doorway farther down the hall.

"He's in the study," Jack said. "Come on."

Sally bumped her knee against a table as they walked down the darkened hall. She was rubbing it as she stepped through the doorway to the study. She stopped, suddenly, and gave a small gasp of surprise. Lying on the floor, face up, his head resting in a spreading swamp of blood, was Robert Forbes Aiken. He was clutching something in his hand.

"Oh God!" Jack gasped. He ran to his uncle and put his hand on Robert Aiken's chest.

"He's breathing. Sally, call the police."

Robert Aiken's eyes fluttered open. "Jack," he croaked, his voice a weak, hoarse rasp. "Jack."

Sally had already run to the phone, but the line was dead when she put the receiver to her ear.

"The line's been cut!" she said to Jack.

"El—" said Robert Forbes Aiken. "El—"

He was gasping desperately to get the words.

"Don't talk, Uncle Robert. We'll get you to the car. Sally, help me."

"No. El—El—"

"What? What is it?" Jack said.

"Seth, he—" There was a sound like a gurgle in Robert Aiken's throat.

"They killed Seth! Is that what you're trying to say?" Jack slid his arm under his uncle's shoulder, trying to elevate his head, to clear his throat and make his breathing easier.

"Didn't know . . . all came . . . unraveled . . . sorry . . . sorry . . . be . . . be . . . be . . . care—" And then the gurgle in his throat became a bubble, a strange, fluid rasping sound. His body tensed, and he lay still. His head lolled back against Jack's chest.

"No! Uncle Robert, no!"

Sally was kneeling on the floor next to Jack. She put her hand to Robert Aiken's neck. There was no pulse.

"He's dead, Jack."

"No. Maybe I can—" He let his uncle's head slide to the floor and began to give him mouth-to-mouth resuscitation. He worked until he was sweating and his body heaving, but his uncle's form was still inert on the floor.

"He's gone, Jack," Sally said. She pried the object Robert Aiken was cluthing out of his hand, and looked at it. "Oh my God," she said.

"It's no use," Jack said, his face bathed in sweat. "I can't—can't—" He was finally able to focus on the photograph Sally was holding up for him to see; it was smeared with blood, but he could see two tanned young men in khaki smiling out at him. There was an inscription.

"Oh no," he said. "Elliott Andrews!"

"He was trying to warn you, Jack. He knew he was going to die, and he crawled to get that picture."

"They killed him," Jack said. "The bastards. The *bastards!*"

"They're desperate. Jack, they know we have the list! They know—"

Jack held up his hand to silence her. She asked the question with her eyes.

"Front stairs," he said. "Step squeaks."

"The killer! He's still here!" Her voice was a hoarse whisper.

Jack grabbed her hand and they moved quietly out into the darkened living room. They crouched down behind the couch.

"Should we make a break for the door?" she whispered, hearing the thumping of her heart.

"No. He'd see us. There's a hunting rifle upstairs. Loaded. I can get up the back stairs to get it." There was another squeak from the stairs. Someone was moving down them, slowly.

"Get behind the curtain. Stay there. I'll get the gun," he

whispered, and she slid quietly behind the curtain as he disappeared into the back hall. By now, her heart was pounding so hard it seemed it must be heard all over the house. She held her breath; even her quiet breathing sounded thunderous to her ears.

She stood, still and silent. How much time was passing? A minute? Five? *Oh, God, Jack, where are you? Please, God, let him be all right!*

Suddenly she heard a cry and a thud from the floor above. "Jack!" she gasped, and she ran out from behind the curtain, with the idea of moving toward the back stairs. But after she had taken only two steps someone grabbed her from behind. She felt a hand clamp heavily across her mouth. She tried to cry out, but only a muffled sound emerged. Then two hands were around her neck, squeezing hard. She tried to take a deep breath, but could not. Panic welled up inside her; she fought it.

Stay calm. Think! Her self-defense instructor at the Cambridge Women's Center had drilled it into her class. *Think. Remember the weak points.*

The pressure on her neck was intensifying, cutting off the supply of oxygen. *Little fingers.* No matter how big a person was, his little fingers were vulnerable.

Her hands reached up, found the hands grasping her neck. There was a ringing in her ears. In a few seconds she would lose consciousness.

She found the man's little fingers and tore back on them with all her might. She heard the bones in his fingers crack like twigs. With a yowl of pain, the man released her, and her knees buckled under her. The next thing she heard was a deafening explosion; a piece of the front door splintered and flew into the air. She looked up the stairs and saw Jack, a rifle to his shoulder, firing at her assailant, who had disappeared out the front door.

Jack ran out the door, rifle in hand. There was no moon, and the figure of the running man was hard to make out in the darkness. He put the rifle to his shoulder and fired again. Staying close to a line of hedges, he began to move carefully around the side of the house where the man had disappeared. Suddenly, he heard the sound of an engine leaping to life, and in a few seconds a car came roaring out of the section of the driveway that ran beside the house. He braced himself on the wall of the house and fired as the car, the driver gunning its engine, sped past. He fired again; there was the sound of shattering glass. The side window had broken, but the bullet had missed the driver. Jack leapt into the driveway and got off one more shot, but the car disappeared on the main road. Then, there was a sudden silence; only the crickets punctuated the warm summer night.

Sally ran to Jack and threw her arms around him.

"Jack! I thought he got you! I heard you cry out!"

"I tripped over a goddamn plant in the hall. Are you all right?"

"Just barely."

"What did he do to you?"

"Choked me. The son-of-a-bitch. But he won't be doing *that* for a while. I broke his little fingers. Jack, we have to get the police."

"No! We have to get out of here."

"But they killed him—"

"Sally, what are we going to tell them? That it wasn't a break-in, it was an execution ordered by the Attorney General?"

"Oh, Jesus, who'd believe us?"

"The minute we walked into a police station, we'd be sitting ducks, Sally. Maybe they'd arrest *us*. How comfortable would you be, sitting right where Elliott Andrews knows where you are?"

"You mean 'Lovers Commit Double Suicide in Jail Cell'?"

"Exactly. Sally, he's the fucking Attorney General of the United States!"

"Oh, Jack, I hate to just—leave him there."

"So do I, Sally. But he's dead. We can't help him now. We have to get out of here. They're going to be coming after us now."

They walked quickly to the car, and Jack sped down the driveway to the main road.

"I know a back way to town," he said. "If they've got anybody after us, they wouldn't expect us to go this way."

"Jack," she said, "we can't go home."

"No. We can't. They'd be waiting for us."

"We've got to spend the night somewhere."

"The Ritz."

"What?"

"Last place they'd think of looking for us."

They drove into the center of Boston, and Jack pulled the

BMW up to the curb on Arlington Street and gave the car to the doorman for valet parking. They walked into the hotel, and Jack registered them as Mr. and Mrs. Jonathan Cabot. He pulled himself to his full height, and his voice marked him as unmistakably Yankee. The desk clerk did not even smirk when he said they had no luggage. They walked upstairs to the room in silence. It was a lovely room, well appointed, with a view of the Public Garden, but they barely noticed their surroundings. Jack went to the phone and dialed the Ipswitch police. He said he had heard gunfire as he drove past the Robert Aiken residence. No, he did not wish to give his name.

Sally sat on the edge of the bed, and suddenly she found herself shaking all over. "Delayed reaction," she said.

He put his arm around her. "It all happened so fast." He shook his head. "I'm still trying to sort it out."

"Yes," she said.

"It was all so . . . confusing, what he was trying to tell me—"

"That he knew, Jack. That Andrews would have to kill you too."

"They killed him because he found out, or—" He shook his head.

"What did he say, exactly, Jack?"

"He said he didn't know . . . about Seth. He said—it sounded like—'all came unraveled.'"

"He had worked with Andrews in Intelligence. Who would be the logical man for Andrews to come to with an undercover plan?"

"My uncle never would have condoned the murder of Seth. I know he did some dirty stuff during the war, but murdering Seth—"

"He didn't know about that, I'm sure. I remember how shocked he was when we told him Seth had been murdered. I'm sure he didn't know that."

"But you're saying that he was part of it."

"Yes. He had to be. That's what he meant by 'all came unraveled.' I think everything went wrong with the plan."

"He was part of it. My God, I can't believe it!"

"Not all of it, Jack. He didn't know they killed Seth. He wasn't part of that."

"No, but—"

"He died trying to warn you. Whatever else he did, hold on to that."

"What did he tell them? To close it down? To cut their losses and run?"

"That would be my guess. They could have dismantled the unit in a few days. Without that, who could prove it ever existed? Us? We were a laughingstock already."

"Why didn't they do it?"

"They couldn't take a chance on what we knew, I guess. After they found out we knew where the unit was, they couldn't risk having us alive. And they knew your uncle would never agree to murdering us."

"So he had to die too."

"Yes."

"Now they have to get us. We're the only threat to them that's left."

She shivered and he pulled her close. "We're safe now. No one followed us. We're safe."

"For how long?"

"We're both in shock," he said. "We can't think straight. Let's try to get some sleep. We'll figure out what to do in the morning."

They crawled under the covers and she curled her body next to his. She was still shaking as she burrowed her face against his chest. She thought that she would never sleep, every nerve in her body seemed as tight as a scream, but she felt the warmth of his body creeping into her own. The events of the past few weeks had taken their toll. She fell into an exhausted sleep, and she did not dream.

She awoke, much later, to see Jack sitting up in bed beside her, staring into the darkness.

"Jack?"

"He was his friend, Sally. He signed the picture 'To my best friend Bob.' And then he had someone beat his best friend's brains out with a club. Left him to crawl across the room like an animal, dying every inch of the way. My God!"

"I know," she said.

"He was a decent man, Sally. A good man. Whatever led him to this . . . craziness, that's not what his life was about. The end of his life wasn't all of it."

"And he loved you, Jack. He did love you."

"In that room. They did it to him in *that* room. I used to play there, when I was a kid. I'd line my soldiers up, and just play quietly, for hours. He'd play with me, sometimes. He was so patient. When I think of him, crawling across that floor, bleeding to death—Oh Christ!" He was not able to keep the tremor from his voice.

"Cry for him, Jack," she said. "Go ahead."

He did cry, then, and she held him against her until his breathing no longer came in large, tearing rasps. Then they were quiet for a long time, huddled against each other.

"It all seems like a nightmare. It's too crazy to be real," she said.

"It's real. My uncle is dead, and they have to kill us too. They can't let us stay alive any longer."

"We have to be smarter than they are. Figure this out. But in the morning. Go to sleep, Jack."

"All right." He put his head down wearily on the pillow.

"In the morning," he said.

33

■

Dave Levinsohn walked through the door of his apartment, poured himself a beer, and dropped into a chair. He was exhausted and demoralized. The division had more than enough evidence of voting rights violations in four states to move ahead, forcefully, to send a message that the Federal government was going to be tough on the voting rights law. It wasn't going to happen. The word had come down: Go slow.

Levinsohn sighed and took a swig of beer. Maybe it was time to get out. What was the point? He'd worked himself into a bleeding ulcer as it was. Did he want to wind up like Seth Chaffee, driving himself crazy with paperwork and frustration?

Poor Seth. Dave still felt guilty about him. If he had done something when he picked up the signs that Seth was starting to crack again, maybe Seth would still be alive. Dave should have insisted that Seth get back in touch with his doctor. But Seth's manner didn't seem that alarming. Not like the last time he cracked up and had to be hospitalized. Dave had excused his neglect of his friend because of his own problems—the pain in his gut and the growing frustration of seeing things done wrong when it would be so simple to do them right. He had even thought of calling Seth's doctor himself, but put it off. Then he awoke one morning to discover that Seth's body had been found floating in the Potomac River. Why had he been so slow in seeing what was happening? *Damn.*

He rummaged around in the disorderly pile of mail, newspapers, and magazines on the coffee table to find the TV guide. As he did so, his fingers brushed an envelope that had been sitting there for two weeks. It was the envelope Seth had given him the day before he died. He should have known, by Seth's remark, that the paranoia was back. He'd said, "If anything happens to me, get this to the *Boston World Herald.*"

Dave had tried to joke with Seth. "Hey, buddy, nothing's going to happen to you. Except maybe you'll get riffed. And that would be a stoke of luck."

Poor Seth. His mind finally broke under the strain of it all. He was so intense. Never learned to put the job behind him, to relax.

He picked up the envelope. He had forgotten it was there. He thought about the time he had visited Seth in the hospital, and Seth had thought he was on a mission for world peace. He was way out in the Twilight Zone. He ought to read what Seth had sent. More paranoid stuff, probably.

Oh, the hell with it. He'd had a rotten enough day already. Seth was dead. There certainly wasn't any rush. He'd read it later. It was time for the news.

He picked up the remote, and the TV flickered on. "This is Dan Rather," it said, "with the CBS Evening News."

34

■

Sally and Jack lay in bed, their bodies close together, taking comfort in the warmth of each other's familiar feel. Though it had already been light for several hours, they had made no effort to get out of the bed. There it was safe, but outside was a world that the events of the past night had changed beyond recognition.

The day was sunny and warm, one of those perfect days New England so often serves up in early summer to atone for the chilly rains of spring. Through the window they could see the swan boats gliding serenely across the pond, men and women hurrying to work, and two young men in running shorts tossing a Frisbee back and forth. It was odd, Sally thought. By all rights, the landscape should be reflecting the horror that had erupted in her world. There should be peals of thunder and venomous grey skies. The sunshine was a lie. The world was not like that.

Finally Jack sat up, picked up the phone and asked for the morning *World Herald* to be delivered to the room. When it came, he spread it out on the bed. The story was buried, deep in the metro section. FORMER AMBASSADOR MURDERED IN ROBBERY ATTEMPT.

"Signs of a struggle," Jack read. "Police believe Aiken may

have surprised the thief. An upstairs bedroom had been ransacked. Aiken had had dinner with neighbors earlier, and they believe he may have entered the house while the thief was inside. Police surmise that Aiken encountered the burglar in the den. There was a struggle, and the former ambassador received a fatal blow to the head with a blunt object."

"So he was upstairs, searching your uncle's bedroom," Sally said. "That's where he was when we came in."

"Yes. Probably looking for anything Uncle Robert had on Seth's memos. Or any other evidence, I guess."

"We can't go to the paper, can we," she said.

"Waltz right in and say, 'Hey you know that break-in at Robert Aiken's house? That was just another murder in this conspiracy of ours.' "

She sighed. "Yeah, it would be like Janet Cooke saying to the *Washington Post*, 'I've got this *other* eight-year-old heroin addict.' "

"Even if we told Bob Ames what happened, what have we got? How can we prove the man I shot at wasn't just a burglar?"

"Jack, what if we just held a press conference and laid it all out. Accused Elliott Andrews of murder. Told everything we know about Neurodyne, Brady, Corrin. They couldn't afford to kill us then."

He shook his head. "Who'd come to our press conference? *The Black Voice*. The *Phoenix*. Maybe *The Daily Worker*. We'd just be written off with all the other conspiracy buffs. The ones who know who killed Marilyn Monroe and JFK and Judge Crater."

"They could get away with killing us, making it look like an accident, couldn't they?"

"You bet they could. Oh, a few people might ask questions if we turned up as corpses. *Mother Jones* or *The Village Voice* would run stories saying 'Were Reporters Killed for Knowing Too Much?' Some lefty songwriter might even write a ballad about us."

"Like Karen Silkwood."

"Yes. Sally, nobody knows for certain who killed Kennedy, and *he* was the president. We'd be a two-day story. That's it."

"We could disappear for a while, Jack. Get on a plane and hide out."

"I thought of that. But they'd find us. They have a lot of

resources. That's probably what they expect us to do, now that we haven't shown up at home or at the paper."

"OK," she said, sitting cross-legged on the bed, still wearing the bra and panties she had slept in, "we have to do something they'd never expect."

"They'll expect us to panic."

"The best defense is a good offense. I have an idea. Tell me if it sounds too crazy." She explained her plan to him. He listened attentively.

"I like it," he said. "God knows it's risky, but it *is* the last thing they'd expect. If we can pull it off."

"Let me make a few phone calls. I can get the stuff we need, I think."

"I'll go pick it up. In the meantime"—he opened the drawer and took out sheets of the hotel stationery—"write it. Write everything we know. Then call the paper and dictate it into the blower. Have them send it to Kevin later this afternoon."

"Insurance policy?"

"Something like that."

Three hours later, Jack was driving a rented car with Sally along the Massachusetts Turnpike. He pulled to a stop in front of a grey stone building—the town hall in Bradley, the town that was the homebase of Neurodyne, Inc. They walked into the building, and Jack asked the clerk where the records on building and wiring permits were kept.

"Room 2A. Upstairs," she said.

As they walked up, Sally said, "I hope this isn't a waste of time."

"They did a lot of renovation. Someone would be bound to notice if they tried to get around the codes. Why attract unwanted attention?"

Upstairs, another clerk told them that the permits were filed by the month, not alphabetically. Sally bit her lip.

"Shit!" she whispered to Jack. "This could take forever!"

"It couldn't have been too long ago." He handed her a folder. "You take this one, I'll go through the second one."

Sally riffled through two folders, wanting to race ahead in the pile but afraid of missing the crucial piece of paper. She had just started on a third file when Jack said, "This is it!" He pulled out a sheaf of paper clipped together, labeled Neurodyne, Inc. He spread the papers out on a table in the room and they both started to examine them.

"Architect's drawings are Greek to me," she said. "Can you understand this stuff?"

"I think so. Look, Sally, here we go. This must be the dormitory. Let's see what they've done here. Torn out a couple of walls, and added a shitload of wiring."

"What's this room? It's a funny shape."

"It's labeled 'laboratory.' Let's see the wiring diagrams. Jeez!"

"What is it?"

"They've put enough juice in here to run Disneyland. Lots of piping as well. See here, the specs call for ceramic tile. Take a guess as to what this is."

"An operating room."

"Yes. Illegal, of course. Any facility like that is supposed to be inspected by the Department of Health and Hospitals."

"But you wouldn't know what it was just by these specs."

"No. You'd have to know what you're looking for. It could just be some kind of lab facility."

"Here, Jack. Is this a back stairway?"

"Yes. It leads directly to the second floor of the renovated dorms. That's where their subjects would be."

"If I could get in that door, I could go right up the stairs."

"It's bound to be locked."

"Yes, but we can get through locked doors."

"It's risky as hell, Sally."

"But there it is, Jack. Right under our noses. The proof we need. Without that, we're just a couple of moving targets."

"All right. Let's find a gas station, so we can change."

They drove until they found one, and Jack took one of the boxes out of the back seat of the car and Sally took the other. They went into the bathrooms, which were side by side.

"Jack," Sally said, "can you hear me?"

"Yes."

"It's filthy in here. Yuk. The country is turning into a pigsty."

"It stinks in here too. Somebody peed all over the place."

"Americans are pigs. Whatever happened to good manners?"

"What a time to be worrying about manners."

"Well, it pisses me off." Sally slipped quickly into the white trousers, shirt, and jacket that Jack had bought earlier, standard nurse's gear for hospitals and labs. She gathered her own clothes in a ball under her arm and stepped out the door onto the gravel at the edge of the concrete. "Hurry up, Jack. I feel conspicuous out here like this."

"I can't get this damn thing buckled. OK, I think that's it." He stepped out of the men's room into the sunlight, blinking at the sudden brightness. Despite the tension building up inside her, Sally had to laugh.

"Oh, Jack, I'm sorry, but you don't look like a cop. It's that goddamn nose. You look so *Yankee*."

"Maybe with the hat."

"Oh no, that's worse."

"Authentic or not, this is the best I can do."

He was outfitted in a blue serge shirt and trousers, a black military belt around his waist. "It's the uniform Arrow Protection Services uses," he said. "I told the guy I was starting today. I've got an Arrow patch, but that has to be sewed on."

"I've got a couple of safety pins. I'll put them on in the car."

As Jack drove, Sally held the patch to his arm and tried to pin the emblem to his shirt.

"Ow!"

"Sorry. I'm no good at this. Stubby fingers. That'll do. Jack, did you have any trouble at Meyer's place?"

"No. I told him I came to get the stuff you called him about. He gave me a funny look, but he gave it to me."

"Meyer was a good friend of my father's. I knew he'd give it to us, no questions asked."

They drove along the highway and Sally rubbed her palms on her jacket to dry off the sweat.

"You OK? You know what to do?" he asked her.

"I know. I practiced in the hotel room. That was really weird, learning to use a rifle in a room at the Ritz. I felt like two-gun Moishe."

"He has to believe you'll use it."

"I couldn't, though."

"Neither could I. But he has to think we'd kill him in a minute."

"I'll convince him."

"Here we go. There's the driveway."

Sally scrambled over the back seat of the car and crouched low behind the seat. She took Robert Aiken's hunting rifle and held the barrel with her left hand and supported the stock with her right, the way she had seen John Wayne do in movies.

The gun felt cold—alien—in her hands, as Jack drove the rented Ford directly up to the chain-link gate, the front fender nearly touching the gate itself. He got out and pushed the red button that would summon the guard from Arrow Protective Services. Crouched in the back seat, Sally gripped the rifle and waited, staring at the grey woolen fabric of the back of the seat. She knew she would remember that pattern for the rest of her life. What if the guard was stupid and went for his gun? She hoped for a middle-aged family man, not some macho kid who didn't have the brains to know this wasn't *High Noon*.

She could hear nothing but silence outside. She stared at the weave of the fabric until her eyes ached. Then, she heard it; the sound of a car approaching. Her stomach gave a violent lurch. She took a deep breath. There were a thousand things that could go wrong. She heard the sound of a door slamming.

"Hi," Jack's voice said. "Mac sent me out. Package from D.C. for Dr. Severn. I have to deliver it personally."

"OK. But you have to sign in before I open up."

"Sure." Jack's voice seemed normal and calm. There was silence for a minute, then Jack said, "There you go," and she heard the sound of the gate opening. She opened the back door of the car and jumped out, crouched and aimed at the startled guard, an overweight man in his forties.

"Make one move and you're a dead man," she said. "I mean it."

"Do what she says and you won't get hurt," Jack said. "Do it fast. She likes killing people."

"You're crazy!' the guard said. But he did not move.

"Don't make any sudden moves," Jack said. "Put your hands over your head and move five steps to your right. Do as you're told and you'll stay alive."

For an instant, the guard hesitated, and Sally's heart skipped a beat. *Please, God, make him move!* Then the man walked five steps, and Sally gave a large exhale of relief.

"Now just stand still," Jack said. "We're not going to hurt you, if you cooperate. Walk to the car, and put your hands on the roof."

"I've got a wife, kids—" the man said.

"You won't be hurt," Jack said. "Stay still. Don't turn around."

From his pocket, Jack took out a bottle and poured some of its contents on a handkerchief.

"What are you doing?" the guard asked. Sally noticed that his voice trembled, and she felt a wave of pity for him.

"Don't resist. This won't hurt you. I promise. Cooperate, and you'll just have a story to tell your wife and kids at dinner."

Jack stepped up quickly behind the man and forced the handkerchief against his nose and mouth. The man tried to squirm away, but Jack held him, firmly. In a minute, he slumped limply in Jack's arms.

"You're sure this won't hurt him," Jack said.

"No. Meyer gave us the right amount. He'll be out for a couple of hours, that's all."

They carried the unconscious guard to the Ford and bound and gagged him securely, making sure that his breathing was unencumbered. Jack drove the Ford off the road to a spot where it was hidden by thick underbrush. Then they walked back through the open gate to the Arrow car. The keys were in the ignition. Jack pushed the button to close the gate and turned on the engine. He drove, and Sally crouched low in the back seat as they drove into the Neurodyne complex.

"I see the building we want," he said. "The road runs right behind it. I only see a couple of people around, walking to one of the other buildings."

"Let's hope our luck holds."

Jack drove the Arrow car behind the dormitory building and pulled it to a stop by the curb in front of the back door. He looked around and saw no one.

"I'll check the door," he said. He got out, tugged at the back door. He took out one of the enema bottles, squirted the clear liquid into the lock, did the same with a second bottle. Then he pretended that he was checking the trash cans at the rear of the building. He waited for what seemed to Sally a very long time, and then he went over and pushed on the door. It swung open. He looked through the door and saw the back stairs. The stairs led to a corridor on the second floor.

"All clear," he said.

Sally got out of the car, slung her purse across her shoulder and walked quickly to the back door. At the bottom of the stairs he said, "I'll be right here." He set the rifle against the wall in the corner. "Call me, and I'm up there."

She walked to the top of the stairs, paused, and looked down the long, narrow hallway. She saw no one. There were six doors off the hallway, leading, probably, to the dormitory rooms. All the doors were closed except the one nearest her. She walked up to it and looked inside. The room was small and plain, but there were pictures on the walls and a huge box radio on the dresser. On the bottom bunk of a two-decker bed sat a very young black woman, who was absently leafing through a magazine. The woman's head was completly shaven, and, on two sides of her head, thin wires protruded from her skull. Sally couldn't suppress a sharp intake of her breath at the sight. She had seen it in pictures, but that did not prepare her for the reality. Sally tried to imagine the face with a head of hair, to match it with one of the pictures she had studied so intently of the missing women.

She walked into the room and smiled at the girl. The young woman gave her a wan smile in return.

Dottie. Dottie West.

"Hello, Dottie," she said.

Despite the smile, the girl's eyes were glazed and dull. Sedated. Sally opened her purse and took out a small Polaroid camera. She raised the camera and began taking pictures of the young woman.

"Just a few pictures, Dottie."

"Don't hurt me," Dottie said. "Sometimes they hurt me."

"No, I won't hurt you. I'm here to help you." Sally moved very close and took a picture that clearly showed Dottie's shaved skull and the wires. The first of the pictures were developing now, and she saw that they were clear and in focus. She waited just a minute to make sure that they were dry, and then she shoved the prints and the camera back into her purse.

"Will you make them be nice to me?" Dottie asked. "Sometimes they make me feel good but sometimes they hurt me."

"Nobody's going to hurt you anymore," Sally said. She took Dottie's hand and squeezed it and, as she did so, heard voices— male voices—in the hall. Her whole body went rigid.

Don't stop. Keep going. Don't come in here!

But the voices kept moving closer, and Sally took a deep breath, trying to keep calm. One tactic she had used often as a reporter—in places where she wasn't supposed to be—was to act as if she had a perfect right to be there. It usually worked;

few people questioned her. She set down her purse and began to arrange the bottles and personal items on the top of the dresser in the room.

A man walked into the room; a large man wearing a white lab coat, a pleasant expression on his round, inoffensive face. It was the same face she had seen across the table in a French restaurant one night that now seemed eons ago.

She tried to control the shaking of her hands as she arranged the various items on the dresser.

"Good morning, Doctor," she said, hoping that he did not notice the slight tremolo at the end of the last word. She took a quiet, controlled breath.

"How is the patient this morning?"

Nurse talk. How do nurses talk? "She was somewhat agitated a bit earlier, but now she is quite calm."

"Good." The doctor looked at Sally, really seeing her for the first time. "Are you Roberts's replacement?"

"Yes, I am."

"What's your name?"

"Prince," she said. "Diana Prince." The name had just popped up out of her subconscious. It was familiar. Who the hell was Diana Prince? Then she remembered. Diana Prince was Wonder Woman's alter-ego. Great, Sally, why not tell him you're Queen Victoria.

But Theodore J. Severn did not react. He picked up a chart that hung on the edge of the bunk bed where the young woman sat. He studied it for a minute.

"She needs another injection of B-1. Will you give it to her, please?"

"Certainly. As soon as you're finished, doctor."

"Now, please."

Sally's stomach gave another violent lurch. She looked around. There was a white cabinet in the corner of the room, and she opened it. Inside, she saw a box of disposable hypodermic needles, and picked one up and tore off the wrapper. On a shelf was a row of assorted bottles, all bearing labels. She picked one up to examine it, but it slid out of her fingers, which were slippery with sweat. She caught it before it fell to the floor. Her hands were shaking so badly she wondered if she could hold the needle.

Calm! Stay calm. Breathe!

She found a row of smaller bottles on a lower shelf, and looked at the labels. *Vitamin B-1. Pre-measured dose.*

"Would you hurry it up, please," said the doctor.

"Be right there, Doctor." She tried to think about the shots she got when she went to Mexico. How did the nurse do it? She couldn't remember. She looked at the bottle, which had a thin rubber top. *Fidel!* When Fidel got that strange cat virus, Sally had to give her shots. It was a bottle just like this one.

Sally plunged the top of the needle into the bottle, and turned it upside down, withdrawing the plunger, slowly. The needle filled up with amber liquid. What else? Alcohol. She took a cotton ball from a jar in the cabinet and soaked it with alcohol. Then she walked over to the young woman on the bed.

She thought about Fidel. A quick motion, firm but not too hard. She took Dottie West's arm and smeared a swath of alcohol on it. She held Dottie's arm with her left hand and plunged the needle in with the right. Dottie West did not make a sound. Thank God she was so drugged up. Sally pushed the plunger on the needle and the amber liquid disappeared into Dottie's arm.

"Thank you," said the doctor. "You can finish here later. I want to have a chat with the patient."

"Of course, Doctor." Sally picked up her pocketbook. She saw, with horror, that it was gaping open and one of the pictures of Dottie was sticking out. She pushed it shut and shoved it under her arm. She walked out of the room, and by the time she reached the hallway, her legs were feeling rubbery. Jack was waiting at the bottom of the stairs, his face tense and drawn. He took her arm and they hurried out to the car.

"Sally, for God's sakes, where were you?"

"Let's go, Jack. I got it. I got the pictures."

He started the car and drove away from the back of the building. Sally hunched down in the front seat until they were clear of the buildings, then she sat up and told him what had happened in the room.

"It was him! Severn! I thought I was going to pee in my pants."

"Good God! But you got the pictures."

She took a Polaroid snapshot out of her purse and held it up for him to see.

"We've got it! That's our proof. Good work!"

"Should we go to the paper? Maybe somebody will be waiting for us there."

"We'll go to a pay phone and call Bob Ames. Get somebody to meet us who can take the pictures back. They ought to be enough to get the state troopers to move in."

"That poor girl. I hope they'll get her in time. She looked so grotesque, Jack. She was all drugged up. She asked me to make them stop hurting her."

"They're finished now. We've got them dead to rights."

Jack drove the Arrow car up to the gate, jumped out, and pressed the button that would make the gate swing open. Nothing happened. He pressed it again.

"What's wrong?" Sally called out.

"Jammed. The gate won't open."

From a distance, Sally heard the hum of a car engine, moving fast.

"Jack, could they jam it by remote?"

"Yes."

"Quick, Jack, climb over. Someone's coming. I'll throw you the gun and then climb over."

Jack scrambled to the top of the fence. He was agile and well coordinated, so it was not hard for him to do. The car was getting nearer now; he could hear it. His shirt caught on the barbed wire on the top of the fence, but he ripped it free and dropped to the other side. Sally had taken the rifle and run to the fence, and thrown it over. She was scrambling up the fence as the other car hove into view and scrambled to a halt. She was at the top of the fence and would have made it over, except the white lab coat caught in the wire, and she had to try to struggle to get out of it. Three men, with pistols drawn, jumped out of the car, and one of them grabbed at her foot. She kicked his hand away, but another man grabbed the other foot and they began to pull her off the fence. Jack picked up the rifle and tried to sight, but there was no way he could get off a shot without risking hitting her.

"Run, Jack!" she screamed, as they pulled her struggling body from the fence. One of the men pointed his revolver and fired at Jack, but Jack dodged and made a run for the safety of the thick brush a few yards away. A bullet whistled past his ear and he plunged into the thick growth past the road. He crouched down and kept running, low, until he found a spot where he could see the men and Sally. He dropped to the ground, brought the rifle to his eye, waited. The three men had Sally pinned face down on the ground, but he did not have a clear shot at any of them.

"Search her," said one of the men. Another patted his hands along her body and the third poured the contents of her purse on the ground. The pictures were not there. Jack had them in his hip pocket.

"Not here," one of the men grunted. They were all dressed alike, in tailored grey business suits. *Feds*, Jack thought.

"The one outside. He's got a rifle. Be careful."

He watched as two of the men dragged Sally to her feet. They pinned her arms behind her and turned her to face the gate, using her body as a shield.

"We know you're out there!" one of the men yelled. "Come on in here if you don't want to see her hurt."

"Go, Jack! Don't listen to them!"

One of the men slapped her hard, across the face. She did not cry out.

"Go!" she yelled again, and the man hit her again, harder. An animal rage surged through Jack. He wanted to kill the man, kill all of them, mercilessly. He wanted to have the man's neck in his hands and squeeze until all the life was gone. He looked through the cross hairs of the rifle. He was a good shot, but without a sniperscope he couldn't be sure that his shot would not hit Sally instead of its intended target.

"Come in, and bring the pictures with you," one of the men called out. "You'd better do it, fast."

He started to unbutton Sally's blouse. "It's not going to be nice for your girlfriend," he said. He thrust his hand down the front of her blouse. She sank her teeth into his arm and bit him, hard. He yowled with pain and pulled his hand away. He slapped her again, hard.

Jack clamped his teeth in frustration and anger. Oh, for one clear shot! Just one!

He could make it to the car, he knew. He might even get away. But would they have killed her by then? Yes, the chances were good that they'd kill her. What did they have to lose? What would one more murder do to their chances?

"You'll never see her alive again if you don't come in!" one of the men yelled. "Watch this!"

He punched Sally, hard, in the stomach. Jack saw her knees go slack. The man drew back his fist and hit her again. Jack fired a rifle burst over their heads.

"No good," the man hollered. "You can't get us without killing her. The man pulled back his fist to hit Sally again, but Jack screamed, "No!"

"She'll get worse if you don't come out here with the rifle over your head."

"All right. I'm coming. Don't hit her."

He stood up and walked into the clearing, the rifle held high over his head.

"Throw it down."

Jack dropped the rifle. One of the men pressed the buzzer on the gate, and now it swung open, easily.

"Come in here. Nice and slow."

Jack walked through the gate.

"The pictures. Give them to me."

Jack took the pictures out of his pocket and handed them to the man. The other two men had released Sally, and she was sitting on the ground, trying to recover her wind. He went over to her, knelt down, and touched her face, where a large bruise was starting to form.

"I'm sorry," he said. "I couldn't go. I couldn't let them hurt you. How do you feel?"

"I'm OK," she said. "Oh *damn*. We were so close."

He helped her to her feet, and steadied her.

"Get in the car," one of the men snarled at them.

"Lousy little Nazi," Sally snarled back. He shoved them toward the car, an unmarked black sedan. One of the men in the front seat kept his revolver aimed at Jack as the driver backed up the car, turned it around and drove off into the Neurodyne complex.

The car moved through the complex, down a road that led to a large oval building some distance away from the main cluster. It came to a halt near a door in the side of the building. Standing there, waiting for them, was Theodore J. Severn. He looked very pleased, Sally thought, seeing him out the car window; a hunter of small prey savoring his windfall.

The men dragged Jack and Sally out of the car. Dr. Severn looked at her, the trace of amusement still on his face.

"Very clever, young woman. If our patient hadn't asked me

why that nice lady took her picture, you might have gotten away with it." To one of the men, he said, "The pictures?"

The man handed him the pictures Jack had pulled from his back pocket. "Nice resolution. Good focus." He ripped them to shreds. "I take it this is Miss Ellenberg and Mr. Aiken. Correct?"

"No," Sally told him. "We are the Duke and Duchess of Windsor. It's over, Mister. We know about the unit, and Dottie West, and Elliott Andrews. Party's over."

The three men exchanged glances. Jack said, "We filed a story before we ever came out here. Do you think we'd be so stupid as to come out empty-handed?"

"I don't think there is any story," the doctor said. "You had to be desperate to come out here and try a crazy scheme like this. If you know so much, why didn't you go to the police?"

"This isn't the Kremlin. Police can't just go storming in places without evidence. We wanted to give them solid proof," Sally said, "but we have the story. All of the pieces. They fit together.'

"Only to you. I think your newspaper might be pleased to be rid of you. You have caused quite a pack of trouble."

"If you think you can kill us and get away with it, you're crazy. You'll have every reporter in town on your trail," Jack said.

"I think the two of you will just vanish," the doctor said. "It will be a curiosity for a time. But people forget. You will be— disappeared."

"Oh, don't be an asshole," Sally said. "You can still cut a deal. You think your pals in D.C. won't throw you to the sharks? Like Williamson at State? Come in with us, agree to testify, and you could get some immunity. Otherwise, you could get the death penalty. You're involved in murder in several states."

"You do have brass, don't you? There is no evidence linking me to murder, and in a short time much of the work at this facility will be transferred elsewhere. It will go on, but in another place."

"Your friends panicked. They killed my uncle. Things are way out of control now. You can't stuff this whole thing back in the bag now."

"You're the science writer, aren't you? Good. *Good.* I think what you are about to see will interest you very much." The amiable expression on the doctor's face had vanished; his eyes narrowed to slits. For the first time it occurred to Jack, *This man is not sane.* Theodore J. Severn lived in his own World, one so filled with menace and terrors and unfathomable dread that constant attack against unseen enemies was his way of surviving. Jack felt a stab of panic grip his bowels. You couldn't reason with a man like this. The colors of his own world were so much more vivid than the real one.

The doctor nodded toward the men in the suits. They pushed Jack and Sally toward the building's side door. Then they were shoved, roughly, through the door, which shut with a clang behind them. They found themselves in pitch darkness. Suddenly the whole room was flooded with light, fluorescent lights had been switched on. Sally looked around her in bewilderment. The room was huge, but empty, with a layer of sawdust covering the floor.

Sally looked around in surprise at the odd surroundings. "Jack, what is this place?"

"It's the old riding ring. I was in some shows here when I was a kid. But they've redone the whole place. What the hell for?"

"I've got a feeling it isn't Ringling Brothers," Sally said.

"Now, Mr. Aiken," the doctor's voice boomed over the PA system, "I have a question for you."

They looked around to see where the voice was coming from. Jack pointed to a loudspeaker high up on the wall.

"Look, Jack. Over there."

A panel at one side of the building was silently sliding open to reveal Theodore Severn behind a glass partition. They could see his lips moving, but only heard him over the loudspeaker.

"This is our animal research facility, Mr. Aiken. Quite essential for the work we want to do. I think you'll find it fascinating." He paused. "Have you heard, Mr. Aiken, of José Delgado?"

Sally heard Jack draw his breath in, sharply.

"I see by your expression that you have," the voice said. It sounded extremely smug.

Sally looked at Jack. "Delgado? Isn't that the guy—"

"Yes," Jack said. "Listen, what time did you tell them to send the story to Kevin's terminal?"

"Five o'clock."

"Too late. He'll never get it in time."

"Do you see any way out of here?"

"There used to be windows. But it looks like they've sealed them. I don't see any other doors."

"The glass partition. Could we get to him?"

"The glass is sure to be triple thickness. We'd have to find something to smash the glass. Maybe we—"

Jack stopped in mid-sentence. A second panel opened in what appeared to be the smooth side of the building, and a huge bull trotted out. It stopped, shook its head, and then trotted out to the center of the ring. Sally stared at it in amazement. "Oh shit! Electronic hamburger." On its head, the bull wore what appeared to be a circular disk.

"Turn right," the voice on the loudspeaker commanded. The bull obediently circled.

"Turn left!" said the voice. The bull reversed itself.

"Oh God, Jack, he's going to send that thing after us!"

"And now—" the voice on the loudspeaker said. The bull shook its head, once, twice. Then, suddenly, the huge animal began a furious charge, directly at Jack and Sally. Sally stood and watched it for an instant, transfixed.

"Come on, Sally, run!" Jack screamed at her, and she whirled to get out of the path of the oncoming bull. But the heel of her shoe caught on the rough edge of a board under the sawdust and sent her sprawling on her face. She looked up and knew it was too late to scramble out of the way. She felt the floor shaking as the enormous animal bore down on her. She curled up and covered her head with her hands, waiting for the impact.

It didn't come. The taste of sawdust was in her mouth and she could hear the frenzied panting of the bull. She looked up, not believing what she saw. The bull was standing still, a few feet away from her. It was so huge it seemed to fill the room.

Jack grabbed her hand and pulled her to her feet.

"What happened?" she asked, still dazed.

"He stopped it! He stopped the goddamn bull like it hit a brick wall."

Sally was shaking all over; she suddenly felt a warm trickle of urine down the side of her leg. "I thought I'd bought the farm on that one. Sorry, bad pun."

Jack shook his fist at the man behind the panel. "You're crazy. A lunatic! You'll go to the gas chamber!"

"Nice try, Mr. Aiken. Are you afraid now? Do you know, now, what fear is?"

"Jack," Sally said, "he's really getting his rocks off on this."

"I didn't hear you, Mr. Aiken!"

"Yeah, I'm scared shitless. Does that make you happy?"

"Ah, but we've just begun."

"He's playing with us, Sally. Like a cat with a mouse."

The bull was shaking its head again.

"Sally, wait till it's nearly here, then dive out of the way. We don't know when he's going to stop it."

The bull began its headlong charge once again. The floor quaked under its ponderous weight. Jack and Sally stood, immobile, as the animal approached.

"Now!" Jack yelled, and Sally dove to the right and Jack jumped out of the way to the left. But as the bull came to a thudding halt, it tossed its head. Jack was too close to the animal's sharpened horns. He gave a cry of pain as a horn raked his arm, ripping open his sleeve and tearing a six-inch-long gash in his arm. He staggered away from the panting, confused animal. The blood was soaking his sleeve and he suddenly felt faint. He sank to his knees, holding his arm.

Sally ran over to him and pulled off her white jacket and tore a strip of fabric from it. She used the piece of cloth for a bandage, winding it around the gash. "It's not that deep," he said. "I'm OK."

"Jack, does a bull only see red? Is that what it goes after?"

"No, that's not true. It's motion. It's the matador's cape moving it goes after, not the color."

They crouched, on the floor, talking quietly for a while. It was obvious that Severn was going to savor tormenting them. He wasn't going to kill them . . . yet.

Then the bull began to shake its head.

"Oh, God, he's going to do it again," she said.

"Wait until the last minute to get out of the way. It won't be able to change gears that fast."

"You go that way, Jack. I'll go to this side. We're harder targets if we split up."

They moved in opposite directions and the doctor chuckled. "It only makes it more sporting," he said. The bull circled, to face Sally, shook its head and flung itself into another charge. She waited, watching it come and, as it was nearly on her, dove out of the way and rolled as far as she could from the path of the bull. The bull came to a halt, and she scrambled up, backing away. Every move she made, the bull turned toward her.

"Stop it!" she screamed "Stop it!"

"Are you getting nervous, Miss Ellenberg?"

"I don't want to die this way, dammit. Stop it!"

"Why should I stop it?"

She walked a few steps toward the glass partition. "Oh God, I don't want to die!" She fell on her knees. "You can have me. Do anything to me. But don't kill me."

"And what about your boyfriend, there?"

"Sally, for God's sakes, don't let him win! If he breaks us, he wins!"

"Kill him. Not me." She began to unbutton her blouse. "You can have me!"

"You bitch! You lousy bitch!" Jack yelled at her.

Sally had her blouse completely unbuttoned. She put her hands to her breasts, cupping them.

"Mice in a cage, when they perceive a threat," said the voice, "often fall to attacking one another."

She had her hand on the clasp of her bra. "Do you want me to take it off for you? Do you want to see me naked? Tell me what to do?"

"Female primates often use submissive sexual gestures to ward off attack," the voice said. "We are all animals, aren't we?"

Sally leaned forward, touching her breasts provocatively. She could see, through the glass, that the man behind it was watching her, intently. What he did not see, until too late, was that Jack had moved up quickly behind the bull and vaulted onto its back, as if it were a polo pony. He grabbed the metal disk and pulled it, as hard as he could. The wires ripped out of the bull's brain and the animal, in pain and rage, began to throw its body about in a wild fury. The animal threw Jack, hard, to the floor of the ring. Sally grabbed the white lab coat and ran to the enraged animal, flailing the coat around.

"Tora! Tora! Tora! Over here, you dumb Big Mac! Come on, *bubbie*, come after me!"

The animal, blood running into its eyes, frenzied with pain, caught sight of the moving fabric. It snorted with fury, lowered its head and began, once again, to charge. Sally ran, as fast as she could, directly toward the glass partition. If the bull had not been slowed by exhaustion and confusion, it might have overtaken and trampled her. As she ran, she saw the man behind the panel, his back turned, reaching desperately for a button on the control panel. As Sally reached the glass, she flung herself with a last burst of energy to the side, and the bull hit the glass in full charge, splintering it into a million pieces. She heard a scream of agony from behind the glass. Severn, clawing desperately at the control panel to close the sliding doors, was caught in the lower back by the horns of the bull, impaled on them. The side of his body opened like a Ziploc bag, and his entrails spilled out on the floor. The bull, further maddened by the blood, raked its horns again and again over the mass of blood and flesh that until seconds ago had been recognizable as human. Finally, the bull, confused and exhausted, collapsed, panting, on the ground.

Sally stood up, looking briefly at the scene behind her; she felt the taste of bile in her throat, She looked around for Jack. He was trying to get to his feet, still stunned by the impact of his fall. He got up unsteadily, but his legs turned to jelly and he sank down again to a sitting position. Sally ran to help him, her own legs not very steady, and as she did so, she heard a muffled *crack!* outside the building. Then another one.

"Jack, come on, we can get out through that door. There must be stalls in there. Hurry!"

"Sally, my legs don't seem to be working. Wait a minute."

She put her arms around him and helped to lift him to his feet. Then she heard a banging on the outside of the wall and a voice: "Sally! Jack! Are you in there?"

"That's Kevin!" Jack said. "Sally, it's Kevin!"

"Here," Sally yelled. "In here!"

The door at the far end of the building swung open, violently, and three Massachusetts State Troopers, guns drawn, ran into the building. Behind them came Kevin Murphy and Bob Cunningham. The two men from the *World Herald* came over to Jack and Sally.

"Help me with Jack! He's hurt."

"I'm OK. Just my knee."

"Kevin, one of the missing women is in the other building. Dottie West. She's—"

"We know. She's all right."

"You got the story," Jack said, "and figured we were here!"

Kevin looked at him blankly. "What story?"

"The one we left on your terminal."

"I didn't get any story. Jesus, you two were right all along."

"But how—"

"A friend of Seth Chaffee's called Bob Ames. He had Seth's memos. Knew they were authentic. We put the whole Washington bureau on it."

"They admitted it?"

"Harold Williamson at State broke down and told us the whole story when we confronted him with the memos."

"Elliott Andrews? Did they get him?" Jack asked.

"We never got to him. He put a revolver to his mouth and blew off the back of his head. In his office. Quite a mess, I understand." Kevin looked around. "What in the hell went on here?"

"You won't believe it."

"This time, I will."

After Jack and Sally gave a full report to the state police, they rode back to the paper with Kevin and Bob Cunningham.

"Hey," Kevin Murphy said, hanging up the car phone in the *World Herald* staff car, "the word just came over the wires. The President has appointed a special prosecutor. And that, boys and girls, will make Bob Ames smile. *We* got the story. The *Washington Post* did not."

"Know what Ames will say?" Bob Cunninghan asked.

The other three chanted in unison: "Eat your heart out, Ben Bradlee."

Jack thought of something. "Sally," he said, "exactly what was it you said to the bull when you were waving that jacket around. I'm not sure I heard right, because I was seeing stars at the time."

"Matador talk. I read Hemingway. I said, 'Tora! Tora! Tora!' "

"That's what I thought you said."

"That's right, isn't it?"

"No. It's *toro*. In Spanish, *toro* means bull."

"So what did I say?"

"Tora! Tora! Tora! is what the Japanese pilots said when they bombed Pearl Harbor."

"I got his attention, didn't I? With all those wires in his head, maybe he thought he was a Datsun."

Much, much later, Sally and Jack lay side by side in bed, their stomachs curdled from uncounted cups of machine coffee, the adrenaline quiescent, and Jack's arm still faintly throbbing.

Of the conspirators, one had taken his own life, two were

talking to the special prosecutor after a plea bargain, one had been apprehended trying to cross the border into Canada, and several others were huddling with high-priced lawyers, considering a range of options, from the insanity plea to sincere denials of knowledge of wrongdoing. One of the plea-bargainers had already talked to Harper & Row about a book contract in six figures. He would be on the "Today" show in the morning.

"I understand Severn," Sally said, leaning wearily against Jack. "It's the others who puzzle me."

"You understand him? He was *nuts.*"

"Yes. Not clinically mad. A sociopath. Like Mengele. A family man who could do the most dreadful experiments on people, and it didn't bother him. He was never really capable of feeling anything for other people."

"The sciences can be a hiding place for people like that. They can bury themselves in technology, things that go buzz and gleep."

"But the others," Sally said. "Elliott Andrews. How did he get so far away from everything that was real? And good. He was the best and the brightest."

"So were the people who dreamed up the strategy of dropping napalm on kids in Vietnam," Jack answered her.

"OK, but there was a war on. And it was another country. That doesn't make it right, but maybe comprehensible."

"I don't think they started out intending to do what they did. But the unthinkable becomes normal, very fast, when you think you're saving civilization."

"Barbarians at the gates?"

"Yes. Step by step, one thing led to another. They never thought it would get out of control."

"I don't understand the mind-set that makes you assume you have the right to make life and death decisions about other people," she said.

"I do. I was supposed to grow up believing that. We govern the lower orders. It's never quite said that way, of course. But it's why my uncle couldn't believe that Elliott Andrews could ever harm him. Or me. We were just like *him.*"

"Power isolated them. They lived in their tight little privileged world, talking only to each other. The outside world became more and more distorted. They weren't monsters. Just ordinary men, who wound up doing monstrous things," Sally said.

"There will be more. Who knows who or where they'll be? Attorney General? Chairman of a House committee? In the CIA? The military? Ordinary men. There will be more."

"There always are," she said.

From "Anatomy of a Scandal," Boston World Herald *Outlook section, by Sally Ellenberg and John F. Aiken:*

It was a key miscalculation that led to the unraveling of a covert medical unit that performed illegal experiments on human subjects, operated by high government officials. The unit, the major issue in the "Braingate" scandal that has rocked the Ellard administration, was set up after Federal officials heard reports of Russian gains in the technology of behavior control. But when it was used as a vehicle to interrogate well-known black activist Hakim Abdul, the stage was set for the revelations that have sent shock waves through the U.S. Congress, the administration, and the scientific community.

In an exclusive interview with the *World Herald,* Harold Williamson, the former assistant secretary of state who helped set up the unit, explained the bizarre series of events that led to the indictment of seven senior Federal officials and one prominent scientist, as well as to the suicide of former Attorney General Elliott Andrews. Williamson was the major witness in the special prosecutor's investigation.

The decision to "activate" the unit came, Williamson said, when a Soviet defector revealed advanced work Soviet scientists were doing on a computer tracking system linked to implants in the brain. Secret and illegal experiments were conducted on the grounds of Neurodyne, Inc., a Massachusetts medical facility. It was never intended, Williamson said, to be used to control political dissidents in the U.S. He told the *World Herald* that he had vigorously opposed the plan to abduct Hakim Abdul and interrogate him, that this operation was conceived and ordered by Elliott Andrews.

Williamson said he told investigators that Andrews

had been convinced that Hakim was a major conduit of arms and money from sources in Libya, who intended to destabilize the U.S. government.

"Elliott had this exaggerated idea of foreign control of American dissident groups," Williamson said. "He really didn't understand the problems and tensions in the ghettos."

Andrews was obsessed, Williamson said, with the notion that revealing a Libyan connection to the anti-war movement would discredit the entire movement with mainstream America. As Andrews more and more took on the role of spokesman for the hawks in the Ellard administration, discrediting the movement became a personal crusade, Williamson believes. It was this zeal that led to the abduction of Hakim. But Williamson argues that there never was an intention to assassinate the black leader.

The plan, he said, was to extract from Hakim the details of the Libyan conduit, and then to inject him with memory-blocking drugs as well as with heroin. He would be found wandering the streets by police, who would be tipped off by an anonymous call. Hakim would be thoroughly discredited, both by his return to addiction and the Libyan revelations. He never knew the location of the unit, and his memories of his interrogation would return only months later, in dreams and memory fragments. But who would believe the ravings of an addict?

"I argued that it was much too risky to use the unit for that purpose,'" Williamson said. "The unit worked only because it did what it was designed to do and nothing else. But Andrews convinced the others in the group that the risk was worth taking—that Hakim's past erratic behavior would act as a shield against any revelations, that the memory drugs were working well enough to be used strategically."

But Hakim died, unexpectedly, from the heroin injection, despite the frantic efforts of medical personnel to revive him. So his death from an "overdose" had to be staged. And the Libyan connection? "It turned out to be minor," Williamson admitted. "The stuff Elliott thought was there just wasn't. A few contributions to the New Panthers, but not the major cache of money and arms we expected."

It was the Hakim affair that eventually led to the murders that have shocked official Washington, as the conspirators tried to cover their tracks. Williamson claimed that he opposed the "termination" of Justice-Department lawyer Seth Chaffee, and that he did not know, until afterwards, about the murder of former ambassador Robert Forbes Aiken. "I was way out of the loop by then," he said. "Elliott didn't trust me."

Asked why he had silently acquiesced in the plan to murder Chaffee, instead of warning the President or other officials, Williamson said, "I panicked. We all did. I guess I thought if I just closed my eyes it would all go away. It seemed so . . . unreal. I'm a bureaucrat, for God's sakes, not somebody who murders people. I was frightened. I didn't know what to do, so—God forgive me—I did nothing. It just got so . . . out of control. It was never meant to happen."

35

■

The bellhop unlocked the door and Jack picked Sally up and carried her across the threshold.

"Jack," she said, kissing him, "what a neat surprise. The Ritz for our wedding night."

"I want us to have good memories of this place. Forget the bad ones."

"Oh, it's a beautiful room. And look, champagne."

"It's from Bob Ames."

"Oh my. Dom Perignon. And the flowers are from Mary Ellen."

"Nothing but the best for John F. Aiken of Pride's Crossing and Wellfleet and his bride, Ms. Sally Ellenberg, of the Back Bay and Brookline."

"That story was sort of pretentious, wasn't it? I had such a fight with the society editor. She kept trying to call me 'the former Sally Ellenberg.' I told her I was just getting married, not disappearing. You don't mind, do you, Jack, that I'm keeping my name?"

"Of course not. I'd feel ridiculous calling you Thelma."

She kissed him again. "I love you. And I love this room. I

think I'll sleep a lot better in this place when I know somebody isn't trying to kill me."

"Sleep? Who said anything about sleep?"

"And just what did you have in mind?"

"First, the champagne. Just enough to get a glow. And then a rerun of my favorite fantasy."

"Which one?"

"You know."

"Italian starlet? She gives hot-eyed looks to Sergio the handyman while he repairs the transmission. He is overcome with lust?"

"Not for the Ritz. Too Mediterranean. But I think I do a pretty fair Sergio."

"Jack, your Italian accent sucks. You sound like Leverett Saltonstall doing Mussolini. The only part you get right is the lust."

"Speaking of which—"

"OK, I know. 'Hi theah, Ah am Miz Honeydew Melon and Ah am a cheerleader and Ah love doin' sinful things in the back of a Chevvy with the l'il ole football team.' "

"No, that's tomorrow night. I mean my real favorite."

"I give up."

"The golden oldie."

"Oh, you mean the one where you are in the middle of a story on laser satellites and I come in and rip your clothes off et cetera?"

"Umm, I love it. It's so kinky."

"Jack, we are in the postsexual revolution era. That is not really kinky. They do it in Des Moines after Wednesday night Bingo. Baptist ministers and their wives do it."

"I may not know kinky, but I know what I like."

"You Yankees make a tradition out of everything. You just find what you like and stay with it."

"Oh no, this time it will be much different. This time it will be how proton decay is related to antimatter and the big bang theory of the universe."

"God, I can't stand all this sexual variety!"

"See. I am not a fuddy-duddy."

"OK. Tell me about proton decay."

"The dematerialization of protons to lighter materials, and ultimately to pure energy—" he said, as she slipped off his grey morning coat and unbuttoned his white starched shirt. By the time she had undressed him, he had reached the theory of the origin of the universe.

"Jack," she said, undoing the mother-of-pearl button on her honeymoon outfit ($99.99 in Filene's basement), "you are the first person who could ever make me learn science. I am going to be smarter than Einstein if you keep this up."

"You don't look like Einstein. You're not built like him either," he said, as the 38-C beige lace bra ($4.99 at Loehmann's) came off. "Are you interested in the big bang?"

"Now," she said, moving her body close to his, "you are talking my language."

"In the beginning of the cosmos, there was—"

"Jack, what I learned in journalism school, remember?"

"Yes," he said, "I think I do. Show, don't tell."

"You got it," she said.